APRIL IN PARIS, 1921

APRIL IN PARIS, 1921

a kiki button mystery

TESSA LUNNEY

PEGASUS CRIME
NEW YORK LONDON

APRIL IN PARIS, 1921

Pegasus Books Ltd
148 West 37th Street, 13th Floor
New York, NY 10018

First Pegasus Books hardcover edition Summer 2018

Interior design by Sabrina Plomitallo-González, Pegasus Books

ISBN: 978-1-68177-775-7

10 9 8 7 6 5 4 3 2 1

Printed in the United States of America
Distributed by W. W. Norton & Company, Inc.

To Hannah, for the negronis, and Bridie, for the whisky

PROLOGUE

21 rue Delambre, Montparnasse, Paris. The little studio at the very top, just a whitewashed attic really, just a single room. With a low ceiling, only just high enough for a man without his hat, windows that stretched to the floor and opened straight out into the Paris air. They opened straight out into the view, down the street, over the four corners, down to the river, over the cartwheel network of streets to the Eiffel Tower. A dizzying view laid out like a model for a Montparnasse genius. I can still smell it, the street scents of freshly baked baguettes and galettes, sour wine and faint piss, salty frying and cheap tobacco. The hall smells of disinfectant and sweat. My studio, whitewash and Gauloises, geraniums in the window pots, old wine and cheap candles and sex—the smell of freedom. Have you also been cooped up in a house, restricted by uncomfortable clothes, hemmed in by social expectations, poor pay, and relatives, colleagues, even friends, with no imagination? Then you know what it means to run away to your own special place, to live in your own flat and earn your own money and every hour is yours to do as you choose. And that's what Paris was like in the 1920s. Utterly free.

"AIN'T WE GOT FUN"

I arrived in London in the slushy February of 1921, so cold and gray that I had to grip the radiator in my hotel to warm my fingers. I'd taken a cheap little room near Victoria Station, with faded floral wallpaper that peeled with damp at the corners and so small that I'd had to leave my trunks at the station. I'd taken a cheap little room as I didn't expect to be in it for more than a minute. Bertie would never let me stay in such a dive if he knew I was here. Which he didn't, yet, so I changed my woolen gloves for my fur-lined leather ones, tied my coat more tightly around me, packed my handbag and set off for the Strand.

The city greeted me with intermittent sleet, weather rarely seen in either of my Australian homes, but it wasn't a shock. It wasn't my first time in this city. I'd lived here in 1914, doing the rounds of debutante balls with my boring cousins. Then I'd been here on and off all through the war, relishing the precious hours out of my nurse's uniform. I didn't finally leave until January 1919. It was cold and gray then, too, a gray that stayed with me even when I sailed south to Sydney sunshine. But now I was excited—and nervous and confused and amazed—to be back. The energy of the city, electric and dangerous, warmed me more than the rattly radiator I gripped ever could.

London bustled and jostled, and in this part of town, the ticket sellers rubbed shoulders with puffed-up businessmen in their bowlers; loud boys in flat caps winked at the smart secretaries who affected disdain; big-lunged flower girls set up a chorus to cajole fat old men with their mustaches. The streets were gray, the buildings were gray, and life moved with the swift ebb and flow of the Thames. I walked quickly—the city demanded it—towards the office of the *Star*.

The *Star* sold celebrity gossip. The star of the *Star* was copy editor Bertie Browne, my friend, confidant, sometimes lover and ofttimes savior from the worst moods of the war. Bertie's uncle was a newspaperman who could have established Bertie in a somber and respectable broadsheet. But what Bertie liked best, what he was best at, was chatting over cocktails in underground bars. He was very happy with his little entertainment rag. The offices were at the other end of the Strand, on Fleet Street, in order to be closer to Soho and all its celebrated types. The building's facade was forbidding gray stone, but the little door had number 72 painted in gold and led to a narrow wooden staircase, covered with playbills. I climbed up to the top floor and waited in the dark smoky foyer.

"Kiki Button!" He burst through the door in an explosion of green check. He ran over and picked up me up, swirling me round as he said my name.

"Darling Bertie."

"When Mavis at reception said it was you, I couldn't believe it, but then I thought, No, I can believe it—it'd be just like Kiki to turn up unannounced. And in pure peacock blue too—right down to your shoes! All right, turn around, let me get a look at you." He spun me around carefully as Mavis at reception gawked.

"Peacock-blue wool coat, fur-trimmed, navy stockings, navy button-up heels, peacock cloche, and is that"—he whisked off my hat—"a bob! Your hair is short, Kiki!"

"I had it cut when we stopped in Constantinople. I walked into this

little barber's shop and chopped at my jawline with my hands. I had a full
five minutes of pantomime with the barber before I could convince him
that I really wanted it all off. People watched at the window—"

"The Turks smirked?"

"They laughed! And clapped, when the final lock came off. They
insisted on buying me coffee and cake before I reboarded the ship."

"A blond woman with a man's haircut. You always were novel."

"I just feel so . . . free." I rubbed the back of my head with my hand.
I grinned.

"That's your naughty grin, Kiki."

"I have a little proposal."

"Propose to me."

"Let's get out of the office and somewhere more gossipy."

"I'll get my hat."

◇

We walked arm in arm through the backstreets to Soho. His coat was a
very fine cashmere in pine green, just the right shade to match his three-
piece suit. Even his hat was green. He kept lozenges on him at all times, as
he loved to smoke but hated the taste on his tongue. He popped one in his
mouth as we left the building, and I smiled—even the lozenge was green.

I nodded at it. "Mint?"

"Lime."

"We're two bright parrots in a world of pigeons, Bertie."

"I think you mean we're two discerning citizens in a world of timid
muck. I just don't understand Britain's obsession with mud colors—didn't
we have enough of that in the war?"

"Khaki, gray—"

"Brown, buff, taupe—ugh! Thank Bacchus for pink cocktails with twists
of lemon. Here, just around this corner."

We'd cut through the winding streets of Soho. In a little lane off a little lane was a tiny house. The upstairs shuddered with cacophonous singing but the basement blew ragtime up into the street.

"Down here. I think it's called something preposterous like the Mountain Rest Stop or the Wonder of the East, but we just call it the Old Standby."

"Because it's always open?"

"It opened up as we all got demobbed. It's tiny, a tad dingy, but yes, Dixon can always be summoned from out the back to pour a whisky."

The ragtime came from a rather beaten gramophone that sat on the bar. The bar itself was a bench, but the wall behind was decorated with a long mirror, just like a Paris café. The walls of the room were covered in posters—playbills, mostly, but also exhibition notices, newspaper articles, job advertisements, for-sale notices, political pamphlets, and lewd graffiti. A fire crackled cozily to one side, with two fat armchairs in front of it. A mix of odd chairs and tables were squashed in next to one another from the door to the bar, so we could hardly move even through the half-empty room. I sat down in one of the armchairs to warm myself. Bertie went up to a bespectacled man scribbling at a table, made an appointment to see him tomorrow, and came back with two doubles.

"Proper whisky. The owner has a cousin's friend's sister-in-law's canary's something-or-other in the Highlands who sends down the most delicious single malt. Half the price you'd get in the Savoy."

"Who was that?"

"An out-of-work actor who's been sleeping with . . ." He stopped and winked at me, "You'll have to read the magazine, Kiki. How's the dram? You're licking your lips like it's soaked into your skin."

"Would you believe that no one would drink whisky with me on the ship over? The barman didn't think a woman alone was deserving of single malt. And in Sydney I was living with my aunt Constance, whose strongest beverage was a particularly dark tea. In other words, the dram's divine."

"As are you." He reached over and smoothed my bobbed hair. "I never thought I'd see you again."

"Whizbangs and flu pandemics couldn't keep me away."

"I was sure they would."

I raised my eyebrows at him.

He shrugged. "You know, British fatalism and all that. When you left . . ."

His big brown eyes reflected the Kiki of 1919. Wan, worn-out by the war, I was almost mute. He'd found me three years earlier behind the casualty clearing station, teary in my grubby uniform, cursing the matron and the registered nurses and in dire need of a cigarette. He provided the smoke, a bon mot, half a music-hall ditty made dirty with frontline wit and joined me in cursing the upper ranks. For years he provided the laughter, but by the time I left, none of us had the energy to joke. I certainly didn't have the energy to know what I wanted, let alone to resist my parents' demands that I return home. Bertie sensibly feared I'd succumb to the Spanish flu. Instead, I nursed passengers all the way back to Australia. I squeezed his hand.

"When I left, we were all too used to final goodbyes. I'm here now."

"And as wicked as ever." He clinked my glass. "So what's your naughty proposal?"

"I need a job."

"No," he gasped. "Don't you have money? Pots and pots of it?"

"My father has money, which I can only use to catch a husband, and then the money will be my husband's. I need my own money."

"And you want a job—in the theater?"

"At the paper. At your magazine. Specifically, I want to be your society gossip reporter."

"We have one of those—"

"But not in Paris."

"Oh—Paris! Yes, Kiki, yes, I love it—"

"Look at these." I opened my handbag and shook out the contents. Twenty different cards, notes, and letters fluttered out. Bertie picked them up.

"'The Honorable Mrs. Hanley-Sidebottom cordially invites you to Miss Letitia's ball on February twentieth.' 'Dear Katherine'— Katherine?"

"It's my birth name. Katherine King Button."

"A solid, respectable name. It doesn't suit you."

"Why do you think I adopted Kiki so readily?"

"Because you despise your family and all they stand for?"

"Well, technically I only got rid of my mother's influence—King is her surname and Katherine is her middle name, after my grandmother. I'm still a Button."

"I never picked you as Daddy's girl."

"If I were Daddy's girl, I'd marry the son of the neighboring wool baron and combine the properties, all while making babies, looking pretty, and doing what I'm told. Instead, I'm here."

Bertie kissed my hand in delight.

"So, 'dear Katherine'"—he cleared his throat and put on a posh accent—"'when you get to London I insist that you visit me for tea at Belgravia Square'—'Dear Miss Button, I'm a friend of your father's (well my father is at any rate, ha ha),' blah blah, et cetera, et cetera—are all of these invitations?"

"I have another thirty telegrams in my trunk of people to look up."

"But you're not posh. How do you know all these people?"

"Through Father's business contacts. He was here in London when I left Australia and spread the word that I was coming, with a fortune for the highest bidder."

"I thought you weren't—"

"I had to say that I was coming over, for another season, to find a husband. It was the only way I could stop my parents from calling the navy on their runaway daughter."

"Ooh, sailors—if only they had."

"Well, quite. I'm also meant to be staying with my cousins, but . . ." I shrugged and grinned. "My letter must have been mislaid. Anyway, the men want money, and the women want any available men. The invitations flooded in."

"But which are for Paris?"

"If I attend these three"—I sorted through the invitations to find the gilt-edged cards—"then I will have all the Paris contacts I need."

"Americans?"

"I love them. They're even richer than Father. The boys don't need my money, and most would rather have an American girl. The American girls all know that and so consider me an ally, not competition. They're the best fun."

"Apart from me, of course."

"That goes without saying, the best of all Berties."

He smiled and tapped the invitations on his knee. "You know, my Aussie minx, I think this might just work."

"I haven't crossed the seven seas for it to fail."

"Now, you'll need to send me a column every week. . . ."

We spent the rest of the afternoon working out the details. Gossip columnists report on the rich and famous, which in those days was mostly aristocrats and the idle rich and whichever Hollywood star breezed into town. I would spend some time here in London in order to secure my Paris introductions. Bertie would help to set me up in a little studio, preferably in a bohemian part of Paris, which I could afford on my income; I insisted on proper independence. I would send a column a week by the express post, to be printed each Friday—Monday was the London gossip, fresh from the weekend, and Wednesday was for the transatlantic tidbits (always, unfortunately, a few days late). My column would necessitate at least two parties a week—"But Kiki, as you're doing nothing else, I think you can squeeze that in, don't you?"—and while I was in London, Bertie insisted that I stay at his flat.

"I have to make sure you know what you're doing, Kiki. It's my professional responsibility to show you how to party."

And with that, we headed for a more exciting underground bar for a bottle of champagne and some illicit tickles. We downed it in double-quick time, but as it was still office hours and the place was empty, we moved our loose limbs to Bertie's favorite dumpling house on Wardour Street. The steam was spicy, and our heads were cleared with hot chili paste and cool green tea. Uncle Wu's nephew, Young Wu, joined us for a little tumbler of rice wine at the end of the meal, his skin golden and his shoes shiny in the half-light of the restaurant. But he had to take his golden tones back to work, so we headed out into the chill night, browsed tipsily through the secondhand book stalls until, clutching cut-price vorticist poetry, we wormed our way into the 43 Club. Mother's ruin came in every sort of cocktail and concoction and we danced and laughed until the poetry made sense, until we forgot our bloody yesterdays, until we were hungry again and had to head back to Bertie's for late-night biscuits and whispers. We fell asleep with the dawn, stinking of booze and tobacco and sweat, in his tiny unmade bed.

London was a revelation, with its fancy stores and dingy bars, with its posh Bohemians and serious barmen, garrulous booksellers and polite whores. This London I'd never seen before; it'd been off-limits to a debutante and hidden from a nurse behind rows of khaki-clad lads. The footpaths were cold, but Bertie's attentions were always warm as he helped me to get ready for my parties. He would often run to the flower seller downstairs to buy me a corsage so that he could have a matching boutonniere. I developed a taste for fruity lozenges and he learned how to darn a silk stocking. We mostly woke up in the same bed.

Then it was the end of the month and time I stopped scandalizing Bertie's neighbors. I loved being with Bertie. We were so free, without our uniforms and our seven-day passes and our mandatory rush back to barracks. But much as I loved the city, it was all too close to Father's business contacts and Mother's vast network of cousins. I knew if I stayed too long I'd be press-ganged into marrying some titled dullard before I had time to finish my champagne.

Bertie saw me off at Victoria Station. He'd bought my ticket, first-class.

"Start as you mean to go on, Kiki."

He looked like a painting, set against the sooty and smoky rising roof of the station. His sandy-brown hair slicked under his hat, his military bearing, long limbs and slender body somehow both louche and polite, as though they weren't really part of him. He wore a light-gray suit, set off with a lavender shirt and a suffragette-purple tie. I half expected him to yell out "Votes for Women!," but in a puff of steam he grabbed me and kissed me.

"Blackcurrant today." I could taste the lozenges on his tongue.

"Don't forget me, Kiki."

"How could I? You're my boss."

"I don't think you can have a boss, Kiki. You just have people who give you money to do what you want."

"We all need a reward after the war."

"Can you be—?"

"I can't be your reward, Bertie."

"Of course not! Good grief. No, I mean, can you be sure to . . . to . . ." He looked almost embarrassed. He straightened his shoulders and took both of my hands.

"It's been wonderful to have you here. I've been missing a true friend—all I have are colleagues, contacts, and casual concubines."

"A hellish triumvirate."

"Quite. So don't just send the column. Write to me as well."

"I'll be too busy." The horn sounded and I kissed him quickly. "Come and visit me instead!"

"I'll be at the Ritz!" He waved with his hat as the train pulled out of the station. Then he was gone. I was on my way to Paris.

2.

"ALL BY MYSELF"

It was the first time I had seen the English countryside out of uniform. There were no troop trains and no barricades, no convoys of khaki trucks or beautiful, doomed horses as they cantered to the coast. It was the pure Kentish countryside as the tracks rolled on to Dover. Fields fallow with winter, and the fog that settled close to the ground. Villagers that bustled around their little station, porters too young to have fought, women in faded black dresses selling newspapers and currant buns. Then Dover, seagulls crying into the ship's horns, the sea gray, then blue, then black, as we left the train for the ferry to Calais. Every time I had crossed that channel before, it was towards the guns. On a clear day, you could hear them as you sailed, their boom over the clack of the wheels as the train rolled towards them over the tide. Only the clamor of London could drown out their peal of doom. Now all we heard were the waves lapping the ship and the gulls that followed us over. I went outside to the bracing air and breathed in big lungfuls. No tears on my face, no cordite in my memory. Just soft, salty sea air.

A shiver ran through us when we docked. We were in France! Tricolors hung on the jetty, on every platform. The dining car of the Blue Train didn't offer ham sandwiches and custard but *baguette au jambon* and crème brûlée. I was too excited to eat. I nibbled at cheese and crackers, sipped at some strange-tasting red wine, and stared out the window. I knew these fields so well. All the rubble, the squat little huts, the profusion of poppies like blood spots in the sun—these were all still there, no one had blown them up or knocked them down. Young men took their young women to the places where they fought; old women took their old men to see the shallow graves of their sons. The train emptied as couple after couple drifted onto the fields for a battlefield tour. I overheard them, they proclaimed at how the fields looked stripped, pocked, full of metal still. I couldn't see it. I saw only that all the men were gone, the sisters and cooks, the horses and dogs. I saw the stillness, the absence of hurry and *schnell*, the absence of uniforms. I heard nothing but ordinary civilian sounds, the murmuring song of quiet conversations, porters and postcard sellers, the occasional toot of a tour guide—no yells, no shells, no orders bellowed from the end of the platform. The sun touched the field stubble and lingered, coaxing the crop to grow. Birds weaved in loops; swallows and sparrows and crows, they called into the empty air. My heart was full. It was a struggle to keep my eyes from filling as well.

◆

Thank heaven for Paris. The train pulled into Gare du Nord with a sigh of smoke and steel. Uniformed porters, so smart in their red and gold, hurried up to the unloaded trunks. Flower girls and newspaper boys gathered in a semicircle and yelled in their broad French. Bearded old men and crisp young women, nannies with toddlers and languid couples in silk and wool, clipped over the platform behind them into their own Parisian lives. I wanted to savor this moment and just watch from the carriage window. I wanted to jump out and kiss all the porters and street sellers. I controlled myself and hopped discreetly from the train to my trunk, from my trunk to a cab, from my cab to rue Delambre, Montparnasse.

My new home.

The cabdriver just smiled when I gave him the address. It was already a favorite place for foreigners. Rue Delambre was the street with Café du Dôme and Café de la Rotonde across the boulevard, with studios and bars and bookshops full of writers, artists, and bohemian tourists. My skin tingled as we wound through the streets. All the ordinary things struck me again as wonderful—all the signs were in French! You could buy baguettes in every bakery! Well-dressed couples drank their coffee on the street!—so obvious, so novel; I'd seen it all before, but somehow it felt new. It wasn't until I saw the advertisements for Dubonnet and Gitanes cigarettes and booksellers by the Seine, those markers of daily life, that I fully understood: now I live in Paris. I was there for myself, by myself. All the smells that wafted in the window, of fresh bread, old wine, unwashed beggar, burnt sugar, salt, fat. All the sounds of French yelled, muttered, sung, and laughed. Even the men on the street corners, dignified in their wheelchairs, tin cup in one hand, nodding at each centime and franc that rattled their metal—it was just them, and me, and all the other war refuse, human flotsam and political jetsam that could only be saved by Paris.

Number 21 had a pale four-story facade with the attic on top like a metal hat. Long windows looked out on the street, framed with shutters and baskets for window pots. Bertie had organized, through his contacts, a cheap little studio for me. I knew from the price that it would be on the top floor—I was to live in the little metal hat.

A stout old woman with a fed-up expression greeted my knock. She jangled the keys on her belt, handed me one, and directed two boys from the street to carry my trunk. She looked me up and down and sighed, but never said a word to me. What on earth had Bertie told her? The boys, in between cursing each other as they heaved my trunk upstairs, were more forthcoming.

"You're the blond *Australienne*?"

"There's only one blond *Australienne*."

"You're a war hero."

"And a wealthy mademoiselle in disguise."

"And a writer! Will you write about the war?"

"Where is Australia? Is it as far as Marseille?"

"As far as the Dardanelles? My father fought there—"

"I have a cousin from Marseille; it took her three days to get to Paris!"

"My father never came back from the war . . . he's a hero too."

All this was exchanged in rapid patter. They made such a racket that people poked their heads out of their doors to look. Most were mothers, who gave a cursory glance and bonjour and popped back inside. This way I found out where the bathroom was—on the third floor, just a toilet and a sink—with a toilet on the ground floor as well. A young man, not much older than the boys, lounged in his doorway and smoked, his waistcoat open and his sleeves rolled up. He gave unwanted directions to the two boys and winked at me.

Finally we reached the top floor. There was nothing in my flat but a saggy old bed. One wall held two windows that, due to the low roof, reached from the floor almost to the ceiling. I opened them and found they had a little sill, but otherwise dropped straight to the street. I kicked off my shoes, swung my legs over, and lit a cigarette. The view over the city stretched on and on, over chimney pots and attics, over the Luxembourg Gardens and the Sorbonne to my right; to my left, over streetlamps and metal roofs to the Eiffel Tower. The light was silver, the city rain-shiny and lit up with a changeable sky. Paris stretched in front of me and all I could do was worship her winding ways. I leaned back against the window frame and smoked.

Bright, laughing people walked down my street to the cafés. They wore parrot-colored scarves and long coats slick with sudden showers; they wore enormous hats or no hats at all; they spoke loudly and their feet seemed to skip over the footpath. Some of them even waved up to me, complete strangers. The Rotonde's tables spilled up the street and around the corner, each chair full, the lamps and heaters from the restaurants keeping the patrons as warm as the wine. I never even made it inside, that first evening. I was hailed by an American who'd seen my feet dangling over my windowsill—"Look! Hey, leggy lady! Hello! Do you drink champagne? Pink champagne? Of course you do. . . ." No chaperones, no invitations, no introductions. We were all here for the same reason. We were all here to escape dull parents and scant options and bad memories. We were all here to explore art, music, sex, and travel. We had already begun, just by being here, just by sharing a drink with a handsome stranger for no other reason than fun. Father's bluster and Mother's frown were very far away. Bloodied bodies and uniforms were just as lost. My stomach fluttered with excitement, bubbles, kisses and a feeling that I was flying.

I felt alive.

◈

Then it was April, with soft light on the chestnut blossoms shaken over tables by the breeze. The squalls of winter rain had faded; the sun said hello for more than a minute at a time. On the street people had swapped their heavy winter coats, leftover from the war, for more colorful, carefree models. I saw ankles and necks again, unwrapped from boots and scarves. Café heaters were not turned on until dusk, and we could sit outside without shivering. In the patisseries, fresh strawberries—"From my grandmother's hothouse, mademoiselle, very sweet"—appeared on the fruit tarts. Sparrows and swallows returned to their nests in the eaves, awnings, and boulevard branches. They sung into the dawn, earlier and earlier each day. As I stumbled home from bohemian nightcaps in nude studios, I found myself greeting them more often.

After a month, my routine was established (well, as much as one could have a routine in Montparnasse). Each night I would head out into the city for a party. I would wear my most extravagant outfit, offset only by the pencil and notebook in my purse. Society reporters are professional partygoers. I wrote tactful, tasteful tidbits that had as much relation to reality as *Alice's Adventures in Wonderland*. Actually, *Alice* was like a philosophical discussion at a party with drunk five-year-olds, and so had more reality than anything I would write for Bertie. Here's an example:

> Who would have thought that Lady Langborough sang opera? She delighted the assembled guests at railway-millionaire heiress Miss Cordelia McNeill's twenty-third birthday party on Saturday night. Lady L wore a beaded silver dress, with silver shoes and long silver gloves, and sang as clearly as the bell she so perfectly resembled. And what better tribute to Paris, this city that continues to give us joy and delight? The sweet, sad sounds of Puccini's *La Bohème* was a touching present for her friend Miss McNeill. Miss McNeill herself was radiant in pink silk chiffon layers that made her as ethereal as the spring dawn over the city. . . .

And so on. I had to sit through hours of bad music played by people with more money than sense. It was all just details sewn together with bits of fluff. If I were being truthful, I'd write something more like this:

> Lady Langborough—the self-styled title of Jane Hotham of Boston— tortured us all with her sentimental rendition of Mimi's aria from *La Bohème*. Although no individual note was off-key, the sense was decidedly out of tune. It was clear that the lady felt starving artists to be as real as fairies or mermaids. She only needed to walk three blocks north or south of her gilded perch to find the Mimis still dying of consumption—but why let reality ruin a solid performance? For solid it was. All Puccini's airy lightness was squashed by good, honest commonsense, in good, honest tweeds and button boots. But at least she had commonsense, which is more than could be said for

the host, Miss McNeill, who clearly couldn't see that every guest was only there to partake in some of her father's money. . . .

But of course, that would mean I would never be invited to another party. While that was tempting, the independence that this job bought me was too valuable. I made meticulous notes on the dresses, food, and the layout of the sumptuous apartments. I asked so many questions that the hosts thought I was genuinely interested in where they bought their rugs and who was related to whom. Usually the best bit of the party was when I found the prettiest young man and retired to a bedroom or back room—or once even a stairwell—with a bottle of champagne for a swift game of hunt-the-slipper. I added "spice," as the parties were "not nearly so lively" when I wasn't around. People performed for me, apparently. Heaven help them when I was absent.

If I had been to an aristocratic party, the type I wrote about for Bertie, then at midnight I would perform my Cinderella act and disappear, usually to Montmartre for jazz or back into Montparnasse for late-night gin and giggles. If the party started in Montparnasse . . . well, I would come home whenever the artistic talk, or political dancing, or licentious party games would release me. I would rise just before midday, sometimes entangled with a bright young thing and sometimes deliciously alone, and rattle down to my favorite breakfast café for multiple cups of coffee. I would write up my notes in the afternoon, and each Wednesday send them express post to arrive, by Thursday, with Bertie in London. One invitation would lead to the next, one party to another, the days brightening and lightening as we floated towards summer. I was untethered and delirious on French wine, scurrilous talk, and the view from my little garret. I slipped into this city as though I had never left. As though it had always been home.

3

"APRIL SHOWERS"

One night, just as the sun was setting, I wandered down to the Rotonde. I had no party and no plan, just a wish for a drink in company. I put on a simple dress, a deep red silk with a low, square neckline and a long waist sash that fluttered as I walked. It was still just cold enough to wear boots, so I wore my black suede pair, along with a black, faux-astrakhan coat with a shawl collar and large cuffs, and a deep red cloche over my bob. No jewelry but a dripping red heart brooch pinned to the coat; I was only hopping down to my local, after all. The café was usually full of all my new friends, artists and writers and muses and tourists, but this evening I knew only one person. She carried her native California with her in her big blue eyes and breezy attitude, but went forward in her chosen artistic milieu by electing only to be known by her mother's maiden name, North. Her work was all talk, but her talk was all smiles and sweet gossip. She was enthusiastic about everything and everyone, and was always at a footpath table with a drink. I waved to her, and she waved me over.

"Oh, honey," she breathed, "it's just fabulous. I mean, I only know Manuelle, who once almost modeled for me, but she's Picasso's current model, and he's so generous, I just . . ." North couldn't stop gushing, even by her effusive standards. A series of tables had been pushed together and in the middle of this gathering sat Pablo Picasso. Picasso was shorter than the other men around him. He was broad-shouldered, and his hands moved often, with energy and confidence, as he spoke. His eyes were the most arresting. Huge and dark, they pinned his companion to his sentence, they took in the group in one big swallow. For any café habitué, as I was fast becoming, aperitifs with Picasso was the very height of fashionable bohemian society, the inmost of the in crowd. The café group drank and chatted, sometimes to Picasso and sometimes to one another. They shared cigarettes and kisses and dipped their fingers into little bowls of olives that were scattered around the tables. As I stood next to North, I was included in Picasso's gaze. He spoke to someone next to him and nodded at me.

"Oh, oh, Kiki, Manuelle wants to speak with you," said North, excitedly patting my arm. She pointed to a lovely woman, all dark hair and dark eyes and glowing olive skin. She waved me over with a smile. I weaved through the tables and pulled up a chair next to her.

"Tell me," she purred—I hadn't understood how a person could purr until I heard that deep, burred voice roll from her rosebud lips—"tell us who you are, what you do, where you're from. We want to know everything."

"I'm Kiki—"

"You're the *Australienne*?" a man opposite cut in. "The blond *Australienne*, you must be her—Max, this is the *Australienne*."

"Who?"

"The blond Australienne."

"Ah, the other Kiki of Montparnasse! Bonjour! So wonderful to meet you." He took my hand and kissed it. "I'm Max."

"I'm Jean," said my first interrupter. He took my other hand and kissed it, so both my arms were stretched across the table.

"Manuelle, feed Kiki a sip of rosé," said Max. "We require her hands for the moment." Manuelle poured a tipple down my throat, cleaning up the spilled drops with her soft fingers.

"Now, Kiki," said Jean, "tell us what brings you all the way to Paris."

"Freedom," I said.

"Perfect!" cried Max. "She will do."

"Paris is the home of *liberté*!" said Jean. "Mademoiselle, you have come to the right place."

"I know I have."

I couldn't imitate Manuelle's purr, but my bright accent with its Australian twang delighted them. They laughed and imitated me, still holding my hands. Both were handsome, slender, and dark-haired, Jean with a cheeky smile, Max wide-eyed like a romantic poet. Both, scandalously, had German accents, though while Max's was obvious, Jean's was only noticeable when he spoke a German name. They instructed Manuelle to feed me and interrogated me on my living circumstances, my work, my opinions on art. I was clearly being interviewed for the post of bohemian groupie, but in the midst of it—*quelle horreur!*—we ran out of wine. They finally let go of my hands to chase up a waiter to order more.

It was dark, and the lights all around the corner of Boulevard Montparnasse glowed. Everyone huddled into their coats and chatted, except for North, who was somewhat agog. I winked at her. Manuelle put her hand on my arm.

"Have you met Pablo?" she asked. I held my breath as I faced Picasso. I thought I would feel skewered, like a pinned butterfly, but his eyes held laughter, as though we shared the most marvelous joke, just the two of us. He put out his hand.

"A pleasure to meet you. Kiki, is it?"

"It's my Paris name." I smiled.

"She's Australian," said Manuelle.

"Kiki Kangaroo," said Picasso. He looked at my face with such intensity it was as though I could feel his gaze. I'd thought it must've been his taste for brothels, but perhaps this was how he got his reputation as a ladies' man. Such intense attention was unusual, and I wasn't sure if I was nervous or excited. He reached over and turned my face this way and that. Manuelle raised her eyebrows, but he just grunted.

Jean and Max arrived with the waiters and made a great show of placing a feast on the table—rosé, bread, olive oil, four types of sausage, five types of cheese, more olives, pickled onions, prawns fried in garlic, anchovies, and chips—as well as cigarettes and matches.

"A pauper's feast!" declared Max, as he flourished a champagne bottle.

If this was how a pauper ate in Paris, I thought, may I never be rich.

"Most of it is on the house," said Jean. "Well, some of it anyway—due to our illustrious guest."

Picasso gave a mock royal bow, and everyone clapped.

"The only catch is"—Max winced—"that Victor's American cousin is here and wants a photo."

"Who's Victor?" I said.

"Libion, the owner," said Jean. "Excellent man, but it seems that even Victor is cursed with vulgar relations."

"I'll have Manuelle on one side and Kiki Kangaroo on the other," said Picasso. "It will be a pleasure."

Which was exactly how it ended up. We drank and ate until most of the other tables were empty. Picasso became progressively looser, giving imitations of various surrealists and Postimpressionists—his Matisse was hilarious, apparently. We played a particularly artistic version of charades, which involved drawing a title of a book or film or play and the others had to guess. Max and Jean held a mock battle with the anchovies that turned into a drinking game. Picasso played with Manuelle's hair, and she had her hand on my knee. The manager's cousin took his photo, fussy and obsequious as he gathered us together or arranged us in "natural" poses. I smiled for the camera as Picasso patted my bum.

The midnight hour struck, and the party started to disperse. Picasso whispered to Manuelle, who turned to me.

"We are buying some strawberries on the way back to my apartment."

"Strawberries? In spring?"

"They're special, from the south."

"Who sells fruit at midnight?"

"The midnight fruit seller, of course!" she laughed. "Join us?" Her hand slipped under my dress and stroked my thigh. I grinned; how could I refuse?

We wobbled down the road like a crab, arm in arm, as we sang bawdy songs—I think I ended up singing "Never let a sailor get an inch above your knee" in appalling French, which had Manuelle demonstrating just how many inches per verse as we walked. The midnight seller was an invention, and the old man had to be shaken by his whiskers to wake him up. He bristled with crankiness, until he saw Manuelle, and then he grinned a gap-toothed grin and opened his cart. A kiss and a little squeeze from Manuelle got us an extra basket of strawberries.

She had a bottle from her uncle in Cognac, Manuelle said as we wobbled up the stairs, but we never got that far. Candles lined the edges of her room, each one stuck in an old wine bottle, and as she bent down to light them her skin shone. I followed her lead, also lighting the three oil lamps that sat among the candles, their red shades adding a rosy glow to the room. Picasso—Pablo, I called him now—set up a running commentary on the shape, movement, and intricate colors of our limbs in the candlelight, comparing them favorably with the strawberries he held. When just the right number of candles were lit, Manuelle stood in front of Pablo, blew out her match, and dropped it on the floor along with her coat. Pablo took one of the strawberries and placed it just in front of her lips, teasing her with it. She leaned forward and bit into it, so the juice dripped down her chin. He watched, and as he did I came up to her and licked the drop where it ran along her jawline. Manuelle took a strawberry from Pablo's hands, teasing me with it until I caught it between my teeth, just as she had done. She let the juice run all the way down to my collarbone before I felt her lips on my neck. Pablo was covered in shadows in the candlelight. I fed him a strawberry, and both Manuelle and I kissed the juice from his stubbled chin.

I followed Manuelle's lead in everything. She fed him strawberries with one hand and took off his jacket with the other. She took off his shoes, I fed him, he took off my dress so I stood in my stockings—"Ooh la la, Kiki Kangaroo wears no knickers! Is that how they do it in Australia?"— Manuelle fed him and undressed him, and I undressed her—"Kiki, undo me, would you? Mmm, just there." Her skin was so smooth, her curves pushed back when I touched them. Pablo couldn't keep his hands off her. She grabbed both of us by the hand and pulled us onto her large bed, covered in a velvet bedspread, just inches from the floor.

In bed with Pablo, Pablo was king. He directed Manuelle, and I followed her, and it wasn't long before he flopped onto the cushions and murmured, "I'll be ready again soon," and dropped off to sleep.

Was that it? I was in bed with Pablo Picasso and he was asleep!

"It's all right," Manuelle called from where she was cleaning herself. "He won't wake up for another half an hour or so. We have plenty of time."

"For what?"

"For each other," she said, "of course."

She kissed me so softly, so tenderly, that I couldn't help but lean forward for more. She grinned.

"We will have some fun before he wakes up."

The room seemed to expand, then disappear, so that all I was aware of was her tongue, her lips, her fingers, her breath, and the waves of pleasure they raised in me. Pablo woke up and joined in. Seeing stars, is that the cliché? The world turned? Whatever it was, I was complete. Then he was, then she was, and I kissed her as I calmed down. We lay on top of each other, sweaty sticky limbs all over the blanket.

So that was sex with the famous Pablo Picasso, I thought.

That was sex with a woman.

The room slowly came back into focus. A dais at one end held a chair, presumably for modeling, and a huge bunch of white lilies. Their smell filled the room. Another table held a mirror, a hairbrush, and other toiletries. Her clothes spilled from a dark trunk. A jug and a basin, in cracked white porcelain, stood beside it. Although the room was small, the ceilings were high and bare, with huge windows from hip height to far above our heads, so from my prone position her room seemed enormous. The red lamps and golden candles made every shadow hold possibility.

It took some time before we heard the thumping. Pablo growled.

"Is that your neighbor?"

"Oh, she's old," sighed Manuelle. "She's telling us to keep going—she'd never get any fun otherwise."

"She spits at me when I walk past!"

"Only because you don't come over often enough—or last long enough."

Then Pablo grabbed her and tickled her as she shrieked. The thumps continued from the flat below.

I watched him as he dressed. He seemed to be made of muscle, even though I was sure he did nothing but paint. This was exaggerated by his lack of height, as he wasn't as tall as I was in my heels. He had slender fingers, which I knew, now, were sensitive and deft. But his shoulders, back, thighs, the rest of him was powerful. As for his smell—so important in a lover—all I could detect was sweat, strawberries, tobacco, and wine. He kissed us both as he left.

"Kiki, you will model for me. When I finish this canvas with Manuelle—the day after tomorrow. Manuelle will tell you where."

"What about his wife?" I asked when he'd left.

Manuelle waved her hand in a dismissive gesture.

"Olga's busy with the baby. That's why he comes here." She winked. "One of the reasons."

She handed me a bowl of water and an odd rubber contraption. "Do you need this?"

"A douche? No, I'm wearing a rubber cap."

"Oh, very modern! So much better than this." She squatted over the basin as she washed herself out. "It's so tedious!"

"And less than effective. And no good on the run."

"You make love while running?" She laughed so hard she almost spilled the water.

"No, I mean, in the war . . ."

"Ah." She smiled and dried herself. She put her contraceptive douche away and knelt by me on the bed.

"That is why I prefer women." She held my face between her hands. It was a perfect fit. "One of the reasons."

She ran her tongue around my lips and we started all over again.

4

"I'VE GOT MY CAPTAIN WORKING FOR ME NOW"

Thank goodness it was only a few blocks, as the next morning I positively wobbled home. I needed coffee and breakfast and a wash and possibly more wine, as I couldn't quite believe what had happened. But I had an appointment to model for Picasso—Pablo, I had to remember to call him Pablo or else forever seem like a tourist. I told myself that if I turned up at his studio and he had no idea who I was, I'd know I'd been dreaming.

Inside the front door of my building were letter boxes, each with a little key. I hadn't checked my post for some days and in the dark wooden box were three letters. Who doesn't adore letters? They're a type of magic, the handwriting so intimate and the stamp indicating how far it has traveled to reach the reader. The first letter was stamped from within Paris this morning. I ripped it open as I trooped up the stairs.

My Kangaroo,
   Manuelle tells me that you are a type of journalist, yes?
That you report on the rich and famous for some London paper.
I have an urgent job for you. I need you to do a little detective
work in those rich-and-famous apartments for something that

27

*has been stolen from me. Come to my studio tomorrow, model
for me, and I'll give you all the details.*

Pablo

Detective work. For Pablo! I knew I'd say yes, even before I knew what
I was supposed to be detecting. I flung open the windows and chucked
my bag and coat on the bed. The little sparrows jumped around the sill
in rhythm with my ragtime thoughts. Who better placed than a gossip
columnist to snoop around? And Picasso! Could I really model? But then,
how hard could it be? Certainly not harder than washing a half-dead
soldier at 2:00 a.m. with only a guttering candle to see by, surely nothing
could be harder than that.

I peeled off my sweaty dress and stockings. There was a little water left
in the jug, cold enough to splash some sense into me. My skin tingled as
I washed my face, neck, arms, and soft places.

I had a black velvet opera cape with me—I was not an advocate of
sensible packing—and I wound it around myself as I sat by the window.
I lit a cigarette and watched the day stroll through its Sunday. Gossip
columnist was a light job, frothy and airy, that demanded almost nothing
of me. That's what I'd searched for, after the war, after the flu pandemic,
after the heavy expectations from my mother and father. A life that I held
lightly. Detective work was more solid. Stronger perhaps, but also more
structured. More restrictive, like all the most interesting work. I sighed.
I had to face up to it sometime—I was not made of froth. A bubbly life
was only mine to visit, not to live in. Whatever this job from Pablo really
meant—a new life as a lady detective, as Picasso's confidante, as simply
the juiciest gossip this side of the war—I would do it.

The next letter had a stamp. I recognized the handwriting from the
envelope. It was sent via London, but I couldn't make out the original
postmark. It didn't look like Sydney GPO, or whatever tiny country town
Tom had ridden his horse through. Thomas Arthur Ian Thompson, my

lucky Tombola. I shivered, though it wasn't cold. My Tom-Tom, my drumbeat—Tom always took my full attention, and I could never give him anything less. To be fair, he gave me all his attention as well, in estaminet or club, at the dinner table or dining car, at the helm, at the wheel, in the saddle. It was just the way we were with each other. I itched to read his letter. But I could still smell Picasso's sweat; I could still taste Manuelle's olive skin. I was too full of Paris right now; the letter would whisk me away, take me back. I tucked it under my pillow as a treat for later.

The third letter made me laugh. It also had no stamp, but the loopy handwriting flourished my name, "Her Royal Highness Kiki of the Buttons," across the expensive paper. It was folded like a puzzle and popped open with my touch.

Kiki,

I trudged all the way up to your ivory tower, only to find my princess was still in her pumpkin carriage. I'm over here to see you and oversee you. I'm staying at the Ritz and I'll be here all afternoon, so come and find me as soon as you can. I have the company checkbook and a _bath_.

Bertie xoxo

A bath—there was no better way to get me to meet him than the promise of a private soak. Suddenly I found I wasn't worn out after all. I hung last night's dress over a chair to try and get some of the sweat and smells out of it and hunted for something cleanish. My generally cavalier attitude to underwear meant I had some cream camiknickers that were barely worn, and I slipped an ivory silk dress over the top. It had a yellow trim at the collar, the hem, and the sleeves, little embroidered daffodils with a tiny bead inside each bloom. Just the thing for tricking the hotel staff into thinking I was sweet and respectable, right down to my two-tone shoes. My cream coat had a big stain on the lapel—white wine, perhaps, or a cream sauce, or something more carnal, I couldn't tell—but I resolved to pin some fresh flowers over the top and no one would notice. Hopefully no one would notice that I looked somewhat underslept, either. Except Bertie, of course.

◆

"Kiki!"

I hadn't even made it past reception before I saw him bound through the foyer. He was dressed in a sky-blue suit and shirt, with a navy tie and navy pocket handkerchief. He even wore two-tone blue brogues, the whole ensemble making his sandy hair look even paler. I was a cloud against his sky. We might've been siblings, if it hadn't been for the big kiss he planted on my mouth.

"What is that lozenge flavor I taste? Rose?"

"Forget-me-not. I couldn't wait to see you. I only got in this morning." He took my arm and swept me into the Ritz bar. "Our crossing was delayed due to the bloody English weather. Mmm, jonquils." He sniffed at my lapel. "They hide the tobacco-and-seduction smell so well!"

"Cheeky."

"Now sit down and tell me—is it a champagne, whisky, or gin-and-tonic kind of afternoon?"

"Hot toddy."

"Goodness me, you have been having fun. You must tell me all about it as payment for your bath."

"Then we can have a cocktail—we have to celebrate our first Paris trip, Bertie."

The bar was warm and dark and gave the impression of being entirely covered in velvet. The seats were dark red and brown, including the sofa-like bench I sat on. The walls had a dark striped wallpaper from just above head height, pinned down with lithographs of the Ritz, with a warm wood below it and across the floor. There was a mirror behind the bar, in true French style, that reflected the golden glow of the lamps, high enough that each face was deliciously vague. Every surface, from the golden metal of the barstool legs, to the wooden bar, to the dark wooden tables, reflected warmth.

"Now, Kiki, tell me what's been happening."

"I can't here, people will think I'm boasting."

Bertie laughed and rubbed his hands. We talked shop and London gossip until the toddy went down. He was shocked that I still hadn't seen my name in print and promised to send me the magazine. This would mean that he'd also send me little presents from London. Shortbread and silk stockings, if I gave him the right hints. When he came back with our cocktails—a Tom Collins for me, of course, I couldn't have anything else, not with that letter in the back of my mind—our bubbly chat became serious.

"Now, Kiki, if I said 'Fox,' what would you think?"

I hadn't heard that name since 1919. But no, he couldn't possibly mean—

"Furry red animal, loves chickens, known for its cunning."

"What if I said Dr. Fox?"

I froze. He did mean Fox. My hands shook.

"Kiki, are you all right? You've become alarmingly pale."

"Light me a cigarette."

He lit up and waited for me to gulp a few lungfuls. The tobacco smoke hung between us with everything that was unsaid.

"Bertie . . . have you met him?"

"I was called to his office in Westminster—"

"Parliament or civil service?"

"He never said, and I was too embarrassed to ask over the leather desktop and aroma of self-importance. He has the most wonderful silver hair, which really set off his charcoal Savile Row suit—"

"Did his secretary wear spectacles?"

"Why . . . yes! How did you know?"

"He's a fox, and bespectacled women are his hens. He likes them in his henhouse where he can get to them. Thank God I never needed glasses."

"Kiki, who on earth is he?"

I gave him a piercing look—what did he know? and how?—and he blushed.

"He, ah, he gave me a message for you."

Something broke inside me and sank to the bottom of my spine. It really was Fox. I closed my eyes and leaned back against the wall. I thought I'd left all that behind. Even the scent of Gauloises and gin, the sounds of clinking glass and tinkling French, couldn't buoy me up.

"Kiki, I didn't think that an old government paper pusher would be so shocking."

"He's not that old. He's had the silver hair since his twenties." Maybe if I kept my eyes closed, then this message would evaporate.

"He makes you shake and go pale! I haven't seen you like this since . . . well, you know . . ."

Since the end of the war. He didn't need to say it; I could hear it in his tone. I also couldn't hide from Fox forever; I had to open my eyes some time. When I did, Bertie was frowning at me. His face was so mobile that his frown was always clownish, as though even his concern amused him. It gave me hope.

"Take me to your bath, dear Bertie. Let's see if there's a chance I can outfox the Fox."

Bertie's bathroom was a temple of marble and gold, where each gleaming surface worshipped the hot, naked body. Actual steam rose from the gushing gold taps. There was rose-scented soap, and I sprinkled some drops of lavender oil into the swirling water. I sat on the toilet lid and held myself tightly, to stop the shaking in my knees, to halt the cold thought that Fox had found me. The bath filled; Bertie kissed my nose and went to order room service. Thank goodness modern clothes dispensed with all the buttons and laces of my prewar wardrobe, as otherwise Bertie would've had to undress me like a child. The silk fell in a pale heap on the marble and I slipped under the water.

How is it that something as simple as a tub of hot water can make you feel safe? That all is right with the world and nothing can harm you. Is it the closed space of the bathroom, private and steamy? Is it the warm embrace of the water? Whatever it was, the hairs on my body rose up to greet the water, and sighed, and settled down with me as I floated in its soothing, scented warmth. I hadn't had a bath this wonderful since I'd left my family home, with the servants to bring in all the water I needed. This bath was a feat of plumbing and engineering and modernity, but it had all the force of simple truth. I slid under the water until all I could hear was my heartbeat. Fox couldn't claim me. Whatever message had come from over the water, I had already found my freedom and no one could take it away.

The little window opposite the bath was ajar and the sounds of the street floated up to mix with the steam. I hoped Bertie would come in with the food soon, as the two drinks I'd downed in quick succession had made me woozy. As I waited, I examined my form—I didn't usually; I preferred my lovers to do that for me. I was still too thin. My hip bones jutted out sharply and there were hollows at my knees and my wrists. My breasts were efficient, compact, where they sat above my appearing and disappearing ribs. My body had lost its prewar plumpness, that late-teenage ripeness. My face too—my jawline was sharp and the slight dip in my cheeks made my cheekbones shine through my skin. All that bad food in the mess huts—bread and tinned meat when I could get it, but most often I finished my shift once the mess had closed and I had to make do with biscuits I'd brought from town—all that irregular eating and stress had ruined my appetite. I still forgot to eat. When I did remember, the food was often so rich that I could only stomach a few mouthfuls. I wouldn't admit that perhaps I smoked and drank to forget my hunger. All my hungers.

"Princess of the Buttons," Bertie called through the door, "the food is here. May I interrupt?"

"You'll be interrupting nothing but the growling of my stomach. I have a hole in my belly the size of Mons."

He brought in an enormous tray.

"I have an omelet, fresh baguette, butter and jam, Brie and Roquefort and pâté with those little toasty things, Florentines, and some madeleines. Oh yes, and a huge pot of Earl Grey tea, that I insisted they bring with milk."

"You're a wonder, Bertie. Why can't you live here in Paris and take care of me?"

"Because I have to live in London and take care of your income."

He placed the tray on the floor and sat crossed-legged in front of it, his waistcoat open and his socks getting wet.

"It's a bathroom picnic, Bertie."

"And here I was, thinking I'd come over for a night in the Montmartre hot spots."

"It's Montparnasse now, darling. Montmartre is so last century."

He laughed and poured the tea. He handed me a cup with a madeleine perched in the saucer.

"Take a sip and a nibble and talk."

"Is that an order?"

"Never again, Kiki."

I reached out and he squeezed my hand. The tea tasted of comfort and the madeleine of strength, both of them citrusy and spicy and light. I sighed.

"What was the message, Bertie?"

"Well, he . . . It was very odd. He was very polite, but he had this, it was a steel, no, a menace—yes, there was a threat behind his words. They seemed to imply my swift demise if I didn't comply. Although he was very charming—lovely manners, beautiful whisky from his own Scottish distillery—"

"Oh God . . ." This was Fox at his best, which meant he was up to his worst.

"Anyway, he asked me, ever so nicely, to give you this." He slid a letter on thick cream paper out of his pocket. "It's even sealed with wax! Otherwise—you know me—I'd have read it already."

Bertie placed it gently against one of the taps. I was glad that my hands were wet as I could hardly bear to open it. He pushed himself up and went into the bedroom.

"He also asked me to give you this, Kiki," he called. "Although I've no idea why."

He handed me a dirty handkerchief.

"Those aren't your initials."

Embroidered in the corner were the initials T. A. I. T.—Thomas Arthur Ian Thompson. It was Tom's hankie, and judging by the mud stains, it was from the war. That meant that Fox knew the truth about Tom. My heart skipped. I held the hankie to my face and it smelled both of Tom's tobacco and Fox's cologne. I didn't want to, but I burst into tears.

"Kiki! Kiki, Kiki, my darling, shush now, there there." Bertie kissed my forehead and stroked my wet hair.

"Bertie . . ." I looked into his brown eyes, so friendly and trusting—so unlike Tom's clear blue, so unlike Fox's opaque gray. I pinched my eyes to push the tears back down and sat up.

"Pass me a towel. I need to open that letter." I pushed my wet hair back, dried my hands, and tore it open.

Darkling,
And many a time have I been half in love—now more than ever—to take into the air my quiet breath while thou art pouring forth thy soul

*abroad in such an ecstasy! Still wouldst thou sing, and I have
ears—perhaps the self-same song that found a path through the sad
heart of Ruth, when, sick for home, she stood in tears amid the alien
corn; the same that ofttimes hath charm'd magic casements—*

*Forlorn! The very word is like a bell to toll me back from thee
to my sole self!*

Fled is that vision. Do you wake or sleep?

F to V.

I swore loudly. I could hardly believe it. But here it was, in his cal-
ligraphic handwriting.

"What is it?"

"My summons."

I passed the letter to him, and the hankie that I was still clutching, and
sank down into the bath. Fox had told me at the beginning that there
would be no end. And again, when I left two years ago, he sent me a
telegram: *There will be no end, V.* I'd thought he was talking about the war,
how close we were, how much closer he had tried to make me. I never
thought he meant that my work for him would never end. That there was
no end to his power over me. My hair floated about my face like seaweed
around the drowned. Perhaps I would do it, I would just breathe in and
never breathe out, let this marble room be my tomb. There would have
to be an end then.

But not for Tom. And even, I guessed, not for me; he'd somehow use
me from the grave. But this wasn't the war, he couldn't order me, he
couldn't tell me when to sleep and when to wake, when to eat and when
to starve. Whatever his power, I was in charge of how far I'd let it hold
me. I'd fought too hard to stay alive through those years and to be here
again in Paris. I wasn't going to give up this life for anyone.

Bertie was waiting, with a Florentine and another cuppa, for me to
reemerge.

"For strength, so you can tell me what the Fox is going on."

"What the Fox—I like that." The chocolate on the Florentine was smooth, the almonds soft, the caramel chewy, and the whole biscuit a mix of bitter and sweet. I moaned in appreciation.

"Whoever the Florentine was that inspired this delicacy, I salute her."

He sat in front me. He had put on his Captain Browne face, his no-nonsense, demand-and-command, interrogation face. He held up the letter.

"Keats?"

"'Ode to a Nightingale.' His favorite."

"A love letter?"

I laughed and it sounded bitter even to my ears.

"It's code. I have a mission."

"For what?"

"I don't know yet. Did he say anything else to you? Any small talk, about the weather, about France—"

"He said . . . yes, he said it twice, which was odd. He said, 'Midnight in Paris is the best time to rendezvous, wouldn't you agree, Browne? Midnight at the Rotonde.' No one's called me Browne since the war. I never even mentioned Paris."

Midnight at the Rotonde. Bertie watched me, and his Captain Browne faced slipped.

"What does it mean?"

"It's my rendezvous."

"For what? You're being very mysterious."

"I thought you liked mysterious."

"I like your velvet dresses and seductive stories, Kiki. But this is too much like home leave: all shadows and the echo of tears."

He stroked my hair back, smoothed my eyebrows down so they made neat arches across my face. His hair curled haphazardly in the steam, and his collar had become floppy. I held out my hand and he put pâté toast into it.

"Do you know Fox from the war?" he asked.

"Unfortunately." I put out my hand for more food and was rewarded with Brie.

"You worked for him? You work for him still?"

"Apparently. So do you."

"Not possible."

"You relayed the message. You're his Hermes."

"I didn't agree to this!"

"None of us ever do."

"But who is he?"

I hesitated. My first instinct was to say nothing, keep my head down, deflect direct questions and imply by silence. But this wasn't a Somme field, and Bertie wasn't a clueless VAD, a German POW, or nosy senior officer. He was my delicious friend, caring and funny and discreet as a locked box. He refilled my tea with just the right amount of milk. I could trust him.

"He was the doctor in charge of surgery in my first unit. He trained me."

"As a nurse?"

"No. As a spy."

"Spy! What, the entire war?"

"No, from 1916. Towards the end of the Somme."

"But at least as long as you've known me."

I nodded. He stared.

"You know, I always thought there was something. You weren't like the other nurses, you never told stories of the wards, you just drank fearlessly and laughed at the men who tried to make you their little woman. You were tougher, somehow."

"He made me so . . . no, he made me understand how to be tough. You know, he kept me on my feet for forty hours straight once, until I collapsed."

"Charming!"

"That was nothing, compared to later."

"And the Keats? Why Keats? What does it mean? It's just a bunch of jumbled lines."

I couldn't meet his eye. I turned to the taps, the gold now garish, and ran the hot water. He tapped his teaspoon on his knee. I could almost hear his frown in the muffled paradiddle.

"You should've told me, Kiki. Although, if you were a spy, I suppose you couldn't. You're not even telling me now, and the war is over." He looked into my face.

"More cheese, please."

He smeared the Roquefort over the baguette and handed it to me.

"So if he trained you, then he must be a spy, too. What's a spy lord-and-master called?"

"Just Fox will suffice."

"And in the letter—'F to V'?"

"Fox to Vixen."

"You're his lover?"

"Only in his fantasies. But I've often had to play his counterpart."

"Did you give him that scar on his cheek for his trouble?"

"That was a mortar. He was so happy when he got it, he told me not to treat it so it would scar properly. He said it made him look like a proper Prussian."

"Don't tell me he's German."

"Very well then."

"Jesus wept, Kiki—"

"He's English now. He was English in the war. But he's a German native."

"Can we trust him?"

"Not a whit."

"I don't suppose we can ignore him?"

"No." Fox's cold smile seemed to chill the bathwater. "I can't, anyway. If you just relay the messages, as he asks, you might get away with doing just that."

"And the handkerchief?"

"That's my leash, my blackmail, my . . . my 'spectacles,' if you will. The man to whom it belongs is . . . a dear friend in a terrible situation. Fox must know the truth. I didn't even know he knew about . . . but as he clearly does, then he probably has the power to clear my friend's name. If I do as he asks."

"You know all this from the letter and the hankie?" Bertie's raised eyebrow seemed to want to crawl off his head.

"I know all this from . . ." From what—his hot-and-cold moods? His mania for secrets? His desire for power over all the living world, including me? "From years of working for him."

He refilled my teacup and tucked some omelet into the baguette. But I needed more than nibbles, I needed a proper sit-down meal with beer and pudding. I needed time to smooth out Bertie's frown.

"You still haven't told me very much, Kiki."

"But have I told you enough?"

He looked me over under the water. It wasn't a look of lust, or judgment, or even pity. It saw the mole on my inner thigh with its wiry black hair, the scars on my knees and forearms, the calluses on my fingers that would never recede, and accepted them. It made me feel seen.

"Yes. I suppose you have. For now."

"Good. I'm cold, Bertie. I need you to warm me up."

The old ways are sometimes the best ways—he warmed me up in bed. I was a little tender and sore—in mind, body and soul—but he was the perfect gentleman. I was the focus of his attention; so much so that he didn't even get properly undressed.

"But what about you?"

"Next time."

"Do you have a new boyfriend?"

He blushed a deep scarlet.

"What's his name?"

"Hamilton Houseman. But he prefers to go by his middle name, Edward."

"Oh, Bertie—"

"Teddy to his friends—"

"My poor dear."

"How can I help it? He's even blond. Other than that, he's nothing like him. He's his own man. Or boy, I should say."

"How old is he?"

"Twenty-two."

"Did he fight?"

"For about ten seconds. I suppose that's why he's still here."

Unlike Bertie's first Teddy, his true love, Edward Greene, who'd been fertilizing Flanders for the past five years with his very own version of blood and bone. I squeezed Bertie's hand. This boy wasn't the first unsuitable Teddy replacement and I guessed he wouldn't be the last. By Bertie's embarrassment, he guessed it too.

"What's the time?" He stretched lazily to his wristwatch on the bedside table, and started. "Oh, I have a dinner engagement, Kiki—"

He jumped up and began dressing for dinner.

"I thought you came here for me."

"I had to justify the trip with the editor, so I'm dining with Uncle Maxwell's aunt's daughter-in-law's—"

"—sister's lover's—"

"—second cousin, or some such. Anyway, Mabel is a great admirer of the paper and a great benefactor. I'm to supply her with gossip and flattery."

"Sounds like fun."

"Like being the organ grinder's monkey. Will you be roaming the den-izens later? After ten? I should have escaped by then."

"I'll be at the Rotonde at midnight."

"Very good . . . oh!" He stopped dressing and looked at me. "I see."

"Yes. Quite."

"Will you want company? What's in store for you?"

"I have no idea."

Except that not only was I a detective, I was now, once again, a spy.

5

"BOY WANTED"

My ivory dress gleamed in the twilight as I slowly walked back to my studio. Cafés were lighting their heaters, and the streetlamps stretched and blinked awake. Ladies of the night lounged in their doorways and windows, chatted with one another or called and winked at the stray men passing by still in their good church suits. The smells of salt and cream, potatoes and garlic, mixed with the street stench of piss and rotting vegetables. The sky was purple like lilacs, like royalty, like a bruised mouth, as it slowly passed into darkness.

My hips were sore, my legs were sore; I felt as though every limb had taken a battering. I'd smoked too many cigarettes and sharp little pains in my stomach warned me off eating properly—it had enough work, it said, with all that cheese and chocolate. Usually the Parisian night soothed me and revived me, the lights all the way up to the tower, the river in its stone bed as it brought gossip to the sea. But tonight I needed time alone; I needed to read my letters again and again, I needed a sweet draught of vintage with purple bubbles winking at the brim—

I cursed. There it was, a line from "Ode on Melancholy," Keats in my steps and my cadences. Fox was already in my head, already shaping my thoughts. He knew how my mind worked, so he knew what that letter

would do to me. But I wasn't in uniform now— I wondered if he'd cal-
culated just how much that meant to me.

I almost ran up the stairs to my studio, with anxiety, with anger, with a
desperate desire to be in my own place and alone. I opened the windows
to let in the cool night air, stripped off to my camiknickers, and flopped on
the mattress. The room smelled of geraniums and dirty clothes. I poured
myself some water from the washing jug and felt under my pillow. There
it was, my treat—Tom's letter.

Button,

So, how are the mademoiselles? Do you hinky-dinky parley-voo,
or do the Yanks and the Brits sing that as you saunter by? How is
the Seine—does it still glitter in the lamplight, does it still ripple
like a snake in the sun? Have you gone back to that little café
where we taught mah-jongg to the proprietor's daughter until
dawn? Have you grown fat with croissants and éclairs and other
rich food bought for you by rich suitors? I think I'd like to see you
with a little tummy, dimples in your plump cheeks and fat arms
swinging like a tuckshop lady. But I don't think you have grown
plump. I think, instead, that you're sitting in a little garret, legs
dangling out the window, smoking a cheap cigarette as you read
this letter. Am I right, or am I right?

I could practically hear the laughter in his voice.

I'm writing to you from a little table in the Old Quarter.

I started. There are no "old quarters" in any city in Australia.

The goats clatter over the cobblestones and the carpet sellers
yell in time with the call to prayer. The smells are just as they

were six years ago, four years ago; the coffee still like a bullet
to the brain and the baklava so wet with honey it tastes like a
dirty joke.

I exclaimed so loudly that a man looked up from the street and waved
his hat.

Does your mouth hang open? Have you sat up straight, with
that "What's all this then?" frown, at the mention of these un-
Australian details? Have you said "What!" loudly enough to make
people look up from the street?

What a cheek! He knew me too well.

So you should. I'm not in Sydney—or Bathurst or even
Melbourne—I'm in Gaza. By the time this letter reaches you, I'll be
almost in Paris. I'm coming to see you, Button. Well, to be more
precise, I'm taking up a position as junior foreign correspondent
for the Herald, to operate out of London but to cover all of
Europe and the Middle East. Possibly also North Africa, but
that depends on the senior correspondent. Possibly also small,
bohemian studios in Paris—but that copy might not be written up
until my memoirs. Not if you're involved.

I can give you all the details when we meet. I will only give
you the details when we meet, in fact, so if you want to know
where, when, how, then you'll have to leave all your arty parties
and spend some time with me. I travel, and write, under the name
Thomas Arthur, for reasons that you know full well. I don't know
where I'll stay yet, but probably some dodgy hotel around Gare du
Nord, which is where the train gets in from the coast—but you
know this too.

What do you say, Button? Feel like a ramble down rue de
Rivoli with yours truly? Feel like a riotous night out paid for by
our hometown's most illustrious rag? Send me a telegram via
the <u>Herald</u>—they'll find me, wherever I am. If you don't, I'll come
and find you, just like I used to—I'll say, send me to the blond
<u>Australienne</u>! And the lads will know precisely where to find you.
So you may as well send that telegram and turn up at the station
and get ready to be on the receiving end of the biggest hug this
side of the equator. It's coming for you.
I'm coming for you.

Tom-Tom xxx

My Tom-Tom. His name beat in my heart like a drum, a call to arms,
the pulse of the dance. The last image I had of him was as I left Woolloo-
mooloo dock. It had been an unseasonably cold December, so his collar was
turned up against the wind and his shoulders hunched as he glared at the
departing ship. He hadn't said a word on the tram to the dock. He hadn't
waved as the ship pulled into the Pacific. Had he known that he'd join me
in Europe before long? Or had my departure challenged him, just as I had
dared him to race further on my father's horses, to leave the comfortable
squattocracy for the city lights of Sydney, to leave university and run away
to the war? He'd looked haunted on that dock, dark hair plastered to his
face, as though my departure was a betrayal. There wasn't a hint of that in
this letter, just bright smiles and sharp teases. The Tom-Tom of old, before
the war made him fearful and thin, before his silence in the ship's wake.

He'd be here in a couple of days. The past four months suddenly
felt like years. I wanted to know, right now, whether he still rolled his
cigarettes in his left hand or if he now smoked a pipe, if he still liked his
waistband to sit an inch lower than the fashion, if his cowlick still made his
black hair pop out of its pomade and flop over his dark blue eyes. If the
scars on his back had healed properly. If he still coughed. If he missed me.

I started—how long had I been daydreaming? It must be time for me to get ready, and I needed a drink before I spoke to Fox. If Tom-Tom was almost in Europe, then I could help him; we could clear his name. But only if I showed up at the Rotonde at midnight. I rootled through my clothes again—ivory silk was too pretty for nighttime, but there was precious little else that wasn't stained or stinking, I promised myself to do some laundry tomorrow—my navy-blue chiffon would have to do. It was cut very modestly, with a high collar and long sleeves that buttoned at the wrists so tightly that I struggled into it. But of course, it was semisheer, so the outline of my slip, camiknickers, and garters was visible in the right light. My favorite kind of tease. I threw my opera cape over my faux-modest outfit, hopped into my boots—I had to have some warmth, after all—and clattered downstairs to the café.

I could see the lights of the cafés spill down the street. Tonight, it was the Rotonde that had the tables out the front with the artists and party people. The cafés were my second home. I knew that Madame Fujita had a one-eyed cat and the waiter Henri at the Rotonde had fiancée trouble. I knew where the Parisians sat, the Americans, the British, and the Spanish, and the space this left for the tourists. I'd been here just long enough to be able to walk in and find a friend at any time of the day. Everyone was so excited to be in Paris, it was infectious; coffee saucers stacked up, wine flowed, we shared *frites* and baguettes and cigarettes from Turkey, America, and Egypt. Soon the lights started singing, the accordion-accented jazz spilled out the doorways, and multilingual chatter flared with the lamps. Did I hate Fox for spoiling this place with his assignations, or was I secretly glad that at least I had a spot of warmth in this cold work? I couldn't decide, but the jazz set the pace, and I walked faster towards my fellow travelers.

North was there, as usual. She took off her hat to wave to me, showing off her newly bobbed hair. At that moment, I loved her big smile and big inheritance and bigger Francophilia.

"What do you think, Kiki? Am I a modern American woman or what?" She shook out her hair as I applauded. "Anyway, sit down, and have you met Hermine? She's back from New York."

Dark-haired Hermine extended her hand, calloused and covered in ink.

"A 'andshake—it is the American way, no? New York was exciting, *oui*, but I'm so very glad to be back in my Paris."

"Aren't we all."

"But you are *Australienne*, no?"

"I was here as a nurse in the war."

"Ah." She clasped her hands and looked out at the street. A hard, basalt feeling stuck in my chest—loss and grief—that little *ah* seemed to trap it, to encase it in the fat ring on her gnarled left hand.

"Hermine's an artist. Kiki, honey, sit down, I'll order you a drink."

I checked my wristwatch, slender and silver and delicately decorated with my father's condescension, "Time to settle down, eh?" and he laughed at his own joke. He never considered that I'd been working shifts as a nurse for years, with a watch permanently pinned to my uniform; time was anything but settled. 11:20 p.m.—I still had a while to wait.

"You speak French?" Hermine looked relieved when I nodded. "We had to leave for New York. Jules . . . he would have had to fight for Bulgaria. Unthinkable. So we waited—"

"Jules is Jules Pascin," North interrupted in English. "Have you met him? He's just a darling. So talented! They both are."

Hermine bowed her head at the compliment. The music inside flickered with the light over her coiled hair, her big, wide-set eyes, her long fingers. One eye rolled sideways, as though it looked to the past while she looked, through me, to the future. I lit up a cigarette and she took one with gratitude. Gitanes, this time, to fit with my gypsy life.

"We didn't know, of course, what it would be like. . . . I think if we had, we may have stayed, to help our people, to save this perfect city. But the Bulgarian authorities—truly, they are barbarous. Jules would've been blown up over Russia and I would've been left selling my work on the street like I did when I was twenty."

She looked down her long straight nose at me.

"We never thought that leaving would . . . we thought everyone would do it. Now we are back, we realize how many suffered."

"And how many never made it home—Apollinaire is still mourned. Perhaps you did the right thing."

"Perhaps," she sighed. "At least there is a home to come home to. I feel for those whose homes have disappeared—all these Russians—although there seems to be more than one type of refugee from this war," Hermine said, giving me a once-over. "Counts from Russia, fleeing the workers. Workers from Germany, fleeing the counts in their brown shirts. Society girls from Australia, fleeing . . . what, I wonder?"

"Not brown shirts, just stuffed shirts." I raised my glass and smiled.

"What's wrong with a brown shirt?" asked North, "I mean, sure, it's dull, but—"

"It is the terrible uniform of the new bullies in Germany," said Hermine. "Jules told me about them from his friends in Bavaria. These young men in their brown shirts, they beat up workers who strike, they stroll the streets with their batons and whack anyone they think might be Communist—"

"They're part of a political party."

"With one of those long German names that I can never remember—"

"National Socialist German Workers' Party," I said, draining my glass, "but I don't think they have much to do with socialism." I had read about them in London whilst flicking through Bertie's morning paper.

"They have more to do with France than I would like," said Hermine. "You have heard of Action Française? My angry young nephew recently joined them—"

"Isn't that a nationalist group?"

"More than that now. I had coffee with my nephew and he spewed forth invective on the government, Jews, the Church, French honor—truly, I was disgusted—and then some strange questions about how much my work would fetch at auction, whether it would fetch more here or elsewhere in Europe—"

"Oh, politics," North sighed. Hermine started, then smiled.

"Exactly so! And all this talk is too bad, too sad, even for my French sensibilities. Tell me, how can you be another Kiki de Montparnasse?"

I grinned. We talked about her work and all the artistic gossip from her time in America, about her upcoming exhibition in London, 'the "*Day-vid Soh-loh*," they call it, in their English way.' The street clattered with chatter. The lights from the café played over the velvet and silk, the rough wool and corduroy of the sinuous, vital patrons. It teased our tousled hair and winter-pale skin. There was an undertone of chill in the air, but my drink's blackcurrant kick warmed me almost to my fingertips. I was about to order us another round when the waiter Henri appeared at my shoulder.

"Just who I wanted." I smiled, but his face was grave.

"Mademoiselle, there is a telephone call for you."

"A telephone call? Here? How novel!" North exclaimed. My desire for a cocktail vanished. I lit up another cigarette as I followed Henri through the crowded café to the back office. It was surprisingly quiet in there, as I could only just hear the noise from the kitchen and nothing at all from the bar. The walls must have been solid brick.

Henri refused a tip. Something in his face, his manner, said that he knew what this was about. Perhaps Fox knew his war record and had threatened him. He gave me a look that was part pity, part fear, part protectiveness, as he closed the door behind me.

The receiver waited on the table. I finished my cigarette, stubbing it out in the copper basin by the lamp, before I picked up.

"'Darkling I listen.'"

He laughed, deep and rich. I hated that laugh, though it was exactly what I wanted. I heard him inhale and couldn't help but see him at a desk, suit pressed razor-sharp, one of his favorite gold-tipped Sobranies between his thin lips. He used to make me collect the ends, as their glinting foil on the ground would reveal where he had been.

I continued. "'To cease upon the midnight with no pain—'"

"'While thou art pouring forth thy soul abroad in such an ecstasy!' You could certainly choose a worse place to expire than Paris."

"Better than Flanders, at any rate."

"But 'thou wast not born for death,' immortal Vixen."

"Because I'm part of the hungry generation?"

"Because I need you. My heart aches."

"Then go to the doctor."

"Through envy of thy happy lot—"

"I knew it—"

"And 'being too happy in thine happiness—'"

"How can I be too happy, with you sniffing at my heels?"

"Vixen, that's unkind. Our first words in two years? Say you're happy to hear from me."

"You're happy to hear from me."

"That's true. I missed my little Vixen."

"Not so little."

"You've grown fat?" I heard him light another cigarette. "I didn't think so. You're too sleek, Vixen, too much the huntress."

"I hunt nothing."

"Not even young men?"

"They're hens in a henhouse. No hunting involved."

"Ah, so you're bored."

"Rubbish."

"I had hoped so. I'd hate to truly envy your 'happy lot.'"

"You'd hate nothing if it brought me closer."

"Too true, Vixen. It's been two years—"

"And four months." I cursed under my breath. Why did I have to remember so exactly? He made a satisfied little murmur down the line.

"It's been too long. It's time you sharpened those teeth."

"How did you find me?"

"Tell me, is this just for me or do all your men appreciate such banter?"

I didn't like this turn in the conversation.

"I know your London man, Captain of the Soho Seas, enjoys your repartee. But what about that handsome farm boy? Wouldn't he prefer a little wife baking scones or—what is the Australian equivalent? Lamingtons?—to a fiery-tailed vixen?"

He wasn't right, about either man, but that he knew about them at all meant that he knew about too much. I lit another cigarette, my nervous anger needed a physical outlet.

"How did you get that handkerchief?"

"I won it at White's."

I choked back a gasp. "How did you know what to wager?"

"We foxes have sharp ears, don't we? I knew something like this would come along if I was patient. The previous owner had a loose tongue and several exploitable weaknesses."

"But . . ." But this means he must've known about Tom for a long time, that he knew I had helped him to desert and escape back to Sydney. If he knew what to listen for—evidence of Tom's innocence and who would have it—then he could well know everything. He knew enough, at least, to keep me on a very tight leash.

"Yes, Vixen?" I could hear the laughter in his deep voice. "Is there something you don't understand?" He was a tease. I wanted to slam down the receiver; I wanted to interrogate him until he told me everything. He loved this, I hated it, but I couldn't keep away. Even if I wanted to.

"I don't understand why you would wait this long to rein me back in."

"You're not a horse, Vixen, even if you do have the bit between your teeth."

"If you know about the handkerchief, then you know about its owner." I wouldn't mention Tom by name.

"And the part you played in his treason." A shiver ran over my skin. "I do, Vixen."

"You could have me put away."

"I could."

"So much power, Fox. Why wait to use it?"

He paused. I could almost hear him think—to tease or tell the truth? I was so angry, so nervous, that I could hardly breathe.

"Because I knew you'd come back."

"How—"

"Once you'd rested, you would become bored and return to Europe. Life here is much too exciting. Life, here with me. I just had to wait until you knew it too."

I hated his games, I couldn't stop myself from playing.

"How did you find me?"

"Vixen"—his voice dropped low—"do you really think I'd lose you? After all we've been through. You're much too precious."

A tiny admission—this was as close as I'd get to a show of vulnerability from Fox. His next words would be a tease or a threat. I sighed.

"Such a sigh, Vixen."

"What's my mission?"

"Nothing to sigh over."

"Why do you need me? Surely you have enough men to do this work."

"But they're men, Vixen. They can't get close enough to their prey."

"I see. And you have no other predators in your pay?"

"There can only be one vixen, Vixen." There was a strain in his voice that confused me. There could only be one vixen? That little vocal wobble, that was real. Surely that was not an admission of love—

"Darkling, do you listen?"

"With a pencil." I fished one from my handbag and took a sheet of paper from the desk.

"Good. In some melodious plot of beechen green, with shadows numberless, there is a mole. The mole quite forgets the weariness, the fever, and the fret, where men sit and hear each other groan, where youth grows pale and dies. More than ever seems it rich to die, not for the warm south, but for the lands forlorn. Tender is the night, and he cannot see what flowers are at his feet. His plaintive anthem fades, his high requiem becomes a sod. The murmurous haunt of flies treads him down. The faery lands are too forlorn, and the word will toll him back from thee to my sole self."

He paused. I heard nothing but his cigarette and the ticking clock on the desk.

"Vixen?"

"Why have you given me this mission in code? The war is over."

"And the new war has begun."

"Oh, please—"

"I must protect my little huntress." He tried to be playful.

"You just want to play games with me."

"No one plays better."

"And if I won't play?"

A pause and his voice went cold.

"Where do you keep the handkerchief? In your handbag? Or under your pillow, where you can smell my cologne as you sleep?"

Ay, here's the rub.

"You're a bastard."

"You don't like that smell? It used to be your favorite."

"This is blackmail."

"This is protection. Trust me."

"Impossible."

"And yet what choice do you have?"

None, and he knew it. I had to trust him, at least for the moment, at least until I could help Tom. I sighed. There was nothing for it but to sink my teeth into the mission.

"So, these clues—they're a Dada poem with Keats. Artists and espionage—am I on the right track?"

"Oh, Vixen, I'm disappointed. You know 'Ode to a Nightingale.'"

I read over the message.

"A mole . . . there's no mole in the poem," I said, and he murmured assent. "What's a mole?"

"Don't you know your spy lore? Sir Francis Bacon used that term back in the seventeenth century."

"You used to call them double agents."

"And I still do. But 'mole' seemed more poetic."

"I don't rate your skills. You're no Romantic."

"You'd be surprised."

"I'd have to be." And he laughed, which pleased me, which haunted me.

"Too kind. But I expect more from you in the future."

"If there is a future. Maybe this terrible enemy will get me."

"You wouldn't waste my time by getting caught. Not if you value your little farm boy." I could hear him swallow. He must be drinking whisky; he was enjoying himself. All his little habits were so familiar—which meant, of course, that mine were to him. I bet he even knew which cigarettes I smoked today.

"Now, you know I find it such fun when you resist me, Vixen, but it's time to work. Expenses have been wired to you."

"I don't need your money."

"Buy some stockings. Or a warmer dress—that little sheer number you're wearing must be very draughty."

"How do you know? Actually, don't tell me. I don't care."

He laughed.

"This little chat was so good, I think we should do it again."

"When?"

"Is it Monday already? Then midnight, the day after tomorrow."

"To say what? You've given me nothing to work with."

"Hunt quickly, Vixen"—his voice was at its silkiest, which always put me on my guard—"and don't get too distracted by the hens in the hen-house." He hung up without a goodbye.

I sat on the table. Everything was still. I was embalmed in darkness, to think is to be full of sorrow and leaden-eyed despair—there it was again, Keats in my cadences—I'd seen his other spies quote Wordsworth and Shelley, barely aware of it. They didn't know I knew who they were, as they never suspected a woman could be a spy. They didn't know that when I saw them slick their hair back and give that twitchy half smile that I could see how Fox was inside them, directing them. It used to happen to me. Was it happening again? He had me in his power, and he'd keep that power as long as he could. If I didn't want Tom hung as a traitor—if I didn't want to be jailed as an accomplice—then I had to obey. I had a mission, but what scared me most was that I liked it.

I pushed my way out of the office and almost ran into the café. I needed people, lights, music! I needed a drink—or three. I blinked at the brightness and the sound as it overwhelmed me, as it took me in its arms and kissed me all over my face—

"Bertie?"

"Kiki! I've been waiting for an age, sitting alone like little Jack Horner without his pie. Where have you been?"

"The phone is in the office."

"What? Oh! Of course. Oh yes, I got this letter at the Ritz on my way out. It's from Fox, look."

The beautiful paper was decorated with Fox's black loops. His attention to every tiny detail was beautiful and chilling.

Ever since I put on a uniform
I have just one heart for just one boy
Dream on, little soldier boy
We're on our way to France
Why don't they give us a chance?
Goodbye, France
I'll take you back to Germany
A man is only a man
With Alexander's Ragtime Band
F to V.

"Kiki, what on earth does it mean? They're all Irving Berlin songs."

"He couldn't tell me too much over the telephone—"

"Why? Wait, you need a drink. You're far too pale. Garçon!"

Bertie took me by the waist and led me to a corner table. The seats were plush and there was only one little lamp nearby, so we were very sheltered. He lit my cigarette and stroked my knee. Henri hurried over with a very large brandy and a very serious *Mademoiselle*. This second message shocked me. Fox had planned too much—two messages through Bertie, the telephone call, Henri—he must have been planning my return for a long time. For longer than I had. I tried to tell myself that this was just his arrogance, just wishful thinking, but I couldn't shake the notion that he brought me back, that he somehow controlled me from afar. Bertie stroked my knee and chatted about nothing until I had imbibed enough to speak.

"Was it that bad, Kiki?"

"No, but it will be."

"I'm here to help."

"No—the less you know, the better. Hide in your trench of ignorance, Bertie, it'll keep you safe."

"I'd rather go over the top with you."

"Let's just be over the top."

"'Knees up Mother Brown'?"

"Rouge your cheeks and roll your stockings down."

I gulped the rest of my brandy and Bertie lit me his last Gauloises.

"I hope you know that I've no intention of letting you cope with all this . . . whatever it is, on your own."

"Bertie—"

"Not that you couldn't—you're the most capable woman, no, person, I've ever met."

"Thank you, but—"

"But there's just no call for it." He stroked my hair. "Friends in need and all that. Besides, we're alive, we're together, and we're in Paris."

"We're in Paris!" I grinned.

"Now, tell me about the songs, Kiki."

I sighed. "They reference soldiers, Germany, and Berlin."

"They're a code?"

"Of course. Fox only speaks in code. He can say 'milk, no sugar,' but every other sentence has a second meaning." The café lights glowed, but they seemed so far away.

"This note must relate to the message he gave me over the telephone."

"Right. Well, I'm a whiz at the cryptic crossword. Let me give my brain a workout before we descend into debauchery."

"All right, but we have to be quick." I handed over the message from Fox. "I can see my other friends looking around for me. They're terrible gossips."

"I don't understand this at all." He stared at the paper.

"I have to find someone—a traitor—who works for some terrible but unspecified enemy. I've no idea yet who that might be. This second message seems to suggest that this traitor is German, or the enemy is German, perhaps a former soldier . . . Part of the clue is the code itself. We're not at war, so the enemy has to be someone who's good at ciphers."

"Like a spy?"

"Like one of Fox's former underlings." I enjoyed working out the clues with Bertie, it made these letters from Fox feel like a game. "Which is another clue—why me? Why wait for me to arrive in Europe to undertake this mission? I was his only female spy. The only men who saw me were dead, or about to be. Therefore, no one will suspect me and I can get close to this mole. There is no other reason that he would need me." No other rational reason, at any rate.

"Gosh!"

"Golly—"

"My giddy aunt—"

"Crikey. Streuth." I played up my accent. "Stone the crows."

"But—"

"But more next time." I nodded at North, who was weaving her way between the tables. She yoo-hoo'd as she made her way to the lavatory.

"So that's where you're hiding! And who's this? Don't keep him all to yourself, Kiki—come and join us outside. Pascin's arrived with three models, and they're debating bolshevism and its relation to the avant-garde—it's so exciting!" She sighed. "I just love Paris, don't you?"

"Love it." I looked at Bertie. "Don't you?"

"Love it." He took me in his arms and started to foxtrot, humming "When I'm Out With You." More Irving Berlin—I couldn't help but hum along.

"I AIN'T NOBODY'S DARLING"

Sparrows woke me later that morning. They landed on my windowsills to chat, preen, and gossip. When the days were bright and clear like this morning, they flocked in for the summer, setting up nests in every available eave. It was so European, it was so particularly Parisian—the sparrows in the geraniums, the tin windowsill in the stone wall—I couldn't help but feel in love. I rolled out of bed and sat, my velvet cape around me, in the window with a cigarette.

Fox's messages sat next to Tom's letter on the trunk that I used as a table, held down from the breeze by an empty wine bottle. Lines from the notes played through my head, like a song I half knew but couldn't quite remember. I was sure that my instincts were right—the mole had to be one of Fox's protégés, which is why he spoke in code, and why he needed me. It also occurred to me that if Fox needed me, then he also needed me as a gossip columnist and café patron, as it was through my Parisian life that I would find the mole. Otherwise the clues were simply too opaque. I needed time to work through them all.

The morning mist had burned off, and the view was clear to the river and beyond. It was the perfect light to be Pablo's model for the first time. I shoved all the notes in my handbag and splashed my face. I needed coffee, lots of it, and some really quality breakfast. I slipped on a blue cotton day dress, patterned with swallows, and headed down to a café.

◆

Everyone knew where Picasso's studio was. It was one of the things foreigners learned almost as soon as they arrived in Paris, along with the opening hours of their national embassy and the number for Western Union. It was practically a place of pilgrimage, and if you hadn't gone there under your own steam, then some enthusiastic Brit or American would drag you to rue la Boétie to hang around outside the big double doors, hoping for a glimpse of the great man. I spent an entire afternoon there just after the war, when the soldier I spent my afternoon leave with—a certain Paul Nash, official war artist and modernist firebrand—wanted to knock Picasso down for not joining the war effort but couldn't bring himself to ring the bell. We sat on fruit boxes, with a bottle of red, a packet of cigarettes, and two army blankets, and watched the sun go down in the December afternoon.

So I knew where to go. I made my way over the cobbled streets, past the fruit and flower vendors, through the market, over the Seine, along the grand boulevards. The sun shone, the chestnuts blossomed, and I felt as light and carefree as a child's balloon. Not even the limping newspaper boy, who seemed to follow me around every corner, could pull me down.

I pressed the little buzzer by the olive-green doors. A boy in a ragged uniform appeared at the tiny half door cut into the bottom.

"*Oui, mademoiselle?*"

"I'm here to see Monsieur Picasso."

"Your name, please." He spoke with such Gallic weariness, all four feet seven of him, that I struggled not to laugh.

"Kiki Button. The *Australienne*."

He sniffed and closed the little door. I heard nothing for some moments, and was beginning to worry, when the main door rolled open and I was let in. I tipped him and he suddenly smiled, huge and innocent like the child he was. I wanted to hug him and feed him, but someone else was at the door and his cynical *"Oui, monsieur?"* fell onto the cobblestones. I headed over the courtyard and up to Picasso's flat.

"Kiki Kangaroo! What time is it? Ah yes, excellent," Picasso was effusive. He kissed me on both cheeks as he held his wet paintbrush away from me. I'd been ushered into his studio by the stern housekeeper, along with a pot of coffee and a plate of plain biscuits. Pablo was surrounded by sketches of dancers in striking poses, arms flung up, skirts swirling, frowns on their faces. As soon as he kissed me he turned back to his work, some type of quick sketch for a theater. It was red and yellow, with his typical bold lines and what looked like bull horns. I poured some coffee, took a biscuit, and watched the painting in front of him transform from a few lines into a full theater, complete with curtains and seating.

He sighed and flung down his brush. He turned to me, hands on hips. "Café?"

"Right here. What's this?" I indicated his work. He shrugged.

"For the Ballets Russes. They do a flamenco show, *Cuadro Flamenco*, with some friends of mine from Barcelona. Diaghilev, he doesn't know how to talk to the dancers; he treats them like furniture, as he did with all his Russians." He stuffed two biscuits in his mouth and gulped his coffee. "You know that Olga is a dancer? My wife?"

He rolled a cigarette with one hand and drank coffee with the other, talking at me the entire time.

"Yes, that's how we met, when I began to design for Diaghilev. But he doesn't understand." He shrugged again. "He has reached his limit. He has no *duende*, I see that now—or else he lost it—or else he just glowed with the reflected light of Olga's talent, of Nijinsky's and Stravinsky's and all the rest." He put down his coffee and walked over to a mirror that sat on top of the mantelpiece. He painstakingly cleaned all the crumbs off his face, chin, smock; he checked his teeth and smoothed his hair. He stubbed out his cigarette and turned to me.

"So, Kiki Kangaroo, I want to paint you as a can-can girl once the show is over. The step is over there, and a drape. Sit on the cushion and I will begin."

I'd never been an artist's model before. Did I just strip off here, in front of him? Did he even want me naked? More important, what about the detective work he needed me to do for him?

He was busy getting a sketchbook and pencils together. Next to a window was a little raised platform, very similar to the one at Manuelle's. On it was a chair, a side table, a jug, and a large white cotton sheet that looked more than a little grubby. I picked it up gingerly.

"Do you want me to wear this?"

He looked up sharply and frowned. I stood there for a long time as he considered.

"What underthings are you wearing? Do you wear a camisole, something like that?"

"Yes, and stockings."

"Then forget about the sheet. Just take off your coat, dress, hat, gloves—leave the shoes on. Let's see them—ah, yes, leave them on."

My shoes were new and shiny. They were patent black leather and more suited to evening than daytime, but I loved them so much that I wore them all the time. They had little silver stars along the side and a silver heel. They didn't even match my cotton dress, let alone my blue silk camisole. But when does that ever matter? I was glad that my camisole was clean though. It was a present from my mother—and by "present," I mean that she wired me some money for sensible shoes to wear to work and I had this tailored for me instead. The blue was bright, almost electric, and stopped just under my bottom. There were black lace panels on the knickers, which could be seen through the slit at the side of the slip. I wasn't wearing a corset either, as I'd conveniently left them all behind at Bertie's flat. My stockings were clipped to suspenders that hung from a little band around my waist. When I turned around to sit on my chair, Pablo was staring at me.

"Do you dress like this all the time, my kangaroo?"

"Mostly, yes. Shall I sit here?"

"Ah . . . yes, yes." He seemed distracted. "Just drape yourself over the chair. Yes, put your hand on the table, tip your head back, yes, just like that—now, put one leg over the arm of the chair—"

"Much better for movement." I was spread over the chair like a lady of the night as she waits, tired but awake, for her next man. Pablo looked me up and down, not really checking my pose at all, just looking at me. He came over and put his hand on my knees, moving my legs apart so the angle was more intense. He stroked the inside of my knee with his thumb, almost absentmindedly. Then he breathed in sharply and turned back to his seat.

"Very good. Sketches first . . ."

He worked very quickly. He seemed to finish sketches like they were cups of coffee. He looked at me but only saw me half the time, the other half I was a collection of angles and lines. It was odd, to see him see me, and the tension built between us, then suddenly disappeared so I was nothing more than a pose. Despite the lasciviousness of it, the pose was quite comfortable, as if I'd just flung myself down after a long night. I had expected to become one of Picasso's flat-planed women and so hold a tortured naked pose for hours. As soon as he sat me down I realized that was preposterous—the planes were in his mind, not my body—and I could easily hold this pose for a long time.

I had a good view of his studio from my chair. It was a mess. There were paintings and sketches and sculptures stacked everywhere. Piles of paper, both art paper with drawings and newspaper, lay in rumpled heaps. Jars of old water lined shelves like biological exhibits. Pencils were heaped in jars that held down tablecloths splattered in paint. All the paintbrushes seemed clean, standing to attention in beautiful, if splattered, vases. There were also many swatches of fabric and a model of a theater, and various photographs of flamenco dancers pinned to the walls and scattered on the table. A window was open to let in a breeze and to let out the paint fumes. Despite all the clutter at floor level, the high windows and higher ceilings made the room seem airy and light, some kind of optical trick, not unlike Picasso's own work.

"Kiki, turn your face to—ah, yes, very good."

I rested my chin against my shoulder and he looked me straight in the eye. His eyes were so large and dark, smart and wild, their image seemed to last longer than his gaze. Maybe it was because their image was constantly refreshed, as he kept looking at me as he drew. He drew less and less and looked longer and longer, a smile creeping into his face, until he put down his pad and pencil and walked over to me.

"Now, my Kangaroo, the sketches are over. Time for a break."

He leaned over and kissed me. It was so different to the last time, tender where that was urgent, attentive where that was demanding. I could taste the coffee and tobacco on his breath, it mixed with the smell of paint in the room. He smiled as he knelt down between my legs and started to undo all the clips of my suspender belt. It was the first time I noticed that he was almost forty. He was so sure, so active, that I thought of him as someone agelessly virile—but of course, he was just a man, with skin rough from decades of shaving and white flecks in his dark hair. His hands were lined and calloused, with nails bitten down to the quick. They moved with swift purpose though, as they rolled down my stockings and held my legs apart so he could bite the inside of my thighs. I gasped.

"It doesn't hurt," he said into my leg as he bit again.

"No, but . . ." It didn't hurt actually, he was very gentle, but it was a shock. He bit me gently again and again, along both thighs, until they tingled. He took off my shoes—"Such pretty shoes, Kiki,"—took off my stockings, and pulled me up by my waist.

"This chair is too small," he said close to my ear. "This way." I still wore my suspender belt, and he slipped his hand under my chemise to grab it and pull me over to a couch under a far window. The window was open and a sharp breeze blew in with all the sounds of the street. He half knelt on the couch so his eyes were level with my waist. He unclipped the belt, undid the buttons that held up my knickers, and grunted with approval as the silk fluttered to the floor. My chemise only just covered my bum, so as he turned me around, I could almost feel him looking at what was revealed. I certainly felt his little bite, and I jumped.

"Jumping kangaroo! You're so sweet, I can hardly help myself."

When our pulse had stopped thudding in our ears, Pablo strode over to his table. He had strong thighs, muscled shoulders, and a confidence to every gesture that you can only get from a few decades of knowing your own body. He grabbed his pipe, his sketchbook and pencils, and threw me my handbag with my cigarettes. He sat on the couch, pipe in his mouth and book on his lap, and sketched me. I had a cigarette between my lips and wore only my chemise.

"Pablo . . ."

"Hmph?" He saw nothing but the curve of my breasts. He pushed the silk aside so that my nipple popped out and continued to draw.

"Don't you have a bit of detective work for me?"

"What?" He looked up, and his expression cleared. "Ah, yes! Of course. Yes, you must do something for me. Olga's portrait has been stolen. She's—oh, you know how it is—she thinks I gave it away, or lost it, or something. She's gone to her friend in the country and won't come home until I have it back. As proof that I love her." He waved his pipe hand in a dismissive *and all of that sort of thing* gesture.

"What does the painting look like?"

"Like Olga, by Picasso." He kept drawing, as though that was enough.

"I've never met Olga."

"Haven't you? No. So. It's . . ." He frowned, then flipped to a new piece of paper and began to draw. "It looks like this." An elegant woman emerged on the page, with dark hair and an arresting gaze, long limbs gracefully draped over the divan she sat on—probably the one I was draped over now. Pablo jumped up and grabbed some chalks and sketched in the colors as well, blue and violet with mad splashes of vibrant yellow. He gazed at it critically, then ripped it out of his book and gave it to me. He must have trusted me, to hand over such a valuable sketch without a second glance.

"That's a fair imitation of my own work."

"How big is it?"

"Just small." He indicated with his hands a canvas as big as his head and shoulders. "It was a present, when she told me she was pregnant. That's why it's so important to her." He shrugged, picked up his pencil, and began to sketch me again. He gently pushed me back into my post-coital position.

"When did it go missing?"

"We discovered it was missing yesterday. We had a few people over on Thursday, some rich people Olga knows. Stupid, except that they like my work. We had the party, I worked on Friday and Saturday, I met you at the Rotonde . . . then when I tried to work on Sunday morning, Olga was crying and yelling at the maid, little Paulo was screaming, the house was in uproar. She left in a noisy huff yesterday morning, which is when I sent you the note." He looked at his sketch of me and nodded as if in approval. He closed his sketchbook.

"So you need me to find it."

"In one of those rich houses."

"Why don't you call the police?"

"And let everyone know that my work can be easily stolen? Have those philistine police sneer at me? No. You are much better placed to find it."

"Well, you'd better tell me who was at your party, then."

As we dressed, he gave some names, some of which I recognized—"Tamara, Lydia, Michel, Leonid, Olga's dancing friends; Igor, of course; and Léon, Léon Bakst, I mean"—and some I did not—"Those two British, Olga's cousin and her lover; some French duke; oh yes, Arkady Nikolaievitch, and his partner in crime, sorry, in art dealership, Pavel Arsenyevich, tiny little rat of a man; some pale wisp of a woman, Russian as well, I can't remember her name." I wrote all the names down on a piece of paper that I salvaged from Picasso's floor. When we were presentable to the outside world, he rang for the housekeeper.

"Some coffee, Kangaroo. Now, Olga won't return until you find that painting. When will you come back to pose for me again?"

He ran his fingers over my inner thigh and smiled. As soon as possible, I suspected.

"CRAZY BLUES"

It was close to dusk as I left Pablo's studio. The sky had turned lilac and lemon, those delicate sunset colors that made Paris famous. Office workers were taking their shopgirls for coffee, secretaries were being romanced by the fruit sellers on the corners, and booksellers chatted along the Seine. I loved walking through the streets at this time of day, as the city unwound from its anxieties and settled into being properly French. It was quite a walk to my little garret, but between the street scene and Pablo's fingers, I couldn't manage more than a stroll.

"Coo-ee!"

I whirled around. Who'd sent that Aussie bush call through the courting couples and denizens of dusk? It bounded off the French facades and half the pedestrians turned around. A tall, dark woman made taller by her mass of curly brown hair parted the crowd and almost ran up to me.

"Maisie!"

"Katie King!"

My wonderful friend wrapped her arms around me and lifted me off the ground with her enthusiastic hug.

"You know, the French all call me Kiki."

"I know"—she smiled—"but you'll always be Katie King Button to me."

"My Maisie George."

"The French call me Chevallier." She lifted up her hand to show the ring on her finger. I clapped my hands together and squealed.

"Married! Right—we need a café. You're under strict orders to tell me everything."

"So the war finished and we were about to be shipped home and those Bluebirds were advertising for nurses, and I thought, why not?"

"Those French Red Cross nurses are so sweet!"

A final ray of sunshine found us where we sat on the street, a firelight on the fake-marble tabletop and the unruly ends of Maisie's hair.

"So sweet. They even took me with my terrible French. Probably because there was so much to do, with all the returned soldiers."

"*Certainement.*"

"What? Oh, exactly. God, my French really needs work."

"But you have an excellent teacher, yes?"

"Oh . . . *oui.*" She blushed. "Raymond. Sorry, *Ray-mon*, as it is in French. He grew up in Senegal. The first thing he said when he saw me was, 'You remind me of home.' He loves all this"—she gestured vaguely to her body—"he says it reminds him of his first kiss. Can you imagine anyone saying that at home?"

Maisie almost hadn't been allowed in the nursing corps, despite her years of experience nursing on the North Queensland coast. At home, if they'd seen us, they'd have hissed "Touch of the tar" as they walked by. She went to five different recruitment offices, working her way down Queensland's coast, but no one would let her join up. She ended up enlisting in London with me; her journey to the frontline is as much testament to her stellar qualities as her work ethic and sunny nature. But in Paris none of the people who walked past, richly dressed or in their stained overalls, young flappers or white-haired old men, looked twice at her, or at us together. We belonged as much as anyone.

"Or in London. Or anywhere in the Empire."

"I know. I'm just a golliwog to them. Even if Raymond did mistake me for jungle drums and bananas, still, it's better than going back to Queensland and working as a maid." She sighed. "I'm free here, Katie. I could be partly Spanish, or Italian, a bit Moroccan, no one cares . . . I could even be myself."

I squeezed her hand.

"The world's changing, Katie."

"And Paris is leading the way."

"About time too."

"That calls for a drink."

"About time too!" Maisie leaned back and let out her enormous hooting laugh. I loved the way her smile spread right across her face, her hair bouncing out of its set, her eyes crinkling. She picked up her glass of rosé in one large, capable hand and clinked mine.

"And how do the other Chevalliers like you?"

"They're all still back in Senegal. We haven't met yet." She shrugged. "Ray can't get enough of me. Never could. He lay there on the hospital bed, leg bandaged and unable to move, trying to hook me into chatting by using everything he knew from Diggers he'd met on leave."

She started to laugh again.

"The way he says 'G'day, mate' and 'Streuth!'" She imitated her husband, his soft French vowels and pouted lips, until she was giggling too much. She shook her head and sighed.

"Anyway, he thinks that my, what does he call it, my 'exotic looks,' will improve his chances at the foreign office." She raised her eyebrows.

I grinned. "Maise, you've landed on your feet!"

"Don't I know it. Now you, missy, what on God's green are you doing back here? And why didn't you write to tell me? Although you never were the best correspondent. . . ."

Over another glass of rosé, and delicious vegetable soup with freshly baked baguettes, and soft little cherry pastries to finish, I told her all about my job as a gossip columnist, Picasso, Bertie, Tom-Tom. She clapped and laughed exactly on cue, until she frowned.

"And?"

"What do you mean 'and'? That's my life."

"You're holding back. There's some . . . shadow across your face. Is everything really so rosy?"

What could I say? I'd had no intention of telling her about Fox. Fox was like a rumor; the more I mentioned him, the more real he became. Right now, I was happy to keep him as a voice at the end of the receiver. Maisie cut up the last pastry, ate one bite, and pushed the rest towards me.

"If you don't tell me, Katie, I'll just winkle it out of you."

"You wouldn't—"

"I would, because you need me to. How much better was it after you told me all about your Tom fella? You were a sniveling wreck, dripping rain onto your uniform, when you came back from Paris that time."

That time when I'd fed Tom and dressed his wounds, when I'd given him a fake limp and a fake pass home, and I'd then come back to camp, worked a double shift, then almost collapsed in the tent I shared with Maisie. I'd forgotten to eat, of course, but afterwards I remembered my appetite. Yes, it was much better after I'd unburdened myself.

"You can certainly keep a secret, Maise."

"So can you. Just not from me. Madam!" She called for some tea, with milk, "English style."

"So what is it?"

"Do you remember Dr. Fox?"

"What, the khaki svengali? I'll never forget how he leered at you over

the operating table. Somehow it made his handsome face look sinister."
She gasped. "Don't tell me that he's tracked you down!"

I poured the tea and breathed in the sweet, spicy scent of it.

"He isn't a fox for nothing."

"Oh, Katie, you only just managed not to marry him! How did he find
you?"

"He wouldn't tell me. He contacted me through Bertie. Let's hope he
hasn't been following you as well."

"He won't have," Maisie scoffed. "He may be wily, but he'd never
pay attention to a brown girl. He never even saw me. You were the only
woman who existed for him."

"It seems that some things never change."

We drank that pot and another as I went through what Fox had said.
I hadn't thought how much it would strengthen me, to tell a good woman
like Maisie of my fears. I hadn't realized how much I needed a friend here
in Paris. The streets were kind, the artists were kinder, but Maisie was a
piece of home. She reached over and took both of my hands.

"Anything you need, anything at all, just call, or call over. And Ray,
you know . . . he loves a bit of intrigue."

"He wouldn't like this."

"He doesn't need to know everything." She winked.

◆

My life had changed so much in the last forty-eight hours that an anchor
like Maisie was heaven-sent. With her at my back—and by my side, and
in front if need be—I could take up my new role as gossiping spy-detective
with only the slightest of qualms.

I lay on my bed, smoking a cigarette before getting ready for that
night's party. How much better was it to go into these gilded cages as
a detective? I hated to admit it, but how much better again to be there

as a spy? I couldn't help going over Fox's coded instructions. I held the mission in my hand.

Tender is the night, and he cannot see what flowers are at his feet. His plaintive anthem fades, his high requiem becomes a sod. The murmurous haunt of flies treads him down. The faery lands are too forlorn, and the word will toll him back from thee to my sole self.

Why is the night tender? Tender—soft, softhearted, sentimental, loving, affectionate—there had to be a synonym that would make sense. Was it tender like meat was tender? Or was it a business proposition, a tender for a contract? Was night how I was contracted to find this person for Fox? Was it a multiple play on words—something to do with my feminine softness, his softheadedness or sentimentality, my "tender" for this man's deliverance and Fox's feeling for me? That would be just like Fox, to put all those ideas in the one phrase, including the little "love note," and make me work it out.

The Parisian sparrows hopped and chatted around my geraniums on the windowsill. "He cannot see what flowers are at his feet"—was that an allusion to his grave? Was I supposed to kill this man? No—"the word will toll him back from thee to my sole self"—Fox clearly wanted this man delivered. I knew from experience that he hated DOAs. If someone was going to die, then he had to see it happen, on the operating table, on the ward, or in the field. No, these flowers—fleur-de-lis? Was he French? No, that wouldn't make sense with all those references to the war and Germany through Mr. Berlin. Maybe it had something to do with blindness—and muteness, as "his plaintive anthem fades, his high requiem becomes a sod"—the Keats poem is "become a sod," a nothing, it suits the sod. But a sod is also a reference to a grave—

I pulled my blanket over my shoulders. I would not become an assassin. A spy, it seemed, couldn't be helped. But I wouldn't do more. . . . I had done more, of course. Hadn't we all, all of us who'd been in that dreadful war?

I folded up the note and put it in my handbag, and with it tried to put away memories of blood spilled in the dark and lonely cries for mother. The sky was relaxing into twilight, the birds had flown to their evening perches and the night reached its purple fingers into my little studio. I lit the candles in their wine bottles.

Fox had made it clear that he could always find me. The thought gave me leaden-eyed despair and something else, a feeling of flight, a sense of midnight on viewless wings. I dragged deeply on my cigarette. A sparrow cheeped from behind the flowerpot and fluffed its feathers in sleep. I finally had a moment to myself and I had to admit: the mission excited me. In a world where I was just a blonde, a gossip, a little woman, Fox's enticements were irresistible. Despite the drawbacks. Or perhaps because of them—the secrecy, the risk, even the telephone calls with Fox himself. I hated that he knew what I liked, but how could I be other than myself? And yet, how could I let myself be chained to him again? I had fought so hard to be here, to be away from the marriage market and all the traps of family (especially of my family), to be mistress of my own time, my own body, and my own mind.

But I was—of course—I was! Was there a uniform? Were there orders? Were there shifts and supervising matrons? Yes, there was blackmail, a nasty little thorn—he couldn't do without power completely. But there was also banter, a playfulness, and that little vocal wobble. He wanted me; no, he needed me. His need gave me some power. The handkerchief showed that Tom could be freed from the charges, so really, even the blackmail gave me hope. And the final thing: my life was more exciting with this mission, I was enjoying myself. That enjoyment itself was freedom.

The lights across the city sat up and blinked, yellow and white in the deepening violet. It was almost as though they heard me. It was almost as though the street hawkers selling *frites* heard me, the prostitutes and dancers who lounged in doorways heard me and cheered. What else could freedom be, but Paris in springtime? We all had to work, we all had to stoop to sell what we had—but if you enjoy it, if you did it willingly, what more could there be?

I stubbed out my cigarette with a smile on my face. I didn't have to work quite as hard as the street girls but I still had a party to go to. I wished Bertie was coming with me, but I knew he'd be haw-hawing himself hoarse in the Press Club by now. With the way he drank gin, I also knew I wouldn't hear from him until tomorrow. I rifled through my dresses, heaped at the bottom of my bed—I must get a wardrobe or clothes rack or even just a couple of chairs, the dresses were getting more and more creased and I relied on them to make the right impression at my parties. My Bloody Mary dress saved me. It was deep red velvet, with a tulip skirt that bloomed from a dropped waist. It had a black taffeta border around the hem; the neckline and the back plunged in a sharp V to the dropped waist. It was one of my favorites, as the plunged back prevented me from wearing any underwear. I'd sewn little clips to the inside of the skirt to keep my stockings up. I pinned a huge silver dagger brooch to the front and put on my starry shoes. But it was the makeup that made this look—blood-red lips and kohl-rimmed eyes and my bob tamed until it was slick. Long black opera gloves and a fur-trimmed hat would help to keep me warm. I wrapped my opera cloak around me and set off.

8

"JELLY BEAN"

All the rich parties were on the Right Bank. Bankers and merchants, aristocrats and heirs from America and England gathered there, away from the mad, penniless Bohemians. More and more Americans came each year, adding to the congregation at the Protestant churches set up last century. That's how they all knew each other—if they weren't shaking hands in the factories and boardrooms, they were sharing tea after the Sunday services. It was a wonder that I was invited at all, seeing as I spent last Sunday as I spent most Sundays, in bed with a new lover. But I had been included in the first few parties that year and was now a fixture.

But parties were not life, and a fixture of my Parisian life was my friendship with Harriet Harker. Tall and statuesque with a penchant for purple, she was one of the belle epoque Bohemians. She had been sent on a grand tour by her hardware-magnate father, packed off to Europe to catch a husband by her society mother, and had never returned to Chicago. She went AWOL in the wilds of Montmartre; she found Natalie Barney and Winnaretta Singer and made herself a home. When she came into her trust fund at thirty, just as the century dawned, she knew that she wouldn't need to sail the Atlantic for a long time.

I met her at the Front—the only time I have seen her out of her cus-
tomary purple. She was one of the corps of volunteer ambulance drivers
who worked as tirelessly as any nurse—although they got to wear trousers,
drink wine, and sleep under the stars in the stifling August nights. She'd
cut her hand fixing her engine, a huge gash across the right palm, and we
spent a long time on the ward after my shifts, chatting about literature,
art, Americans in Paris, the aphrodisiac properties of champagne, the
deliciousness of silk against the skin. She gave me the address of her huge
Parisian apartment: "Stay there whenever you're in Paris, darling, even if
I'm not there—everyone else does, at my invitation! I have to justify the
maid somehow."

I had contacted her as soon as I arrived in Paris, but she was in Rome,
then Barcelona, then London, then "too too exhausted, Kiki darling, you
know how enervating all these male-dominated dinners can be." I hadn't
seen her—until now.

"Darling Kiki." She opened her arms and gathered me into her ample
bosom. Her strong, dark features made her look like a middle-aged Diana.
She kissed me on both cheeks and held me out to look at.

"So soft and velvety, Kiki. You always did love luxury."

"Only now I can indulge. Wait until you see my dress, Harry."

"More velvet?" she laughed. "You've become such a Wildean! I always
knew you were a secret aesthete. It was only that nurse's uniform that prevented you from giving your proclivities their full soft-jacket, green-carna-
tion wearing, sugared-violets-for-dinner expression." She kissed me again
and took my arm in hers.

"Oh, Kiki, it's so good to see you again. Now, before we go to this
party, I'm going to buy you a champagne cocktail and you're going to
tell me everything."

She swept me into the famous Café de la Paix, finding a table right
at the back, where we had less chance of being found by one of Harry's
friends. The café was warmly lit, candles on every table complementing

the electric lamps, and soft, plush chairs that you could almost sink into. I'd had interrogations before, from men with pips on their shoulders and hair partings so sharp they seemed cut into their skull. To them, I gave only the bare facts, but to Harry I could give almost everything. Harry's face was expressive, stern and kind and disapproving and loving, just as I needed it to be.

"You're looking very thin. How often do you eat? How much fruit do you eat? I know it's very American, but orange juice really is the thing for keeping away coughs and colds—why do you think the English are called 'limeys'? Because of their love of citrus! Oh yes, stomach pains, those rations were really terrible, we've all had a bit of that. But it's time to get over it. And girlfriends here? Tell me all about Maisie! Excellent. I know you won't have a problem with lovers, but are you taking care of your health? Hmmm, that Dutch cap will do as a first stop, I suppose. But come over and use my doctor. She—yes, she—is very discreet, no-non-sense, we met her in the war, you know, an absolute expert in women's health, as you can imagine. Most importantly, she doesn't indulge in all that nonsense that men do when they don't understand women—shame, blame, and diagnoses of hysteria. No, even if you had syphilis—you don't, do . . . no, of course not—well, she'd just tell you that you'd had too much fun. And who are you reading? What did Sylvia recommend for you? What do you mean, you haven't met Sylvia Beach? That must be rectified immediately . . ."

She set me up with a series of appointments—her doctor, her dentist, her diet guru, Sylvia Beach of Shakespeare and Company, Elsa Maxwell and Natalie Barney, "but not Gertrude Stein, darling, you'll have to conquer her set on your own." She insisted I come over for a bath at least once a week, with a pile of laundry and a pile of gossip. I laughed at her industry, but a private part of me cried with relief. It felt so good, so warm, to be wrapped up in Harry's busybodyness. I was sick of sitting cross-legged on the floor to wash my hair with cold water; it didn't feel exciting and new when I was dizzy and shaky and hungry. Besides, Harry knew me and knew what I neglected.

She sat beside me with a purple velvet coat, trimmed with fur, over her chair. Her dress was more subtle, its black silk embroidered with crocuses and violets around the wrists and wide neck line, around the waist and all along the hem that fell almost to her ankles. Her shoes were such a dark eggplant that they almost looked black. Her hair was longer than the fashion and she wore it up, white streaks through the brown and twisted in swirls. She had insisted on a plate of fruit, regardless of the waiter's frown, and waved pieces of melon and apricot about as she spoke.

"But I must tell you about Wendy. From Gwendolyn, which she hates. Yes, I met her in the ambulance. English, and my age! Which hasn't happened since I was in my twenties. Somehow I got older while my women remained the same . . . but it is just wonderful to have a peer. A true equal—she's even tall enough to look me in the eye. I recommend it. No, I insist on it, Kiki. Anything but an equal is merely settling. She's an artist, she's so technically skilled but avant-garde too; her eye for color is like nothing you've ever seen; no, not even with Picasso. She even has me painting—yes me, after all these years. Such liberation! And the way she wears a suit! George Sand can't rival her. We have a salon every third Sunday—so make sure some of your baths are on these Sundays, you absolutely must come . . ."

No wonder Harry has insisted we meet at sundown. By the time we left, the café was full and the streetlamps beckoned us out and on into the night. Our chat had taken almost two hours, "and we just skimmed the surface, darling! Thank goodness you're here to stay."

The uniformed doorman let us in to a wide and winding marble staircase. This was going to be a lavish party, unusual for a Monday night. The marble glowed from the inside and music hummed from the golden handrail.

"Wait a moment, Kiki darling, I need to fix my hair. Why I still keep it long, I don't know. I must get one of your bobs . . ."

Mirrors followed us up the staircase, from railing to ceiling and sparklingly clear. Harry looked perfectly turned out as usual, the silk of her dress fluttering around her calves. I always felt small next to her height and solidity, like a fluffy canary that chirps for a feed. She tapped my arm.

"Stop it, Kiki."

"Stop what?"

"Stop judging yourself. You're incomparable. We all are. Now, come along. I heard there might be some interesting people we can recruit for the salon and I want to speak to them before they drink too much."

We climbed up the stairs, slowly and elegantly, arm in arm.

"Kiki Button," I said as the door opened. I always introduced myself first, just in case the host didn't know who I was.

"Of course, blond Kiki, the society reporter." A slender young American held out his hand. He had nice hazel eyes above his tuxedo, but alas, his handshake was weak.

"Indeed. And this is—"

"Miss Harker"—he opened his arms with a warm smile—"such a pleasure to see you again."

"I warned you, Joseph, call me Harriet or Harry, or I'll call your mother and tell her what you're really up to."

"You wouldn't dare!" he said with a smile.

"Don't try me. Now, where is Margaret?"

"She's over by the window." He pointed out a round brunette who looked for all the world like a plump fairy. She was swathed in soft pink chiffon that seemed a little too tight around her arms and waist. She even wore pink shoes and a little pink bow in her hair. She saw us and waved.

"Oh, Harry! You came!"

"Of course, little one." Harry greeted her with kisses, but the pink fairy embraced her without restraint.

"And you brought the gossip columnist!" she exclaimed, her American vowels wrapping around the words, "Oh, I'm just so excited to have you here! It means this is a real Parisian party."

"Glad to hear it," I said.

"Oh yes, now look, let me give you a few tidbits for you to write up. Joey, he let you in, he's a Vanderbilt on his mother's side a couple of generations back—"

"Three, but who's counting these days?" said Harry with a smirk.

"My mother," said Margaret, and Harry laughed. She was greeted by a tall woman in trousers and an American accent.

"I wanted Harry to come, so I made sure I invited all her wartime pals. Besides, they seem like a fun bunch." Margaret leaned in and looped her arm in mine. "Anyway, Joey's been having an assignation with that other Kiki, you know, the dark one? Those three over there are poor British aristocrats who want to latch on to Father's money—and those two are French aristocrats, here for the same reason. I'm trying to make the French *duc* fall for the British baroness, but I think the *duc* would rather have Joey, if you know what I mean—"

Even if her dress sense was maximum froufrou, her sense of gossip was sharp as a scalpel. The pink puffery must be a disguise and she was really a black-clad Bohemian or a purple-clad sapphic. Maybe I was just a little too prejudiced against these rich Right Bankers.

"—and I just love it when you put in all those veiled barbs about us—"

"I'm sure I don't know—"

"Oh don't be coy—how boring! You know you do. Everyone thought that *La Bohème* recital last week was just dreadful, and your praise was so lavish that it had to be satire. Brilliant! And there are so many odd bods here, I mean, only those who have nothing better to do can celebrate a twenty-third birthday on a Monday night, right? So it should be an interesting party. Joey!" She called and waved her hand in the air. "It's so dull in here! Let's have some music."

"On your new gramophone?" he said, on cue.

"Why, of course!"

Joey unveiled the gramophone, a beautiful object with flowers engraved on its enormous brass phone. Margaret and Joey pretended to argue about which recording to play, but in the end they remembered that they were young Americans and put on jazz. Racy, jagged ragtime filled the room and people pretended to look horrified or delighted or licentious, as they thought the music demanded. Margaret picked up a French aristocrat and started to teach him to jig walk.

"She makes him look ridiculous, doesn't she?" Joey had loped over to me, slicking his hair back where it refused to stay in its pomade. "Do you dance, Kiki Button, society reporter?"

"Everything but ballet." I looked him over. He was tall and gangly, his tuxedo seemed at times too short in the arms and legs and too broad in the chest, his smile fraught with innocence.

"I'll have to find another way to see up your skirts then." He put his arms around and lifted me so that I almost left the ground. He danced an odd jig walk that I could barely follow and his poker face made me laugh. He clenched his lips together, determined to be serious, but his eyes gave him away.

"Is the expression part of the dance?"

"It's a game I play with Margaret. This is the face her mother wears when she waltzes, so we use it for every dance, regardless of tone. We're second or third cousins or some such. Our mothers are great friends back in New York. I think we were planned for each other but we're not each other's type." He sentences came out in little puffs of ragtime.

"And your types?"

"She prefers girls. I prefer anyone who's not American."

"Like Kiki de Montparnasse?"

He blushed. "Oh, that. It's not serious. I'm not bohemian enough for her! She just likes to be fed properly every so often and I fill her with American-imported meat."

"I'm sure you do." He blushed again, more violently this time, but kept his poker face. Despite his weak handshake, he might be a good ally.

"How well do you know the other guests?"

"Oh, not well at all!"

"So you wouldn't know if any of them were friends with Picasso?"

"Oh, yeah, I know that! Anyone who knows Picasso talks about it, especially if it's their only fortune left."

The song finished. I saw Margaret reach over to change the disk, lock eyes with a young American girl at the gramophone, another plump brunette with a razor-wire voice. Harry raised her eyebrows at me. It seemed that our host was set for the time being. Joey led me over to the drinks table, crammed with bottles and jugs of orange, red, and purple, and manned by a dour Frenchman in uniform.

"Two glasses of punch, Pierre."

Pierre nodded, but I couldn't help but notice his twinkle as he looked at me.

Joey handed me the punch. "Pink and fruity, just like our host."

"To Paris," I toasted.

"To Paris!" He took a swig. "That Violet knows Picasso, or at least went to his house last week sometime, she can't stop talking about it. And I think the Duck Orange knows him too, or knows his wife, or something."

"Who's the Duck Orange?"

"Some French duke. One of his many names is Orange, so we call him the Duck Orange. He's that one, and Violet's two along on the couch." He nodded at a middle-aged man, slender to the point of skinny, who stroked his lapel with long fingers. He leaned against the couch and had his listening face on, but there was no one speaking to him. Next to him was a woman in impeccable modern dress, waved hair, skirt to the knee, all in black. Next to her was a man with a fierce face, who looked directly at me in a way that sent a shiver through me. Violet was talking to the fierce-faced man even as he stared at me. Joey had begun to dance with another guest; Pierre managed to soften his features as he handed me two fingerbowls of champagne—"Excellent choice, mademoiselle." I took them over to the Duck Orange; I needed to build up to that fierce-faced stare.

"This will soothe your jazzed-up nerves," I said to him in French. I loved the music, but I stopped my foot from tapping and left the shock to the Americans.

The Duck Orange thanked me graciously and sipped. "Ah, yes, it takes me back. To more civilized times, before the war."

"Before the Americans."

"The Americans have been here all through my lifetime"—he spoke in a soft murmur—"but usually they were more grateful for French culture. Now all they enjoy is the absence of their Puritan American mothers."

I took a sip to stop myself laughing at him, as it was those "Puritan mothers" whose money he clearly needed. He'd worn his tails, his shirt-front so white it glowed, but the jacket and trousers were frayed at the cuffs. His shoes shone with a recent polish but I could see the leather worn down at the sides. His hair was streaked, gray, white, and deepest black, and held down in perfect waves. But a tiny muscle at the side of his eye twitched, he was so thin, and he stroked his clothes nervously.

"Were you a soldier, during the war?"

He looked at me sharply, almost frightened.

"I was a nurse."

"Ah." He relaxed. "Yes, these ones"—he waved a hand over the host and her friends—"they say they want to know, but what can we say . . ." He looked at me properly, over my blond bob and skinny shoulders and the nicotine stains that marked my fingers. He smiled sadly and it made me aware of what the war had cost me, how I could be known, even by a stranger, as a survivor.

"Much better to reminisce, is it not?" he asked.

"I prefer jazz to memory, but to each their own."

"I prefer dignity to jazz, but unless one joins Action Française or some such group, there aren't many other options for restoring our national pride."

"You're a member?" It seemed strange that I'd heard of this fierce nationalist group twice in two days.

"Oh, no, they're not my type," he sniffed. "They're in trade."

His snobbery knew no bounds, but he still hadn't introduced himself. Thank goodness my profession let me barge past all these Gallic inferences.

"I'm Kiki Button. I write little columns on these parties for a newspaper back in London."

"Oh." The champagne was clearly more interesting.

"I'd love to put you in my column, but I need your name."

"I am Antoine Armand Victoire Pierre Guillaime de Tallifer, heir to the Duc de Orange de Orleans . . ." But we both got bored before he reached the end. I played on his snobbery and for my sins got a lot of tedious chat about French honor, family names, buying titles, and the degrading need for American heiresses. The chat turned to Russia, its horror and scandal, and his distant relative by marriage, Olga Khokhlova Picasso. He'd been at Picasso's home on Thursday night, but he paid no attention to Picasso's work.

"Olga and Pablo, they are . . . modern people." He threw so much disdain into that word *modern*. "I won't comment on the art, but Pablo can keep Olga in style, so I suppose someone thinks it has value."

"Who else was there?"

"These two." He waved a languid hand over the fierce-looking man and his black-clad friend. "I forget their names but they're proper people."

Before I could ask who "proper people" were, Margaret clapped her hands and cried, "Food, everyone! Please help yourself."

"So American, this 'buffet' style." But he sprang up to the recently laid table and heaped his plate with cold meats, asparagus spears, little savory pastries and bread. He sat in a corner to eat as quickly as was polite. He gave me one furtive glance and looked away, pastry stuffed into his cheeks.

That left only a spare seat between me and the fierce-looking man. He raised his eyebrow and handed me a deep brown drink.

"You look like you need something stronger than champagne," he said in a cut-glass English accent. *I will with you*, I thought.

"You're English."

"Born and bred," he said. "Bottom's up."

It was single-malt Scottish whisky and it tasted of comfort.

"How did you know I needed whisky?"

"After his nibs, every girl needs a stiff one."

I laughed. He held out his hand, unconcerned by its missing fingers. He was missing his ring finger on his left hand and his middle finger and ring on his right.

"Hugh Fernly-Whiting, but everyone calls me Ferny. Why don't you come sit by me? It's a little undignified to lean across this enormous divan." He patted the seat and revealed the brown bottle.

"You brought the whisky with you."

"Had to. These American parties only have that sweet American stuff, if anything." He smiled and I saw a silver tooth. "But I have a Paris supplier that I set up in the war, so I haven't had to suffer too much."

"Who needs five fingers when you can have two of Islay's best?"

"Well, quite." He grinned. "And I've always been light-fingered."

"You must be butter-fingered now."

"Only in the sense that I'm smooth and rich and go down easily."

"You'll get five fingers of a different kind if you're not careful."

He barked a laugh, open and friendly. His gaze unsettled me though, as did the scar on his cheek.

"That looks like a dueling scar."

"I spent some time with my Prussian cousins, before they became my enemy," he said, "and they liked to play rough."

"It makes you look . . ."

"Like a Hun." He grimaced. "I know, but as everyone's cut up nowadays, I thought it'd be all right."

"No, it makes you look . . ." I was going to say, *like a spy, like a villain, like my boss.* But he turned his gaze on me, brown eyes staring right into mine as though he wanted to unwind me and set me ticking to his own time. It made me feel slightly sick.

"It makes me look how?"

"Just like someone I used to know." I shrugged. "So who do you know here?"

"Get out your notebook, this might take a while."

He gave me detailed histories of the British aristocrats whom he'd known since childhood: "A Baroness? Our host exaggerates. Minor titles and second sons only here." He tapped me on the knee as he did so, familiar and strange—Fox used to tap my knee, just so, as if to tease me, or to let me know that I was his. As Ferny outlined the rise and fall of their family fortunes, he leaned right in so that I could smell his breath, expensive whisky and Sobranie tobacco, just like Fox. Or rather, like Fox on his days off, as in the hospitals he smelled of mud, blood, and disinfectant. The whisky I could understand but not the tobacco, as he smoked Woodbines where he sat on the couch.

"So, you see, I know all the worthless people in Paris."

"And who do you know who's worthwhile?"

"Well, we met Picasso the other day, didn't we, Violet?" he appealed to the woman on the other side of him, as if he'd just remembered her. "That was quite a meeting."

"Hello"—she extended her hand—"nice to meet you, Kiki— Oh yes, I know who you are— Yes, Picasso, what an extraordinary man! I think we must've caught him on a bad day, he barely said a word. Darling, I'm parched." She turned her dark eyes to Ferny.

"Duty calls." He bowed, almost with a click, and picked up my glass as well. He walked off to the drinks table with a pronounced limp.

"Has he been trying to charm you? He's hopeless about blondes; it'd be a nuisance if we knew very many." She looked after his straight-backed figure. "I tried to dye my hair blond once, but it went green. I had to pretend I'd gone to the country as I spent the next five days dying it back."

"Black suits you."

"Well, it has to." She looked me up and down. "Nice little job you have, going to parties and being paid for it."

"Very, but unfortunately it means I can't refuse an invitation."

She smirked. "Yes, sometimes it's too much, even if you have known the host forever. Perhaps especially when." Ferny looked at us together. He smiled at me but his expression darkened when he looked at Violet. She seemed to stiffen. I almost didn't want to intervene.

"Tell me more about Picasso."

"Oh, yes." She looked at her hands. "We were at his party on Thursday night. His wife was lovely, although she only spoke French and Russian, and half the party was in Russian, so it was a bit rough for the rest of us. She went on and on about how talented her husband is—as if we were there for any other reason. She made him give us a little tour of his studio. So many paintings! Some very, ah, modern, but others just perfect. Wouldn't you say, darling?" She'd perked up talking about Picasso, enough to appeal to her lover. She took the champagne from his hand.

"Some that even philistines like us could understand? Yes, indeed." He handed me another whisky. "A particular one of his wife that captured her elegance just so."

"Oh, yes, that one—the most extraordinary colors! For a portrait, anyway."

"She showed it off with great relish—"

"Picasso seemed most embarrassed that she did so—"

"Although I hear that she's not in rue la Boétie to show it off now—"

"Where did you hear that?"

"I have spies everywhere." He winked at me.

Violet looked at Ferny with an odd mix of adoration and fear, but he had his relentless gaze on me, his eyes almost black, a beckoning abyss. I almost wanted to be sucked in, just to see what was at the bottom. Was this Fox's influence? Was I still fatally attracted to the bad boy, the dangerous job, the wild risk? I thought I'd moved away from running into the bullets and flirting with the enemy and all that destructive behavior. That's why I was here, in this city of light, to move away from the darkness inside men. But that darkness was here, in the pretty pink parlor of a rich American on a Monday evening.

"Well, that might be the first time I've heard of a great man being embarrassed by praise."

Ferny smirked and Violet giggled. I felt that Pablo's dismissal of them was justified.

"You know, the best person to speak to is that Russian fellow," said Violet. "What do they call him, one of those long Russian names . . ."

Ferny shrugged.

"Oh, yes, you remember, darling, you remember everything. . . . Lazarus . . . no, Lazarev, that's right. But Olga called him something else—"

"His Christian name and patronymic, most likely."

"What's that?"

"Like in Dostoyevsky's *Crime and Punishment*—"

"Oh, darling, you know I don't read that type of thing—"

"Raskolnikov is called Rodion Romanovich—"

"This isn't fiction, even if it is Russian—"

"So Olga would refer to him as that, Something Something-avich—"

"Oh yes! She did too . . . Arcade, no, Arkady . . . Nikolaievitch?"

"I didn't pay attention," he murmured into a Woodbine.

"Rubbish. You always pay attention; I don't know why you're claiming ignorance now. Anyway, it was something like that. He's Olga's cousin."

"A connoisseur of modern art." Ferny raised his eyebrows. Somehow he managed to address his remarks just to me.

"Bored us all to tears, exclaiming and declaiming in the most ornate French you've ever heard—and that's saying something! He just couldn't get over Picasso's work, kept kissing his hand. If one's behavior is too affectionate for the Spanish, well—I mean!" Violet snorted in derision. I suspected that her British snobbery would remain untouched by her stay in Paris. The same could not be said for the host's stock of champagne, or for Joey's virtue, which I valiantly assailed for the rest of the night to great success.

9

"SHUFFLE ALONG"

I woke to a knocking at my door.

"Mademoiselle! Mademoiselle!" The telegram boy had run up the four flights of stairs and stood, chest heaving, in the doorway. His eyes boggled as I stood only in my bedsheet, Joey having left just moments before. Thank goodness he had, or the telegram boy might never have stopped staring.

ON 4.25 FROM CALAIS BE AT GARE 7.30 TOM-TOM NEEDS TO DRUM UP WINE WINKS WHISPERS FROM A PARIS BUTTON SO BE THERE OR I WILL COME AND FIND YOU STOP

Tom would be here tonight! When had he sent this telegram? He must be just down the coast, or perhaps he went to London first—my pulse beat in my ears. Tom-Tom, my oldest, dearest, most beautiful friend. We'd be in Paris, together, again. I wore a grin I couldn't ungrin, I felt light and flighty. This might have suggested to me that Tom was more than a friend, but I wasn't about to listen to those kinds of suggestions. Otherwise, tiredness might suggest that I needed to sleep, or the pangs in my stomach would hint that I should forgo cocktails for food. I'd learned long ago to ignore my body's chatter. The war taught me to pay attention only when the chatter became a screaming tantrum and I had mere moments to save myself before I fell down in a faint. There was no party tonight that I couldn't miss, but I knew that I'd miss every party before I missed Tom-Tom's arrival at Gare du Nord.

The birds tra-la-la'd and ooh-la-la'd and hopped a jazzy two-step on my windowsill. The mist over the city rose like a bridal veil. Even my hangover was suddenly sunny and fine.

◇

"Kiki! Darling!" Bertie hooked his arm around my waist and kissed me flamboyantly. "Is it my mind or my body that you missed the most?"

"Bertie, your taste—have you opened the champagne already? Nine o'clock is early, even for you."

"Is my breath like the fumes of hell?"

"Like trench foot and fear."

"How ghastly!" He ran in to the bathroom, his robe flailing behind him. His room looked as though it had been shelled, with every surface covered with clothes, shoes, papers, dirty glasses, empty bottles, and cigarette stubs. Beautiful objects, all of them—Savile Row suits, fluted champagne bottles, papers with the crests of various newspapers and government departments on them—but none of them as beautiful as the boy's head that rose from the pillows. Big-eyed and smooth-skinned, he nodded and murmured bonjour, before putting on his trousers and slipping out the door.

"Bertie?" He grunted in reply to me. "Who was that?"

"Has he gone?" Bertie poked his head out of the door. "Just a diversion. He's on the hotel staff, I'm sure he can be diverted again."

"And is he diverting?"

"Quite. But the mission was never in danger. Now, you're here for the laundry, correct?"

"And a bath."

"And food, no doubt. I'll order and we can exchange information."

Hearing him speak French made me smile. It was stilted and clipped, just like the British soldier he used to be, but it could at least rustle up croissants and coffee. I cleared the bathroom of the remains of his rendezvous—it certainly wasn't beneath me to get rid of dirty socks and hair, not in order to have a proper, pampering soak. I opened the little window to let in the chill air and cobblestone chatter of Paris. The bubbles rose as my clothes fell to the floor and I slipped under the water with a sigh.

"Are you sunken?" Bertie called from the door.

"My treasure's at the bottom."

"Your treasure is your bottom," he said, sitting on the edge of the bath. "The food will be here soon. Now, tell me what happened yesterday, and I'll tell you what I've heard from the rich and ribald."

As I recounted the last few days, he clapped his hands in delight.

"Picasso gave you this job in between modeling sessions?"

"Of course. He's sure the painting is with some rich society people who were at his place last week. So as well as Fox's mission, I have this too. The society party I attended last night was full of lost fortunes and improbable heirs, but I did get a couple of names. Do you know a Hugh Fernly-Whiting? Violet Trelawney-Wells?"

"Never heard of them."

"You're not posh enough."

"Or rich enough. I've had my ear to the ground for tidbits of gossip about Berlin and Romantic poetry. No one speaks of Goethe and Werther, mists and mellow fruitfulness, but they do talk of the Weimar Republic. Specifically, the most recent uprisings."

"I read in the papers that they were more like rebellions."

"In Silesia, yes; in Saxony, less so. My dinner parties are full of the sorts of people who can't help but talk shop. They talk of Germany, mainly.

Then they get sick of talking about Germany, so we talk of France and then wind up, via borders and refugees and inflation, to Germany again."

The bubbles whispered as I swirled them around the water.

"Those Irving Berlin songs," I said, and he nodded.

"Those song titles and the rumbles from across the border—it can't be a coincidence."

I sank down until the water came up to my chin. The street-hawker cries rose through the window, including one that sounded familiar.

"You know, Kiki, those titles were all patriotic songs written—"

"Yes, I remember—"

"So this does go back to the war." Bertie raised his eyebrows. "Fox knows the mole from then."

"The mole has to have been one of his protégés—the clues practically scream it. Not least because, why else choose me? It has to be because of what I alone know." Alone and unknown by all but Fox. "Oh—'He cannot see what flowers are at his feet'—it's because I can remain unseen. Because only Fox can see me."

Bertie was the opposite of Fox—open and warm, slender and graceful—and therefore a relief. I reached out and gave his hand a bubbly squeeze. But it was Fox who ambushed my mind. The steam opened my thoughts and conjured him up, his strong body, his sharp glance, his cruel smile. His reliance on me, trust that was mixed with the threat of punishment. He knew I wouldn't let him down, even if it killed me; except, of course, that being killed would be the greatest disappointment of all—

"He'll never let you go, will he, Kiki?" Bertie smoothed the wet hair from my face. His sad smile caught at my throat. I shook my head and sighed.

"Have I told you that he proposed?"

"What? Your spying surgeon!"

"More than once. The first few times were in the field. He'd say, at the end of the mission, 'And we'll marry in the morning,' or book us into a hotel as Mr. and Mrs. Fox. One time he even instructed me to go to the registry office in Chelsea for a marriage license. But they were just tests. His real proposal was my farewell."

"What did you do?"

"I left for Australia."

I swirled the water, willing it to warm the chill memories of that night.

"Well? You can't leave it there, Kiki. You're a gossip columnist, for Pete's sake!"

His exasperation made me smile—I had a new life now, in a new place, with better friends than ever—it gave me strength.

"It was at the end of the war. You know how we all were. I could hardly tell night from day." Or heat from cold, or love from cruelty. "He picked me up in his sleek silver Vauxhall. The drive to his country house in Kent was long and wintry, each tree a skeleton in the barren fields. All I saw were crows. I must have been chilled to the bone, because when we got to his mansion every room felt like a dream—so warm, they smelled of woodsmoke and old leather, the aroma of freshly baked bread floated over the carpets in the hall. He even had a cuckoo clock, with a man and woman who came out at the hour and danced. He sat me down, handed me the most vibrant, soft, wonderful whisky I've ever tasted, and proceeded to charm me. I actually laughed—I don't think I'd even smiled for him during the entire war."

"So he isn't all evil, then."

"He smiled too, a proper smile. That was the true end of the war for me. I felt human again, I could taste the roast goose and chocolate mousse he served, it tasted . . . you know, with the texture of the mousse on my tongue, soft and creamy and rich, I came back to life. You know the feeling—"

"Oh yes. You can hear again. Your days come back into focus."

"Exactly! When the war was like a nightmare and you realize that you are alive, that you made it. I understood who I was suddenly; I felt the power and strength in my body and knew it was mine—not his, not the army's, not the nursing corps'—just mine. After the dinner there was a small star shower, and we watched the white flashes from the window seat in his library. Then he wound his arm around my waist and kissed me."

"Doctors and nurses"—he grinned—"you wouldn't be the first."

"Master and slave, more like. But it was such a kiss! Firm grip and featherlight lips, passion and restraint—he was clearly very experienced. As I regained my breath he whispered that I would stay the night."

"Did he now?" Bertie raised an eyebrow.

"Quite. That was his mistake. If he'd asked, or even if he'd said nothing and kept kissing me, everything might have happened as he'd planned. But that order—it was an alarm bell through that fairy tale of good food and perfect manners. I remembered, in a flash, one dark predawn when I'd washed a young man's teeth through the wound in his face, blood and saliva dripping through the flap as he groaned. We were by the side of the road at the end of some failed mission—Fox had sent him to do the work and then sent me to clean up. I'd said to myself then—no, I'd promised myself—'No more orders, Katherine King Button. Once you remove this uniform, you will never take orders again.' And he ordered me." I shrugged. "He was so shocked when I said no that he watched me walk out the door and take his car, all the way back to London."

"And now he wants you back."

"According to him, I never properly left. I just took a little holiday."

Bertie frowned and swirled the water.

"Kiki . . . do you think he loves you?"

I laughed and it sounded harsh as it bounced off the tiles.

"He doesn't know what love is."

"Do any of us?"

"Bertie . . ." When he looked up, his expression was almost sad. "Bertie, you survived. There's no shame in that."

"I know . . ."

"You are made for love. You'll find it again—but probably not with the porter."

"No, probably not." He smiled. "Or with an ex-nurse, spy, detective, gossip columnist."

I stroked his face. He took my hand and kissed my palm.

"You'll always have my love, Bertie Browne."

He breathed in the scented steam and sighed. There was no need for him to avow his love for me. He smiled.

"But, Bertie, this water is getting cold and I'm hungry. Let's eat—"

"And gossip."

"I'll swap French dukes for German rumors."

"Deal. Speaking of food, our breakfast should have arrived by now. . . ."

Over crisp croissants and bowls of milky coffee, I filled him in on all the people I'd met last night. We sat at the window, golden sashes pulled back to reveal the bustle of Place Vendôme, the room high-ceilinged and flush with pale light. Our chairs were soft and striped and right next to each other, and he touched my knee or hand or foot as we talked. He laughed and smiled on cue, without fail. This was the comfort of the body, and he seemed to need me as much as I needed him. Was he lonely? I knew how a full bed could be a symptom of an empty heart. He missed me in London, certainly, he'd told me more than once. But there was something else underneath this gossip. I poured him more coffee and decorated the saucer with a flower from the vase on the table.

"Why, thank you, Kiki."

"What else is going on?"

"Else?"

"There's something more. I can sense it. Gulp your coffee for fortification and tell me what it is."

"It's nothing, really." But he gulped his coffee just the same. "It's just . . . these businessmen keep mentioning the name of Hausmann."

"And?"

"That's Teddy's surname—Hamilton, my latest paramour—or at least, the German version of it."

"Your new boy mixed up in this?"

"No! Well . . . I don't think so. They never said 'Edward Houseman' or even 'Hamilton Houseman,' and the man they spoke of was definitely German."

"What did they say about this Hausmann?"

"Well, that's the funny thing. Some of them thought he was a rabble-rouser, some kind of agitator. Others thought he was a salesman. At one dinner there was quite an argument—was Hausmann a Bolshevik or a businessman? Whatever he is, he's been busy."

"Does this sound like your Teddy?"

"Not at all. I rang his father's house, just to check, but he acted just like the silly boy I picked up in Soho last month."

He fidgeted with his coffee cup.

"So why are you suspicious, Bertie?"

"I'm not really, I just . . ."

"Bertie . . ." I used my warning tone.

Bertie grinned. "Yes, yes, all right, Kiki. I'm suspicious in case anyone has seen us together. You know men like me always have to be suspicious on that count—"

"But?"

"But I remember that Teddy had said his family used to be German, but I can't remember if that was one generation ago or several. It was one of the reasons Teddy waited to be called up instead of volunteering—that, and he was only a child."

"What else was said about this Hausmann?"

"What we discussed around those dinner tables were German politics—the uprisings and their consequences, the Communists, the Brown-shirts—"

"The Brownshirts?" My ears pricked up.

"Yes, they were called the Freikorps last year, during the Kapp Putsch, but officially they've been disbanded. Unofficially . . . " Bertie gave a mock shiver. "Most of the businessmen I spoke to seemed to support the Brownshirts in some way or another. There was a lot of ridiculous talk about Jewish bolshevism and the Red Menace as a threat to business. The Brownshirts are meant to stop all of that."

"What, Jewishness, or bolshevism?"

"Both—ha! No, the bolshevism part—I assume—in the minds of these businessmen, they're connected."

"Who are the brownshirts, exactly?"

"Exactly? The reports say that they're old soldiers who can't accept that Germany lost the war."

"And your Teddy . . . does he still have family in Germany?"

Bertie shrugged and looked dejected.

"So . . . it's not impossible that he, or someone in his family, would support the Brownshirts?"

"After the war, is anything truly impossible?" Bertie sighed. "His people are old Junkers, so who knows what connections they still have to Prussia. I'll have to keep digging. I may even have to introduce myself to his father." He gave me the look he gave when he had to go over the top, eyebrows raised, lips pursed, mock shock mixed with real fear. I squeezed his hand.

"Bertie, be careful."

"Anything for you, Kiki."

The light from the window, soft and white, lit up every hard-earned line on his forehead. He could've looked like such a boy with his lanky limbs and his features too big for his narrow face. But his skin was taut over the jawbone and the line of his lips was set. He was only thirty, but he had seen too much to ever truly be young again.

"Anything but jail, Bertie."

"Oh, don't worry. My green carnation is hidden away, pressed between my passport and my reporter's card. Now, I have to go back to London today—"

"Boo."

"And hiss. But we'll keep in touch via telegram and telephone and other modern inventions. Will you see me off at the station?"

10

"A NIGHT OUT"

In the end, I spent all day at the station, walking to and from the station, drinking coffee at the station cafés and reading station newspapers. Bertie and I had a long, warm goodbye, as only we could. I'd miss the food—whenever I was with him, I was relaxed enough to eat a proper meal. I'd miss his company—but it was just like the war, always saying goodbye. Except somehow, this was harder than the war. Bertie looked pinched and anxious as I saw him into his carriage, a look that corresponded to the tightness in my own stomach.

"Don't forget me, Kiki."

"What a ridiculous thing to say."

"I just have a bad feeling, some presentiment of doom."

"Then book your passage back as soon as you reach Victoria."

He sighed and visibly unwound. "Yes, I will. A few weeks—no, days—and we'll be in the cafés again."

I walked back to my garret to change my clothes. In a week of troubles, Bertie's words occupied me all the way home. Did we need each other so much that we couldn't say goodbye? We weren't really missing each other, I didn't think—so what were we missing that the other filled? But as soon as I started to think of all the holes in our lives, the dead rose up and marched over the cobblestones, staring from their broken faces. I had to stop and hide in a drink before I even reached the studio. The purple winked at the brim and I forced myself, with every sip, not to feel forlorn. I needed Bertie and he needed me. Why that was so was not something I could think about.

But I could think about Tom. In fact, I couldn't stop thinking about Tom. I dressed carefully, in my peacock-blue outfit, with matching blue camiknickers and my favorite star-patterned shoes, brushing my hair and applying my red lipstick with luxurious excess—I wanted to look brilliant, delicious, divine. I even tidied my little flat in order not to be early to the station, but I was early anyway. I was standing by the newsagent to buy a paper when a paperboy ran up to me.

"Mademoiselle, you must buy this paper."

"I'm not sure that I want—"

"No, you must, you must!" His face looked pained. Other men tried to buy a paper from him, and he just shoved copies in their hands without looking at the change they gave him. One particular copy he held out to me.

"Haven't I seen you before?"

"Please, mademoiselle. This paper."

When I took it from his ink-stained fingers I noticed his withered hand on the other arm. He saw me notice and ran off. I had that familiar jolt; I was being followed, by Fox almost certainly. I would have to pay closer attention.

I sat at a café, perched on a stool at the end of the bar, with a Florentine and coffee. The bustle of the platforms was mirrored by the bustle inside, the glass walls of the café showing every train, the door open to let in every announcement. I broke the almond flakes off the Florentine one by one, placing each on my tongue and letting the caramel dissolve in my mouth. Fox must have organized for this particular paper to be put into my hands. If so, then there was a clue inside. Would it be in an article, a classified advertisement, a personal message? I didn't want to read through the whole paper, I was far too distracted with thoughts of Tom-Tom. I glanced at the station clock: 7:05. Did Tom have a hotel? Would he expect to stay in my tiny, ill-equipped flat? Was my hair neat? Was I too thin from living on cocktails and kisses? I worried over every tiny thing that I usually couldn't give two hoots about—well, maybe one hoot, but certainly not two. 7:10: the wait was excruciating. I forced my attention back to the newspaper, just for some relief.

It was in the third page, next to articles about European politics. It almost fell on the floor—a photo. It was a group shot of several British Army officers, not posed or formal but all laughing, as though at a joke someone had told. The photo was clearly from the war as right in the center, in nurse's uniform, was me. Next to me, standing straight, barely smiling and looking straight at the camera, was Fox.

It made me feel sick to see him, as though my memory had suddenly taken physical form. He stood at ease, hands behind his back, legs apart. He was slightly taller than me and it was clear that under his jacket he was strong. His stare seemed to bore into me, as though he knew this photo would be a missive to the future. He had sent this image as a reminder: here you are, Vixen, next to me, where you belong. I looked around at the station café, all happy chatter and scents of smoke and coffee. I couldn't shy away now. I took a deep breath and steeled myself to look at the photo more closely.

I didn't remember it being taken and I barely knew any of the men gathered around me. Was this a ward of convalescent men? Three men were total strangers, darkish hair and even features, smaller than Fox but clearly enjoying the joke. One dark-haired man I remembered, with a shock, dying quickly and noisily in my arms. Another man looked very much like Hugh Fernly-Whiting. He was standing next a very pale, thin man whose smile was more like a sneer.

I flipped the photo over. There was Fox's handwriting, in a single line:

Hungry generations tread thee down . . . F to V

More Keats. But the line should read "No hungry generations tread thee down"—if Fox had changed it to the positive, then this wasn't about the war but about something new, a new hungry generation. I peered more closely at the man who, I was increasingly sure, was Hugh Fern-ly-Whiting. There was something about him that didn't look right. He didn't stand like the other officers, with their loose slouch, rolling ciga-rettes in one hand. He was too straight, straighter even than Fox, and he stood with his heels almost clicked together. Was he the mole? Had Fox just told me? I wanted to believe it, but it wasn't his style to be so direct. Ferny was definitely part of . . . whatever it was, but only part. The other part must have to do with this meeting during the war. Would I have to follow Ferny to find out? What would Fox expect me to do, what had he trained me to assume? But my mind wouldn't recall those months of subtle indoctrination. Instead, it focused on Fox, his face projecting mem-ories, the way his silver hair shone under a full moon, his gray eyes with their turbulent expressions, his thin lips in a sneer. Those times that he scrubbed his arms until they bled. Those times when, too tense to sleep himself, he would sit by my cot when Maisie was away and watch me as I slept.

I tucked the photo in to my handbag and scanned the pages it had been inserted between—its placement would not be a coincidence. An article about Germany caught my eye.

The uprisings in Saxony last month brought the German govern-ment to its knees. All industry in Mansfeld has stopped and there is no coal for the entire northeast. President Ebert says he is negoti-ating with the strikers for a swift resolution. Meanwhile, inflation of

the mark gallops ahead. If it continues at this rate, the paper won't
be worth the ink. Leader of the recent strikes, Mr. Hausmann, said
they would bring down the government if they had to, they would
get what they needed for the workers . . .

Hausmann—I paid attention to that name. I took down the name of
the reporter. Michel Martin would get a little visit from me in the next
few days. I needed to know what he'd seen. And I needed a photo from
Bertie of his latest Teddy.

A train whistle blew loudly and there was commotion outside. The
Blue Train from Calais had come in. I ripped the article from the paper
and stuffed it into my purse along with Fox's photo, then ran out to the
platform to wait with the others.

I saw him as soon as he got out of the carriage. He was a head taller
than everyone else, his hat jaunty over his eyes. He looked around at the
station as he walked slowly towards the concourse. I could almost see him
remember when he was last here, with me, in that cold November. I saw
him straighten up; he wasn't in uniform now, no khaki or gray, no pips
or puttees in sight. He was in a navy suit with a wide lapel, with just the
sweet sounds of Paris and me.

I was too excited to wave. He caught my eye and grinned, now a little
boy, now a dingo. He stepped up the pace and almost ran towards me.

"Tom-Tom—" But he picked me up before I could finish. With his
arm around my waist, he lifted me high, looking up at me like I was a
star as he whisked me around. I wanted to laugh, but I was almost too
full of laughter, it caught in my throat. He dropped his bag and held me
tight against him, his face buried in my collar, my feet not quite touching
the ground.

"Button." He said it over and over. I closed my eyes and breathed him
in—tobacco, train dust, the wool of his suit, soap, and his smell underneath it all. He smelled like home. Finally, he let me go, and I saw that

his eyes were as misty as mine. I laughed then, both of us so silly to be overwhelmed.

"Oh, my lucky Tombola—"

"Button."

"Picking me up with one arm, really! What have you been doing, shearing sheep?"

"Maybe, or maybe you've just danced yourself into a skeleton." He pinched playfully at my elbow and ribs.

"Hey! . . . Actually that's not too far off the mark."

"Then it's time I fed you up, some proper food—roast lamb and potatoes and scones and custard—"

"Oh, not custard!"

He laughed; he knew how much I hated it.

"I'm sophisticated now, Tom!"

"And Yorkshire pudding and corned beef sandwiches and rock cakes—"

"Stop!"

"And jam toast and bananas and beer—"

I couldn't stop laughing and he couldn't stop grinning; he couldn't take his hands from my waist or his eyes from my face. He looked me over, from hair to skin to shoes. I returned his gaze and his touch to the waist. I felt his muscles twitch and tense through the suit. Everything about him was big and strong. It spoke of sunshine on paddocks and country cricket and sailing round Sydney Harbour in his uncle's little dinghy. His eyes, a deep dark blue, were the endless sky of home. If I was ever homesick, then he was all I needed to be content.

He squeezed my waist, his hands big enough to span half of it.

"Well, Button, did you miss me?" His smile wavered and I choked up. If his eyes were home skies then, like a Sydney sky, they could also rain torrents and darken with storms. He put his palm to my cheek. I felt the calluses along the ridge of his palm and on his padded fingertips. I closed my eyes and breathed in the scent of his skin, tinged with expensive

American tobacco and sweat. I turned my face to his palm and kissed it. I heard him let out his breath in a rush; nothing more needed to be said.

"So, Button, are you living in some poetical garret like a true Bohemian, or is there room enough for me?"

"Poetical garret. But you're welcome to stay. We'll just need to fashion another mattress . . ."

He laughed and squeezed my shoulders. "It's all right, the newspaper's paying for this visit. You didn't think I came all the way from Sydney with this one suitcase, did you?"

"I've seen people come farther with less."

"Not farther, surely—you can't know that many Kiwis."

"Chileans." I grinned. "Tasmanians."

"Take me to a hotel near you, Button."

"Oh, so not the Ritz then."

"Not on your nelly!"

"Which newspaper's paying?"

"The *Herald*. But I'm only a junior."

"Then why are you here without your senior? What are you reporting on?"

"Paris life." He grinned.

"You do mean the *Herald* back home, right?"

"I'm one of the Europe correspondents." He puffed out his chest in mock pomposity, then leaned in to me. "The editor's nephew was in the first fifteen with me at—"

"Oh, don't tell me, I've heard it before."

"I'm on my way to Germany, actually."

"Germany! Saxony or Silesia?"

"You know about all of that? What do you— Actually, don't tell me. That's work, and work is for tomorrow. Tonight, I'm here with you."

He twirled the ends of my hair where they curled around my cheek.

"Bobbed hair, Button. You are modern."

"I live alone and smoke cigarettes and walk unchaperoned through the streets."

As we were doing now, arm in arm, making our way out of the station slowly as we chatted. People moved about us, brisk women, old men, young girls, limping veterans. Tom took my hatpin out and removed my blue cloche, fluffing and smoothing my hair so he could see the full effect. He looked wistful, comparing my new hair to the memory of the long blond plait that I let loose when I was last at home. He leaned forward with a little frown and sniffed my hair, so close and so soft it was almost a kiss.

"Lavender?"

"My bath this morning was scented."

He nodded. Very solemnly, he took off his own hat, plonked it on my head, and placed my cloche over his black, slick, short-back-and-sides. He stood to attention and pointed forward.

"Button—to the champagne!"

◆

We found him a room only a block away from my garret, where we dumped his suitcase and headed straight out for the city's bright lights and brighter people. Tom wanted to see it all, with me—"Just like you do, Button. I want your Paris."

We landed first at the Rotonde. Oysters and artists: what more could a tourist want? By the best of luck, Pablo was there, and Tom's face was priceless as I introduced him. Shock, covered with an odd smile as he tried to look nonchalant. Pablo shook his hand perfunctorily and turned to me, his hand on my elbow.

"My Kangaroo, when will you sit for me again? Even just looking at you now gives me ideas. . . ." His eyes searched mine and, as always, when he looked at me the world disappeared and it was just the two of us.

"My friend is here now, so . . . the day after tomorrow?"

"What day is that, Thursday? Good, because I'm busy tomorrow. Come on Thursday." He kissed me on both cheeks and the lips. "And wear your little starlit shoes. I have an idea." He grinned, nodded farewell to Tom, and went back to his table. I couldn't help but smile.

"You model for Pablo Picasso," said Tom, unbelieving, envious, awe-struck.

I gave my best impression of a Gallic shrug. I had meant to show off, to show Tom that even on an ordinary Tuesday I was sophisticated and bohemian, but this was even better than I could have planned. He leaned back in his chair with a cigarette. We were sitting outside, the late spring chill lessened by the heaters near us. I wore my coat and nuzzled into its fur trim. People chatted all around us—to our right, a pair of young lovers trying so hard to be private, a British pair to our left trying even harder to look bohemian, Americans behind us achieving both as they spoke French to their friends from L'Ecole Grand-Chaumière down the road. The light from inside the café spilled through the windows in spots and wheels, through the signs and patrons, covering Tom's suit with golden freckles. He had an odd expression on his face, somehow both shrewd and sad, his leg crossed in a pretense of insouciance. And it was a pretense, I could tell straightaway; I could almost feel the tension where it brewed just under his breastbone. I reached for my glass of champagne.

"What is it?" I asked lightly; I could pretend too.

"You model for Picasso," he exhaled in a plume. "So you—you have to . . ." He waved his hand as though waving away my clothes.

"Sometimes"—I took a sip—"and sometimes not. Light me a cigarette, would you?"

He lit one, and another for himself, with a frown. He handed me the cigarette without looking at me and spent the next few minutes looking at everything and everyone but me.

"And why should that make you jealous?"

"Jealous!" he sputtered. "I'm not jealous, I—"

"Oh, come on, you can't lie to me."

"It's just— It's not seemly for—"

"Seemly? Seemly!"

"Not respectable—"

"Who are you, my chaperone? Some emissary from my parents to make sure that I still have a marriageable reputation?"

"You don't want to get married?"

"Not by reputation! Not to some stuffed shirt who wants his little wife safe in his pocket where she belongs."

"That's not fair, Button. That's not me!"

"Isn't it? 'Seemly,' 'respectable'—whatever you used to be, it appears you're now just as small-minded—"

"All right." He gripped my wrist and leaned forward. I pulled back instinctively. His grip was too strong, his eyes were dark and stormy; it made me want to fight. He flipped my hand over and kissed the wrist he gripped. Not lightly, not a peck, he pressed his lips hard to my skin and breathed in deeply. He couldn't look at me until he'd let go, swigged his champagne and poured us both another glass. His cigarette dangled from his mouth and he squinted at the smoke in his eyes. My heart pounded, I couldn't take my eyes from him, I wanted to yell at him and slap his face, I wanted to rip his shirt open and dissolve into him. He picked up his glass and leaned close to me. His eyes held mine as firmly as if he held my chin in his large palm.

"All right," he said. "I am jealous."

"I hate jealousy."

"He's seen you . . . and I haven't." He clenched his jaw as he fought to keep his voice down. "It's what . . . It's . . ." But he closed his eyes and looked away, a flash of pain over his face. Ah, my Tom-Tom. That look told me more than a dozen half-formed phrases. I ran my finger over the stubble that prickled his cheek. He closed his eyes, not in pain this time, but in release.

"Not naked, nude," I said softly.

"What?" I still stroked his jaw and his eyes were still closed.

"He's seen me nude, a model, an object"—I traced just under his jaw-line, the skin soft beneath the stubble—"not naked, vulnerable, and truly myself. It's work, with Pablo. Everything for art." It was a bit of a lie, but a bit of truth as well. Pablo didn't know me, certainly not like Tom did. And the modeling, being nude, was about freedom. I couldn't explain it to Tom just then. I could hardly explain it to myself, not with half a bottle of bubbly in me and surrounded by artists and tourists and wannabes. Besides, this man under my fingers, his sensitivity to me mirrored my sensitivity to him. It was as though I knew what he tasted, knew how the air entered his lungs. He took my hand and laid it flat on his cheek as he looked up at me.

"You're a modern woman, Button."

"I am."

"That might take some getting used to." He smiled faintly.

"For you and me both."

How did we get over this little tiff? With more champagne, of course. We finished the bottle, the finger bowls winking at us through the night. I regaled him with long and detailed stories of some of my more raucous society parties, turning each aristocrat and heiress into a caricature, com-plete with accent. I made Tom-Tom smile again, then grin, then laugh with his head thrown back, deep and loud enough that people turned to look. That laugh was always worth the effort of my performance. His long legs stretched out and his black hair, flopping out of its brilliantine, caught admiring glances with the light. There was something between us now—or the something between us had come more into the open—a little promise, that I wanted desperately and yet rebelled against. His smile said, *Tell me more*, and I obliged. He watched me, face alight, the French champagne creeping up his neck in a soft blush beneath his tan, his white teeth now like a dingo, now like a little boy; in a flash he'd look at me with hunger and then the flash was gone. My pulse raced, it felt like Paris in the war, when everything had to be done this night because there might never be another, we had to swallow the whole world—the champagne bottle was empty. The lights along the street beckoned us out into the soft night.

"Another bottle, Button?"

"I have a better idea."

"What could be better than champagne?"

"A jazz club in Montmartre. La Gaya—it opened just a few months ago. I've heard that it's always full of artists and dancers and stays open until the last surrealist has cracked an egg on his cat and wandered off with his beast into the dawn. I've never been and I'm dying to go."

"We can't have you dying, Button, I couldn't bear it. La Gaya it is!"

He didn't take my arm, he took my waist as we walked over to the road and hailed a cab. He kept his arm round me in the cab all the way to Montmartre as we chatted and laughed. Of course I let him. This little promise—I wanted him, I needed freedom, I could neither say no nor compromise. People and lights popped up through the cab window as we trundled past on the cobblestones. We tried to be the first to point out various landmarks as he tested his memory against my recent knowledge. His face was so close that I could feel his breath, his skin, every time he moved.

The cab bundled us out at rue Duphot. It was too easy to spot La Gaya. People spilled onto the street, bohemian types, the fashionable rich, men in suits and waiters chatting over the piano inside. I hooked Tom's hand into my suspender belt over my dress and led him through the door.

We ordered two surrealist cocktails, one blue and served in a piss pot, the other green and served in a glass skull, both intensely alcoholic and indescribably awful. I grimaced at my green concoction.

"It'll do the trick though, Button," Tom yelled over the music and chatter.

"Let's do some sightseeing," I yelled back. We were at a table against the wall, opposite the piano. It afforded the best view of all the patrons inside and on the street. The roof was decorated with large golden lamps hung at different heights, so people's faces glowed in spots. There were mirrors on each wall so we were reflected infinitely across the floor. I lifted my hat and Tom wobbled his head to the music, our gestures repeated again and again in the mirrors. Our little seated dance attracted the attention of a group by the piano. One man shrugged his shoulders in time to the music, another lifted his hat up and down, another flapped his glasses, dancing to us across the room. We got up and moved to one another on the dance floor, in perfect rhythm, so that we became like a machine, each one of us part of a multipart dance robot in the middle of the dance floor. Others joined in until the little dance floor was crowded, people waving their surreal drinks above their heads. Our dance mutated, Tom flapped his jacket like a flasher and I flapped my cloak like a bird, as notes bounced off the mirrors and off our skin. In the middle a man with a long nose in his long thin face, his head topped by a sprig of curls, turned to me and took my hand.

"You have a dreamlike sensibility. You inspire me to the depths. What is your art? What is your name?" We kept jigging together in time to the syncopated rhythms.

"I'm Kiki—"

"Oh, Kiki Kangaroo?" Another man jigged in. "The *Australienne?*"

"Yes, that's right—"

"She models for Pablo," said the second jigger.

"Ah, Pablo! He has impeccable taste in models." He smiled and waggled his eyebrows. I didn't know if that was a surreal wink or if he was dancing with his face. It seemed best just to keep dancing.

"I'm Jean," he said, "You must come here more often, we're here most nights."

"Just us," said the second jigger, "Les Six. Pablo too, and his wife and the other dancers. Come back tomorrow, we're having a hat party for my un-birthday." I flapped my coat and he moved in a jerky shimmy to the jazz. We danced around each other—Jean danced with Tom, I danced with the second jigger, we shimmied into a circle and out again. When the music stopped, we clapped and cheered and someone poured champagne on the pianist's head. The music started up and Jean kissed my hand.

"Kiki, until tomorrow." He bowed and went back to his seat.

I flopped into my chair and picked up my green skull drink. I needed a rest.

"Who was that?" asked Tom, none too discreetly.

"I think that was Jean Cocteau. We're going to meet him here tomorrow. Bring an outrageous hat."

"A fez with a pelican?"

"A beehive with real live bees."

"A baguette with two bicycle wheels hanging from it."

I laughed, but his smile didn't last long.

"What is it?"

"Button, I'm not here tomorrow."

"No, Tom-Tom, no no no." I kissed his hand. "I don't want to hear it. Only happy things tonight. Only the outrageous, the surreal."

He pulled me onto his lap and raised his piss-pot cocktail.

"To pelicans!" he proclaimed.

"To kangaroos!" I rejoined. We downed our drinks in one long draught and ordered something more civilized.

We danced and drank until well after midnight. We waved goodbye to Cocteau and his coterie as we swayed out the door, drunk on music and freedom and friendship and sexual tension and lots of French liquor. We couldn't find a cab, so we just walked home. We spent almost two hours slowly meandering across the city, sobering up and calming down, hand in hand, arm in arm, entwined together. He gave me all the gossip from home, the good stories and the bad, my father's health (rude as ever) and his sister's (delicate and worrisome), which school friends had married and which were shipwrecked forever from the war. I was glad that I was drunk when we talked about this, that it was dark and in the chill of the small hours I had Tom-Tom wrapped around me. Otherwise I might have reeled with the proliferation of all these parallel lives; I might even have cried over a life that had almost been mine. Or maybe I would have taken it calmly, like a story from far away and long ago—except that Tom-Tom was the messenger, his body a reminder of all I had left behind to be here.

I didn't know how late it was, or how early, but by the time we approached Montparnasse the sky had begun to lighten. Just the faintest tinges of gray on the horizon, making the air seem fuzzy. Our outlines were soft, the predawn cold made us clutch each other tightly, and even more tightly as we came to my front door.

"I live in this garret." I pointed at the geraniums with the sleeping sparrows next to them, little feathery balls against the chill. Tom looked up, his face opening further and further until I was sure all his love and tears would fall out and splatter the footpath with glorious color.

"That's where you read my letter."

"Not quite with my legs over the edge, cigarette in hand, as you described . . . but almost. You know me too well." I choked on the last words. He stroked my disheveled hair and I couldn't stop myself, I flung my arms around his neck and buried my face in his collar. He held me tightly, my feet off the ground. We clung to each other and stayed that way as long as I could hold it. I had to let go eventually, but he only lowered me enough to stand. He didn't let go, and through his shirt I could feel his pulse, his blood drum against his ribs, as though his heart tried to break free of its bony cage.

A rooster crowed somewhere. A cat prowled out of the alley, scar-faced and regal, as shifty and suspicious as a fox. Fox—

"What is it, Button?" He'd heard me catch my breath.

"You can't go yet—"

"Oh, Button, I want . . . I want—"

"No, really, you can't. I have to tell you . . ." He stroked my hair, I held my hand to his chest. I didn't want to break this tender moment. I kissed the button on his shirt and breathed in his smell, and he made a little noise when he sighed. My Tom-Tom. I had to steel myself.

"I think I might have some information about the end of the war."

He breathed in sharply.

"*My* end of the war?"

"Yes, I— From a war contact. It's . . . it's absurdly complicated."

He frowned at me. He still held me tightly, but his embrace was more like a grip.

"So you can't leave tomorrow—today—you have to stay so I can tell you everything."

"So tell me."

"Not now—"

"Why not?"

"Tom, look at us." I pointed to our appearance. His hair was a mess, his tie askew, and somehow he'd lost a cuff link and a shoelace. My stockings were full of ladders, one suspender had broken, and my hat was dented over my sweaty hair.

"You need a bath, I need a bath, we both need rest. There are so many details. . . . We need coffee and breakfast and some semblance of a clear head when we talk about this."

"But, Button—"

"We need some semblance of a stout heart to talk about this, and my heart . . . my heart is . . ." But of course I couldn't finish the sentence. I didn't need to. He pulled me close and kissed my hair, my ears, my neck, my cheeks, he pulled me up and kissed me very gently on the lips. That blue gaze, it was home. I had to close my eyes and just breathe him in.

We stood nose to nose; if I gave in I would just tumble down into him, out of Paris and freedom. His pull was magnetic, my pull for him was equally strong; he could neither put me down nor look away. It wasn't a little promise between us, it was a big promise, bigger than I could hold in my body in this pearl-gray dawn. He felt it too, and with a sigh of relief and disappointment, he crushed me into an embrace.

"Be back here at lunchtime."

"Button." He kissed me chastely on the hand, pulled his hat down over his eyes and set off towards his hotel. I felt a small pain in my chest as I watched him lope over the cobblestones and out of sight.

"WANG-WANG BLUES"

I thought I would pass out as soon as my head hit the pillow. I thought sleep would overtake me like chloroform and I'd be dead until Tom-Tom knocked on my door. Instead, I undressed and slowly washed, including my hair. I sat at my windowsill, bare legs dangling over the street, and smoked my last three cigarettes. My hair curled up and around the warming day. I watched the clouds part, the fog lift off the river, the gray give itself up into blue.

Tom-Tom had unsettled me. Those blue eyes, that changeable grin. His kiss on my wrist, his hand on my waist, that slight brush against my lips. The way he made me forget everything else made me dizzy and I wasn't sure that I liked it. I could feel his passion with his pulse. I didn't think I was lonely. But Maisie, then Harry, then Tom—perhaps I was and I just had no idea what lonely meant anymore until I was overwhelmed by a desire for home. Not the physical place but my true home, the home I could only find in people. The kind of home that Fox could never provide.

Fox—there he was, intruding on every thought. I sighed. I remembered that day in Amiens when he first revealed his smile, a real smile full of delight. It's so addictive, to make a frosty face finally warm. Much better, by far, to stick to the work. Like the newspaper boy with the withered hand—he would report to Fox that I had recognized him and I'd have a new watcher tomorrow.

The sky was a soft blue, the hawkers were out, I could smell bread from the boulangeries. I had no more cigarettes, my mouth felt fuzzy, and my body felt poisoned with too much partying. If Tom-Tom was going to be here at lunchtime, demanding an explanation, I told myself that I at least had to rest. I crawled under the covers and sunk straight into sleep.

◆

How did Tom manage to look handsome when rough, unshaven, and grumpy? His hair flopped over his face, he had dark circles under his eyes, and his black stubble shaded halfway down his neck. He frowned and slumped in his chair, feet stuck out onto the footpath, the collar of his navy peacoat turned up. He wore the striped shirt of the Breton sailors, comfortable morning-after wear, and only acceptable here in Montparnasse. He'd bought one for me too—work wear was the latest fashion, he'd been told—and it lay in its brown paper package in my lap. We weren't thinking about that now, or the other presents he said he'd brought from home, or his train that afternoon. We were thinking about his handkerchief on the table, and Fox, and the return of the war.

"You never told him anything?"

"Never. Don't you trust me, Tom-Tom?"

"'Tom-Tom.'" He shook his head. "I'm not that name anymore, am I? Because of this." He picked up the hankie and flung it angrily back on the table. "Button, how could you let him back into your life?"

"Let him—! Do you think I had a choice?"

"You always have a choice."

"He presented me with this." I copied his action with the hankie. "You know as well as I do, it means *Follow me or I let him hang*. Is that what I should have done? Left you to skulk around the gallows for the rest of your life? When I might have a chance to—"

"I can save my own skin." He leaned forward and growled at me, "But Fox—you promised me—never again, you said, never under any circumstances—"

"And you would have preferred that?"

"Infinitely—"

"Than that I save you? You hypocrite—"

"Save me! Oh, please. All I need saving from is your hero complex. And I'm not the hypocrite! You're the one who breaks her—"

The waiter came to clear our coffees away and it put a stop to our squabble. I ordered more coffee and a midday breakfast. There were enough Americans who came to this hotel that they would serve baguettes with jam, or bowls of fresh fruit, at any time of day. However old Parisians might grumble, I would always be glad of the American tourist for that.

Tom smoked, not looking at me, not looking at anything. I shivered into my Chinese-style coat; its burgundy brocade was too thin for his cold shoulder. Not even its gold peonies, so perfectly matched to my new dress, could brighten this moment. I hated his moods; I always had. They weren't brooding or dark, they showed no hidden depths—they were just selfish and grumpy. I took one of his cigarettes and lit it myself.

"You promised me, Button." His voice was small.

"I promised myself. But your life was more important."

He looked at me then. Stormy waters—his blue eyes held such turmoil. He knew all about Fox. One night in Paris, just before he went AWOL, he'd had to hold me as I shook, whimpered, cried, and moaned. He'd had to feed me and nurse me for his full day of leave. Fox's mission had left me bruised, inside and out. He'd placed me in a frontline brothel. Madame Rouge was an informer for the Germans, using the girls to send messages. I was only meant to usher men in, to give them drinks and sexy small talk. To avoid the real business, I pretended to be only fourteen, a good seven or so years younger than I really was. But there were so many men that Madame Rouge converted the broom closet under the stairs and put to me work. Fox's watchers watched it happen. They were my first customers, but they wouldn't sneak me out. I made a lot of money and my information led to three arrests, instead of just the one we had been aiming for. I never forgave Fox. Neither, it seemed, had Tom.

He held out his hand, a peace offering, and when I took it he held my hand tightly. I'd done the same for him, nursed him when he turned up in Paris shaky and skinny after his escape. I'd procured him the forged ID and passage home—through Fox's contacts, of course—yet another reason why Tom couldn't forgive Fox. Which was why Tom wanted us to have nothing to do with him—Fox had too much power over us already.

"What else could I do, my Tom-Tom?"

He kept hold of my hand as the waiter brought out our bread, jam, orange juice, and coffee, our arms a link over the circular table in the spring sunshine, as the lunchtime life of Paris clipped neatly by. The coffee steamed, rich and creamy; the citrus tang of the juice mixed with the subtle scent of very fresh bread. My stomach growled, but I didn't want to let go of his hand. If any of this was going to be worth the effort, then I needed Tom to be on my side. I needed him to forgive me.

He sighed and stubbed out his cigarette. The stormy-waters look had gone, and the grumpy frown, and all the horrid moodiness. I almost wanted it all back when I saw the sad, defeated look that had replaced them. I squeezed his hand hard.

"All right, Button—"

"We'll fix it together—"

"Whatever you need—"

"I need you, Tom." His name caught in my throat. I hadn't realized it until I'd said it, but it was true, it was too desperately true. He stroked my cheek. His open look asked *Really? You really need me?* and read the truth of my words in my face.

"You have me, Button. Always," he said softly, "as I need you."

Suddenly he flashed me his dingo grin. "But perhaps not quite as much as I need this breakfast."

"*Mon Dieu!* I'm so hungry, Tom, I thought I'd faint before you mentioned it."

He laughed then, his head tilted back, all the worry fled in that moment. We were a team. We'd clear his name and clear Fox from my life.

◇

I had to hold on to the platform lamppost to stop myself from running after his train. It was so much worse than when Bertie left—perhaps it was made worse because Bertie had left only yesterday. I clung to the lamppost as I clung to our plan. He was off to Berlin, to join his senior reporter, before they traveled around Germany, reporting on the political turmoil. He'd send me regular updates that hopefully would help with this mission from Fox. But even if they did not, it meant that Tom would call often and telegram oftener; it meant that he would be back in Paris before long.

But that didn't help right now, with the great gaping hole left by the train, the air full of smoke and regret. Paris, my beloved city of light, felt cold and gray. Even with the chestnut blossoms littering the holiday tables with fallen petals. It was just after lunch and a sleepiness hung over the platforms and taxi ranks. I needed some work to help me get my Paris feeling back again. I needed a distraction.

◇

I gazed at the cracks in Manuelle's ceiling, half-dressed and completely undone, as she hummed in satisfaction beside me. She had been washing her hair when I turned up, wet and clad only in a dressing gown, ruby satin and deliciously short. It took some time, and a number of kisses, a good glass of Madeira and two cigarettes, before we could think of going back to her hair. Water warmed in a kettle on a gas ring on the floor. She leaned over me in the late-afternoon light and placed a pair of scissors on my bare chest.

"Like your hair," she said, still naked, her olive skin gleaming in the sunlight from the window. "I want a kangaroo cut and I can only get that from you."

Apparently a kangaroo cut was a straight bob that stopped at the jaw, as mine did.

"And it's so modern, Kiki! I want to declare how modern I am with my haircut!"

"Are you ready?" I laughed. "Here's the first chop." I snipped off a foot of her hair and handed it to her. She gasped, stared, and burst out laughing.

"Yes! Chop it all off! Freedom for women!"

Each snip earned a portion of her life history in sweet, bubbly phrases. She'd moved to Paris during the war to escape the local pimp, her soft curves and free spirit making it easy to settle into the life of a Montparnasse model. She liked the Brits, put up with the Americans, thought the Spanish were dreadful—"except for Pablo, but then, Pablo's Pablo"—but loved the Russians. "So handsome and strong and soulful—except for Olga, of course, she must be the most venal Russian this side of the Danube—but Osip and Igor and Michel . . . most of the time they just want to drink with me and lament their lost homeland." They toasted her eyes, they wrote stanzas to her bum, they got too drunk and wobbled home to their wives. They came from all over the Empire, a stream in 1918, but now, with Russia gripped by civil war, there was a flood. Not all of them were bighearted musicians; many of them were "tight-fisted aristocrats who want the world to go back to kings and slaves—or the next best thing." But she couldn't say what that was except for some confused sentences about honor, pride, nation, and Mother Russia.

"They hate the Bolsheviks."

"Of course."

"They'll do anything, join anyone, to oust them—I've heard Olga and her cronies say so."

"Which cronies?"

"Oh, you know, the ones who hang around Pablo all the time and try to steal his sketches—Arkady? Is that his name? Tall man who thinks he's God's gift. He's some distant cousin of Olga's. He's boasted that he has contacts, men with money, but he never names them. Yet he turns up every so often and buys a little sketch of Pablo's or Fujita's. Where does the money come from?"

"Where indeed?"

"Who knows? Who cares? Is my hair done yet?"

"I'm just going to give you a few little layers, Manuelle, as it'll be easier to look after with your wavy hair . . ."

"You can call me Mimi," she said, her dimples deepening.

"Mimi"—I kissed her neck—"where would I find this Arkady, if I wanted to?"

"Those Russians drink tea on the Right Bank. There's a teahouse there." She knew it only as the Russian tea room.

"I'M A JAZZ VAMPIRE"

It was the end of sunset by the time I left Manuelle. The empty feeling, the gnawing feeling of absence, was hard at my heels. I had to keep working, keep going, find more distractions until it completely calmed. Until Paris was mine again.

I leaned against a streetlamp and lit a cigarette. I loved watching the lamps flick on one by one, their puddles of light on the footpath, making golden the fishermen and street walkers who passed through them. The windows of the apartments were an Easter celebration, bright squares with their shadow-puppet play inside them. There was a mother calming one child as she scolded another. A young man leaned through the window frame and smoked. An old woman twitched her curtain corner as she surveyed the street. The streets quivered with a thousand stories.

On my third proposition, I knew I had to move on or else start my new life as a prostitute. I checked my silver watch in my handbag—6:00 p.m., Michel Martin would no longer be at his desk at *Le Figaro*. But it was only 5:00 p.m. in London, with this new British Summer Time, and Bertie would most likely still be at his desk. I walked into the nearest hotel and asked to use their telephone.

"Put me through to the *Star*, London."

"One moment, mademoiselle."

I had another six hours before Fox would call the Rotonde. I had to keep working or I'd drink myself into a stupor.

"The *Star*, Browne speaking."

"Bertie darling, you sound so professional!"

"Kiki! Don't tell me you're in London."

"I won't, because I'm not."

"Oh—"

"I'm in a scungy hotel foyer, sweaty and slightly sticky, after a long, erotic afternoon with Picasso's model."

"Mmm . . . Is this advance notice of your column?"

I had almost forgotten—my deadline was noon tomorrow. Thank goodness the phone wouldn't register my surprise.

"No, it's just a tidbit for you. What I need now is the name of a bar."

"Aren't there more than enough to choose from? Just find the nearest one, walk up to the juiciest man, and—"

"I need the bar where the *Figaro* reporters go for their after-work aperitifs. I'm hunting down a particular man before Fox calls tonight."

"I see! Well, from what I know, they go to the bar at the foot of their building, it's called something obvious like Le Journal or Le Journaliste."

"That should be easy to find."

"Either that, or they wander into Montmartre to dirty their conservative souls."

"Bertie, you're a star."

"The star of the *Star*, eh?"

"A guiding star. Come back soon."

◆

Le Journal was dark and smoky. The smell of salty *frites* and beer mixed with sweat and news ink and pipe tobacco. Men lined the bar under the low lamps, chatting earnestly in pairs or threes, or frowning into their solitary drinks. I saw no other women. Every eye turned to me as I made my way to the bar. I slid in next to a young loner, who nursed his beer like an Englishman, and ordered a beer of my own. Only when I took my first sip did the chatter start up again.

The young loner glared at me. "What are you doing here?"

"What does it look like?"

"It looks like you're plying a trade, but whether you're a whore or a spy, I couldn't say."

I smiled. "I'm looking for Michel Martin. Is he here?"

"What, does he owe you money?"

"I need something from him."

"What's it worth to you?" His eyes, dark in the shadows, became hard, and a nasty smile curled his lip. I took note of that smile. If he quoted Keats or Byron, I'd have to find out his name. I cursed Fox yet again. Wherever he sent me, my body ended up as barter.

"Martin?" A plump boozer leaned over and put his beery mustache in my face. "Martin's just back from Germany, so of course he legged it to be with his bohemian mistress. Skirt above her knees and eyes like an enchantment. I told him, take me with you to those cafés, all the girls are easy, but he said I wouldn't like it." He burped loudly and it smelled of yesterday.

"No, you wouldn't," I rejoined.

"He calls her Justine, you know, after the Sade novel."

"Not her real name, then."

"He told me her real name," the lone wolf said, "but information doesn't come cheaply."

"Oh, is this one up for sale?" the boozer breathed. "We could tell her Paulette's real name when she . . . oh." His face fell as the lone wolf growled at him. I wanted more information—what did Martin look like, how long had he been in Germany—but I felt it would be safer if I slipped away before the lone wolf could grab me.

Martin had a bohemian mistress called Paulette, who most likely lived in either Montparnasse or Montmartre. Someone would know her, especially if she brought her conservative lover with her to the cafés. I just had to ask the right questions.

◆

But the right questions eluded me. No one at the Rotonde had seen a Paulette with a reporter from *Le Figaro*. I asked as discreetly as I could, but Henri was too busy, North was too interested in the gossip from home, and the rest were not regulars. I'd have to keep my questions for tomorrow, as in a few hours I had to receive more instructions from Fox—and then find the best place to obliterate his influence. Dread and loneliness nipped at my fingers and toes—where was Bertie, or Tom-Tom, or Maisie, or Harry when I needed them?

"Kiki, you look lost." North looked up from her gossip.

"Forlorn. The very word is like a bell—"

"Like a bell? You're being morbid and poetical, Kiki."

"My heart aches—"

"Well, we have the cure for that—wine!" She held up a bottle. "Sit down and have a glass of this, what is it, Beaujolais."

Why not? I needed something and I still had hours to wait until Fox's call. Some of her companions were old soldiers, Californians who'd run off to Canada to join the fight and knew Paris in the way I did. The hours relaxed with the wine, and when I saw Henri come towards me, I smiled, ready with my next drink order. Despite my mild flirtation, his expression remained glum. I looked at my watch; it was exactly midnight.

"Mademoiselle," Henri leaned over and whispered in my ear, "you have—"

"Yes, yes, I'll come now."

The office was a tomb, and Henri wouldn't come farther than the door. I lit a cigarette before I picked up, as something to do, something to calm me, to pretend I was in control. I blew out smoke into the telephone receiver.

"Woodbines, Vixen?" purred Fox. He was in one of his filthy flirty moods.

"I'm not that nostalgic." Woodbines were the smoke of the trenches.

"Not even Sobranie?"

"Gitanes," I said. "I bought them with the newspaper yesterday."

"Do the French newspapers include photos now?"

"Just the one."

The clocked ticked on the shelf. The sounds of the café were blocked by the heavy stone wall of the office.

"Vixen."

"Fox?"

"'I cry your mercy—pity—love! Aye, love!'"

Oh, this game. "'And what is love? It is a doll dress'd up—'"

"'Ye may love in spite of beaver hats . . .'"

"Fox, are you just bored?"

"Bored? I could play this game all day!"

"But not all night and night it is."

"And is the night tender?"

"'Tender is the night, and he cannot see what flowers are at his feet.'"

"Do you know it by heart, Vixen?"

"I'm working on it. Am I the flowers at his feet?"

"You're one of them."

"Along with the man who took that photo?" I wanted to know how many other agents the mole could not see.

"Do you like it? It's one of my favorites. I have so few of you laughing."

"So few of me? How many did this photographer take?"

"That photographer is me." I could hear that he was delighted with my confusion, with his own technical ingenuity. "I'm as dexterous with a box brownie as I am with a scalpel, Vixen."

He was also more intimately involved with this mole than I had originally assumed. The man who had died in my arms was one of Fox's
protégés, as I was. . . . I thought I had known most of his agents, but
apparently not. I took the photo out of my handbag and stared at it. I still
only recognized a few faces.

"You look very pretty in it, don't you think? A Queen-Moon clustered
round by her starry Fays." His voice was silky but it chilled me that he
knew I was looking at the photo again.

"'But here there is no light,'" I countered.

I heard him exhale. "'Save what from heaven is with breezes blown.'"

"Who's listening to us, Fox?"

"'Darkling I listen—'"

"Who do you think is eavesdropping on the line?"

"'Men sit and hear each other groan . . . youth grows pale—'"

"'And dies—' That sounds like a hospital ward."

Fox made a satisfied noise down the line.

"It seems rich to die for the lands forlorn"—I connected the two sets
of clues—"Germany is a bit forlorn at the moment. Is this goodbye,
France?"

"Why don't they give us a chance? The faery lands are too forlorn—"

"Because they don't have shadows numberless to hide a mole?"

"Not quite yet."

I could hear him light another cigarette. I was right—the mole was a
double agent for Germany or some German organization. I had to look
for a man with German connections. I hated the way Fox made me play
his games, but I couldn't stop myself. If I was brutally honest, I didn't
want to stop—but I wanted to play on my terms.

"Do you have more clues for me, Fox?"

"Oh, Vixen, I was just beginning to enjoy this match—"

"'Beauty cannot keep her lustrous eyes—'"

"Lustrous or lusty?"

"Or her wandering mind—"

"Beyond tomorrow—and you don't have many more days beyond that to complete this mission." He sighed theatrically. "As you wish, Vixen. But before we go, tell me, was the owner of the handkerchief glad to receive his property?"

Tom. I had to protect him, and I had to force Fox to surrender his information.

"He'd be gladder if everything was returned. As would the messenger."

"Such as what? His name?" His voice was cruel.

"His good name."

"But is it really so good, Vixen?"

"I trust—"

"Ah, trust. Such a fragile thing. The slightest suspicion and it disintegrates."

I cursed under my breath. To trust Fox, to let myself be trustworthy to him, would betray too much vulnerability, would leave me open to his lies and cruelty. But without it, how could I get what I needed? I had to work for Fox and trust that he'd deliver, and trust that what he delivered to me would help clear Tom's name. I stubbed out my cigarette. There was nothing else for it; I had to gamble on trust and all that it entailed.

"But trust is the basis of love, Fox. And I only work for love."

Silence. I strained to hear him, but all I could hear was the clock on the table and the muted sounds from the other side of the door.

"I know." But his voice wasn't cold, or sharp, or cruel. It sounded almost sad. I had expected more jealousy from Fox. He hated to be second best, in anything. So what did he know that I didn't?

"Vixen"—his purr was back—"open the table drawer, the top right. There is an envelope addressed to Mademoiselle Renarde. Use that name when you go to the address on the back."

"Why? To find what?"

But the only reply was a click. The line was dead.

The envelope was not written in his ornate handwriting but typed. Just the name on the front, and on the back, an address in a part of Paris I didn't recognize. Inside was another photo, but not of Ferny or Fox or anything related to the mission. It was of me and Tom, both in uniform, somewhere in Paris during the war. We weren't looking at the camera, we weren't even aware of it, as we held hands over the café table, forehead to forehead, eyes closed. I had to light another cigarette to stop the tremble in my fingers; I sucked hard on it to stop myself from crying. When had this been taken? Had Fox always had me followed? Or had he taken this himself? Had he followed me in person? How many other photos did he have? I flipped it over, but this time there was nothing written on the back. Fox was the master of understatement. Nothing else needed to be said—he was watching me; he had always been watching me. He was trying to make me believe that he knew everything. I slipped the photo into my handbag and stayed at the table for a moment, blotting my tears and staining my hankie with makeup in the process. He was trying to poison my most precious relationship and replace it with himself. The mission was exciting, yes, but this was why I'd been so desperate to get away from him. Another reason. And now I couldn't get away because that meant losing Tom too—I gasped; of course—if I wanted Tom, I had to take Fox too; if I abandoned Fox, then I abandoned Tom too. It was ingenious. I almost admired the perfect trap Fox had made for me.

I looked at the photo again. Tom and I were in focus while the waiters, other patrons, pedestrians were blurred figures around us. We looked so happy, our heads together, at peace in a bustling sea. Envy of thy happy lot . . . Fox must want this; he must be envious, or sad, or jealous. However deeply he hid them, his pursuit of me revealed his feelings, and that gave me a tiny morsel of power. A tiny window through which I might escape his trap.

Henri was waiting at the end of the bar. When he saw me he came over and bowed.

"Mademoiselle, please, a drink on the house."

"A double whisky would be lovely."

"Scottish, *oui?*"

I reached out to touch his shoulder in thanks, but he grabbed my hand and kissed it, giving it a squeeze. He knew Fox somehow and knew what he did. I'd have to get the story one day, but right now I just needed that drink.

"And a packet of your best cigarettes."

"*Oui, mademoiselle.* They are expensive but Sobranies are handmade in London and serve the kings of Europe." I knew all about that; Sobranies were Fox's favorites. Henri opened up a packet to show me cigarettes colored blue, yellow, pink, and green.

"These cocktail cigarettes might entice you." They still had that distinctive golden tip, but the bright, jaunty rainbow beckoned. I took one and smelled it; it didn't smell like Fox's tobacco at all. That decided me.

"Kiki! We're off to a party—are you coming?" North called as I paid a vast sum for the pretty tailor-mades.

"Is it Cocteau's hat party?"

"Why, yes, how do you—"

"He invited me himself." I grinned and pulled a cloth contraption out of my handbag. I had converted a camisole into a black lace veil that fit tightly over my entire head, with only a hole cut out for the mouth. Across the lace I had sewn little bumblebee buttons that I had found at a flea market stall when I'd first arrived.

"How do I look?" I smoked through the hole in the veil at North's shocked face, "Suitably Dada? Suitably surreal?"

"Oh!" Relief made her smile. "Yes, Kiki! Yes, absolutely."

I turned to Henri, but he just shook his head. I whipped off my "hat" and kissed him on the cheek.

"Thank you, for everything." He blushed as I swigged the last of my whisky.

◆

La Gaya was alive when we finally arrived, in a cab that included North and all her friends sitting on each other's laps. A doorman policed the entrance—no one was allowed inside without a fancy chapeau. My veil reflected exactly how I felt—I wanted both to stand out and to hide, I wanted to party and to stay alone in the dark. I pulled it over my face and lit a pink Sobranie through it. It was my passport to the party.

Inside, the jazz was faster than last night's and the dancers were wilder. Our hats had given us leave to take leave of our senses. I could hardly see people's faces under their headwear. There was a straw hat with a bunch of flowers in the top like a vase. There was a stuffed pelican that perched on a pudding bowl, the contraption strapped under the wearer's chin. There was an enormous wineskin with a tube that went down into the dancer's cup. Hats were bloodred and crushed silver and electric blue. Hats flashed with bits of tinsel and tin foil and one wearer had to stay near the wall, so that he could keep the Christmas lights he was entwined with plugged in and lit up. Even the barman wore a hat—a bowler hat turned upside down, the crown concave so it perched on the back of his head as he poured drinks. I ignored his offer of cocktails—the crowd was mad for a purple mess served in a white mug that reminded me too forcibly of a blood clot. I ordered more whisky instead. North and the rest were still outside, adjusting their hats, mostly made of flags and hankies and scarves like fortune-tellers, greeting North's friends who spilled out onto the street. I took a sip and looked around for Cocteau.

He was by the band in a beekeepers hat. I expected a couple of live bees to be attached to him, but instead he had a drink that looked like it was a block of honeycomb. I lifted my veil and waved and he waved back, then continued to conduct the dancers. I joined the throng on the dance floor.

"Oh! Very modern. I love it!" A tall pretty woman wearing a colander touched my veiled face. "You look so . . ."

"Ghoulish," the man holding her said disdainfully. He wore a sub-editor's visor with some tags sticking out of it. He only came up to her cleavage, which made him even shorter than me. She didn't seem to notice or care.

"Yes, ghoulish. It gives me shivers."

I took a drag of my cigarette and let the smoke fill the inside of the veil, so it wafted out of the lace on my cheeks and forehead. She laughed and he coughed. One song ended and as we applauded she held her hand out to me.

"I'm Paulette," she said.

"Kiki. Cocteau invited me last night."

"Oh, yes, he loves to invite all the interesting ones." She smiled. "I've known him since I came to Paris, before the war." The man beside her coughed. "This is Michel."

He held out his hand.

"Do you write for *Le Figaro*?" I asked.

He looked startled. "Yes, how—"

"You wrote an article about German unrest—"

"It was published yesterday. Why—"

"I need to know—"

"If you're going to talk work, I'm going to dance with Dadaists." Paulette waved her hand dismissively and wiggled over to a man with a monocle. Martin looked jealously after her.

"Why do you ask about the strikes?"

"I need to know about Hausmann." With that phrase, he looked at me properly for the first time. I took off my veil so he could see my face.

"Hausmann's an interesting man," he said. "Everyone knows of him but no one seems to know him. I managed to talk to him—though I didn't see him. No one has."

"Then how do you know he exists?"

He scoffed as we pushed our way to the bar. The barman served us more whisky, which Martin drank with relish.

"That voice of his isn't a fake. That's how I knew it was him—simpering, high-pitched, somewhat revolting—"

"You spoke to him in French? I thought he was German."

"He is. His French is rubbish. But the tone of his voice . . . it gave me the creeps." He looked me up and down. "Why do you want to know?"

"I'm investigating the Brownshirts in Paris—" I bluffed with the truth.

"Those Jew-hating fascists," Martin spat. "Just like Action Française. I don't want to have anything more to do with them!"

"More? What have you had to do with them until now?" *And*, I thought, *what's a fascist?*

"Nothing! . . .Not much, just . . ." He looked into his drink. "A lot of us were angry at the end of the war . . . so many had died, France was a mess, no one seemed to care but Action Française. But then I found out they have connections with the *fascisti* from Italy—"

"Fascists—"

"Yes, like the Brownshirts in Germany." His face turned sour. "Germany! Such a betrayal. And those thugs coming over here, bringing their ideas to the people with clubs and guns, the lot of them swarming over France's wounds like flies on a corpse—"

Flies—"the murmurous haunt of flies treads him down"—could these right-wing nationalist groups be the flies?

"I almost think they'd betray their own country to further their beloved cause," he continued, with only the merest nod of encouragement. "They don't care about our glorious traditions, freedom, democracy—France has been a democracy for a long time, Germany should be the same!" He was properly worked up now, eyes bulging, tapping his empty glass on the bar top. "But how can it succeed, when it's the Germans who run it? How can they build a land of liberty and fraternity when they have the blood of so many millions of Frenchmen on their hands?"

A shriek of delight rang across the dance floor. Paulette had climbed up onto a young man's shoulders and was being bounced around in time to the music. Martin visibly jerked. The music increased in intensity. He said something to me that I couldn't hear, never taking his eyes from Paulette. He gave me a wave of dismissal or goodbye, I couldn't tell, and moved towards his ecstatic lover, leaving me with just enough information to make Fox's clues murmur and haunt the back of my mind.

The rest of the party was exactly what I needed—mad, wild, weird, and wonderful. North and company finally joined me on the dance floor with their fashionable cocktails. One handsome veteran had a surprisingly good foxtrot and a very smooth waltz, and we danced until his wife cut in for the slower songs. We swapped hats with every song and my veil ended up smeared with lipstick and kisses. I introduced myself to everyone who wore it. The monocled man was Tristan Tzara and he wore his monocle on top of it. He was a delight to dance with, his movements odd and jerky but with a nervous charm. We tangoed to a waltz and did a polka to a foxtrot. He stood next to two dancers from the Ballets Russes. I couldn't catch their names, but they took my veil and danced with it, making it a shroud, a ghoul's mask, a puppet's face and a sleepwalker's blank stare as they passed it between them. The lights bounced off the mirrors and the marble tabletops so everyone seemed to shine in double, triple, infinite replication. Hats ended up on the floor and purple drinks spilled like blood down shirt-fronts and onto stockings. Faces pressed against the glass from the night outside. Cocteau kept conducting the dancers and sipping his honey. North's companions ended up in a tight, cozy corner while North flitted between different groups. As she passed, she shot me a look that went right through me and all the ghosts rose up from their muddy graves to crowd the conversation. I was aware of all the absent people—Bertie, Tom, and those who would never return. Did North feel it too? Even in the midst of such a festival, with the air full of jazz and laughter and the room smelling of all the tobaccos and drinks and sweat of the world, did absence also haunt her like a half-heard melody? She was off again, attending to her guests, swilling her drink like the lifeblood it resembled—perhaps that was how she coped. For me the only cures were booze and sex, but I'd had enough of them. I kissed Cocteau on the cheek and North on the lips and, with my now soggy veil, headed into a taxi and home.

"LA BELLE EXCENTRIQUE"

The morning bells woke me. It was my favorite way to wake—bells ringing from Église Notre-Dame-des-Champs down the road, then hearing the trucks and horses clatter on the cobbles, the newspaper boys and flower girls, the smells of bread and frying and old wine and cabbage floating up from the street. I would become aware of each sensation one by one as I stretched in my sheets, as I wound a robe around me, as I grabbed my cigarettes and a glass of water and sat with the sparrows at my windowsill. There she was, in front of me in her elegant workday attire—Paris. The sky was a delicate blue, not quite sunny and not quite warm, just flirting with summer. The sparrows swirled over the gray rooftops, with chimneys like sentries guarding the secrets in every studio, swooped from the tips of my toes and down the hill, over the streets, loop-de-looped over the river to the Eiffel Tower, until the little birds were part of the air itself. I thought I had lost her, but I was merely blind-tired. She was here, Paris, as she always had been.

I never went to the Rotonde or the Dôme for breakfast. There would always be someone I knew there, and then breakfast would turn into lunch and there would be drinks, and before I could check my watch I'd be drunk in the afternoon and no good to anyone. I reserved champagne breakfasts for feasts and holidays. The start of the day was mine, to think and write and plan, to read the paper, to daydream, to stretch my legs and think of nothing at all. I went to the little café down the street, open to local workers who spoke of politics and foreign writers who didn't speak until the day's work was done. It was called simply Petit's, and petite Madame Petit, with her enormous bosom and tiny bun, greeted me with a kiss on each cheek. I always had the set breakfast menu with a large black coffee, which she set in front of me sometimes with a smile and an aspirin, sometimes with just a wink. Today the aspirin came with a little pat on the shoulder and a face full of pity. I must have been carrying the previous four days under my eyes.

I checked the newspapers lying on the counter; thank you, Goddess of Single Ladies, it was only Thursday, I hadn't slept through my deadline. I wrote my gossip column over coffee and fresh baguette, the crust crunchy, the coffee rich, the butter smooth, and the apricot jam just the right mix of tart and sweet. Crunchy, rich, smooth, tart, and sweet—inspiration for my column, to make those crusty aristocrats tastier in print than in the flesh. My column was due in Bertie's London office this afternoon and I'd have to send it by telegram, or telephone, or some such expensive magic. I'd have to be more organized next week if I didn't want to spend my entire income on getting the work to Bertie.

◇

"Ah! Blond Kiki!" the telegraphist at the local post office blushed beneath her rouge, making her face a very rosy pink. "I have a telegram for you." She held out the slip of paper and I flashed my widest smile. I could see the blush extend down her neck.

It was from Tom. It was marked from Kattowitz in Silesia.

BUTTON CALL ME 1800 AT HOTEL MONOPOL HAVE NEWS OF HAUSMANN

No one else called me Button and it caught me every time. I could feel the telegrammist watching me and I was glad that I was not prone to blushing. I slipped the telegram into my purse and turned to her.

"*Cherie*"—I could never remember her name—"could you send this telegram to London urgently? 'Bertie must call with column'—"

"Do you need to use the telephone? You can use the one here." Her eyes almost sparkled.

"Oh . . . yes! May I really?"

"But of course! We all love you here, Kiki—I mean—"

"Thank you." I placed my hand on hers. "Where is it?"

"This way." She was so proud in her pink-cheeked fluster. I couldn't help but admire her. She led me to the telephone in the back office. It was clearly meant only for the postmaster general—her crush must be deepening. She scurried back out to the queue at the telegram booth before I could thank her properly.

"Reverse charges to the *Star* magazine in London, please."

After an agonizing exchange, first with the switchboard and then with the secretary, I was finally put through to Bertie.

"Browne."

"Browne, it's Button."

"Kiki! Two calls in two days. You miss me enough to charge the *Star* for the pleasure?"

"Ha! I'm late with my copy."

"You certainly are. Where is it?"

"In my hand. Have you sharpened your shorthand?"

"It's as unreadable as the best of them. Fire away."

If he had been angry when I rang, he wasn't by the time I finished. He laughed all the way through the column, adding flourishes here and there as I described the Duck Orange and the Sapphic Ambulance Corps reunion, as I skimmed over the hat party to describe the one aristocrat there.

"I'll have copy from the Russian exiles next. I'll visit the teahouse as soon as I can. And I'll make sure I post it in advance."

"Sounds good, Kiki. But the reverse charges are worth the argument I'll have with the chief. He can't fault the sales increase on the day your column comes out."

"I'll drink to that."

"I would too, if you were here."

"Why don't you have a drink with Teddy?"

There was a long pause on the line.

"I haven't seen him in days."

◈

Pablo's housekeeper, a gray-haired woman with a down-turned mouth, showed me in to his studio. He was engrossed in his set designs for the ballet. I watched him for ten minutes as he painted, on huge sheets of rough paper, the arches and architraves for the set over and over, sweeping loops and swirled columns with only a hint of variation. He'd paint one sheet, then tear it off and lay it on the floor, before beginning an almost identical one in the thin, dilute paint he held in a jar. When he finally sighed and stepped back, I coughed to let him know I was there. His look of surprise became recognition, which became delight, his big-eyed expression moving rapidly through the changes. He strode up to me and kissed me on both cheeks and the lips.

"Sweet kangaroo."

"Hello, Pablo."

"Good to see you. Just at the right moment too. Shall we begin?" It wasn't a question, as he immediately faced the set designs to the wall and picked up his sketchbook. He just smiled at me as he guided me towards the seat on the dais. It was a warmer day today and he was dressed very simply: his rough white shirt brushed my arm, his leather slippers slip-slopped on the floor, his blue cotton trousers crackled with stiff old paint splatters. I wore the same shoes, stockings, and underwear as I had previously, I'd even washed the camiknickers by hand to make sure they were clean enough for daytime viewing. I wore a simple navy shift over the top—so simple that I only had to use one movement to pull it over my head and be halfway to naked. He arranged his own chair and then arranged me on the dais in the leg-spread slump. He smiled but he didn't see me. He seemed to look through me or past me, to see only the surface of my skin. He was entirely in his own head, my body a jumble of angles that he rearranged as he watched, checking the light and his pencil. He nodded and mumbled "*Bon*" before he began to sketch furiously, a frown deepening on his face. He went through half a dozen pages of his sketch-book before he threw down the book and hunted through his studio.

"Pablo? Is everything—"

"Don't move." It was almost a grunt, thrown over his shoulder as he flicked through canvasses stacked against the wall. He found one with only a few stripes across it and half an eye in blue. He studied it for a moment, then cleared an easel of a display of his sketches to make room for the canvas. He rolled up his sleeves and arranged all the paints and brushes next to him, large brushes like those for a child, huge tubes of paint that were so covered in fingerprints that I couldn't tell what color they were. I suppose I didn't need to, only he did, and he seemed to know exactly what he was doing. All I had to do was sit still.

This was quite a different experience from the last time. Then I was a guest he entertained as he drew. Now I was a model and he was the genius artist, and I had to do as I was told. There would be no point in worrying if I'd get to the Russian teahouse today, or be able to call Tom at six o'clock. This was work and I simply had to wait for him to be done.

I went into a kind of trance. The sun slanted through the studio window and I could see the dust swirl in its beam. Outside I could hear the paper-boys begin their calls again with the afternoon news, updates from the morning, along with the rattle of cars and carriages, the old jostling with the new. The room smelled of paint, tobacco, coffee, and turpentine, a heady mixture only slightly alleviated by the air from the window.

I hadn't planned on it, but there was time to think of all I had learned so far. Ideas and facts chased each other through the sun slant from the window. Pablo's painting, a party of poor aristocrats, Russian exiles, German unrest, a mysterious Hausmann, Ferny in the war—the war, the war, and its eternal return. I focused on the slant of light to remember Fox's message.

In some melodious plot of beechen green, with shadows numberless, there is a mole. The mole quite forgets the weariness, the fever, and the fret, where men sit and hear each other groan, where youth grows pale and dies. More than ever seems it rich to die, not for the warm south, but for the lands forlorn. Tender is the night, and he cannot see what flowers are at his feet. His plaintive anthem fades, his high requiem becomes a sod. The murmurous haunt of flies treads him down. The faery lands are too forlorn, and the word will toll him back from thee to my sole self.

I had to find the mole. "He cannot see what flowers are at his feet"—the mole was blind to his pursuers. At least I hoped so, because if he wasn't then no code, however nicely phrased, could protect me. He "quite forgets the weariness, the fever, and the fret"—Fox often spoke those lines after a round of the wards, so it had to do with the war. This was a nice, obvious clue, which meant that it had to have another meaning. The mole forgets the war somehow—but who could? No, it must mean that the mole has forgotten something in the war, or something to do with the war. He'd certainly forgotten the consequences of betraying Fox. Or maybe he didn't care—he was too attuned to "his plaintive anthem" and "his high requiem." Why else would it seem "rich to die" now, more than then? But for the lands forlorn—Germany was forlorn, Fox had pretty much said so—but it was hardly a faery land. And again, I didn't trust any clue that had only one meaning. Faery land, German fairy tales, Brothers Grimm—that all worked. But the message said lands, plural, so the lands were not only Germany but also . . . Austria? Russia? And how did the haunting murmur of flies fit in exactly? Were they some other brown-shirt supporters, what did Martin call them, fascists? How could they tread him down, how could their murmurs haunt him? My thoughts chased their tails and I had to shake myself out of it. The mole was a man. The extra clues from the songs meant I knew that it had to do with Germany and the war; this was confirmed by the photo of Ferny in uniform. Ferny was involved, that was certain—I was fairly sure that Fern was the mole and he couldn't see me because he didn't know that Fox had a female agent— but it was more than just something leftover from the war. The photo was inscribed "hungry generations tread thee down"—"tread down" had been used twice, so the murmurous haunt of flies was also the hungry generations—the mole was involved with something new and something en masse. This unrest in Germany, perhaps? But why would Fern be in Paris if the unrest was in Germany?

"Kangaroo." Pablo called me to attention. "Ring the bell. We need coffee and sustenance."

I heartily agreed.

But sustenance came in more than one form. Before the housekeeper had properly closed the door, Pablo strode towards me and bit my bum. I was stretching and moving, my limbs stiff from the long pose, and when I squeaked I thought I could see her roll her eyes. Pablo swigged a small cup of black coffee and took hold of me by my suspender belt.

"This garment is very useful," he said, pulling me closer and kissing my neck. "I can manipulate you just like a puppet."

"Only because I let you," I said with a fierce nip on his ear. He drew his breath in sharply. "Never forget that."

His eyes lit up. He took the suspender belt and hauled me over his broad shoulder to carry me to the lounge. I squealed and fought, just like he wanted me to—but it was fun, all the way down.

We were both sweaty and the breeze from the window was a caress. I sat and leaned against the window frame, naked except for my shoes, stockings and suspender belt. Pablo laughed and collapsed on the lounge.

"Giving the street an eyeful, kangaroo?"

"They've already had an earful. What more can I have to hide?"

"You should hide nothing, lovely blond one. Your lovemaking is a delight."

I smiled at him. I knew he meant it. There was something about this city, this life I was living, that meant I could let go and fully enjoy myself. Sex in the war was always furtive and flirted with death. Sex in Sydney was near bloody impossible with Aunt Constance hovering around my reputation. London with Bertie was better, but here, I could be free. The city had seduced me and it was too easy to persuade others to surrender.

"Is there still coffee?"

"Bring it over, kangaroo, and tell me how you're getting on."

The coffee was completely cold but with enough sugar it was still drinkable. There was a plate with a variety of delicate biscuits, some golden and crumbly, some dark, some with pale crusts. I wrapped myself in one of the blankets from the dais and told him about the halting progress of my search.

"Yes, the teahouse, very good. I know you can be discreet. But please hurry up. Olga sends angry letters and they interrupt my concentration," he said, and shoved another biscuit in his mouth.

14

"AVALON"

The sun was setting as I left Pablo. It hadn't rained for days, and the sky was stained gold, bronze, and blood above the rooftops. I wanted to sit and watch the sun die dramatically over the city. I wanted an evening at home, to read and think and plan. I wanted a simple meal of vegetable soup to soothe my stomach. I'd get none of it. Instead, I wandered. It was almost six o'clock and I had to find a telephone to call Tom.

I found myself only two blocks from the Ritz. Their telephone was in a little room with a plush chair, pad and paper on a table. I flirted with the concierge, "accidentally" showing my stocking tops, and he let me use the telephone for free. Five past six—it took an age to connect to the hotel, the French and the Germans refusing to understand each other. My skin felt sticky and my limbs felt heavy. Finally I heard a cough and a thank-you in a voice I recognized. I forgot Pablo instantly. My body remembered only Tom's breath.

"Thomas Arthur."

"Hello, Tom-Tom."

"Button! Excellent. Listen, I've been reporting on this recent plebiscite in Silesia—"

"To see if they'll remain part of Germany or become part of Poland, yes?"

"Yes. They voted remain, but there are rumors and rumblings in the streets."

"And what do they say?"

"They say Hausmann."

"The mysterious Hausmann who nobody's seen?"

"I've seen him."

"And?"

"Fair hair, skinny, tall, high-pitched laugh—"

"You've spoken to him?"

"No, he won't meet us—or any reporter."

"What's he doing there? Supporting the Polish against the German oppressor?"

"No, the opposite—"

"He's supporting the government?" He was supposed to be an anti-government agitator—why was he on the side of the Weimar government then?

"Not that either. He's been seen in the company of the Freikorps."

"The Brownshirts!"

"The very same. I saw him come out of one of their meetings."

"What are the Brownshirts doing in Silesia?"

"Causing rumors and rumblings in the streets." He sighed. "We'll be here for a little while longer."

"How much longer?"

"Too long." There was a pause on the line. Could I bear to have him say what I felt—that I missed him, that it was too lonely without him? The concierge knocked at the door and I had to lean right into his bad-breath smile to beg for another minute.

"Button, are you there?"

"Tom-Tom, I have to go. I had to flirt with the Ritz concierge to use the telephone, but I'll have to prostitute myself if I don't hang up soon—"

"When will we talk again?"

"Come to Paris."

"When?"

"Tonight." These calls were too expensive to be coy. "Your voice down the line is not enough." I heard him exhale, although the line was so bad, it could have just been static.

"I can't leave tonight—"

"You know what I mean—"

"Too well. Until soon, Button."

◇

I walked around the lamplit streets trying to find the teahouse. At least, that's what I told myself I was doing. I didn't want to find the teahouse. I didn't want to charm another stranger, to wrangle information from him, to make false promises and then scurry back to Pablo, to Fox, not even to Bertie—to any of the men who felt I owed them something. Five minutes on the telephone with Tom had been too hard. I walked round and around, not seeing any sign for tea, any notice in Cyrillic, looking at my shoes or the sky until I gave up. I needed company, proper company, real friendship where I could cry or laugh or just be silent. Where sex didn't hang in the air, a permanent question that always, eventually, demanded an answer. Maisie would be with her husband at this hour, so I used my last bit of change to catch a taxi to Harry's.

Harry's building rose up majestically white from the street. Even the facade, with its intricately detailed brass metalwork, reminded me of its best occupant. A doorman greeted me with a dignified grizzle and rang a bell. The lift door opened—I'd forgotten about the lift and was suddenly glad I didn't have to walk to the top floor—and a boy in a red uniform ushered me into his wire cage. The lift clanked and spluttered, and the boy whispered to it until we reached the top floor.

"Kiki! Darling! Wait, have you tipped the lift boy?" Harry rushed out of her front door and handed a coin to lift operator. "I didn't think so, none of you garret dwellers think of such things. Let me look at you."

She put her hands on my shoulders and turned me this way and that, inspecting my face and my clothes, frowning at the dark shadows under my eyes in the warm light that spilled into the corridor. I'd barely even said hello, but it seemed that I didn't need to say anything much at all. I'd come to the right place.

"Hmmm, as I suspected. I diagnose determined both-end candle-burning. When did you last bathe?"

"Just the other day—"

"Alone?"

"Well . . ."

"And when did you last eat?"

"I had a biscuit—"

"I'm looking after you tonight and I won't be opposed." She tut-tutted and shook her head. "You're as bad as ever, my dear."

I linked my arm in hers and she kissed the top of my head.

No one was home but her lover, Wendy, who was painting in one of the rooms and wasn't to be disturbed. Harry walked me into her luxurious bathroom, twice as big as I remembered from the war. There were black and white tiles on the floor and up to my head height, then the palest of purple up to and across the ceiling. Her royal purple towels and bath mat set off the brassy fixtures. "I redid it recently, Kiki, I just had to have a bath big enough for two after all those buckets of cold water behind the lines. Do you remember? Of course, how could anyone forget? Ugh, they still make me shudder. You know, I think I ended up paying for hot water for the entire building! But what else was I to do? French plumbing is as reliable as French marital fidelity. I know how American my obsession sounds, but I just don't care—I *am* American and I like to be clean. We haven't eaten yet, so you can join us for dinner, but I'll get Annette to rustle you up a little predinner snack. No, no wine. Well, maybe a bit of brandy, to help the medicine go down. I'll come back in an hour." She left the bath to fill with lavender-scented water. I came to Harry when I wanted, no, needed to be bossed about. She didn't have to tell me that I looked a mess. I felt like a delicate glass figurine. I felt like a swallow caught in a storm. I felt like a nightingale, caged and clipped, made to sing on cue for my masters though my throat was sore and my tongue too dry to swallow. I wasn't in some melodious plot of beechen green, but a twisted, tortured plot of shadows numberless. I sank into the bath with relief.

The steam curled and danced and the warmth massaged my bones. Annette came in with a glass of orange juice, a bowl of apricot halves, and a nip of brandy. A little food and a little booze, sinking under the hot water and letting the lavender into my skin, and I could untether my mind. Thoughts floated up and connections were made that I could never have made without the liquid assistance of bath and brandy.

Fox had changed. Maybe it was because I couldn't see him, because he couldn't stand too close to me or look at me with his ambiguous expressions, but he didn't seem as cruel as he used to be. Had he mellowed? It was more likely that my memory played tricks on me. But if I stopped trusting my memory, if I doubted what I knew to be true, then I was lost. Then I'd be in his power, completely, once again. I couldn't do that. I had to just take what I knew: that he wanted me, and underneath, he needed me.

Fox needed me, but I needed Tom. It was a compromise to my perfect, selfish freedom, but it wasn't something I could ignore. Like not realizing I was hungry until I smell food, like not knowing I was tired until I closed my eyes for a moment, I hadn't known I was lonely until Tom's letter. I hadn't known how precious he was to me until he left on the train for Germany.

And my need for him led him into more danger. If I didn't . . . but I stopped myself there. Whatever I had done and would do, I was not responsible for Tom's charge of treason. To remember the details of Tom's plight was a struggle, partly because I didn't want to remember the war, partly because I kept seeing, smelling, hearing Tom as he was now. I took another sip of brandy and forced myself to concentrate. It was after the final battle at Passchendaele, late 1917. I hadn't heard from him for days when he turned up in my Paris hotel, skulking and sneaky, a man on the run. I remembered getting almost no sensible words from him for hours, until he'd warmed up, calmed down, eaten and slept. Then he told me that he'd been trapped in the mud for days, only to find himself charged, unbelievably, with treason, when he found the lines again. He said he'd had to flee, something about his superior officer, an old enmity; he couldn't return, he needed to escape back to Australia; he needed my help. If I was going to help him again now—if I was going to work for Fox in order to do so—I'd have to get the full, proper story from him when he returned to Paris.

As for the clues . . . Fox talked of the war. Pablo had a party with Violet and Ferny. Ferny and Violet spoke of the Russians. Fox sent me a photo of Ferny from the war. Everyone else talked about Hausmann. I wanted to talk to a certain Arkady Nikolaievitch Lazarev about art. I wanted to talk to Ferny about Romantic poetry. I wanted to talk.

"Kiki? Are you ready? Dinner is almost on the table, darling," Harry called through the door with a knock. Perfect timing.

◆

"So you see, it was just as I predicted!" said Harry, waving her fork about. "That little man knew nothing whatsoever about it, and delayed our departure by hours! So we missed our connection to Venice—"

"Et cetera, et cetera," Wendy cut in with a smile. "We did get there in the end though."

"Yes, and it was wonderful." Harry smiled at her lover and her face glowed. I'd never seen her like this before. I guessed that with Wendy it was "until death do us part." Wendy wasn't her usual glamour-girl style, twenty years younger and enthusiastic about herself. Wendy wore her "good" work clothes, a loose white linen shirt and blue serge trousers, man's brogues, and one heavy gold necklace. Her hair was short and almost white and every laugh line was displayed, unadorned by makeup. I could imagine her digging for weeds, or trekking across Snowdonia, or even shearing sheep. She had greeted me with a handshake that moved into a hug. I liked her immediately.

Perhaps it was Wendy's influence that had changed their eating habits from the decadence of gin and an entire wheel of Brie to the healthy properties of fresh bread and orange juice. Dinner was simple and perfect. Fresh ingredients, all in season, cooked without too much oil or cream. An asparagus soup to begin with, followed by a very rustic steak and salad and baked potatoes. Annette shook her head at the simplicity of it but it reminded me of home. Not where I lived in Sydney with my aunt, but the sheep property I grew up on—when the men came in from the paddocks or the shearing sheds at sundown and Mum had baked two ovens' worth of vegetables, as Dad stoked a fire out the back, where Tom cooked slabs of beef, so the blackened edges smelled of eucalyptus and clean bush air. This steak was fried in a pan, in butter, and not nearly as romantically bloody, but tasty nonetheless. A few others had joined us—some American poets who had just arrived in Paris, and a Russian woman seated next to me. Eva said almost nothing. She only smiled, her pale face a mask, with her pale hair pulled back severely and her icy eyes seeming to pierce the light fittings.

"You're not a fan of Venice?" I asked.

"Oh, yes, many of my countrymen escaped there." She shrugged. "I went there first, but it didn't suit me. Too many Bolsheviks."

"There are a few here—"

"No, they are only socialists, and only with champagne, in a café, after they finish their office work for the day. I mean the men with bombs and the women with poison who are intent on hunting down dissidents and bringing them to their so-called justice." Her face was blank but her hands fidgeted. I had to listen intently, as her English became thicker and harder to understand as she became agitated.

"Those Bolsheviks aren't here in Paris, then."

"Not yet. But they're in Germany—I can read the newspapers, 'between the lines' as you say. A very useful phrase."

"You're a monarchist?"

"Even worse—an aristocrat." She raised a manicured eyebrow. "Only a minor one, with hardly any title and no money. But as a practicing painter whose third cousin was in the tsar's court and who had been seen, and I quote, 'in the company of Imperialists and other enemies of the people'—that is, my sister's in-laws—well . . ." She trailed off.

It was clear that the last few years had been difficult for her and I wondered if her experience was typical. She looked starved, her protruding wrist bones making her arms seem like sticks. I couldn't help but glance at my own in comparison.

"Do you know the teahouse here?" I asked.

"Of course. My aunt runs it."

"I need to meet with someone and I hope to find him there. I was wondering—"

"Meet me at the corner of the street at ten o'clock. We'll go there for breakfast. They do excellent blini." She smiled then, a proper smile that reached her eyes. She patted my hand.

"It's a piece of the real Russia," she said, "without a Bolshevik in sight."

15

"BOLSHEVIK LOVE"

It was a warm day, but I shivered as I waited at the corner of rue Bonaparte. The sun played with the footpath as clerks and shopgirls hurried past me to their jobs. The street smelled of baked bread but I was almost too hungry, it made me feel sick. Or maybe it was the small black coffee I'd downed as I rushed out of Montparnasse, mixing with last night's berries and cream. Or maybe it was the cigarettes that I was smoking to ward off my nerves. Whatever it was, I could do without it. I could do with a clean bed and a warm body and—

"Kiki." Eva appeared at my elbow like a ghost in the spring sunshine, pale and dressed in light gray. She took my newly lit cigarette for herself without a thanks.

"I hope you're hungry, as my aunt has never let a guest of mine leave without consuming three full plates of her hospitality."

"I'm starving—I haven't eaten since last night," I said as I lit another cigarette.

"Very good." She turned on her heel and clipped quickly down the street. Her clothes were scruffy, patched and frayed at the cuffs and heels, but she bore herself like a queen. I almost felt scruffy in comparison, though my hair was neat under my purple cloche hat and, thanks to

Harry, my shoes were polished and my dress was clean. I wore a lavender shift with a sprig of violets embroidered at the shoulder that matched the hat. I had pinned some fresh violets to the lapel of my cream coat, to complete the picture. The dress only just covered my knees, its silk-cotton hem riding up whenever I sat down. I had no idea if this was correct breakfast wear for the exiled Russian aristocracy, but I had to assume that what was popular in Paris was popular everywhere.

Eva's clicking heels led us down three connected lanes to a narrow, unmarked door.

"No wonder I couldn't find it last night," I remarked as she knocked three times in quick succession.

"This is the back door," she replied as she listened. "You should have found the front easily enough." The door was opened by a small boy, whom Eva ignored. We stepped into a dim passageway that led immediately round a corner and upstairs. She talked over her shoulder as we walked.

"Although the front door is not marked with anything so simple as 'Russian teahouse.' It is Café Gogol. So perhaps if you are not educated enough to know that Gogol was a Russian master . . ."

Her disparaging tone was cut off as we entered a sumptuous room. It was on the second floor, with windows that extended beyond the floor, from which I could see Parisian heads near our feet. The high ceiling held aloft chandeliers that, by their snowflake reflections on the walls and roof, I guessed were real crystal. The polished marble floor was arranged with tables and chairs, lounges and a piano on a bandstand in the corner. We had emerged next to the kitchen, by the bar, which held three huge tea urns, piles of pastries, and a wall of vodka, cognac, and other bottles labeled in strange scripts. The middle-aged woman behind the bar turned to us with a severe expression, until she saw Eva and smiled, holding out her arms.

"Eva," she said, and kissed Eva three times. They had a brief conversation in Russian, Eva looking somehow bored and troubled simultaneously, the older woman nodding and looking concerned, her large gold cross bouncing on her black-clad bosom. They both turned to me at the same time, their blue eyes equally piercing.

"Welcome, Kiki," the middle-aged woman spoke French to me and took my hand in both of hers, "Exiles of all kinds, both forced and chosen, are welcome here. Eva says that you're looking for Arkady Nikolaievitch, correct?"

"Lazarev?"

"Yes, it's the same man, but only the British use family names."

"Arkady—"

"Nikolaievitch, yes. He will be in soon but is not here yet. You have time for tea and breakfast. You are hungry."

"Not terribly . . ." Eva frowned at me. "Oh yes, starving. I'd love some breakfast."

"You are too thin, like Eva." She surveyed me. "We don't have any kasha for you, but plenty of cheese. Vanya!" She yelled through to the kitchen and followed the reply with a blast of Russian, going into the kitchen after her instructions.

"Good," said Eva. "You sit there." She pointed at a table near the bar, from which I could survey the entire teahouse. She sat instead at the bar, a glass of tea held delicately between her fingers, and chatted to her aunt, who polished and sorted and arranged. A grumpy waiter brought a mountain of food to my table—black bread, an aromatic hard cheese, pickled cucumbers, little crepes dripping with jam and whipped cream, breadlike pastries that smelled sweetly of apples and cinnamon. Eva placed a glass of tea in front of me and whenever I finished it, she would refill it for me from the ornate urn on the bar. It felt strange to sit in this sumptuous place, in bright daylight, completely ignored. But the food helped—food always helped—in the moments I had to myself before Lazarev walked in.

Which he did with a flourish of watch and cane. I knew it was him as the aunt called his name from across the bar. He was tall and well-built with thick silver hair—he must've been a ladies man when he was younger. He didn't have those piercing blue eyes, thankfully, but big soft brown ones that tempered his dramatic gestures. He put the watch away and swung his cane under his arm. He chatted to the aunt, he chatted to Eva, before turning his gray-suited body to me.

"Kiki?"

"Arkady Nikolaievitch?"

"Please, just Arkady will do." He took my hand and held it, not a handshake, more like the beginning of a courtly kiss. He couldn't turn off his charm, it seemed, especially not with a young woman in front of him. But he didn't kiss my hand, in the end. Instead, he took a glass of tea and sat down opposite me.

"Eva Sergeyevna says that you come from Picasso," he said. "Does he have word for me?"

"In a manner of speaking." I tried to act coy, but his look was too intense. Clearly the preference for coquettish women of indirect speech was for French men only. This Russian almost stared; he wanted passion. I met his gaze.

"He wants to know about his portrait of Olga."

"The beautiful, fierce picture? The one we saw last week?"

"The very same."

"It was extraordinary." He leaned back and played with his tea glass. "That stunning contrast of the gold and blue, Olga Stepanovna's eyes both commanding and caressing, her posture on the couch both inviting and in control. I've never seen her look so regal. I think I fell in love with her a little in that picture." He smiled. "It's another masterstroke of genius. His previous portrait was more traditional, muted, clear, and available. This one is . . . wild, it's modern; it shows the tension and passion within their marriage, that she can do this to him, that he can do that to her." His soft brown gaze rested on me.

"You speak very eloquently."

"I was an art dealer in Saint Petersburg. When it still was Saint Petersburg. I already have a buyer lined up, who would purchase the portrait unseen—this is Picasso's power. Unseen! Just to own a Picasso."

"And it would make your fortune."

"Fortune!" He snorted and waved his hand away. "No single painting can replace the fortune I lost. But I want that portrait very much."

"What would you be willing to do for it?"

"What do you suggest?" His eyes lit up as he leaned across to me.

"If you were to . . . appropriate the picture, how would you do it?"

"I see—"

"Just hypothetically, of course."

"Of course! Well, I would apply to the housekeeper, first of all—"

"The older woman?"

"Precisely. Servants always have grievances; it's just a matter of getting them on the right day. And artists are such hard work, there are more days than usual to catch them on." He laughed.

"And then?"

"And then I suppose I would somehow make it more worth her while to work with me than to be loyal to Picasso."

"With money?"

"Or fear. Sometimes fear works better, especially with women." He saw me raise my eyebrow. "Or I should say, especially with mothers."

"And would you work alone?"

"This is very detailed"—he raised an eyebrow in response to mine—"for a hypothetical theft."

"And if it wasn't hypothetical?"

"No. I couldn't. I know Olga Stepanovna too well." He smiled at me. "Alas, I have too much honor."

"Terrible for business."

He laughed. "Beautiful *Australienne*, why did you want to speak to me? I don't think you have an offer for me from Pablo."

I cursed under my smile.

"I do come from Pablo . . . but not with an offer, exactly, although he may change his mind about you, depending on your answers," I lied, but it worked. Lazarev leaned in.

"Anything."

"Your art-dealing business—"

"I'm an art lover. My passion makes it my business."

"Who is your buyer?"

"Ah." He fiddled with his tea glass. "That is a strange part of the business. I have never met him, but his name is Hausmann."

I leaned forward now, so I was only a foot away from Lazarev.

"He's German," he whispered.

"Quite the secret. How did he contact you?"

"By letter, through my friend Katya—Yekaterina Dimitryevna— although the letter was delivered to her when she was away. It was given to me by the woman staying there, what's her name, a silly, vain woman." He helped himself to my plate of pastries, his large hands articulate and graceful. I pushed the plate farther towards him.

"A flower name . . . Violet, that's it." He pronounced it the French way. "She was at Pablo's the other day, looking very British—scandalized and trying to hide it, like she'd stumbled in on her sister making love with the stableboy."

I laughed but made frantic mental notes.

"Yes, Pablo's work does that to some people," he said. "A little while ago, she called me to say that a letter had come for me at Katya's. The letter was from this Hausmann, asking to procure for him any Picasso. He's a businessman, apparently, and wants portable assets."

"Not an alien sentiment for you."

"Unfortunately not. But this business, no handshakes, all by letter, it does not seem entirely . . ."

"Honorable?"

"*Exactement!*" He spoke French with the same flourish that he swung his cane, "And when the revolutionaries take your house, your history, everything but the raiment you can escape with, honor is the only currency you have left."

"How noble."

He laughed then, throwing his head back in delight at my sarcastic tone.

"We Russians love to be dramatic—that's what you English say, isn't it?"

"I'm Australian, actually. We take an even dimmer view of high feeling."

"I'm glad that I don't disappoint." He gave a mock bow and dropped another piece of pastry in his mouth. He called to the aunt for more tea and cake as he finished off the little crepes.

"Do you know where Violet is living?" I asked.

"The English woman? At Katya's while Katya's in Italy. I believe she's been there for some months already. Do you need the address?"

I nodded, and he scribbled down an address not far from here. He got up and kissed my hand when he saw that I was leaving.

"If you hear from Picasso, dear lady, please talk to me. I'm always here." He waved to the sumptuous marble interior of the teahouse.

"Just one more thing—"

"Anything."

"What is Hausmann's first name?"

"I don't know." He shrugged. "The letter was signed only with an *E.*"

16

"DARDANELLA"

My feet decided where to go. The morning streets burst with spring flowers and sweetheart postcards. They bustled with newspaper boys, and fruit sellers peeked out of laneways. I could smell bread and cigarette smoke, horses and car exhaust, dead flowers and coffee and old wine. I kept a lookout for any newspaper boys who might be following me, but I saw none who left their corner. My feet had decided to take me to the hospital where Maisie George Chevallier had said she volunteered each week. I had no idea if she'd have time to see me—normal people had routines, they had shifts and obligations; they weren't like myself or Harry or the artists of Montparnasse. But I needed her. The lonely chill of last night hadn't quite been chased away.

In the usual ironic style of hospital buildings, this temple of health was a crumbling mansion. The stones needed scrubbing, the iron railings sported a patina of rust, and pigeons nested in the hidden corners. But the windows shone and all manner of people—nurses in blue, clerks in black, patients and visitors in pale tones—walked in and out of the high double doors with purpose. I joined the throng.

As a married woman, Maisie wasn't allowed to do paid work, but she was allowed to be on the wards, administer medicine, sign patients in and out. Most married women worked to raise funds, but Maisie's great skills and terrible French meant she did more conventional hospital work. I heard her before I saw her, her hooting laugh followed by some near-incomprehensible French as she stood behind the registration desk. A young veteran leaned on the counter with his one good arm and had clearly taken on the role of language tutor. She saw me and waved.

"Katie King!" She leaned over the counter to kiss me on both cheeks. "French style, eh? I'm learning, slowly."

The young veteran looked me up and down, bent over, and kissed my hand.

"Louis, mademoiselle." He was as flirtatious as a one-armed man in pajamas could be.

"Kiki," I said with a smile. "If you want to improve her French you have to get her to stop laughing."

"Katie, don't speak so fast, I can't keep up—" Maisie protested.

"How could I ask her to stop laughing? She is laughter itself." Louis smiled.

"She is sunshine, I've always thought," I said, "but sunshine audible is laughter."

"Indeed! And you are a poet!"

"A café philosopher." I smiled. "I know published poets and they're all mad. I prefer my sanity." Louis laughed and Maisie cocked her head in a *Well?* gesture. I shrugged.

"Have you finished your shift yet?" I said in English. "I need hugs, coffee, and gossip."

"Just as soon as . . . ah! Here she is. Bonjour, Eloise!" Eloise looked harried as she reeled off four excuses as to why she was almost late, shooing Maisie out of the way and Louis off the counter just as the sour-faced matron clipped by. We waved goodbye to Louis as he sauntered back to the ward, giving Maisie a second and third glance over his shoulder.

"You've got an admirer there," I said, linking her arm with mine.

"Oh, not really, he's just bored. You know how it is."

"He looked back—"

"He's shortsighted. It's probably why he got the clap." We shouted with laughter as we made our way to a café.

"So, what was it you said you needed—gossip, coffee—"

"And hugs."

"Well, I can deliver there," she said, and before I could sit down she hugged me so tightly that she almost lifted me off the floor. She was taller than me and stronger too, especially as it'd been two years since I'd lifted patients and moved beds. People around us hid their smiles.

"Everyone who went through our war needs a hug, I reckon," she said as we sat down. "Do you think I can order lunch already? Is it noon? I've been working since six, I'm famished."

"Are you asking me to order for you?"

"No! But if you're ordering for yourself . . ."

I ordered a coffee for me and the set lunch for her, with a bottle of crisp white wine to share. The waitress was like the café, old-fashioned and upholstered in velvet. We sat on red velvet seats, two chandeliers hung over the diners, and thick brocade curtains of faded gold framed the windows. Most of the other diners were a generation older than us, but it was the closest café to the hospital building that wasn't full of other nurses, visitors, and patients.

"You've got your hug, you've got your coffee—"

"Now I just need to gossip."

"Tell me." So I did. I handed over all the jumbled thoughts from the bath, from the bed, from my lonely trips around gloomy streets when Paris wasn't my Paris. This was even better than Harry—Harry was the mother I should have had, but Maisie was a sister. She took it all and sorted in out in her matter-of-fact way. All the women in my life were sensible and strong; it was the men who were fragile, needy and sensitive. Yet another strange outcome of the war.

"Well, I can't say I'm sorry that Tom has come back into your life," said Maisie, as she wiped up the sauce on her plate with a piece of bread.

"It makes things more complicated."

"You love complicated."

"Not like this—"

"Rubbish. If anything is settled, you go out of your way to add another lover, another job, a risky bit of Paris AWOL to your nights to spice things up. In fact, if Fox weren't such a bastard, I'd be glad that he was in your life too."

"Maise!"

"I'm serious." She popped the bread into her mouth. "A gossip columnist—really, Katie? You're too smart for that."

"It takes a lot of work!"

"Fine. You're too honest for that, then. You're too outspoken, too fierce. Can you honestly tell me that you enjoy those parties that you write about?"

I humphed.

"And can you honestly tell me that you're not just a little bit excited to be a spy once again?"

I grinned.

"I didn't think so."

"So you know me better than I know myself, do you, Maisie?"

"I wasn't your tent mate for three years without learning a thing or two," she said. "Besides, I'm not living the danger, Katie King. I'm not drunk on risk."

"Ouch."

"You know you love it or you wouldn't have said yes to Fox."

"I said yes because of Tom—"

"No, you didn't, Katie." She finished her wine and refilled our glasses.

"And this thing with Tom—you love it because it's risky. If he was just a farm boy from central New South Wales . . . well, you wouldn't look twice."

"So what do I do about it?"

She clinked her glass with mine. "You enjoy it, that's what you do." She grinned. "And you keep me up-to-date with all your gossip."

"Now that I can promise." This was why I loved Maisie. Whatever she said about me, it was she who was honest and outspoken and fierce. She wasn't afraid of what I might think; she told me the truth and trusted that I would recognize it. I knew, then, that two years without her sunshine had been two years too long.

"So which of your men are you seeing tonight?"

"None. Tonight I have a society party to go to—one of my gossip columnist duties. Care to join me?"

"Would I! I've always wanted to go to one of those posh parties."

"Don't you go to them with Ray?"

"Oh, no, they're bureaucrats, not aristocrats. They talk politics together while the women push their husbands to speak to the right people. Not a foxtrot in sight."

I was finally relaxed enough, or drunk enough, to feel hungry again. We ordered delicious slices of lemon tart to top off the meal. It was just the right mixture of sweet and sour, with rich pastry that melted on the tongue. Maisie entertained me with stories of the hospital, glad that she finally had someone who would understand. The freckles stood out on her nose in the slants of sun that came through the windows. Maisie insisted on paying for us, and I walked her to her metro stop with a promise for tonight.

◆

It was still within the lunch hour and the sun was high overhead. I was full of cake and caffeine and lightened by Maisie's sunshiny nature. With

the address from Fox in my handbag, I bought a fresh packet of cigarettes—Gauloises Bleu, with the little blue helmet on the packet and that
distinctive smell of French trenches and estaminets—and hailed a taxi for
the strange part of town.

The cabdriver asked for the address twice, read the envelope, and
looked at me for a long time, his white hair tinged with yellow, before
he finally set out. He wound through the streets, crossed the river, and
it wasn't until he went farther and farther into the slum areas of Paris
that I understood why. Obviously bourgeois mademoiselles like me didn't
venture into places like this—part dark city slum, part shantytown—unless
they were up to no good. Which was most likely true, although what kind
of "no good" I'd be up to I'd yet to find out. I hoped, at least, it'd include
a pretty young someone with a drink.

The cabdriver stopped at the top of a cobbled lane, narrow and flanked
by dark-eyed houses.

"It's down there"—he pointed into the gloom—"but I wouldn't go
down there if I were you. Mademoiselle, let me—"

"Let you what?" He was silent. "I have a good friend down there!"

"I'm sorry but I doubt that very much."

"Doubting Thomas, you'll have to believe it. How much?"

"Let me take you home. You can pay me then."

"I have no idea how long I'll be—"

"Where do you live? With the other foreigners in Montmartre? Montparnasse?"

"Monsieur"—I put on my wickedest smile—"I do not need you to wait
for me, or protect me, or lecture me on how to live. You can either leave
with my money or without. Which is it to be?"

He sighed and shook his head. I gave him the usual price for a cross-
town fare and got out, not looking back. I heard him pull away and felt a
pang. The old man was trying to look out for me and I wouldn't let him.
But that was the point—what right did he have to tell me who I could

and could not see? I hadn't left my father in Australia to be lectured by a cabdriver in Paris, however well-intentioned. I pulled my coat around me and strode down the alleyway.

The stench over the cobbled path was almost a miasma, as it mixed with the steam that seemed to appear from between the houses. I was hit with a familiar waft of piss and cabbage water and rot; I knew it from the waste trenches behind some of the more "civilized" army hospitals. People openly stared at me, incredulous and hostile and mocking, as I walked along in my star-patterned shoes and cream coat. I flashed one young woman a grin and she smiled back, a ray of light in that gloomy alley.

"Do you know this address?" I couldn't tell if she was younger than me or simply shorter. She stared at the envelope and I read out the address.

"Who lives there?" she asked.

"I don't know, but I need to see them."

"Marie!" she yelled across the alley, and a dozen heads appeared in doorways and windows. "Who lives at number fourteen?"

"One-Eyed Luc," said the called-for Marie, a short, stout girl with a basket on her hip. She looked me up and down and turned to my smiler. "I'm going there now."

"I'll come with you." I picked my way through the street sludge.

"Suit yourself." She turned and walked briskly into the darkest part of the alley. The walls were wet in a way that looked permanent. Although it was as dark and dank as any London slum, the doorsteps of the houses were scrubbed clean, the windows were clear, and half of them had window boxes of geraniums and herbs, their subtle scent alleviating the stench from the gutter. Marie clipped quickly over the cobbles, winding through another alley and then another. They began to widen and lighten, and the boxes of geraniums became bigger and brighter. Some of the windows even had colored shutters as though this part of Paris was a village. But as we turned a corner, the shadows suddenly deepened and darkened. Over the alleys loomed an enormous factory with three black chimneys that blocked out the sun. The houses around the factory were black with soot and spidery metal staircases wound round the outside. Marie clipped onto one with her basket, her footsteps a fierce clang.

I caught a glimpse of a man with a limp. I turned, but there was no one else in the street. The limp was familiar but I couldn't place it.

"Are you coming?" Marie called. I followed her up the staircase. I knew thousands of veterans must be limping around Paris, but there was something in the jaunt, the heft of it, that I'd seen before.

Marie opened a dark door and turned into a tiny room containing the aptly named One-Eyed Luc. Although One-Eyed was kind, as he was also missing both legs at the knee and his right hand. The half of his face that lacked an eye was so scarred it looked like a map of Paris. He stared at me with his one eye as Marie fussed over him, plumping pillows, laying out bread and cheese, pouring wine, putting on the kettle to make tea. The apartment smelled strangely of stale breath, soap, tobacco, and sickness, but Marie made no move to open a window. She glanced at me once or twice but mostly ignored me as she tended her pet. He ignored her and spoke directly to me.

"Who are you working for?" His voice was gravel, strained with injury. I was taken aback, but I decided that honesty would work best.

"Fox. In London."

"Never heard of him."

"That's probably just as well." I stared right back at him. "I'm Mademoiselle Renarde"—his eyebrows shot up—"and I need information."

"What are you offering?"

I looked around, at the cracking walls with their peeling paint, at the gas ring on the floor, at the warped skirting boards, at the threadbare patches on the cushions, blankets and throws. I could offer a lot.

"What do you need?"

"Let's exchange"—he leaned forward as his voice scraped against his throat—"a name for a name."

I didn't know that I had any names, but I put on my most knowing face and took the seat he pointed out with his stump. Marie brought tea and started to massage his legs, but he dismissed her with a gruff "Later." She pouted, sulky, and took out her knitting. I raised my eyebrows.

"She's with the cause," he said. "You can trust her."

I nodded. They must be Communists—maybe they would know about the strikes and about Hausmann. I thought I was here about Ferny, but suddenly I wanted much more. How to get that without revealing that I knew nothing?

I smiled at Luc. "It's your house, Monsieur Luc. Your turn first."

He looked like he wanted to smile, but his face prevented him. "Who sent you?"

"Fern," I bluffed. I almost said *Ferny* but checked myself at the last moment. Good thing too, as both Luc and Marie sat up straighter and looked at me.

"He said that you would inform me of Hausmann."

Marie looked at Luc, who stared at me. He started to fidget, his voice squeaking in panic. "This can't be right—"

"We had a meeting just . . . Fern said nothing—"

"He would have mentioned something, surely—"

"Or maybe . . . Luc, perhaps this is a test. . . ."

"Why would he test me, Marie? He knows how committed I am—"

"But the plan—moved forward to—He said he had to have someone he could trust, someone who would lay down his life—"

"Surely he knows I . . . but perhaps . . ."

I waited as they whispered to each other. I had my best bored Gallic face in place, which wasn't hard, as my nostrils flared and my lips pursed against the smell. But each line was a revelation. If their cause wasn't Communist, it was certainly underground politics, possibly anarchist. They knew Fern well—Hugh Fernly-Whiting was clearly not just a bored aristocratic bureaucrat; it seemed that he was also a revolutionary, a political radical, a fomenter of trouble. Fern knew Hausmann and One-Eyed Luc knew enough of Hausmann to accept an emissary.

Luc and Marie stared at each other in concern and Marie put her hand on his good arm. "I think we must, Luc," she whispered, "because if we don't . . ."

He nodded and breathed in deeply.

"I'll get the brandy," she said.

"So"—he turned to me, back straight like the soldier he clearly still saw himself as—"forget the exchange of information; I'm at your command. You need to know about Hausmann."

I nodded. Luc took the brandy Marie offered and swallowed it in one gulp. I sipped mine slowly, using it to cover my surprise.

"Hausmann contacted us about three months ago. We had contacted the believers on the western border last summer and told them of our readiness. After the war, we knew it couldn't be long before the revolution began. We've spent the time recruiting—Marie came to us in that time." He exchanged a soft look with her. "Most of the people who came had just given up their loved ones to illness from the war. Broken hearts and broken faces, like me."

"Oh, Luc—"

"Shh, Marie, it's true. Fern came to us, not with a broken heart but with a message from Hausmann. We were to ready ourselves for the beginning. It would start in Germany, where conditions were ripe—workers downtrodden, low patriotic feeling, ineffectual government. We would help spread the revolution to France and others would spread it to Belgium, Holland, Spain, and on. Hausmann is the coordinator with a direct link to Russia." His face lit up at this. "Hausmann will send us a revolutionary, someone who can help us to create the right conditions—someone who knows how to—" He stopped himself. "Well, that's secret business. But you must have read about the riots in Saxony." I nodded. "That's Hausmann. That's our man!"

"You've met him?"

"Oh, no."

"We don't meet him," cut in Marie.

"He only speaks to a select few, the true believers. Fern is one of them. We're lucky to have him with us."

"So if you want to send a message to Hausmann—"

"We don't send messages," said Marie. "We receive instructions."

"There's never any question of us not carrying out our orders," said Luc. "We follow them to the letter."

"So that the revolution will come and then we'll all have enough." Marie's face lit up now. "Getting rid of the king a hundred and twenty years ago was only the first step. We have to be brave to take the next."

"Quite." I'd never felt so phlegmatically Anglophone. "I'll speak to Fern about Hausmann. But tell me—how can you trust Fern?"

"What?" Luc looked shocked. "What do you mean?"

"Fern came to you with a message from Hausmann. How could you trust he was a true revolutionary?"

"Oh that's easy." Marie looked relieved. "The same way that we can trust you. He knew the right names—"

"And the knocks and the signals—"

"And 'The Internationale,' and he had word from Russia—"

"He'd been changed by the war too—but he had much better skills than, well, than some of us." Luc raised half a smirk at Marie.

"We—I—grilled him for three days," rasped Luc. "He passed every test. He's a man of the cause."

Or a man with a mission. I nodded with a smile and finished my brandy.

"And he said"—Luc looked exultant at the memory—"he said, 'Bliss was it in that dawn to be alive—but to be young was very heaven!' It's an English poet speaking of the Revolution, but it is just perfect for this new revolution. Even after three days of interrogation, he could quote poetry."

Fern quoted Wordsworth, a Romantic poet just like Keats.

I could hardly sit in my chair. Thankfully Luc and Marie weren't ones for chitchat and I left with only one farewell—"The next meeting is in two days' time. We'll see you there," and Luc handed me the address. I tucked it into my purse and clattered down the spiral staircase.

"I'M JUST WILD ABOUT HARRY"

I got to Montparnasse, even to my building, but I didn't go all the way home. My feet ached from walking, but to lie down would mean trudging up four flights of stairs. To soak them would mean somehow getting hot water from somewhere and I'd have to pay for that. There was some post in my little letter box, so I took the letters to Petit's and settled into a back-corner table. A letter from my mother that a quick scan told me was full of scolding, platitudes, and complaints. A letter from the paper confirmed my pay, always a favorite, and there was a handwritten note in a vaguely familiar hand.

Kiki Kangaroo,

I want you to sit for me again, but I will be away visiting Olga and Paulo today and tomorrow. Come the day after that. You know what to wear.

Pablo

Pablo would be away, but presumably his housekeeper would still be working in the apartment or nearby. Hadn't Lazarev said to interrogate the housekeeper if I wanted the secrets of the house? There wouldn't be a better opportunity. My aching feet would have to wait. I had to get to rue la Boétie.

◆

"He's not here. You're one of his models, yes? Come back tomorrow night." The housekeeper would have slammed the door in my face if I hadn't caught it.

"Actually, it's you I need to speak to."

I'd never seen anyone so short look so forbidding. Her manicured eyebrows framed eyes that glared at me. Her gray bun was held back tightly and her black dress encased her so thoroughly that it was hard to imagine a body underneath it. Her eyes were a pale gray, the type that looked ghostly or halfway to blind. All I could do was smile.

"It's for Pablo . . . but perhaps to your benefit too. May I come in?"

She stared for a moment more, then sniffed and let me through. She let the door bang shut.

"What can I help you with?"

"This hallway is pretty dark and unconvivial"—it was spotless but cheerless, so unlike the studio—"perhaps first we can sit down and share some tea. I have more than one question and my feet ache from walking all day."

"Your feet ache!" she scoffed as she walked briskly into the kitchen. "Try being a housekeeper, to an artist and a dancer, at my age!"

"It must be difficult."

"You have no idea."

"Do you get to soak your feet at the end of the day? Is there hot water in this apartment?"

"I should be so lucky!" She was so efficient; it was amazing and slightly frightening to watch her prepare the tea with so much speed and so little joy. Lazarev was right; her grievances were present in every movement.

"But sometimes, if they don't stay up too late, I can fill a pan with water and sit with a book," she said, "which happens about once a month. Pablo was much easier before he married. He would let me go home at the same time regardless of how late he sat up drinking and talking. He even made me omelets and coffee once, when I came in one morning and he hadn't been to bed at all. Me! His housekeeper! But that Olga, she wouldn't deign to spit on me. She insists I stay at my post until they are all asleep and then insists on a clean kitchen the next morning. As though I'm an army of servants in her Russian childhood home. They don't pay me enough for that kind of service."

"It sounds as though they'd have to pay you enough for two or three people."

"Exactly! Lemon biscuits or ginger? You'll have the lemon—my sister made them, they're much nicer. I mentioned a higher pay rate to Pablo and then an hour later Olga whirled into my kitchen yelling and screaming about my ingratitude, my poor attitude, my lack of professional pride. She even docked my pay! Pablo gave it back to me when she was out, but I mean! That woman is beyond the pale."

I must have touched a nerve. I didn't think it would be this easy to get her to talk, as she'd always seemed so dour when I came to model. I'd spent the walk over here thinking of persuasive sentences to charm information from her, but I needed none of them.

"How long have you worked for Pablo?"

"Oh, years now. I began to help him out when he lived next door and was just another artist come to make his fortune. He was always charming and he would find little treats for my Jean-Claude"—the severe lines around her mouth softened momentarily— "my little son . . ." A spasm went over her face, from sweetness to fear to sadness, before the severe mask came down.

"Not that that woman, Olga, would ever let my son into this house, let alone speak to him—"

"How old is your son now?"

"Twenty." Her mouth was pinched. I waited for the motherly pride to pour forth, but there was none.

"Is he working in Paris?"

"Yes, he's . . . yes."

I waited, but after a moment she turned away from the table and began to tidy the kitchen. I took a guess.

"Was he injured? In the war?"

Her shoulders hunched and she nodded.

"I was there, with the soldiers." She turned and stared at me. "I was a nurse with the British Army. Sometimes I was behind the lines, sometimes I was right at the front. I saw . . . a lot of things. I know what it's like, to come home and have to make a life again."

"But you're not home."

"No, well, precisely. I couldn't live where I was born. I had to make a life here. Anything else was just too hard."

With that, she deflated in a rush.

"He's . . . he looks whole, a missing finger, a couple of scars, nothing serious. But his mind, his dreams . . ." She bit her lip in an attempt not to cry. "It's worse now than it was when he first came home. He has a job now, with other veterans, but how long will that last? He's had so many. He can't work some days, and then he loses his position, and then he gets desperate and does desperate things. . . ."

"And you have to pay for it."

"How can I? Of course I try, but he's a grown man. There are just so many men like him and so few have any sympathy anymore."

"Has he done something lately?"

"What have you heard?"

"Nothing. I'm guessing from the pitch of your anguish."

She threw up her hands and sat down heavily. She reached into a hidden pocket and pulled out a tiny bottle. She poured two drops into her tea and offered it to me. Brandy, I could smell it from across the table. I smiled and shook my head.

"He's . . . he's in with a bad crowd. Not criminal, at least not yet. He met them at work. But someone knows and I—they say . . ."

"They're blackmailing you," I said.

She nodded.

"Who are 'they'?" But she shook her head.

"Does it have anything to do with the missing portrait of Olga?"

Her eyes widened with fear. Bingo.

"You know that Pablo has hired me to find the painting, yes?"

"You're not a model?"

"Not only a model."

She fidgeted with her cup. Poor woman, I hated to put this kind of pressure on her.

"And I think you know how it left this building," I said. She bit her lip and blinked rapidly. "I'm not going to report you to the police, or even to Pablo." She looked at me, her gray eyes underwater. "But I need to know what happened to the painting. Pablo doesn't care how it comes home, as long as it does. So"—I pulled up a chair next to her and took one of her shaking hands, cold and worn to the bone; I rubbed it warm—"I need to know what you know."

"I can't," she croaked.

"Pablo doesn't care—"

"Not Pablo, the other one. He'll kill me."

"Who?"

She shook her head.

"He's not here and he can't know. He won't get to you."

"How do you—?"

"I promise. Just tell me who."

She heaved a sigh so enormous it became a hiccough. "It was one of Olga's guests last week."

"A Russian?"

"No. An Englishman. Ugly, scarred, with a limp. He came with a silly woman who is related to Olga, I think—she must be, as they didn't come for the art. Neither of them can appreciate Pablo's genius."

"But the Englishman could."

"The Englishman could only appreciate how much one of Pablo's paintings is worth on the black market. He came in here"—her voice tightened, but she swallowed some more tea and pressed on—"when the others were gone, when Olga and Pablo were out, he came in and told me all about Jean-Claude, things I didn't know, things that would get him into terrible trouble if the police found out. . . ."

"What did he make you do?"

"He made me"—she shook her head—"I'm so ashamed. . . . But my son, I had to—sorry, sorry. He made me give him the portrait of Olga— that is, give it to my son, Jean-Claude, to give to him. . . ." She started to cry then, sniffing, her clean, pressed hankie rapidly becoming limp with tears. I poured her more tea and pushed it towards her.

"Never, I've never done anything like this before, not in all my years, I wouldn't—"

"This Englishman, he had a limp and scars, you say?"

"And some missing fingers. I don't know his name, but the woman he came with had a flower name, something pretty; it didn't suit her."

Who else could it be but Violet and Fern?

I kissed the housekeeper on both cheeks. "You've been an enormous help."

"You know who he is?"

"I do, and he's a rotter." I smiled. "Now, tell me what I can do to help you, Madame . . ."

"Just call me Céline," she said, and sniffed. "I don't need any . . . well, my Jean-Claude needs help, but how . . ."

"I know a nurse who works with veterans. There might be a doctor at her hospital who can help with his dreams."

Céline nodded, again on the edge of tears. As I turned to go, she grabbed my arm. "I'm sorry, I—"

"Desperate times," I said with a smile. "But I'll be back for more of those biscuits."

◈

It was dusk, that time when the horizon dissolves and my thoughts, my inhibitions, my skin along with it. The streetlamps splashed their gold along the Montparnasse footpaths, mixing with the brass and bronze from the bars, cafés, and hotels. I buzzed, my heart pounded, I was scared and excited. My thoughts chased each other as I hurried to my apartment. Would Fern and Violet be at the party tonight? I couldn't remember who was throwing the party, but they always seemed to turn up wherever there was free food.

The stairs inside my building were dark but I knew them well enough to hurry up to the top floor. I lit my candles in their wine-bottle holders, I shucked off my shoes and coat and sat in my favorite position, leaning against the window frame, legs hanging into the street, glass of wine in one hand and cigarette in the other. The candlelight reflected in the bottles and windows, imitating the twinkle and sparkle of the night city at my feet.

I searched the notebook where I kept all my work notes and invitations. The party was at Harry's. I swore loudly—tonight, of all nights, I needed a party of stuffed-shirts and know-it-all men, not brilliant women—until I realized that this was a benefit for the ambulance drivers, to showcase Wendy's work, and there'd be a lot more people there than her Sapphic Ambulance Corps. That's why she had invited me—"You can write about it in your column, darling. There'll be a Rothschild there and a couple of duchesses. I've promised them a first peek at my Cézanne . . . well, Wendy's Cézanne. It's all for a good cause!" I wondered how well Maisie and Harry would get along. After two glasses of champagne, I imagined they'd get on famously.

◇

Maisie hurried towards me as I waited under the lamplight. I wore a new dress, silver satin with silver beads, sleeveless and low cut and short. The dress was cut on the cross, so the satin flowed like water over my curves. It was a warm night, so my velvet opera cape was open, my star shoes winking at the beads, my blond bob adorned only by a diamanté comb. I'd had two propositions already, but in this part of town that was almost unavoidable. I sent them off with a rude gesture and a sharp "Not for sale." I'd also been approached by a cigarette seller, a boy with bright red hair, who walked up to me so pointedly that I wondered if he was my new watcher. I bought a packet from him, Player's Navy Cut with the hero sailor on the front. As Maisie walked in and out of the lamplight, I could see that she wore a long dress of dark green silk under her fur-trimmed black coat, patent leather black shoes, and green cloche hat decorated with a feather. She waved with her hat as she hurried.

"I'm so sorry, I could hardly get away." She hugged me, panting. "Ray had a bad day at work, and the undermaid girl—"

"Undermaid girl?"

"She has a title, third parlor maid or something, but I can never remember it. She was in tears over some boy—I mean really, how do those posh people cope with all this hullabaloo?"

"Gin."

"Ha! Exactly. I felt like telling everyone to down a drink and grow up, but you know, lady of the house and all that." I laughed and she grinned. "Although Ray would've preferred it if I'd stayed the lady in the house tonight—"

"Don't tell me he's the jealous type."

"Do you think I'd stand for that? No, he just wanted his wife to soothe his ruffled feathers. Some bother in Germany, apparently."

"Germany?" I didn't want to turn Maisie into work, but how could I resist any news?

"Oh yes." She sighed and linked her arm in mine as we walked towards Harry's. "Rumors and gossip. It's the brown hats—"

"Brownshirts?"

"Yes, that's the one. He got into a big fight with his colleagues. It's not even to do with his work! But some of his colleagues, his boss, support them, and Ray is dead set against them. He couldn't stop himself from arguing with them."

"When you say 'support,' do you mean financially?"

"Oh, I doubt it. A Frenchman would never give money to a German. Why?" She stopped and looked at me. "Is this your spy stuff?"

"Shhh, Maisie—"

"Do you need me to find out exactly how they support the Brown-shirts?"

"I don't want you to be involved with my work for Fox—"

"I won't be, don't worry. I'm just being a good wife, that's all. Just being a good friend." She squeezed my hand.

I squeezed it back and kissed it. "You're too good to me, Maisie."

"Rubbish. What about all those times that Captain Severn called me Nurse Golliwog and you stood up for me? Or when the more stupid blokes would recoil because they didn't want to be touched by a n—"

"Insupportable."

"You gave them a sharp scolding. I thought their mustaches would fall off in shock. I don't forget." I hadn't seen her look so serious for a long time. "But I need a drink now, Katie. Are we almost there?"

"We are, in fact, on Harry's street. Are you ready?"

"I was born ready, Katie King."

Harry's party was in full swing by the time we arrived at her purple palace. A string trio played in the corner while liveried waiters carried around trays of champagne and nibbles.

"How modern!" said Maisie as she grabbed a little pie.

"Oh, isn't it though?" said Harry. "I wanted jazz as well, but it would've been too much. Wendy's work is modern enough, and I've found that if you want people to open their checkbooks, shocks are best administered one at a time."

Harry handed us both glasses of bubbly.

"Now, Kiki, I want you to gossip with everyone and write the most scurrilous nonsense about tonight. Say that people spent twice as much as they did, that the waiters were caught with the duchesses, and that the band played the latest dance craze after midnight."

"Yes, ma'am!"

She smiled but looked wistful, and placed her hand on my cheek.

"You're looking better, Kiki," she said. "That bath did wonders for you."

"And Maisie," I said. "Another friend from the war. She's my other Nightingale."

"Another Florence," said Maisie.

"And another Kiki rescuer, I see. Welcome to the club, Maisie." Harry and Maisie were almost the same height, both with piles of hair and big, open expressions.

"Thank you, Miss Harker."

"Harry, please. Any friend of Kiki's is a friend of mine. Now, make sure you eat me out of house and home. This party needs to be voracious. I'm relying on you!"

She kissed us both and whirled away in a twirl of purple.

"Phew, what a place!" Maisie breathed.

Harry had outdone herself. Every light in the place burned, and extra lamps, candles, mirrors, and crystals made her apartment glitter and glow. On every wall was one of Wendy's works, large, vibrant, fierce portraits of female ambulance drivers. Some were in classical poses, some were cubist interpretations of a wartime ambulance with lots of red and gray. Beside each painting was a little plaque with a story, some about the ambulance drivers, some from soldiers who had survived the trip to the clearing station. Harry's Corps friends were stationed between the paintings, in their wartime uniforms, looking modern and strong with their cropped hair and cigarettes. They chatted away with the older partygoers, explaining the plaques in more detail, directing them to Harry when it looked like a sale might be in the offing. Harry put a bright red notice on one plaque—SOLD—and applauded the coy old lush who had bought the portrait. Others turned, inquired, the band played louder as the Corps girls did their best to sell more paintings. Champagne cocktails came out—mimosas and kir royales—and the waiters stayed with the patrons so they could guzzle from the trays. The room seemed to throb, but whether that was the chatter, the lights, or the variety of purples that adorned the place in velvet and brocade, it was impossible to tell.

"This is pure Harry," I said. "The only way to participate is to dive in."

"Lucky I can swim," said Maisie.

I cleared a path through the living room crowd to the parlor. There was a small, surreptitious gathering at the door. A skinny older woman with a bob even sharper than mine turned to me and spoke into her champagne glass.

"We heard there was a Cézanne here."

"Have you seen it?" I asked.

"It's supposed to be in this next room. The housekeeper won't let us through."

I looked over her shoulder and saw the petite figure of Annette, in her black uniform, standing resolute at the door. I moved up to her, the skinny older woman pretending not to listen in.

"Annette, doing your duty. Very commendable."

"Thank you, Mademoiselle Kiki," she murmured with a little bow.

I stood close and spoke as low as I could. "I need to get in. There is someone I need to find, who will only be lured by Wendy's Cézanne. Is it in there?"

"Oui, mademoiselle."

"Harry knows about this little lure, and approves, but only if you guard the painting itself. Can you do this?"

Annette looked into my face, her honest eyes searching mine for traces of deceit. I felt naked, even though I was telling the truth. She nodded, turned, and opened the door to the inner room like a vigilant revealing a shrine.

This was Harry and Wendy's private parlor, with soft carpets and heavy drapes. The wall opposite the door was as bare as Harry could allow herself, just the lavender brocade wallpaper and two lamps. Their light shone on a painting, small enough to hold in your arms, of a still life. Apples, lemons, flowers—the Cézanne. The soft lamplight made each visible brushstroke shimmer as though alive. The purple wall made the yellows of the painting jump into the shadows beneath. Annette stood next to it—really, underneath it, as she was so short—hands folded in front of her, a vigilant incarnate. The little crowd surged through the door and then stopped, moved slowly up to the painting, and gazed.

The drapes were tied back to display the view over the city. I waited by the window as I watched partygoers move into the room. Each looked back over their shoulder, as though this inner sanctum held a robber's haul, an opium den, a harem. None of them noticed either me or Maisie, cloaked as we were by the shadows. I sipped slowly, watching, for a certain Black Violet to make an appearance.

"What's going on?" Maisie whispered as loudly as she dared, as softly as she could.

"I have to find someone and speak to her. All I can do now is wait."

I turned to look at her. She stared at the Cézanne and the room, turned to the window, then turned back to me and raised her eyebrows. I nodded.

"Go on." I gestured to the main room. "Drink and dance. I could be hours."

She grinned, downed her drink, and slipped out of the room in a swish of silk. The light from the other room hit the freckles that speckled her strong shoulders, highlighted the curve of muscle and bone, so that I almost missed the woman who walked in behind her. But even if I hadn't been looking, I would have recognized that sarcastic, bitter expression, fashionably too-pale skin punctuated by eyes that, in this gloom, looked black. Her black dress clung to her bones, a long scarf trailing behind her. She walked right up to the painting, and only when she reached out to touch it did she notice Annette. She started, visibly recoiling from contact, as Annette warned her off. She sniffed and went back to examining the painting, firing Annette a volley of questions without looking at her. I saw Annette suppress a sigh; this was my cue.

"Keen to purchase?" I asked.

Violet frowned at me. "You're the gossip reporter."

"And here to report." I smiled. "But I'm also a good friend of Harriet Harker."

"Who?"

"The hostess." I raised an eyebrow.

"Oh. I came with a friend. I have no interest in any of those ambulance drivers. Morbid, I say."

"But you have interest in the Cézanne."

"What was your name again?" She frowned at me but didn't move from her close position to the painting.

"Kiki Button." I held out my hand, but she gave me hers as though I was going to kiss it. I tucked it under my arm and dragged her away from the painting.

"So, Violet, who's the friend who brought you here? Your piratical mate, Hugh Fernly-Whiting?"

She stared, then let out a little *oh* and withdrew her hand. We stood by the window and her cigarette end made a new lamp to match the ones in the street. I lit one of my own to join her.

"That's right, I remember everything now. You're the blonde he couldn't stop flirting with. Well, one of them anyway." She looked me up and down and I gave her my *This joke is just between us* smile. She huffed and tried not to smile in return. The hurt lover always needs someone to help them mock their beloved.

"Piratical—you mean the scar and the missing fingers?" she asked.

"And the swagger and roguish look."

"Oh yes, he has those in spades."

"He's here tonight?"

"No, he's at some meeting or other." She shrugged. "He never tells me where or why, just ups and leaves me to . . . well . . ."

"To?"

She nodded towards the Cézanne.

"He wants you to buy it?"

She laughed, loud and sharp, and the other people in the Cézanne shrine turned to look. She ignored them. "Yes, sure, let's say that. He wants to buy it."

"He wants you to find out how he can 'acquire' it."

She grinned, then put on a fake-innocent face. "Oh, I don't know what you mean," she said in a high breathy voice. Her expression dropped to one of anger as she dragged heavily on her cigarette. Now was my chance.

"If you wanted to hurt him—really hurt him—what would you do?"

She glanced at me and then lit another cigarette with the end of her first, a nasty little smile playing over her lips.

"That's easy, I'd give him up."

"For another woman?"

"No—to the police." She inhaled with satisfaction. "Or better yet, the government."

"Which government?"

"British, French—it doesn't matter. Of course, if I did that, I'd be locked up too . . . but sometimes I think it'd be worth it, just to thwart him."

"What if I told you that you could do that, without getting into trouble?"

She gave me a sharp look. "How is that possible? He knows—"

"Too much perhaps. But others know more."

"Others know something different but not more. I have yet to meet a man he couldn't wind around his finger and then wring out."

"I have. I work for him." Her eyes were wide. "And Ferny used to work for him too." I prayed my bluff worked.

"His boss. From the war," she breathed.

"The very same."

I was right. Bingo.

"The only man he's afraid of." She blinked rapidly, smoked rapidly, and stared unseeing at the view. Now that her dreams of revenge were possible, she was scared. I moved closer to her.

"You'd be safe and well set up." I looked casual as she glanced at me. "My boss would see to it. Probably not here, mostly likely back in London—"

"I'm sick of this city—"

"He knows the value of loyalty. In fact, it's the only thing he values. And those who are not loyal to him . . ." I let her imagine. By the way she inhaled, I could see that she imagined the worst.

"And if I . . . if I was loyal?" she said in a small voice. She hardly dared to look at me. I could hardly bear to lie to her, but such is the life of a spy.

"You'd be rewarded." It could be true. One never knew with Fox.

She stubbed her cigarette out in the little ashtray by her elbow, a marble bowl on its own plinth—Harry didn't even smoke. She stared at it, at the view, at her hands, all unseeing. She turned to me and nodded.

"Very well. Tell me what to do."

◆

As I made my way to the Rotonde I was happy, nervous, sad, excited—all the usual things I felt when spy work went well. I hated the lying and loved the subterfuge. I hated the manipulation and loved the thrill of getting what I wanted. I hated Fox, hated that he knew how to excite me—but there was no antidote to that.

There were few people I knew sitting at the tables outside. Not even North was there, and she was almost always there. It was only a quarter to twelve, not too late. I saw Henri and signaled to him. He stopped halfway between a smile and a start—he didn't know if I was an ally or enemy. I gave him my best smile and he relaxed.

"Where is everyone?"

"It is spring, mademoiselle. One minute, the patrons are here, the next . . . an American tourist came by with a cheetah on a leash and your friends left for a jazz party in Montmartre." He gave me his best Gallic shrug. "They will return tomorrow."

"It seems that I'm missing a party."

"If I may suggest, this is not a problem for you, mademoiselle." He bowed his head slightly, a knowing look on his face. I sighed.

"No indeed. I think you know why I'm here."

"This way, mademoiselle. Your whisky will be waiting for you when you return."

"You're a godsend," I murmured as he ushered me into the office. The door clicked shut, a tiny lock on a vault.

It was dreadful, waiting for Fox's call. I didn't have his number, of course. I could have asked for his office number but I knew from experience that he wouldn't be there. He'd be at his club, or in a hotel, or even, heaven forbid, in his London home. The quiet atmosphere of the office chilled me. I'd been excited, alive, my body humming with ideas and clues and people and parties—my veins were full of champagne and my heart beat with gossip—but as I waited, all this flattened and stilled.

The telephone rang. I wondered what would happen if I didn't answer. If I let the telephone operator make my excuses for me, if I just walked out of the office and never returned. I sighed. I didn't need to wonder; I knew that Fox would find me.

"'Bright star——'"

"Glad you feel that way, Vixen."

"'Would I were steadfast as thou art——'"

"'Awake for ever in a sweet unrest'? 'With aching Pleasure nigh'?"

"'Pleasure turns 'to poison while the bee-mouth sips.'"

"Such a sad story! That's because you don't take your pleasure with me."

"Monsieur Renard, would I were steadfast as thou art, then in lone splendor, hung aloft in the night, I would watch with eternal lids apart for the mole."

"As you have been."

"But I am not steadfast. My hand is ever at my lips, bidding adieu——"

"To your precious dreams of freedom?"

What a bastardly thing to say; I took a deep breath to contain my anger. "To you."

"Oh no, Vixen. Because then you'd taste the sadness of my might——"

"How? You'd send me to prison as you'd send a certain farm boy to the firing squad?"

Silence. I heard him light a cigarette.

"I didn't think so, Fox."

"I had other ideas——"

"Your games are all very pretty, but this play is almost played out."

"Are we down to brass tacks, Vixen?"

"I need a drop off point and date and time."

"Indeed! You've done well. I'd be impressed if I didn't expect it."

"I need payment."

"Money was wired to you."

"I need proper payment. What will you do for my farm boy?"

The clock ticked and all was hushed. I couldn't pretend now, if I ever could have, that Tom wasn't my weak point. His freedom was what I wanted and I couldn't get it without revealing that to Fox.

"You really do only work for love." Fox's voice was soft. I didn't trust it. And did I really love Tom? As a friend, certainly . . .

"This shouldn't surprise you."

"No . . . it shouldn't." But it clearly did. This was not the Fox I knew. He sounded almost gentle. It made me almost concerned for him.

"Fox?"

"Your farm boy will visit you tomorrow."

"How do you—oh, never mind. Yes, but—"

"If that's what you want as payment, then payment has already been made."

"How? In what way?"

"He'll tell you. He'll also tell you the drop-off point."

"Is this the word? Or does your plaintive anthem fade?"

"I am forlorn."

"Fox—"

But the phone went dead. The room was so still that I could hear my heart beat its unsteady rhythm. I had what I wanted, but I wasn't quite sure at what price. It seemed too easy—I delivered the mole, and then Fox delivered proof of Tom's innocence? That wasn't how Fox worked. There had to be something more.

I stared at the receiver. This was not a public telephone and I should not use it to make a call. Especially not a trunk call to London; that would be too cheeky. Rude, even.

At the Colonial in Soho, the barman yelled over the drinkers for Bertie Browne.

"Hello?" Bertie yelled into the phone. I could just see him squinting with concentration, trying not to ogle the barman.

"Bertie darling."

"Kiki! How did you know I'd be here?"

"Because I'm thinking of you, so you must be thinking of me."

"Oh, Kiki, I am! It's so dull here without you."

"It doesn't sound it."

"Just sound and fury, darling."

"Then catch the early train to Paris."

"Done. I'll bring whisky."

"Good. It'll go with my gossip."

"Meet me Gare du Nord, darling one. I'm . . . I'll be there."

18

"WABASH BLUES"

I was woken by a knock at the door, a brief call of "Mademoiselle? *Tele-gramme!*" and the handle rattling as the telegram boy tried to open the door. I checked my little wristwatch—nine o'clock. Far too early for a party girl and the telegram boy knew it.

"Do you do this on purpose?" I asked as I unlocked the door. I'd picked up a satin kimono dressing gown at a flea market, and it slipped from my shoulders as I jiggled the temperamental lock.

"Do you deliver to me first so that you can glimpse me in my negligee?"

He blushed.

"Here's your tip." His eyes widened at my generosity. "Always deliver to me first, any time of the day or night. If you can't find me here, leave a message at Café du Dôme or Café Rotonde. Understood?"

He nodded, his big brown eyes wide and excited in his sallow, skinny face. I guessed that he was about twelve, although it was almost impossible to tell—he had a cigarette behind his ear, even as his childish body ran bandy-legged down the stairs.

I splashed my face and perched in my favorite spot on the windowsill. My bare legs dangled and sparrows darted here and there near my geranium pots. Three telegrams; I liked being a wanted woman.

The first was from Bertie.

ON BLUE TRAIN HEADED FOR YELLOW HAIR RED LIPS PINK CHAMPAGNE KIKI ETA 1500 FIRST STOP THE RITZ

I could hear the corks popping already. I tingled in all the right places. Harry was good for my mind, Maisie was good for my heart, but Bertie was good for my body. He'd provide food, dancing, and some good old-fashioned bedroom acrobatics. I would be able to relax tonight.

The second was from Tom. I paused, breathed deeply, tried to steady my heartbeat—but even my pause gave me pause. Would this always be the way? Would I always need to steady myself before I even so much as read his name? I hoped not; I hoped so. I sighed and reached for a cigarette. I had the telegram now; that was enough to think about.

HAVE LEAVE SO LDN VIA PARIS ETA TOMORROW PM TOO MUCH TO SAY HERE SO MAKE ME A WILLOW CABIN BUTTON I AM COMING

"Willow cabin" indeed; I told my heart to behave so I could focus on the rest. Too much to say? About Germany? Had he had word from one of Fox's emissaries? Was he thinking of something else entirely? I hoped so; I hoped not. I watched the sparrows fluff themselves and gossip around the flowers. The sounds of the morning rose up from the street; hawker calls, horse traffic, and car horns. He'd be here tomorrow night. Bertie and Tom would be here together. I never liked to mix my men, it seemed boastful and gauche. Thankfully Bertie would arrive first; he would be merely amused by Tom, but Tom would be devastated if I stayed at the Ritz, especially as he was calling for willow cabins. Could I have my cake and eat it too? That depended on the cake, I supposed. Luckily, there was no way that Bertie would envy Tom sleeping in my garret. The only way Bertie would sleep on the floor was if he passed out drunk.

The third telegram had no sender. It held only one sentence.

DARKLING I LISTEN

Not even a stop. Of course not. He never stopped; Fox would never let up. Was I supposed to be his "darkling" now, his darling in the dark, his darling of darkness? He listened to me . . . when, in the small hours? Unseen, unnoticed? He knew that I noticed the newspaper boys who followed me around the streets. So what was he listening for? His soft voice on the telephone came back to me, his surprise at love, but I couldn't tell if these reactions were truthful or yet another way to play games. I needed to see his face to properly understand him, to see how he moved his body, how he looked at me—

I needed nothing of the sort. I ripped up the telegram and cast the torn pieces into the street.

Too many thoughts, too many men, not enough hours with my head on the pillow. I needed more sleep. I used my war training—to sleep anywhere, anytime, whatever provocation—climbed into bed, put a scarf over my eyes and was asleep within seconds.

◈

I had arranged to meet Violet in the morning, though I knew that her morning and my morning would be about the same—midday. When I left her last night she'd been downing her fourth cocktail and following the waiters for food. If I turned up with some croissants I'd probably get a hero's welcome, but I wasn't sure if I wanted to butter her up or put her under pressure.

The sky threatened rain, spitting and dribbling as I pulled on my most jealous-lover-friendly clothes. No open backs or low necklines today, but a dark blue-gray blouse with a white lace collar, cut tight to the body to show curves without showing flesh. It was a soft cotton-wool blend with details of darts around the bust, down to the hips. I wore gray trousers that I'd copied from Bertie, wide-legged and cuffed. My shoes laced up like a schoolgirl's and my coat was thick and navy, double-breasted in a military style. I looked mannish and modern, like nobody Fern or Pablo or even Tom would look at twice. A little captain's hat kept my hair away from the rain. Madame Petit clapped her hands with delight at my outfit as I drank my coffee from the bar. The baker at the boulangerie looked twice, but in Montparnasse, he was getting used to all sorts of sights—men holding hands, jazz musicians and lady artists, a Japanese man in a ball gown—a woman in trousers was no longer noteworthy here.

Violet was staying on the Right Bank, in the midst of the bankers and Americans. A Protestant church was tucked in between a café and a hat shop, and men in suits hurried up and down the street. Unlike when the sun shone, today all the pedestrians looked at the ground, head forward, intent on their warm office and hot cup of tea. Except for my follower, of course: a newspaper boy, with violent red hair, who turned up on every other corner but wouldn't let me buy a paper from him. I listened to his calls instead, but there were no Brownshirts in the headlines today. The river shivered, its gray surface flecked and pocked. I had no umbrella but turned up my collar like a sailor and kept the croissants dry inside my coat.

"Violet."

She looked cross as she answered the door.

"It's the maid's day off."

"I brought croissants." I held up the bag.

A pale smile crossed her face. "You're a sport." She kissed me on both cheeks and left the door for me to close.

Violet's cousin must have escaped early in the revolution, as her apartment, while not sumptuous, was a good deal better than the ones I'd seen in Montparnasse. It had no fancy wallpaper or brocade curtains, but the ceilings were high, and the white walls reflected light. Where you could

see the walls, that is, as most of them were covered in bookshelves. On
the bookshelves were not only books in Russian, French, English, and
German, but also dozens of vases, statues, boxes, and other knickknacks.
The floors were plain polished wood, covered only with exotic rugs held
in place by enormous brown leather armchairs. I had the feeling that
Violet's cousin didn't escape the revolution so much as the overblown
sumptuousness of a life at court. There were no servants or silk curtains,
no crystal chandeliers; this apartment paraded only its wealth of experience and intellect. I picked up an African mask that sat prominently on
the nearest shelf to the door.

"Katya travels a lot," Violet said with a shrug. "She and Dot bring
back treasures from all the countries they visit."

"Dot?"

"Her companion. Another English cousin of Katya's, but one so distant
you need a telescope to see the connection. I think . . . is she also very
distantly related to the royal family? I can't remember." She plunked herself down in one of the armchairs and lit a cigarette. She wore black, of
course, a long slim skirt and a long cashmere top that was belted at her
waist, a jet-black snake pinned high on her breast. Her foot in its elegant
black brogue, with its slightly too-high heel, twitched, and she covered her
eyes with her free hand.

"Rough night?" I asked.

She huffed a laugh and inhaled. "Great night. Rough morning."

"Point me to the kitchen and I'll brew some coffee."

"Oh, no, I'll have to brew the coffee—their little coffeepot is Italian, a
gift from some artist, made by his artisan uncle on a lonely hillside over-
looking the Adriatic, blessed thrice by the priest under a full moon—or
something or other." She heaved herself up with a sigh. "Anyway, they
showed me four times how to use it to make sure I used it correctly. If it
was damaged under my watch . . . well, there would be a necessary trip
to a certain artisan uncle, and I'm not sure if my poor Italian is up to

groveling." Violet threw these lines over her shoulder as she clipped her way to a little galley kitchen.

"You speak Italian?"

"I learned a few phrases from a flirtatious guard in the war. It's not bad, but not to be trusted in polite society." I was beginning to like her, her cigarette dangling from her lips as she washed the pot and ground the coffee beans. She was even thinner than me, her wrist bone like a dome at the end of her arm, her movements jerky and quick. I stood at the door of the kitchenette, a thin sliver of apartment that was just about big enough to prepare coffee and eggs but not much else. A high window at the other end framed Violet in light.

She put the pot on to boil and turned to me, scrutinizing me through her veil of smoke. I smiled my best smile and she snorted.

"Yes, you're very charming, Kiki. I can see why Ferny had a thing for you."

"What, after one night?"

"Oh yes. He spoke of you often after you left, asked everyone he knew about you, went to the Rotonde on several occasions in the hope of seeing you." She stubbed out her cigarette in a saucer; there was a slight strain in her voice. "He even created a little scrapbook about you—one of his dossiers, as I call them . . ." She trailed off as she stared at the stern, concerned look on my face. She remembered our chat from last night and the penny dropped. From the way her mouth hung more and more agape, that penny dropped a long way down.

"My God . . . they really are dossiers, aren't they?"

"They? He creates dossiers on lots of women?"

"Yes . . . or at least, he tells me about the women. Taunts me, if I'm honest. With relish. He can be . . ."

"Cruel?"

"Humph." Violet looked around the room, avoiding the implications of that word, before she turned back to me.

"Might he have dossiers on men as well?"

"I never go into his study. I went in once and—well, I was suitably punished." The coffee started to whistle and boil. "It's just at the end of the corridor." She turned off the pot and poured us both little cups of steaming, strong black liquid. Black gold, it was so delicious. I murmured in appreciation.

"Indeed. We're fortified now, Miss Button. We can violate his private lair."

"Ha! Well he's already violated my privacy. I'm just retrieving what's mine."

She sighed, but in relief or apprehension, I couldn't tell.

The corridor was short. There was one large bedroom to the right, and on the left was the bathroom and then a small study. Violet opened the door to a room barely big enough to hold the desk, chair, and chocka-block bookshelves that threatened to overwhelm it. A thick curtain made it very dark. I yanked it open and the light revealed piles of scrapbooks, notebooks, and newspapers. Ferny appeared to have forgotten some of his training, as the messy room violated Fox's rules about neat work and leaving nothing behind. Books were opened, pencil shavings were in the overfull ashtrays, newspapers were out of order in piles by the chair, thick translation dictionaries held other scraps of scribbled paper. In the center of the table was a pile of lined notebooks, very like the army-issue books we used in the war. I opened one but it held only nonsense.

"It's written in code."

"Why?" Violet was barely breathing behind me, her question just a whispery wisp. I looked at her and raised my eyebrows, but she only looked scared and confused.

"I assume so that people like me can't read it."

She began to realize the full implications of this—that he had some-thing to hide, that he was a spy—and she looked like she might crumble. In fact, her hands shook as she went to light a cigarette.

"Don't." She looked up as I spoke. "He'll smell the smoke and know we've been in here." She dropped her hand slowly. I'd deal with her revelations, and the spilling of secrets this often entailed, in a minute. I needed my dossier first.

I flipped open the next book. It held a similar code. I studied it for a moment, grabbed a piece of paper and pencil and started to transcribe. I swapped every pair of letters, just as Fox had taught me, a simple kindergarten code that could be remembered under duress. My guess was right and the sentences emerged. This notebook was on his meeting with the Communist cell, Luc and Marie and Hausmann featuring prominently. I flicked through the notebooks, looking for one about IKIK UBTTNO, as my name would be written.

"Are you sure he had a dossier on me, Violet?"

"He joked about it . . . that's as sure as I can be." She stood still in the middle of the room, as though by moving even an inch she would shatter what remained of her life. I needed to take advantage of her shock as quickly as possible. The drawers of the desk were locked and nothing was hidden under the desktop or chair bottom. There were no other notebooks around. Either it didn't exist or he had it with him, in which case I was in trouble.

"Let's get some more coffee and eat those croissants," I said softly. Violet nodded and turned to go. Just as we were leaving a book caught by eye—*The Complete Poetical Works of John Keats*. I opened it, but there was not a single poem contained in the pages. It was a notebook, full of times and dates, full of *ikik* and *ubttno*. The code, the poems, the nickname, all confirmed that Fern was a Fox acolyte. "He cannot see what flowers are at his feet"—if he was blind before, he wasn't any longer. Though I doubt he suspected just what his particular flower, Violet, was capable of. Or was Violet not a flower but a fly?

I tucked the book into my pocket as I followed Violet to the armchairs, surreptitiously hiding it as I pulled out my cigarettes. If she didn't know

I'd stolen it, she might be protected. She dragged hard on her cigarette, sucking in her cheeks so that she didn't just look thin, she looked skeletal, tiny in the chair. I ripped open the bag of pastries, poured her more coffee, and pushed the vitals towards her.

"What is all that stuff?" she croaked.

"Information, I assume. Research."

"But why?"

"I was hoping you might tell me that."

She looked anguished. She knew why but couldn't bear to admit it, not even to herself. I'd have to play Dr. Freud to persuade that information out of her subconscious and into the light. I just hoped that Ferny wasn't coming home any time soon.

"How long have you known Ferny?"

"Oh, years." She waved the smoke from her face as she picked up her cup. "Our families know each other. Our fathers were in the same year at Eton, his elder brother boarded with my younger brother—oh yes, there's about eight years between us, not that you'd know it, he looks much older than me. The war did that, to all the boys who came back."

"But when did he become your lover?"

"Lover! We're not 'lovers,'" she snorted.

"But you live together."

"A lover is a man you're intimate with, correct? With whom you share passionate trysts? You know the kind—I know the kind—and Ferny is not of that kind." She inhaled as violently as one could with a tiny tube of flaming paper. "But I let him into my bed about a year ago. It was fun, at first. At the very first. But then we moved to Paris."

"Not the city of love?"

"Ha! Hardly. I was last here with Peter—my fiancé—my late fiancé . . ." She sighed and stubbed out her cigarette. "We were here in 1915. He had two days' leave from the front and we spent it strolling the cafés. . . . I never wanted to return, but Ferny insisted. Said it would be good for me, would lay my ghosts to rest, all that sort of thing. I remember watching the moonlight splash over his skin as he told me these tender lies, the scars on his back like a map to redemption." She shrugged. "Of course, when we got here, he started going off on his jaunts, collecting notes, neglecting me."

"That must have hurt."

"Oh yes, I suppose. . . . It's been hard to care about anything since that little telegram in 1916. . . . But I came here to be with him and then was left alone, or else instructed—no, ordered!—to do this, fetch that, butter up this or that French duke or Spanish artist or Russian dancer while he flirted with every blonde this side of the Rhine."

"Did you gather information for him?"

"No!" She looked at me sharply and frowned. "But by gather information, you mean . . ."

"I mean, you butter up those people, then tell Ferny what they said, how they behaved."

She broke a tiny piece of croissant off and dipped it in her coffee. She looked at it, sighed, and put it down.

"Well, yes, I did that. That's gathering information, is it? If I'd known . . ."

"Ah, if you'd only known—the informant's lament." I gave her a wry smile. "But you have a chance to make amends now."

"How?"

"By talking to me."

"That's it?" She gave a half smile. "Revenge has never been so easy."

"More coffee?"

"Is it too early for cocktails?"

"Never." I grinned. She opened a desk, but instead of writing tools there was a secret drinks cabinet, full of shiny bottles and shinier glasses. She made us a drink she picked up in Italy over the summer and poured out all her frustrations with the gin. With only the merest encouraging *yes?* and *hmmm*, she talked on.

"We came here just after the summer, when all of Paris was heading home from their holidays. It had taken me months to contact Katya. We eventually had to find her in Florence—she introduced us to this negroni, made by Count Negroni himself, slumming as a bartender—to pick up the key and instructions about the maid and Katya's regular suppliers. You've been to Italy? Of course you have. You know how golden it can be. As though the war never happened, as though, since the Renaissance, the purpose of life was to eat figs on a Tuscan hilltop one day and splash in the sunlit Mediterranean the next. I almost convinced myself that I was in love with Ferny. It was certainly lust—he's rather . . . experienced. I was taken aback by how well he performed his role as lover." A secret smile stole over her face. She brought out a bowl of glacé fruit, clearly meant for the cocktails, and popped a cherry in her mouth.

"We took the slow train back to Paris, our own compartment, looking out over the Swiss mountains and Alsace farmland as we . . . took advantage of our solitude. The golden sensations of late August followed us all the way into the city, up the stairs, into the flat, and promptly vanished with a rain squall as we shut the door. A typical northern September. The heat had vanished.

"Ferny badgered me to introduce him to all of Katya's friends, all of my distant relatives, which was odd, as he already knew a number of them. His family was just as old and complicated as mine, although his relations are German—his mother's side is entirely Prussian. I remember my brother going on holiday with his family to Berlin, sending me postcards from Rügen Island about their long days of hiking. I remember it clearly, as that was the summer before the war broke out, I'd just become engaged, it was a blessed time . . . but yes, a lot of those Prussians left Germany as soon as they could—they're fleeing like the Russians—although not many have ended up in Paris, it's true. Too tricky. Ferny told me most of them had gone east, to Croatia and Montenegro and other far-flung parts of the Austrian empire. But still, these French aristocrats and Russian emigrés have always been around . . .

"But in the end, his badgering wasn't the problem. He came to the parties, where he ate and drank and charmed, he even danced with me once or twice. Then we'd come home and he'd interrogate me. Really, there is no other word for it. Who did I speak to, what did they say, what were they like. . . . Then it became more intense. I had to seek out particular people, I had to make them say certain things. . . . I told myself, over and over, of course it feels cruel, everything after Peter would feel less than loving, less than adequate . . . but it wasn't that. He played games. He would boss me about like I was a cadet in his command. He would set me riddles and punish me if I couldn't unriddle them. He would tell me who to talk to and what to say, and if I deviated, I would be punished. The punishments were always some form of humiliation." She stared at a Buddha on the shelf as she blinked back tears. I took a guess.

"Humiliation . . . you mean, like making you wait for hours in the rain, or cold, so that by the time he showed up your anger had been worn away?"

"Yes—more than once."

"And quizzing you like a child on something only he could know—some obscure point of history, perhaps?"

"Prewar German politics."

"And then admonishing you for not knowing?"

"Precisely—"

"Quoting Romantic poetry, but twisted and altered to make you sweat, rather than make you swoon? Something like *If by dull maids our English must be chained*—"

"Yes! How did you know?"

These were Fox's little games.

"I've met his type before." I raised my glass in a mock cheers, and we both downed a large gulp. "What did he do in the war?"

"The war? I never really asked. I didn't want to be reminded of all the men who saw the bullet with their name on it. . . ."

"What regiment was he in?"

"Oh, the . . . actually, I don't know. He's never mentioned it." She popped a piece of croissant in her mouth. "That's odd. All my brother's friends were always going on about the Buffs, or the Queen's Own—the regiments near our estate in Kent—and when a mate from his regiment popped into the Rose and Crown, my brother cried with joy, as though a lover had come home."

"But Ferny has never mentioned his regiment."

"Not that I remember."

"Has he met up with his mates from the war?"

"Just the one. A nasty piece of work. We met him here in Paris, actually, Eddy something. Tall, pale, blond hair perfectly in place, and a nasty habit of stubbing his cigarettes out on the carpet." She rubbed at a cigarette burn on the Oriental rug with her foot, her polished toe doing nothing to hide the circular singe in the pattern.

"I think he's a distant cousin of Ferny's or something. They were very pally—and I'm fairly sure he didn't have an eye for women. That isn't being nasty, no one liked him. He has this odd voice. High-pitched, clipped, sounded a bit . . . well, he sounded a bit German. He had a nasty smile and simpering manners. He had a repellent effect at parties, as though his handsome face was actually Dorian Gray. Women would come up to him with a drink and then draw back in disgust—or in tears."

"What did he say to them?"

"I don't know, but I know what he said to me. 'So how did you get Ferny in your pocket? He doesn't like brunettes. Was it a trick taught to you by the ladies of Piccadilly?' After I expressed my opinion on the waste of life in the war, he said, 'Oh, yes, that's what all the old men say. Tell me, can you form opinions of your own, or did Daddy not give you enough education?' That one made me quite angry."

"As it would."

"So I decided to follow them one evening." She smiled and made us more cocktails, double serves with a twist of lemon.

"They met just near the Rotonde. I half expected them to kiss, or embrace, but they just pulled down their hats and headed towards the river. They caught a cab—I followed, though it was almost impossible, I had to get out of one cab and grab another, as my first driver was rather too chatty. I needed discreet. Anyway, they wound up next to a factory, although it was so dark I couldn't see which one. Big warehouses loomed near the river, their effluent black against the stone. I saw them walk through the gates into a warehouse, including the cabdriver, which I thought odd. I couldn't go in, as it was brightly lit with gas, and even wearing my black uniform, I'd be noticeable. But I caught a peek as the cab drove past the gates. They had met with a group, both men and women, in tattered clothing. I spied a cripple and a woman with some knitting, and a couple of scruffy others. They shook hands, but I couldn't see any more. I had to get the driver to bring me home.

"Of course, I went straight into his room, but I didn't know what I was looking for. I wish I'd known about codes and all of that—how do you know, by the way?"

I didn't want to reveal the exact extent of my work for Fox.

"An old boyfriend"—Fox would be happy with that—"from the war."

"They have to be good for something, don't they? Well," Violet continued, "instead, I sat in here and smoked and tried to remember all the times he'd been away. He was away every Sunday night, until quite late, and always returned home exhausted and stinking of tobacco. This was his regular card night, he said, but growled when I asked what game he played. He went away once a month for a couple of nights and always came home with a present of Swiss chocolate or beautiful gloves—one of the few nice things he did—although he only gave these things to me on the condition that I didn't ask about them. I rummaged through his pockets once or twice, but there were no train tickets or foreign currency or even a packet of matches that might indicate where he'd been."

Ferny hadn't forgotten all of his training, then.

"But you accepted this."

"He wouldn't have told me anyway. And the gloves were really very nice, German made. I kept thinking, although he flirted with other women in front of me, he never came home smelling of another woman's perfume, or with his shirt less than perfectly neat, or even the tiniest smudge of lipstick on a collar or cuff. He came home stinking of tobacco, sometimes with grazes on his cheek, grumpy and growly like a tomcat, but never that blissful, wistful look of a sated lover. So either the blondes he saw were violent and cruel—"

"Entirely possible."

"Especially with some of the places one can patronize in Paris—or else he wasn't seeing other women."

"And your conclusion, as the woman who knows him best?"

"Neither women nor wine is his vice." She slugged back the last of her own vice, "Gambling, perhaps, but he is very meticulous and hates to lose. No, he has a 'something else'—mysterious, strange, and he's made it clear that I'm not to ask." In her excitement, she had polished off not only her own croissant but mine as well. I secretly cheered; I'd take her out to lunch when this was over.

"I started recording his trips in a little notebook—I don't know why, I think I just wanted to know more clearly, you know, to see it all written down—all the times he was away, how he was when he returned."

"You were spying on him." I couldn't help a smile.

"No! Oh . . . yes, I suppose I was. But not for anyone. . . ."

"Except me." I grinned. "That little notebook is just what I need."

She raised her eyebrow and returned my grin. "I'm not useless after all," she said as she went to the bookshelf. She returned with a slim volume that had *The Bachelor Girl's Guide to Everything* on the spine. Instead of a how-to guide for soon-to-be flappers, however, inside was a list of times, dates, and observations.

"Far from it." I kissed her hand and she barked a laugh. "This is beautiful."

"Well, I'm very flattered—"

"And you know what else is beautiful? A set lunch at the Rotonde. My shout."

"If you insist." She went to grab her handbag. Something had dropped away—her sharp edges, the bitter taste of her black clothing—and she had more color in her cheeks. Clearly her secrets, and her lover, had been draining her of energy. She'd unloaded her secrets and I was about to relieve her of her lover.

◈

"Kiki! It's been so long! Where have you been?" North was effusive as usual. She had a cigarette in one hand and a fizzy pink concoction in the other, which she waved around as she kissed me on both cheeks.

"Eating with strangers and sleeping under the stars." I pulled Violet in. "This is Violet. She's a spy."

"A spy!" North gasped, her Californian blue eyes wide. "Who for?"

Violet looked at me and raised her eyebrows. I winked.

"If I told you, I'd have to kill you," she said. "And if I don't get a drink—"

"You'll have to kill everyone," I finished. "Another negroni?"

"No, something a bit simpler this time—just champagne," she said with a wave, as North pulled her towards a table. They both looked as tipsy as each other; she'd be in good company. I hoped, even, that Violet might make some desperately needed new friends, as North was nothing if not friendly.

I ordered Violet the set lunch and champagne—a bottle, just to make sure—and scanned the café. North was lunching with some Americans I didn't know, all of them high on cheap wine and Paris, allowing Violet to play up her aristocratic background. Djuna Barnes was in a corner by herself, although I knew from past encounters that she preferred it that way. Most of the artists I knew didn't come out until dusk, when the work had to finish as the light was gone. This lunchtime it was mostly tourists and bureaucrats. And Henri, behind the bar. He beckoned to me.

"Mademoiselle." He bowed his head. "I have a message for you."

"Oh," I sighed. "Thank you."

"Please, do not thank me." With a very serious face, he handed me a little slip of paper.

"This isn't his handwriting."

"I don't know, mademoiselle. It was delivered, in person, this morning."

"By whom?"

"A man, very large, with a crushed nose and black eyes. I did not recognize him, but his accent, I think he is English."

"What does he have over you?" Henri stared at my question, "Fox—what does he know? How can he play with you like a puppet?"

Henri looked down and blushed.

"My brother," he almost whispered. "He could not . . . he ran away. From Verdun. He was found by a British surgeon—"

"Fox."

"*Oui*, mademoiselle. His secret safe in return for . . ."

"For?"

Henri shrugged. "Whatever he wishes."

I reached out and squeezed Henri's hand, almost squeezing a tear or two from him.

I ordered a coffee and opened the note as calmly as I could. He'd already sent a telegram today—what more could he possibly have to say?

Ever since she put on a uniform
I have just one heart for just one girl
Dream on, little soldier boy?
A man is only a man!
Why don't you give us a chance?
I'll take you back to London

You'll send him back to London
Goodbye, France!
He's on his way to Germany
With Hausmann's Brownshirt Band

F to V

This was the note that Bertie had given me a few days ago, of titles of Irving Berlin songs. But the titles had been inverted and changed. I didn't have time to take this note home and think about it, I had to decipher it immediately.

The first section read, for all the world, like a love note. I could hardly believe it. Was this another game? I couldn't help but think of his photo of me and Tom, of Fox's telegram *Darkling I listen*, of his soft voice on the telephone. I hadn't lied when I told Bertie that I didn't think Fox knew what love was. No, it had to be another game, a way to soften me, to make me as dependent on him as I had been during the war. Wasn't that how it worked—when someone professed their love, you thought of them tenderly, you didn't want to hurt their feelings, you took pains to comfort them—surely this must be his aim. He didn't want love, he only wanted power. Surely.

I ordered some *frites* and a beer for sustenance and skipped quickly to the second section. "Hausmann"—this stood out like it was written in lights. This line tied together what Tom had said on the telephone, what

Martin had said—Hausmann wasn't just involved with the Brownshirts, he was some kind of Brownshirt leader. But how could that be, when Hausmann had ties to Luc and Marie's Communist revolutionaries? They were opposite sides of politics. If Fern was the mole, what on earth was he doing with those revolutionaries, and Picasso's painting, and a Brownshirt Hausmann? And why would Fox choose to give me this information now? Unless the clue was "He's on his way to Germany"—was Fern leaving for Germany soon, today, now? How on earth could I know?

"Him"—this must the mole—I knew he had to go back to London, so perhaps Fox meant with the Englishman that Henri described, with the battered face. I scanned the restaurant again for a large black-eyed man. No one watched me; no man sat in a corner, ready to nod in acknowledgment of my glance. But it had to come, and soon; there would be no other reason for a hand-delivered note. There was still no drop-off date or place mentioned. I'd have to rely on Tom for that.

I dipped my *frites* into the mayonnaise and tomato sauce, Belgian-style, that Henri had provided. Violet had enough alcohol and friends to take care of her; I could slip away to work. I felt for the coded notebook in my pocket, as I left my money on the table and slipped out the door. I needed to decipher the code, to find out what Fern had planned for me, for Luc and Marie, for tonight or tomorrow, as I was sure that whatever it was would happen soon.

The gray sky had turned to drizzle, leaving droplets on my hat and coat. I checked my watch; it was almost three, I'd have to go straight to the station to meet Bertie. He would surely help me to decipher the notebook. I couldn't help it, but I looked over my shoulder all the way to Gare du Nord.

"KITTEN ON THE KEYS"

Bertie's pale face, surrounded by his camel cashmere coat, was a beacon in the dark steel of the station platform. He looked as though all the industrial grit of Gare du Nord couldn't touch the perfect press of his lapel, hat brim, or swish of scarf.

"Kiki! In trousers! My God, have all my dreams come true?"

"It's a dream to see you, Bertie. And how do you manage to look so fresh? Surely you didn't sleep before you jumped on the train."

"No, I slept all the way here instead. Have you put the champagne on ice?"

"You'll have to put that idea on ice. I've only just got over my lunch-time cocktails."

"But how could you start the party without me?"

"It didn't, those cocktails were work. As is this." I let the notebook peek out of the inside pocket of my coat. Bertie peered at the title and gave me a funny look.

"A book of poetry?"

"A book of Keats."

"Oh!" His eyes mimicked the perfect O of his lips. I swallowed a smile.

"Fox and Keats—"

"Not so loud!" I took his arm and held him close as we walked towards the taxi rank. He must have spent last night scrubbing off ink and Soho dirt, as even the skin on his hands looked fresh.

"Well, you know," he said, "if we're going to work, we still need to lubricate the old brain cogs a bit. Coffee with cognac?"

"And cake."

"And biscuits."

"And finger sandwiches."

"And pots and pots of tea."

"And then more coffee . . ."

I filled in all the details as soon as we closed the door to his room. The Ritz wouldn't serve us a high tea outside of the dining room, but the staff were prepared to bring up chocolate éclairs, pistachio macarons, plain butter biscuits, chocolate *mendiants*, mille-feuille, sliced baguette with little bowls of butter, jam, and pâté and a particularly stinky blue cheese, along with a pot of coffee and a pot of black tea, to which Bertie added a little bottle of cognac from the bar downstairs. The feast almost overflowed the table. We had to prop the book against the teapot so that we could keep working amid the treats.

"What am I reading for again?"

"You're reading for my name, Bertie, written like this." I wrote out the coded name for him—IKIK UBTTNO.

"Shouldn't you—"

"I'm looking for the time and place of his next meeting."

Bertie read the left-hand pages and I read the right. The initial code was simple, just substituted letters, but Fern had put a code within that. This line:

YCLCPOS & IVGRNI OSDLEISR TA T IREVR

read *Cyclops and Virgin soldiers at the river*. He had more lines like that:

YCLCPOS & OGSDNO IMSSOIN CAECTPDE F OGSDADY

that read *Cyclops and Godson mission accepted for Godsday*. It was clear that Cyclops and Godson were code names. More confusing were lines such as:

EBRA   ROEDSR   ERECVIDE   5230   OCPMELET   1040
OSDLEISR   I   LPCAE

that translated as *Bear orders received 2503 complete 0104 soldiers in place*. I'd written these lines on the hotel paper when Bertie peeked over my shoulder.

"Kiki, you know how I like to boast about being really quite good at the cryptic crossword. . . ."

"Yes?"

"Well, what I mean is that I'm the Fleet Street champion."

"Self-crowned or won in a Soho backstreet battle?"

"They held a tournament last year—"

"For fun?"

"For a war orphans charity, but yes, it's a wordsmith's idea of fun. It was held over the course of an entire week. All the best crossword writers put in their most difficult clues. The winner was the first, all correct, to the final clue." He shrugged in faux modesty.

"What did you win?"

"Just glory, sweet pea."

"No champagne?"

"The jealousy of the hard-news reporters and their editors' grudging respect was enough for me." He winked. "As was the crate of Drambuie that the sponsor provided. Bought me all sorts of gossip in the wee hours." He took the paper as I reached for more baguette with cheese. He muttered the names to himself, turning them in his mouth, probing them for their secrets, as I poured us both a cup of tea and perched half a biscuit in each saucer.

"They must be code names, Bertie."

"Cyclops—someone with myopic vision? With severe prejudice?"

"Or one eye— Oh! One-Eyed Luc!"

"Is that a new cabaret act?"

"And Virgin—that must be Marie! And Godsday—"

"Clearly Sunday. Although that's more of a quick crossword clue."

"It's also tomorrow."

"We'd better work quickly, then." Bertie gave me a serious look, then nodded, "Godson, son of God, Jesus, Hey-sus . . ." He unpacked the words, the light through the window now bright, now streaked with rain.

I shrugged. "I've only met Luc and Marie. And Fern, of course."

Bertie sliced the chocolate éclair and popped a squishy segment in his mouth, his thinking frown crinkling his face.

"Maybe the names inform each other—Bear . . . a Russian?"

"There's a Russian connection. I'm fairly sure that Luc and Marie are Communist revolutionaries—but with links to Germany . . . so Bear could be a Berliner—you know, after the Berlin coat of arms."

"Maybe it's a teddy bear," he joked, but then he went pale and almost dropped his cup.

"Bertie, we're dropping hints, not crockery."

"Teddy, my Teddy—"

"Edward Houseman?"

"Yes. He's— Did I tell you? No. I ran into one of his friends last night—cronies, really, they hang off his every word—and they said he'd taken a job with his uncle's firm, reconstructing Saxony."

"He's in Germany!"

"Has been for weeks. No wonder I hadn't heard from him. But I didn't think he needed work, much less wanted it."

"What type of firm does his uncle have?"

"They used to manufacture arms."

"Hell's bells—"

"And British-made shells. That was during the war, of course. Now they manufacture steel bits and bobs, for building." He exchanged his cup for a cigarette, unable to keep still even after he lit it, cutting the mille-feuille into messy little pieces, moving to the window to push the brocade curtain further aside.

"Teddy told you this?"

"Oh no," he snorted. "When he's with me, he acts like a regular party boy, pretty and charming and vain."

"Well, you've been with worse . . ."

"Am I bitter? Am I jealous, you ask? I've been lied to, Kiki darling." He poured a slug of cognac into his cup, unadulterated by coffee. "And not just the ordinary lies of a promiscuous boy. I expected those. No, he's someone fundamentally different to who he said he was. A businessman! A cowboy in the wild west of the Weimar Republic."

He gulped the cognac and winced. The plush carpet and brocade contrasted sharply with Bertie's spiky sentences.

"I found out about the Houseman firm myself, with a little journalistic digging—I quite enjoyed it, by the way, maybe I missed my calling—"

"Not when you drink cognac like that."

"Rubbish—have you seen those newsmen drink? It's my pass into the press club." He poured himself some more. "Anyway, through their war contracts, the Housemans' wealth went from substantial to obscene. After bombing the blighters they're now offering to rebuild—for a hefty fee—and, to make it happen, have used distant family still in Germany. Oh yes, did you know that Teddy's family was originally German?"

"You told me."

"The clerk I took out for drinks waxed lyrical about the firm's predatory antics. I almost got bored with all that praise. I don't know what Teddy is up to, but whatever it is, he's up to it in Germany."

"And maybe France."

Bertie stared at me so fiercely it was almost a glare.

"And maybe Paris." I pointed out another Bear sentence. "'Bear Nord

2040.' Something tells me that this means, 'Teddy at Gare du Nord on April second.' Was Teddy, perhaps, AWOL from London on the second?"

Bertie looked stunned as he sat back down with a thud. He was so still that, in his camel-check suit, he looked like part of the furnishings. I squeezed the nearest part of him to me, his knee, to bring him back to life. I knew how nauseating it felt when your world flipped upside down, the violence of one piece of information. I lit a cigarette and stuck it in Bertie's confused face. He smiled, but I felt bad. I'd had an idea, and if I was right, Bertie was in for an even bigger shock.

I handed him the group photo that Fox had sent me.

"Bertie, tell me—who do you recognize in this photo?"

"Oh, here's a little cardboard memory. Well, first off, there's my favorite nurse-gossip-reporter-spy. Is that— Yes, it's Fox, isn't it? Don't know him, or him; lovely jawline, wish I knew him, but no idea . . . oh." Bertie stopped, cigarette halfway to his mouth, his mobile expression arrested. His still face underwent a gradual change: the bubbly life leeched from it, his eyes sank back into their sockets, and his mobile mouth settled into a thin, pale line. A blank face that hid the activity within. A mask that could hide grief, anger, jealousy, love, fear, or joy equally well.

"That's Teddy, isn't it?"

"I've never seen him in uniform. It suits him."

"The man next to Teddy is Hugh Fernly-Whiting, who we also know as Fern. He's the mole."

"You worked out the clues." A smile struggled through the mask of his face.

"Not all of them. But with what I know, we should be able to unlock the rest."

"We?" His mask broke then, an almost-tear appearing in the cracks.

"Yes, we, Bertie." I took his face in my hands and kissed him. "Friends in need and all that."

He pulled me into a big hug, a single suppressed sob shuddering through his skinny frame. It hurt, the passion of that sob, the strength used to rein it in, and I had to think of something else in order not to cry myself. So I thought of pockets—the pocket Bertie slipped the photo into, the big pockets in my great coat, how I wished women's clothing included pockets, as then I could stop pinning emergency money to my knickers. Pockets and heartbreak; the juxtaposition was too absurd for tears.

"Right," he said with a big intake of breath. "Light me another Gauloises and let's get cracking."

"Here are Fox's messages." I put a cigarette in his mouth and placed the messages on the floor so we could see all of them together. We sat, crossed-legged like school children, in front of them. Bertie read them out.

"'In some melodious plot of beechen green, with shadows numberless, there is a mole'—well, that's obvious—'The mole quite forgets the weariness, the fever, and the fret, where men sit and hear each other groan, where youth grows pale and dies.' What does that refer to?"

"The war. Fern is an ex-Fox cub."

"Right. 'More than ever seems it rich to die, not for the warm south, but for the lands forlorn. Tender is the night, and he cannot see what flowers are at his feet. His plaintive anthem fades, his high requiem becomes a sod. The murmurous haunt of flies treads him down.' This is really quite morbid, isn't it? I'd never noticed that about Keats before. 'The faery lands are too forlorn, and the word will toll him back from thee to my sole self'—which word is *the* word?"

"My word to Fox—but I think I've already given it."

"And is that word *yes, no,* or *maybe?*"

"I say *no,* but somehow that's not the word he hears." I raised my eyebrows. "I'm sure that the lands forlorn are Germany—"

"Aren't they though—?"

"But the 'high requiem,' the 'plaintive anthem'—are they something to do with the new tune that Fern's whistling? If so, why is it both a requiem and an anthem?"

"Sounds like 'God Save the King' sung before we went over the top."

"Oh! Yes—nationalism and the war and all the glorious dead. Yes, that would work—and perhaps also something to do with the Berlin song titles?"

"Let's see." He picked up one of Fox's notes. "'Ever since I put on a uniform, I have just one heart for just one boy'—well, I can relate to that—'Dream on, little soldier boy'—that cuts to the quick— Wait, when did you get these again?"

"After my first telephone call with Fox, at the Rotonde."

"Of course! I delivered this little message, didn't I? 'We're on our way to France / Why don't they give us a chance?/ Goodbye, France / I'll take you back to Germany/ A man is only a man / With Alexander's Ragtime Band.' Who's Alexander?"

"No one. That just shows that they're Irving Berlin songs, which is the key to the code—Berlin, Germany—"

"And the clues link France with Germany, yes?"

"If they don't, then I'm not playing ragtime. But they must, because in the search for Pablo's painting—"

"Just Pablo now, is it?"

"It was always Pablo, but rarely 'just' Pablo—it was often Pablo 'as well.'" Bertie laughed. I continued, "But in the search for his painting I was led back to Fern and Violet. The name Hausmann comes up again and again. As do the Brownshirts in Germany."

"What, those violent veterans in lederhosen and tin hats?"

"They are connected to all the rest of this business. Here." I laid out the message that I'd received this morning. "But I just have so many questions. Is Hausmann a Brownshirt or a Communist strike leader? If Fern is a double agent for underground German thugs—which the clues strongly suggest—why is he involved with the Communists? And why, after fighting for Britain, are either of them making trouble here in France?"

"Who are the flies with their murmurous haunt?"

"Exactly! I have some ideas but they seem so far-fetched. . . . And how is Pablo's stolen painting mixed up in this? I'm hoping this notebook will tell us."

"What's this part of the message? 'Ever since she put on a uniform . . .'"

"Oh, that." I waved it away. "That's Fox being mischievous. Or devious. Or even downright dangerous. I don't know." I shrugged and moved away to the table for some more food. Bertie raised an eyebrow and looked at me expectantly.

"Don't, Bertie darling." I wished my voice wouldn't wobble. I popped a chocolate thingy in my mouth, whole, so I wouldn't have to speak. When I finally turned around, his face had a soft expression and he patted the floor beside him.

"Then let's work," he said, as tenderly as if he'd said *I love you.*

We came across my name UBTTNO more and more. Fern had been following me but it didn't say why. Did he know that I'd come from Fox? Was it just lust and a spy's instinct?

"Ooh, that's me!"

"Of course it is, Bertie. He was my shadow when you were my sun."

"A God-sun? Sun-god, Apollo . . . that's not right. . . ."

My name was often reduced to either Button or KB. But one line stuck out:

UBTTNO ON ILKN EBRA ISELISA KF. NOYL ILKN IPACSSO. IMINAML HTERTA RPCOEED A OCED RGEEN

It read as *Button no link Bear Silesia FK. Only link Picasso. Minimal threat proceed as code green.*

"'Only link Picasso' . . . Fern is connected to the theft of Pablo's painting. This is proof!"

"What's code green?"

"It's not Fox terminology. With Fox's orders, you were either successful or dead."

"You were clearly always successful." Bertie looked at me with new admiration. "No wonder your old boss wants you back."

"Humph." I didn't want to think about Fox's intentions just now. "What about this first part—I have no link to the Bear character—Teddy bear?"

"Oh God, Kiki, no, I could hardly bear it."

"Ha! But what about this part—Silesia or FK? In Silesia, from Silesia? What's FK?"

"The Freikorps. Fern knows you're not connected to them, Kiki."

"So he assumes I'm no threat."

"More fool him. But Silesia—that's interesting."

"Too interesting."

We kept reading. Silesia came up often, that northeastern section of Germany that was trying so hard to be Poland. Bear was in Silesia with the Freikorps, for a series of meetings or transactions, though it was hard to tell which.

"What about this?" Bertie pointed to a line:

XEHCNAEG ASUTDRYA MP IRHGT ABKN

"It reads *Exchange Saturday PM Right Bank*."

"Do you have a party on the Right Bank tonight, Kiki?"

"I . . ." I could hardly think of anything but this mission. "Yes . . . you know, I think I do! Something held in honor of yet another exiled Russian prince. The invitation's at home."

"Well then . . ." Bertie leaned back with a satisfied smile. My head buzzed with coffee and sugar as I looked at the notes on the floor, covered in ash and crumbs. The street sounds came through the open window, curled around the lampshades and into our hair.

"Is that it? That there'll be an exchange tonight? Have we just solved the riddle?"

"We'll soon find out. Have you got your handcuffs ready?"

"I might have to solicit for them. Tom is supposed to tell me the drop-off point and time—"

"He works for Fox too?"

"Only as much as you do. But a Fox cub delivered this latest message—I think he's meant to be my . . ."

"Chauffeur?"

"Corpse carrier."

"Jesus Christ, Kiki—"

"Not literally! I only deal with metaphoric deaths now—oh! 'Jesus Christ!'"

"What about him?"

"Jesus Christ, JC—perhaps someone with the initials JC is Godson?"

"James Christopher? Jeremy Clarence? Jellicoe Connaught?"

"Jean-Claude." I couldn't help but click my fingers—*eureka!*—as Céline's face as she mentioned her son popped into my mind.

"Who's Jean-Claude?"

"The link between Fern and Pablo, that's who."

"I FOUND A ROSE IN THE DEVIL'S GARDEN"

I put on my most daring dress. It was golden, a silk shift that hugged every curve until it fluted out around the knees. The neckline dived, the back line headed for hell, both decorated by sparkling beads that swirled away from the seam and down to the hem. A wide sash hugged my hips and its beaded fringe whispered to my knees. It barely stayed on my shoulders and only just covered my suspender belt and knickers. I'd bought new shoes to match the dress, golden satin heels embroidered with flowers and leaves. I twisted my waves into curls around my face; my mouth a succulent red and my eyes dark with mascara. I wound my opera cape around me and headed out into the night.

I had arranged to meet Bertie outside the opera house, as the party was around the corner. The drizzle of the day had stopped and the city felt fresh and crisp. There was a chill to the night, just the right amount to up the drinking and start the dancing, just the right amount to wrap a certain Fern in my opera cloak and sneak him out to . . . But as I clipped along in my satin shoes, I had to ask myself, *Sneak him out to where? Lure him to what?* Unless the Fox cub was at the party, I didn't know what to do with Fern once I had him. Simply arrange to meet him tomorrow, once I knew the drop-off place? In these final moments, it seemed unwise to be caught without a plan.

Bertie stood in the most exquisite white-tie ensemble. His tails were perfectly pressed, his bow tie as precise as a butterfly, every crease sharp. His top hat sat at a rakish angle, so as he leaned against a column and smoked, he was the picture of insouciance.

"Look at you, Bertie! You'd have had no idea your heart was broken this afternoon."

"The war taught me many things, my darling," he said as he kissed me and gave me his cigarette. "How to keep a clear head before a battle is one. How best to follow Kiki is another."

"You're an expert at both." I smiled. He'd given me a Woodbine brought with him from London. It smelled of men—fear, danger, estaminets at midnight—it smelled of the war. He knew it too, as we watched the smoke curl in its thin line towards the stars.

"I've had enough practice. Now"—he lit his own cigarette—"fill me in on what I should know and who I should do."

"And how."

He tucked my arm close into his as we swam in and out of the pools of lamplight to the party.

The apartment was so large it had its own ballroom. A small ballroom, with only a modest chandelier, but a ballroom nonetheless. It had been bought before the war, long before the Russian revolution, when the owner's grandfather could afford a Paris home for his successive mistresses and their children. The wooden floor gleamed, the ceiling danced with a fresco of nymphs and goddesses, and the large windows welcomed the moon. My cynicism evaporated with Bertie's sigh of "Jesus wept! Old-world splendor, this!" If I hadn't had to work, I would've danced and drunk and debated soulfully with any exiled prince or princess who could spare the time.

As it was, I scanned the room for Fern and Violet. The butler had introduced us as Miss Button and Captain Browne, but only the hostess came forward to greet us, an old dame with jewels that sank into her bosom. Princess Drubetskaya held herself regally, her magnanimity towards unfortunate compatriots extending to the likes of rich reporters and old soldiers.

"Next month we will have a fête for the children," she said in too-perfect French. "A May ball to rival the Bolsheviks' disgusting May Day parades. Tell that to your readers."

"A little unpaid advertising?" Bertie asked.

"I would never be so vulgar," sniffed the princess. "But those who wish to come deserve to know. It's for the children."

"Which children?" I asked, for my sins, as I was treated to a long story of train escapes, dolls stuffed with diamonds, titles on the heads of babes as parental limbs were caught in the claws of the dastardly Reds. Bertie slipped off to find champagne and, if possible, a handsome waiter. Eventually more guests arrived, the princess had duties, and I was left with a strange sympathy for some poor little rich kids floating around Paris.

There was no sign of either Fern or Violet, though Violet seemed related to everyone and I was sure that she would turn up eventually. A tall woman, with a fiercely beautiful face and proud bearing, caught my glance. She smiled like the Cheshire cat as she came towards me with two glasses of champagne.

"You're not Russian," she said as she handed me a glass. Her eyes never left mine; it was exciting and unnerving.

"How can you tell?"

"One can always tell," she said. "But your accent confirms it. Where did you spring from? Tell me everything."

She stood slightly too close to me and stared at me as she drank her champagne. I answered her, polite and bubbly in my gossip-reporter guise, but her flirtatious command sounded perilously close to an order—and I didn't like to be ordered. But with her blond hair and blue eyes, it was as though I looked in a magic mirror. Her magnetic charisma, her authority, the way she almost stared at me, was the female version of Fox. I didn't need two of them in my life, but a woman with this much forbidding confidence intrigued me.

"I'm Tamara." She procured us more champagne from a passing tray. "Tamara de Lempicka, for when you have your portrait painted."

"I've been warned about you."

"Excellent—"

"I haven't seen you around Montparnasse."

"You will. Look out for me. Yes, I will paint your portrait." She tucked my hair behind my ear and slipped a strap off my shoulder, lightly holding my arm to inspect me. Now she really did remind me of Fox. I couldn't help it, my chin tilted up in defiance of her overfamiliar touch, and she laughed.

"Oh yes, very good."

I had to swallow my instinct to lash out. "You're an artist and an aristocrat."

"Someone must support the family now that we've sold our jewels. My husband . . . is good for what he trained for."

"Which is?"

"Nothing." She took a little spoon heaped with caviar from a waiter. "This party reminds me of when I met him. Except then, I was a starry-eyed debutante who knew nothing of what she really wanted." She ate the caviar then, keeping the spoon in her mouth as she looked at me. I couldn't help it; I laughed at her brazen flirting.

She smiled. "I wondered when you might relax."

"I wondered when you might let me. You have quite a stare."

"It's seductive."

"If you say so."

"I don't need to say so, I know so." She raised an eyebrow. "Are you trying to tell me that I'm wrong?" Her eyebrow was haughty, her huge blue eyes demanding. The silver satin of her dress made her skin shimmer with danger. Her challenge was so imperious, I could easily see how she would bowl people over.

"When will you model for me?"

"I model for Picasso at the moment."

"Really? Since when? I haven't heard of you."

"Maybe when he's finished my painting." I shrugged.

As she looked at me, an extraordinary range of emotions flashed over her face—shock, anger, deviousness, sadness, a eureka, and finally a smile. She was nettled that her usual techniques had failed but she refused defeat. I made a note to say hello next time I saw her in a café. I didn't think we could be friends, but she would certainly be interesting. Maybe even useful.

"Yes, maybe *after* Picasso. André would like that—André Lhote, my mentor."

"Oh yes?" I knew who he was, of course, but it was more fun to feign ignorance.

"Yes." But she was clearly bored of not getting her own way. She turned, pinching her nose and sniffing, and excused herself.

I looked around. There was still no sign of either Fern or Violet, which was odd—weren't they everywhere that one could find free food and valuable art? Bertie gave me a little cheers with his glass from across the room. He had settled himself in with a group of handsome young men, talking heaven knows what in his terrible French. I could see his hands dance as he spoke to the group, a satisfied smile hiding in his face as they punctuated his story with laughter.

"Mademoiselle Kiki." A deep voice spoke into my ear. I whipped around to find Lazarev, champagne glass in one hand, pickled herring in the other.

"Arkady Nikolaievitch! Of course you'd be here. Now, who should I speak to? Will there be dancing? Is all the vodka chilled? How is one supposed to drink it?"

"Women aren't." He laughed. "You live on champagne. The men, however, are bound to drink the little tumblers at every toast. That usually begins after the dancing, which, if those violin cases are a clue, is about to begin."

A string quartet, in their black-tie attire and serious mustaches, was in

the corner tuning and setting up. At a nod from the cellist, the princess
called forth all the couples for an opening waltz. Young men and old
women, in their frayed finery, began to swirl around the floor. The hubbub
increased, champagne and caviar circled the edge of the dancing pairs.
The chandelier winked at the diamonds that glinted on rings, combs, and
cuff links. Highly polished shoes reflected laughing faces, and the dancers'
attitudes mimicked the ceiling nymphs. Even a seasoned cynic like myself
felt the magic, as I was transported to a world of snowy intrigue in the
Saint Petersburg court. If this was a preview of the May ball, then after
my column was printed the princess may well have a number of my
London readers join the party.

Lazarev watched my delight with amusement. On the third song he
finished his glass, bowed, and held out his hand.

"Would you honor me with this dance, mademoiselle?"

He was as graceful on the dance floor as in the café. This was a far
cry from the frenetic jazz parties I'd attended lately. I had to recall all my
dancing lessons from school, with Miss Piggott tapping the floor with her cane
and yelling instructions from beside the piano. After a few fumbling steps, I
remembered how to follow, and Lazarev's lead let us glide across the floor.

"This is wonderful!"

"It was like this all the time when I was a child"—Lazarev smiled—"except there were many more young people. They took charge of the dance
floor as the old women spun their gossip in the corners. Now, alas, all
those who have legs to dance, must."

The song ended and he bowed.

"I insist on another," he said, with a glint in his eye.

"Well, if you *insist* . . ."

"Have you heard from the magnificent Pablo?" he asked. His expression was unreadable as we whirled around.

"Not recently," I hedged. "Why?"

"I heard some . . . fuss has been made over the painting. By darling

Olga Stepanovna." He looked me right in the eye as he twirled me. "I heard that I couldn't get hold of the painting, even if I wanted to."

He waited for an answer. I didn't want to break Pablo's confidence, but Lazarev could be a good source of information.

"I think . . . there will be an exchange tonight. I thought it would be here, but I can't see Violet and Hugh—"

"The British couple? I should think not! The princess hates them."

"Why?"

"They're too German."

"Too German? How are they German at all?"

"The man—the one with the limp and scar, yes?—has been seen with the former German ambassador's nephew. It isn't clear why the ambassador's nephew has come back to Paris, as no Frenchman would willingly be seen with him. He runs around with some skulking old soldiers from Alsace, who can't marry their French ways to their German tongues. Your Englishman is probably with them now, at the only place that will serve Germans in this city."

"Where is that?"

"It's near the stock exchange. A tiny bar called, naturally, the Exchange. I only know it to avoid it. Wait, mademoiselle, won't you try the herring? The vodka toasts have begun. . . ."

But I couldn't wait. I pulled Bertie away from the pretty princeling he'd found and into the street.

"It's isn't *an exchange* that Fern is making tonight—he's *at* the Exchange."

"Kiki, slow down—"

"We can't! We have to run. He may have left!"

"Wait— What— Why wasn't he at the party?"

"Because the Russians know that he's German—they *know* it—and they hate him for it. He hasn't been as discreet as he assumes—"

"Kiki, stop, you're getting puddle splashes on your dress—I'm hailing a taxi."

It took half an hour of winding around the lanes before we saw the tiny sign to the Exchange. It was down a set of rickety stairs, barely lit, that turned into a dark, smoky room. The hum of voices stilled as we clattered into the bar, and I mentally cursed our hurry and my startling golden dress. Bertie held my waist and whispered in my ear, "There once was a man from Nantucket," every dirty version he could think of, until the hum slowly returned. We groped our way to the bar through the miasma and took the only spirit they had left.

"Oh dear"—Bertie looked into his glass—"OP rum. I can't seem to drink it without ending up under a sailor."

"If you can end up under a soldier—a German soldier at that—all the better."

We clinked our glasses and pretended to be a clandestine couple. It must have worked, as not a single patron looked at us again; it was hard even to get the barman to serve us a second drink.

"You know, Kiki, I've been in trenches that are cozier than this."

"And I've seen battlefields that are friendlier. Hugh Fernly-Whiting isn't here."

But he had been. The barman looked at us like we were swindlers when I asked, not twitching a muscle when I gave him my best smile—he couldn't possibly be French. He answered in gruff tones that Fern had been there earlier but wouldn't say when or with whom. He just topped up our rum with a stingy finger and turned around to the telephone behind the bar.

"Since when do dive joints have telephones? There's only a handful of outside lines at the Ritz!" Bertie buried his observation in his glass.

"The floor's sticky, the bar's understocked, and the patrons haven't got a spare two sous between them—who paid to have it put in?"

"Shall we leave?" Bertie gulped his drink. "Before the rum kicks in?"

"Before something kicks in."

As I headed for the stairs, the barman's stare made the skin on the back of my neck tingle. We had headed down a dead end and I wanted to get away before "dead" and "end" became more than just metaphor. The stairs were as noisy going up as going down, creaking and clanging. If anyone was waiting for us at the top, they'd hear us coming.

Which they did. As soon as I stepped out from behind the heavy door a gloved hand slapped me hard across the face as another grabbed my arm. I was so shocked I didn't scream, but I heard Bertie yell behind me. I twisted around to see him being clubbed over the head by a man in a carnival mask.

"Ber—" But I choked on my call as the gloved hand clenched over my mouth, another twisted my arm behind my back, and both hands dragged me down the alley towards a waiting car. I couldn't see who had hold of me, but the gloved hands were wiry and very strong. The masked man ran past us—Bertie must be unconscious, or worse—to open the doors and start the engine. It was a Paris taxi, black and anonymous, the back covered, the front open, no glass in the window by the driver.

The hands shoved me in the back seat, face-first. I could feel something heavy on my back—a knee, maybe?—holding me down as my hands were tied together roughly and, I suspected, inexpertly as I twisted and yelled in French, English, Italian, even German, anything to grab attention. The hands dragged my head back and tied a scarf too tightly over my mouth, before shoving me by the bum into the taxi and climbing in after me.

The taxi rattled down the alley, its mirrors almost scraping the wall, and out into the bright, wide boulevard. Not that the lights mattered, they didn't reach me where I writhed in the back seat, and even if they had, no pedestrian would take a proper look to see what was really happening— the French could sometimes be too discreet. I had half twisted around when my attacker grabbed me and turned me so that I lay on the seat, my legs over his, held in place by his strong, thin hands.

He sneered—his mouth was the only thing I could see beneath his mask. I could finally get a good look at him. Like the driver, he was dressed all in black. He wore a mask from the Venice Carnival, black with a long beak and teardrop eyes. The mask was attached to a sock that fitted neatly over his head. He grabbed my gag and pulled it down, hurting my lips and jaw as he did. He held my thighs, one in each hand, so I couldn't move my body properly. The taxi drove from one wide boulevard into another, the lights and their safety tantalizingly close.

"You're right," my attacker said. He was French, but his accent wasn't one that I recognized.

"I know I am," said the driver. He spoke French too but wasn't—his accent was definitely English. Who were they?

"She's a feisty one though," said my attacker. "This should be fun."

"There's plenty of time."

"But why wait? She's ready." He ran his hands along my legs.

"Let me go!" I struggled. "Help!" But my yell was stopped with another fierce slap. It stung, and I hated that I could taste blood in my mouth and feel tears in my eyes.

"Now, now, none of that," he said. "We have a little bargain for you."

"You'll get nothing." I spat blood at him, but he laughed even as he flinched.

"Oh, I think we will," he said, "and you'll be glad to give it." He pinched my legs, hard twisty pinches that left red welts on my skin. It hurt, but more, it was humiliating, the way I couldn't help but jump with every touch, the way he smiled wider every time I did. The taxi stood at the roundabout, waiting to go through. Pedestrians smiled and waved at the masked driver, who waved back.

"You're going to tell us who you work for—"

"And why—" cut in the driver.

"And in return, we won't kill you."

"No deal," I said. I wasn't brave; I was just reckless. I should've been more calculating, as my fighting words received their due and he slapped me again, harder this time, so pain flashed through my head, leaving the world high-pitched and ringing.

"Don't be silly," he said. "Now, who do you work for?"

"Is it Fox?" asked the driver. I was still.

"You got her attention there."

"Well?" The driver was tense, his hand clutched the wheel and he had to stop himself from turning around to look at us. He could have easily—my attacker was behind him and I was sprawled out on the back seat, in easy viewing distance—so why didn't he turn? I checked—there wasn't much traffic—

"You can talk to us here and get this over with, or you can come with us to the little farmhouse owned by . . . who again?"

"My lover's cousin, or some such," growled the driver. I twisted around to try to find a street sign or a landmark, though I didn't need to—we were driving out of Paris. Soon we'd be too far out of Paris for help.

We turned a corner, onto a busier street. The driver had mentioned Fox, but I was in no position to interrogate him. Horns tooted and people laughed in their Saturday night finery. Umbrellas popped up—red, black, white—like flowers in the rain that had started to fall. I shivered. Reflected light shimmered in the newly slick roads. Our driver cursed, wrangling the gear stick and the steering wheel over the slippery tarmac. My attacker pinched my tender upper thigh and laughed softly as I squirmed.

"You know, Fern," he said—I gasped, Fern was the driver!—but Fern was too preoccupied with the cranky old vehicle to notice that his cover was blown, "I think I will wait until the farmhouse. I'm enjoying this too much to waste it all in the back of this taxi."

"This fucking taxi." Fern swore in English and ground the gears. The other traffic made a swishing noise in the rain. My attacker squished my face and gave it a little pat. I was quiet and still, and he must have assumed I'd been scared into submission, as he leaned forward, reached into his pocket and brought out his cigarettes, shaking the packet to take one with his lips.

The taxi growled and stalled—this tiny moment of pause was my only chance. As the taxi jumped back into the traffic, I kicked my attacker, bracing my body against the seat for maximum force. My heel hit something soft and he jerked forward into Fern, gasping and choking. His fall pushed Fern into the steering wheel, where his mask smashed into his face. The taxi swerved wildly and clipped an oncoming truck, which then slid sideways back into us, covering the road, the hood, our front seat with cabbages. Those vegetables were a lethal weapon as they smashed the windows, and Fern and my attacker yelled as the cabbages hit their fragile masks. I had the door handle in my hands and pushed down as hard as I could, falling out of the seat and onto the road in my haste. My attacker grabbed for me weakly, but he couldn't breathe—I must have hit his diaphragm, and hard. I slid and slipped like a drunk, climbing over smashed glass and cabbage leaves, desperate to get away as fast and as far as I could. I bolted across the road and was almost hit by a car, the yells following me onto the footpath. I looked back—the truck driver was shaking Fern and my attacker was trying to follow me through the suddenly fast traffic, bent over and clutching his stomach.

I couldn't run, bound and in heels. I had to hide until they gave up and went away. A young woman grinned at me from a doorway.

"Did he hurt you, love?" she asked. Her voice was gravelly with cigarettes. I nodded.

"In here, then." She jerked her head and I slipped behind her.

The room was lit only with a few candles, a soft glow that couldn't hide the stained sheets, the bare wood floors, the grubby Madonna on the wall. There was a mirror at hip height and a washbasin in the corner. I'd been inside brothels—some men liked to think they could shock me with a few feathered women of the night, to say nothing of Fox—but none quite as sad and cold as this. Her voice said she was forty, but she looked only seventeen. I sat on the bed and listened hard, while my rescuer stood guard at the door, business as usual. The commotion went on, the truck driver, Fern, and my attacker all yelling and grinding glass underfoot. The rain swished and swirled. I got my breath back, ragged and painful. I could feel all the bruises along my thighs, the cut in my mouth, the grazes stinging on my elbows and shoulders where I'd fallen on the road. I no longer had my bag—I panicked, but thankfully I'd left all the notes at home after I left Bertie. Bertie! I had to get back to him. I mentally checked, yes, I had pinned a twenty-franc note to my knickers earlier that evening. Always a good idea before an adventure.

The rain relaxed a moment, took a deep breath, then came back harder. People ran from the street. My savior sighed.

"No one's going to walk past in this weather. May as well take a break."

"Is everyone—?"

"Yes, love, your nasty john's run away. Only the cabbages are left. Speaking of, hold on a tick." She ran out and returned moments later with her arms full of dirty, battered vegetables.

"Nothing a bit of water won't fix." She dumped the cabbages in the corner and looked at me, head cocked to one side. "You *are* in a fix."

"Do you think you could untie me?"

"What? Oh! Of course. Do you want to keep the tie?"

"No! God, no—"

"But it's a lovely silk stocking—look!" She held up the end of my bind.

"You keep it, if you can, but be quick—I have to go."

"Your pimp expects you back, does he? And without payment too—that's too bad. I'd give you something, but it's been slow tonight, hardly a soul wandering lost and needing love—ah! Not even a ladder! Are you sure you don't want it?"

I could have hugged her for her workaday assumptions.

"Positive. What can I give you?"

"Give me? Don't be silly. We're in this together—although, if you know a comfortable place, with a bit of class, you know, maybe put in a good word for me. I'm Rosie, do everything and everyone, plenty of experience, specialize in playing the schoolgirl." Up close, I could see the lines around her eyes, two missing teeth, the gray roots of her hair. She smiled and I smiled back.

"By the way, where are we?"

"We're on rue Choron" she said. "Taxi's over there. Ask for Bruiser; he'll look after you."

Bruiser was a hulking man with hair on his knuckles and a witty sideline in grunts. He looked after me by asking no questions, just handing me a towel to sit on and taking off into the traffic. I was going back to the Exchange bar, much as I hated to, in the wild hope that Bertie would still be there. I found the note in my knickers, a bit sodden but still legal tender.

Fern had been the driver. He'd kidnapped me; he and his accomplice were going to torture me. They clearly didn't care if Bertie was alive or dead. How did they know where I was? Who else was looking for Fern? Had Fern been betrayed by someone other than Violet? Had I been betrayed?

I barely had time to go over what I knew before the taxi drew up at the alley. Bruiser waited but kept his dark, beady eyes on me as I wobbled, sodden and sore, down the cobbles. The bar door was almost hidden in the drizzling dark. I wanted to call out to Bertie, but I didn't want to attract any attention. It was too dark to stay silent, but in the end, I didn't have to.

"Stretcher-bearer!" Bertie yelled from a pile of junk. I ran to him as his unusually harsh voice chilled me through.

"Stretcher-bearer!" He flung out an arm.

"Bertie, it's me—"

"Nurse, nurse, they're over there, the lads—"

"Bertie—"

"All six of them, in the wire—"

"Bertie, we're in Paris—"

"Nurse, why are you here, where's the stretcher-bearer? Stretch-er-bearer!" His eyes were glassy, as unhinged as his voice.

"Bertie, it's Kiki, it's 1921, the war's over; here we are, come on now, Bertie—" Over and over I murmured reassurances to him, trying to bring him back to now. I patted him gently on his arm, careful not to shock him. Eventually he lost momentum, sighed, closed his eyes and sank back onto some rapidly disintegrating cardboard. He was very pale and wet, with a huge red gash across his forehead.

"Bertie," I said softly.

His eyes clicked open and he stared at me. "Oh—Kiki . . ." He started to cry. Huge rolling sobs shook his body, a high whine dying in his throat before it could become a proper wail. This was worse, really, than the pinches and slaps, than being kidnapped by the enemy. I could do nothing but wait for Bertie to recover from his nightmare.

"Kiki—what happened?"

"Hell's bells and mademoiselles," I said. "Come on, Bruiser's waiting for us."

"Bruiser?" he hiccoughed. "Haven't we had enough of that?"

Bruiser charged me an arm and a leg, and almost a kiss as well, for the wet ride back to the Ritz. Bertie shivered all the way, and I joined him. We stumbled upstairs to his room, doing our best to avoid the concierge and any mentions of the police. We ran a bath as a first priority and called for room service.

"A whole bottle of cognac or just half?" he called through the door.

"Bertie, do you even need to ask?"

"Sorry, still not quite myself yet— Yes, hello, and coffee, and biscuits, and an extra bathrobe, and . . ."

I stopped listening to his list as I lowered myself gingerly into the water. I cursed as little pink tendrils wound up to the surface from cuts I couldn't see.

"Christ on a bike—Kiki! What happened to you?"

"The same as what happened to you, but without the blackout." I swished away the stained water before Bertie could comment on that too. "Our attackers were the mole and his accomplice."

As Bertie got in the bath with me I went over everything that had happened. Except, of course, for his nightmare. He didn't ask, but I could tell it was with him still; he'd abandoned some of his dandyish grace for tension and precision. He was completely focused on my explanation, not even smiling at the cabbages and silk-stocking banter, much as I tried to make it a joke. Perhaps that made it worse—it did for me, as his concentration made me see how very close we'd been to disaster.

"So if you know a classy joint for the gap-toothed Rosie—"

"I'll ask my cousin, he likes to tread that line between ingenue and child." His quips were quick but his frown didn't lift. "How did they know we were there?"

"Either we were betrayed or Fern was betrayed—"

"Well, we know Fern was betrayed; we betrayed him."

"But he must have set a trap for someone, us or his betrayer, laid false clues, a little path of red herrings that we waltzed down—"

"Ran down, more like it." There was a knock at the door as our food arrived, and Bertie pushed himself out of the bath. "I pity his betrayer. He'll probably end up in that farmhouse with Mr. Pinchy."

"She," I said, and froze. Was it a she or a he? Was it Violet or Lazarev? The initial clue of "the exchange" came from the notebooks, which Fern must know could only have come via Violet. But it was Lazarev who pointed me towards the bar where Fern was waiting. Was Lazarev working with Fern? That couldn't be; Lazarev hated anything German. But why had he sent me to the Exchange bar? Whether he was just an exiled aristocrat or something more, from Bertie's bath I had no way of knowing. I could know, however, that Violet was in trouble. I had to protect her. My muscles protested as I pulled them out of the bath and ran in to Bertie.

"Look at this spread, Kiki! Not bad for a midnight feast."

"Bertie, we have to go—"

"But the cognac—"

"My source—Fern's lover, Violet—she's in danger. He will have worked out who betrayed him, and I'm the only one who can tell her."

I scrambled for my sodden clothes as I spoke, trying to untangle the wet mess of silk and stocking.

"Kiki, you're naked and I'm hungry."

"We have to go and get her."

"Can't we send the telegram boy or something?"

"Oh . . ." My dress was like golden pulp in my hands. My arms shook from the very meager effort it took to hold it, and my feet were still blue with cold. Bertie took the dress from me and replaced it with a very large cognac.

"Yes, I suppose so . . ."

"Excellent. I'll summon my favorite telegram boy."

"Violet may even have a telephone in her building."

"There you go. And we have one here. Now, sit down, drink up, and we'll sort this out in a civilized way."

"But—"

"Kiki"—he put on his Captain Browne voice—"you cannot seriously think that, despite our near escape, the best thing to do is to rush off naked into another probable abduction. I got the bump on the head, not you."

"It looks nasty."

"As do the bruises blooming on your arms, my sweet."

"And my face?"

"No . . . lucky. Still, all this happened, what, an hour ago? Is it likely that, after a car crash in a stolen taxi with an irate cabbage seller, the first thing Fern would do is torture his lover? If it was me, I'd lie low to pick the bits of papier-mâché mask out of the cuts in my face before I went anywhere."

"Yes, but not everyone is as well-groomed as you."

"I should think not. Nonetheless, I insist you stay here. You can die another day, my darling. Now, where does she live?"

How could I recover from such an episode? In the war, I used to go straight back on the wards and let the adrenaline fuel me through a long night of bedpans and pus, so by the time my shift finished I thought of nothing but sleep. Tonight Bertie wanted me to stay with him, in his bed, a glass of cognac in one hand and his body in the other. This was as much for his comfort as my safety, as I suspected he dreaded a return of his war nightmare and wanted a body to ward off the ghosts. But I couldn't do it. We'd left Violet in a suite upstairs, tipsy and smiling at her imminent return to London and home. She wasn't the only one who dreamed of home. Bertie was right in that Fern was unlikely to do anything tonight, and I needed my own bed, my own space, the view that emptied my heart of care and filled it with joy. It was worth putting my wet dress back on, heading back out into the rain, climbing up all those stairs and busting the lock with one of Bertie's tiepins. It was worth it to wash every cut slowly and in private, to wrap myself up in my silk kimono and indulge in a solitary smoke.

I had made a mistake and it cost me my cover. I had been too eager and almost lost my bodily integrity and my darling Bertie as well. I liked this work too much; I was losing my cool. Had Fern set a trap and caught me? Had Fox tipped him off to teach me a lesson? I needed more information before I could know any of that. And I needed sleep before anything.

The lights of the city shimmied and twinkled through the rain. A last wisp of winter blew up from the street and wound around my bare feet. I shut my windows on the damp and the chill, on the paranoid double agents and violent men, on all the nonsense that threatened my place, my part, my peace in this city.

"A PRETTY GIRL IS LIKE A MELODY"

The bells through the city pealed, letting the sparrows know that believers attended Sunday mass. The air vibrated with the joyous, judgmental, dogmatic, divine sounds of a citywide carillon. There was a knocking at my door and my sleepy brain tried to make the door knocks part of the bells' rolling rhythms. It couldn't, and the arrhythmic sounds prized me from sleep.

"All right, all right, hold on!" I called.

The telegram boy was my only uninvited guest. Would he be here on a Sunday? It was the only service that this Catholic country would allow on the Sabbath—apart from the cafés and brothels, of course, which for some were essential after a long mass and longer family lunch. The knocks kept up as I tied my kimono dressing gown around my waist, making sure the huge sleeves covered my bruises. I ached. Why didn't the boy call through the door? I was suddenly wary. He usually did. Unless it wasn't him. Unless—

I pulled open the door and was greeted by that dingo grin I adored.

"Tom!" He dropped his suitcase and I jumped into his arms. My aches were gone.

"You don't half keep a man waiting." His hug was fierce. I almost couldn't speak for lack of breath.

"It's not usually a man I keep waiting, just the telegram boy," I said into his shoulder, "and with the tips I give, he can wait as long as I please."

"Don't get used to it."

"What, you turning up so early? I hope not. I'm not even dressed." He let me down to my feet then, his smile softened, and he kept one arm around me as he stroked my hair out of my face. From the way he looked at me, I didn't think he'd really heard what I said, or saw what I wore. Or perhaps it was the opposite, and he saw everything in an enchanted light, just as I saw that he had to tip his hat back on his head to fit in the tiny doorway. That he had dark circles under his eyes and his gray suit had a crumpled, slept-in look. The stubble on his neck prickled under my fingertips, but his monochrome wardrobe made his blue eyes dark and fathomless. What a word, *fathomless*, like a penny novelette for naughty schoolgirls—when it floated into my mind, I shook myself and smiled.

"What?"

"Nothing." I could hardly say that he made me feel like a naughty schoolgirl. "I'm just delighted that you've come for breakfast."

"Well, it's almost midday, but I know that's early—"

"Abso-bloody-lutely. You're straight from the train? Did you use your coat as a blanket last night? For Pete's sake, come inside, Tom-Tom, the ceiling isn't that low."

"You don't reckon?" He took off his hat as he ducked inside. Even though he had to stoop to fit, he couldn't stop grinning and neither could I.

"Not if you sit down."

"Where? You haven't a chair to hang your hat."

"That's because there's too great a risk a hat would be sat on. I put hats on the floor and my bum on the windowsill." I pushed open the window and the sparrows immediately flew in and hopped about. Tom laughed. I grabbed my cigarettes and a glass of water, and sat on the windowsill, my feet dangling out.

"*Et voilà!*"

"Very pretty, Button." He sat down next to me.

"You have to take your shoes off. Only bare feet may dangle into the street."

"Who made that rule?" he said as he untied his laces.

"My house, my rules, of course." I shook out two of the last cigarettes from my somewhat battered Gitanes packet. He placed his between his teeth, struck a match, and leaned close to light mine, my hands cupped around his so that the breeze wouldn't blow out the flame. How could this gesture be more intimate than a hug? Was it the deliberation, the stillness, the way he watched me breathe in? Was it that we almost touched, and this sparked a desire to feel his fingers, his face, his breath? I only know that he let the match burn down as he watched me, inhaling and lighting his at the very last second. He leaned back against the opposite window frame, looking at me, watching the street, blowing his smoke into the air. He looked wrung out and scruffy, but he looked just right, like he belonged here, sitting on my windowsill, halfway between the studio and the sky.

"You won't believe what happened," he said.

"Try me."

"Look at this." He pulled a piece of paper out of his jacket pocket, worn and brown along the folds. I sniffed it; it smelled of Woodbines and trench mud. I raised my eyebrows, but Tom just nodded. I opened it carefully. It looked like it was written on thin army-issue paper, which meant it'd be quite fragile. It was dated October 18, 1917:

Bobsy—it's done. I hardly had to do anything! TT disappeared— bloody awful show—but that hardly matters. What matters is that he was seen being helped by the Boche. Really! Just out of a shell hole & he was injured or some such—but again that hardly matters. All I had to do was drum it up. The groundwork we laid made *the brass receptive to the charge—treason! From military medal to spy—could we write a penny dreadful any better? That nobody Sergeant Thompson is finished. Fancy a transfer? SJS*

P.S. Burn this when you're done.

I read it over twice more. I could hardly believe it.

"This is proof."

"Incontrovertible." Tom grinned. "The idiot actually wrote it down."

"But Bobsy didn't burn it, as instructed."

"It almost restores my faith in God."

"Who's Bobsy?"

"No idea. Either a fool or a friend."

"Or someone who guessed what this note might be worth," I said, but he just shrugged. He couldn't pull down his smile where he sat in the window, the breeze in his hair and the light on his dark stubble. He was stretched out, his legs so long that they reached me at the other side of the windowsill, but he was only pretending to relax.

"Did you know about all of this, Tom? Did you know precisely what SJS—"

"St. John Sinclair. Golden boy, man fancier, and outright bastard."

"Did you know exactly what he'd done?"

"Not at all—that's the wonderful thing!" He leaned forward in excitement, "I couldn't understand how the charge of treason came about. I mean, I went missing in that mud along with all the other blokes who bought it. If you were looking for a fella, wouldn't you check among the bodies in no-man's-land? Or the POW lists? As he says, I got that silly bravery medal—that I had somehow run off to the Hun didn't make sense. But this explains it—some Jerry helped me, heaven knows why. Someone saw it happen, and the Saint used it against me. Clearly he'd been blackening my name for some time."

"Why?" I put on my schoolmarm tone. "What did you do to him?"

"I wouldn't be his 'special boy.'" He grinned. "Not that I have any-thing against that sort of thing—a man's business is his own. But I won't be ordered into it, especially not by my superior officer."

"That's all? That doesn't seem like enough—he'd surely be used to rejection, if he was trying to find his lovers in the trenches." Tom smiled but looked sad. The Sunday sounds came up from the street, more sub-dued than during the week. There were no newspaper boys yelling doom or fruit sellers dragging their carts along the cobbles. Just the flower girls, the Sunday cafés, the sighs of mothers released from drudgery, and the laughter of factory workers unshackled from their machines.

"He was humiliated in front of the men and blamed me."

"How?"

"It was pretty ordinary—he soiled himself during a bombardment, got the shakes, couldn't even walk himself to the latrine. I had to take charge. Every man would've forgiven and forgotten if he hadn't become nasty."

"He sounds like—"

"A liar, a coward, a snob—oh yeah, and I beat him in a rugby match in 1910."

"Don't tell me this is an old school rivalry—"

"Not really." He shrugged with a smile. "But it didn't help."

I folded the letter up carefully and handed it back. The only way that Fox could have obtained this letter was if Bobsy worked for him. If so, how much of Tom's charge had Bobsy orchestrated, on Fox's orders? Or had Fox merely been opportunistic, and if so, for how long?

"So what will you do with this letter? Do you know who to show it to?"

"Your Dr. Fox?"

"No point. He sent it." Tom stared at me. "As payment—well, partial payment—for the work I'm doing.

"That explains why the man who gave this to me knew your name. In the hotel bar, a tall, burly bloke with face like a smacked arse, sat down with his beer and threw out a few conversational sallies. I wouldn't have given him more than a nod and a grunt, but when he mentioned your name—"

"*He* mentioned it?"

"He said, 'Do you know a Katherine King Button? Then this is for you.' He handed over the note, finished his schnapps, and walked off."

"I got the name Kiki so early in the war that not many people here know me as Katherine King."

"Your full name—I knew then it had to be some kind of intrigue."

A little sparrow hopped onto my leg, but I flinched at its little claws and it fluttered to the other side of the windowsill.

"Intrigue or introduction to purgatory. That note was most definitely from Fox. In which case, what else did the man say?"

"Nothing."

"Rubbish. He must've given you another place, time, venue, rendez-vous . . ."

Tom shook his head and started unloading the bits and pieces in his pockets so he could stretch his legs more comfortably and relax properly. In among the matchboxes, lollipop wrappers, and coins was a clipping from a magazine, folded up and over many times. It was an advertisement for Citroën cars.

"You're buying a car?" I held up the clipping.

"What, to put in my suitcase?"

Under the address of the showroom was a line of tiny handwriting. It read, in English, 'Factory: Quai de Javel. 1900.'

"I don't know how . . . Was that hidden in the matchbox?" He took the clipping and folded it up along the creases until it fit snugly into the top of the matchbox. On the front was a pipe-smoking fox that grinned smugly at us.

"What does it mean?"

"It means at the Citroën factory, tonight, we deliver the mole to Fox."

Tom had insisted that he didn't want a hotel, even if they did have running water. We each looked out at the view as the other washed and
dressed and spruced up for the outside world. It worked better than I
expected; it felt like beach holidays, when we'd turn our backs as we
changed in and out of our swimmers, keeping up the chat the whole time.
Part of me wanted to stay on the windowsill, and I could see that Tom
felt the same. Except that he was sleepy and I was hungry, so to Petit's
it had to be.

The café was always run by Monsieur Petit on a Sunday. He was just
as short as Madame but gruff and stern, nodding curtly to me as I smiled
bonjour.

"He doesn't approve of me," I whispered to Tom after we'd ordered.

"How could he not?"

"He doesn't like my type."

"The modern woman?"

"Independent. Outspoken. Hatless."

Tom laughed.

"And I think his disapproval is in direct proportion to Madame Petit's
wish for just such a life."

"But who wants a life without hats? You'd get sunburned—"

"Or a head cold—"

"Or covered in flies—"

"Or messy hair—insupportable. Oh, Tom, you should have stayed for
that hat party at La Gaya . . ." Over coffee and fresh croissants, I told
Tom everything that had happened. Well, everything that had to do with
Fox and this mission, the other things he didn't need to know. I made a
list of everyone he did need to know as we ordered a second coffee the
minute we'd downed our first. Monsieur Petit might be gruff, but his
coffee was delicious.

"And you? Silesia—the Brownshirts—"

"If I'd known how relevant it was, I'd have brought my notes." He tore his second croissant in half, dipped it in his coffee, and maneuvered the soggy mess into this mouth. For a moment the café disappeared, with its decorated tiles and wall of drinks, and I was back in Sydney the summer after we'd finished school, feeling like rebels as we sat at the Quay among the ferrymen and ate a mountain of cream cakes—

"Button, are you listening?"

"Yes, of course! . . . What?"

He snorted. "This Hausmann character—that's who you're interested in, right?"

"He's as slippery as a whore's virtue."

"Ha! Well, I managed to get a bit more information on him before I left. He is with the Freikorps, most definitely. He's some kind of mover and shaker, knows everyone, people mention his name with awe . . ."

"Yes? And?"

"And . . . he's not German. He's English."

This sounded more and more like a certain Hamilton "Teddy" Houseman. I humphed.

"What, you knew?"

"I suspected."

"I went to so much effort to get that information! The factory worker who told me that Hausmann was English was terrified to do so, and it wouldn't have slipped out if I hadn't soaked him in Slivovitz. Apparently Hausmann's German sounded odd."

"I've been told that."

"That too? Why have I even—"

"This is great, really." I squeezed his hand. "Just tell me everything."

"Fine." But he smiled. "I was trying to talk to Hausmann at one of his political meetings. I failed, due to some zealous German door guards, and only got a glimpse of him orating. However, I did manage to corner a factory worker who left the meeting, and convinced him to have a drink with me. He said that Hausmann spoke English to two men. One looked like a Junker, with his scar and his limp, the other was a big man—with a 'broken face' was how my factory worker put it."

Was this another agent of Fox's? Was this a double-cross of a double-crosser?

"But he said that Hausmann spoke French with a Russian. There were a few Russians floating about the cafés, actually, although they were never very welcome as they were clearly all aristocrats. . . . "

The murmurous haunt of flies treads him down: Fern was being betrayed. But by whom, exactly? More turncoat Brits or furious White Russians? Or both?

"Though I did hear one of the German guards talk loudly about '*diese verdammten Engländer*'—I remember enough German to know he was talking about these damned Brits—and the factory foreman told me that everyone was sick of foreigners. Though who is actually a foreigner in Silesia is another question entirely."

His high requiem becomes a sod—*sod* is a word for *soil, soil* is a synonym for *nation*. His "high requiem" is turning into a nation? Suits a nation? Is the "high requiem" some kind of nationalist mantra—I must be getting close . . .

I scanned the café. There were just enough people, and the right sort of people—old workmen cradling their aperitifs, young foreigners absorbed in their hangovers, middle-aged foreigners absorbed in their books—to give us privacy. Monsieur Petit ignored us where we sat against the dark wall and where, between the two of us, we had a view over the whole café. Tom saw me surreptitiously looking around and obliged me by scanning the tables behind my back. He shook his head; nothing suspicious.

I shook out two cigarettes, lit them, and handed one to Tom. "And on the ground—what's happening?"

"Nothing—yet. There's going to be a riot, I'm sure of it. The Germans can't stand it, that the Poles would rather face the threat of Russian expansion than be a German state. But it wasn't the government who called in the vigilantes. It must've been the good burghers of Kattowitz who called in the Brownshirts from Bavaria. Every day I was there I saw more and more on the streets, strolling around, encouraging German shop owners and directing German-Poles away from Polish shops. The only violence I saw was when one young man kicked a passing Jew. I was amazed—the old man was kicked in broad daylight and not a housewife or fruit seller even flinched! You would expect some acknowledgment, wouldn't you? A jeer, a gasp—but everyone did a sterling job of pretending it didn't happen. I followed the old man, I wanted him to talk to me, but he refused to speak any language I could understand. But more violence is brewing, I'm sure of it. We'll be back in Silesia before a month is out, I reckon."

"And coming back through Paris?"

"If you like," he said with his little boy smile. I could feel a blush in my cheeks. I had to look away; I smoothed down my ivory silk dress, I played with the embroidered jonquils around the cuff. Tom reached over and gently took my wrist.

"Tell me, Button." His blue eyes matched mine. I couldn't look away; I could hardly breathe.

"Yes, I'd like that," I murmured.

He smiled, wide and joyous, and like a mirror, I matched him. It was only us, his fingers on my pulse, the smells of coffee and pastry mixing with memories. I might have kissed him then, I might have done a lot of things, if Petit hadn't come over and asked if we wanted anything more. I asked him politely for cigarettes, my head in a whirl.

"Right, Button, so"—Tom was equally dizzy—"what's next?"

I took a deep breath.

"There's someone I need you to meet."

Thank goodness Bertie was dressed when he opened the door to his hotel room. A cream suit with ivory brogues, a pearl tiepin, and razor-sharp hair parting; it looked like we'd matched our outfits on purpose. He was the too-clean Pom to Tom's swaggering Digger, but he used his Captain Browne handshake and his infinite charm to put Tom at ease.

"Ah, the boy from the bush!" he exclaimed. "Kiki never fails to mention you."

Tom raised his eyebrows at me, but I could tell he was pleased.

"What, in the same breath as 'that bloody,' 'that annoying,' 'that hopeless—'"

"Only in that she might say 'That bloody Tom is so annoying, he won't stay more than a day! He's hopeless!'"

Tom laughed and I breathed out. After his tantrum over Pablo, I was afraid that Tom might act the jealous lover again—which would have been even truer with Bertie than with Pablo. But in the ensuing chat Bertie acted the perfect combination of old soldier and gay dandy, so jealousy never entered Tom's head. He went to use Bertie's bathroom, snooping through the windows as he did so, whistling at the luxury present in every cornice and carpet hair.

"Well done, Bertie," I whispered.

"Darling, of course! I must say, you have excellent taste." He pouted lasciviously. "Any chance . . ."

"Not a snowflake's in hell." I grinned. "Besides, he's a little preoccupied with yours truly."

"Never mind, there's plenty more where he came from." Bertie caught my arm in mock panic. "There are plenty more where he came from, aren't there?"

"Why don't you see for yourself? It'd be a good holiday."

"And miss all the fun here? I told you, I'll have what you're having, thank you."

I laughed and accepted the cognac that Bertie handed to me.

"Private jokes, Button?" Tom asked.

"Just a private stash of booze," Bertie cut in. "Cognac?"

"You'll need it," I said. "So will you, Bertie. We have work to do."

"Don't I know it. I have a luncheon, a high tea, and two dinner engagements today." Bertie turned to Tom. "Persuading rich businessmen to advertise with us is part of my job. However, my editor finds it's best done via the wives and their interminable parties."

"Nice work, if you can get it," Tom said.

"Nice! It's cutthroat. Those businessmen are paper tigers half the time—it's the wives who drive the bargains. They could beat the Turks in the Grand Bazaar."

"So you can't come with us?" I asked.

"Alas, Kiki—"

"Don't you have a free window? We're starting early."

"Kiki darling, it's Sunday," Bertie implored. "Can't we just stroll along the Seine?"

"Seine, yes. Stroll, no. More like roll or haul—or mole." I toasted Bertie's questioning look. "Tom delivered the drop-off place and time."

"It's all on then."

"For young and old. Bertie, can you show Tom that photo of Teddy?"

"Oh!" Bertie glanced between us, but Tom looked nonplussed. "Ah. Yes." He went straight to his wallet to retrieve it.

"Button, that's you and—"

"Yes, I know, but the man in the corner—is that the man you saw in Silesia, Tom?"

As Tom studied the photo, Bertie and I conducted a pantomime conversation. I raised my eyebrow and cocked my head.

Really, Bertie? You keep the photo in your wallet?

Bertie shrugged and looked defeated. *What else can I do? I still adore him.*

I sighed softly and let my shoulders droop. *Poor Bertie-darling. You need better luck.*

He tucked his hands in his pockets and gave a small smile. *Don't I know it.*

All the work of a moment. Tom raised his frown-riven face.

"Yes," he said. "Unquestionably. How do you know him?"

"I don't, but Bertie—"

"Unfortunately, he's a good friend of mine." Bertie sniffed and turned away, hiding his despair by lighting a cigarette.

"With friends like these, mate—"

"Quite." Bertie gulped the rest of his drink and grimaced. "Oh my giddy aunt, I don't think one should swig that stuff. That man is known to me as Edward Houseman, a silly boy from Marble Arch with a penchant for cabaret. Then I found out he was also a businessman with extensive contacts, and family, in Germany. Yesterday, Kiki informed me that he's also a political rebel with a repellant manner. And who is he to you?"

"He's Hausmann, a leader in the Freikorps in Silesia. I've just come from Kattowitz."

Bertie transferred his stare from Tom to his empty glass. The sounds of the street could only just be heard and the room was still as a tomb.

"So Teddy really is behind all this." Bertie was barely audible. I reached out and squeezed his hand.

"But why he is, we don't know," I said. "We only know that he's not the mole."

"EVERYBODY STEP"

The door boy at rue la Boétie recognized me and smiled. With my tip in his hand, he ran ahead, opening doors, knocking on others, giving me the royal treatment. Tom didn't look surprised; he must have thought that this was how Paris always treated me. I didn't like to disabuse him.

Pablo's housekeeper opened the door with her usual sour face but quaked when she saw me.

"Bonjour, Céline," I said with a smile. "I'm back for those biscuits."

"Mademoiselle"—she didn't move, she quivered between anger and fear—"you bring the police?" She nodded at Tom.

"Oh, no! No no, he's my friend. We can trust him completely. Tom, this is the redoubtable Madame Céline."

Tom gave his best smile and reached forward to shake her hand. Her fear thawed as she looked between us, until she finally opened the door to admit us. She bustled us out of the dark hall and straight into the light, warm kitchen.

"Pablo will be home soon," she said as she placed us in chairs, refreshed the teapot, opened the biscuit tin.

"We'll be quick, of course," I said. "Oh, are these biscuits from your sister too?"

"Yes, vanilla cream." Céline nodded, her lips a severe line. "Eat as many as you wish. Madame Picasso does not like 'peasant baking.'"

"More fool her," said Tom, already shoving a second biscuit in his mouth. Céline almost smiled; bringing Tom was always a good idea.

"We've come about Jean-Claude," I said. Céline almost dropped the teacup as she was handing it to me. "Where will he be tonight?"

"Tonight?" She looked confused. "I don't know . . ."

"Who does he usually spend his evenings with? Where does he usually go? It's vital for you to tell us everything if you want to keep him out of trouble."

"Trouble with the police?"

"Or with that nasty Englishman." I sipped the tea, a delicately perfumed black with just a hint of lemon. The food she'd prepared for us was too subtle for my brutal questions. She heaved an enormous sigh.

"Is it as bad as that?" I asked. She responded with a faint smile.

"He is friends with . . . men from the factory. Other old soldiers who 'understand him,' he says. Men who want to change things, what does he say, 'to sweep away the hypocrites,' to 'do away with the warmongers.' I don't understand him." She crumbled a biscuit, unseeing, into her saucer. "He finally has a job, in a place he likes, with a foreman who is understanding of his weaknesses, and he makes trouble!"

She put down her tea and looked away from us, out the window, blinking rapidly.

"Has he ever mentioned the names of these fellow troublemakers?"

"No, never, he's very secretive," she sighed. "But I know he doesn't go to mass. I know he spends his Sundays with them, doing God knows what heathen things."

"Where does he work?"

She smoothed her hands along the table, polished and scrubbed almost down to the grain. The kitchen was neat and tidy, ready for anything, from tea to a banquet. Céline's dress was perfectly pressed and speckless.

But these were her areas of control. Her son, it seemed, was far from neat and left her heart a mess. She wanted to keep him close and under her protection; she needed help to give him independence. Her hesitation told me that she lost out either way.

"He works at the Citroën factory."

◆

The clues were coming together. *Cyclops and Godson accepted mission for Godsday*—Luc and Jean-Claude had accepted a mission for Sunday, today. Luc had told me that the next meeting would be today at six o'clock. I had to hand over the mole at seven. What was I supposed to do with that hour? The mission had to be the exchange of Olga's portrait, as that was the whole point of Jean-Claude being involved—he was the link between Pablo and Fern. That he worked at the Citroën factory, where the meeting and handover were both to be held, only confirmed this. Other clues were still floating around my mind, yet to find their proper place in the puzzle—the Russians in Silesia, that Lazarev sent me into a trap, intentionally or otherwise, who "Mr. Pinchy" was, the Englishman with the "broken face" who was in both Poland and Paris—but tonight seemed straightforward enough. Luc and Jean-Claude would hand over the painting to Fern; I would intercept the painting and hand Fern over to one of Fox's agents. What could possibly go wrong? A better question would have been, what fresh hell was this? I sighed to myself. There was nothing to do but wait for night.

Our late breakfast was followed by a late lunch, as Tom and I spent hours trying to find a camp bed. With all the shops closed, it was a case of knocking on doors, begging friends at the Rotonde, paying the hungrier street urchins to haul the thing up four flights of stairs. Blankets and a pillow were another rigmarole, as Montparnassians didn't generally run to spare bedding. I almost trekked out to see Maisie, but a hotel manager from across the street saved us the trip. All this fuss because Tom refused to relent; he would stay in my garret, come what may. All the fuss to avoid thinking about what terror awaited us tonight.

But in the end, with everything that happened, it was a good thing that we didn't have to sneak past a hotel concierge. That we could sit in my studio in private to clean up the mess.

◆

At half past five, Tom and I made our way to the factory. The sky had darkened with drizzle, summoning foul smells from the grates and gutters. We huddled into our coats as we stepped over the puddles.

"Is there a secret knock, a test, something to declare us?" he asked.

"You're asking the wrong person."

"So, what do we do?"

"We do as the jazzmen do. We improvise."

I wore my trousers and boots and military coat. Tom had raised his eyebrows when I put on my outfit, but he had to admit it was useful, "even a bit flattering, Button. Those ambulance drivers always looked so dowdy, but a well-cut pair of trousers on a woman, nicely fitted around the rump, hmmm, I think I could get used to it."

When we got to Quai de Javel I wished I'd done some more research.

"Jesus, Button, this factory is enormous!"

It wasn't just a building or two but a small city dedicated to the cars and their makers. Warehouse after warehouse, chimney after silo after workshop, stretched out in front of us. The nearest growled with industry and the farthest we couldn't see.

"Where the hell are we supposed to go?" Tom whispered.

"Somewhere secluded, is my guess. They're hardly going to have a revolutionary meeting under the foreman's gaze, are they?"

The first set of gates we found were locked but the next set were open.

We slipped inside and headed as far as we could away from the working machines. We kept near the perimeter, avoiding noise and people, until we finally reached the back of the complex. It was quiet, the Sunday stillness ominous among all these machines. In one building I saw a lighted window, a beacon in the dying light. Dusk was a deadening of light and made each outline fuzzy as we searched the warehouse for a way in. Finally, a little door around the back, like a fairy door in an old castle, revealed itself in the gloaming.

"Do you know how to pick a lock?"

"Button, I thought you'd never ask. Do you have a hairpin?"

I trapped my hair under my hat as he knelt at the lock.

"By the way, how do you know how to pick a lock?"

"Boarding school," he said, frowning in concentration. "Couldn't get into the pantry without it."

"Not enough biscuits from Mummy?"

"You know my mother—a stale orange and a platitude was considered generous. Ah!" The door wheezed open noisily, but I couldn't see any moving shadows in the dark. I climbed in and Tom closed the fairy door behind us.

Car bodies stood in rows in front of us, blind and gutless. The room rose into a ceiling of metal girders, an industrial church, with the last light of day streaming through the high windows to illuminate the mezzanine floors. The only sound was the coo of pigeons somewhere in that secular belfry. It smelled strongly of oil, dust, and diesel. I stood, hardly daring to breathe, in our dark corner of the floor. Tom touched my sleeve and pointed. On the far side of the factory a sliver of light cut through the reverential darkness. We headed straight for it.

We heard voices as we moved closer, and I stopped Tom to listen. It was just a murmur, not violent or passionate or pleading. I held my coat close to my body to avoid knocking any tables, to disturb the least dust possible. The door was closed, but the voices kept murmuring, even as I crept up to it—they hadn't heard us. I needed to see them and hear what they were saying. I could hardly see Tom in the darkness, but he saw me hesitate to listen, and he must have guessed what I wanted. He touched my arm and pointed upward to the wooden floors of the level above. If we could get upstairs, we might just be able to watch them through the wooden slats of the ceiling.

If you want a fun, relaxing time, don't creep around an unknown factory warehouse in the dark. It's spooky and smelly and every corner could cut you open with a clang. We had to move quickly so as not to miss a word; we had to move slowly while our eyes adjusted to the lack of light. Factory warehouses are noisy places, even when empty, with jangly tables and creaky floorboards. Every time we made more than a whisper we stopped, but the voices mumbled on. We can't have been that loud, even if I was sure that Tom could hear my heart pound. It felt not merely unprofessional but childish, and I feared that I was losing my touch— even if I had got my information too quickly, I should've investigated the factory before this crucial meeting. I followed Tom around the corner, up a very tricky metal staircase, across the floor, into an unlocked office. A sliver of light beamed up on the far side of the desk. With our shoes beside us, we lowered ourselves down to look at our quarry through the gaps in the floor.

It was Luc and one other man. They sat at a table, a saucer full of cigarette stubs in front of them, a bottle between them with two small glasses of brown liquor. Luc sat in a wheelchair-type contraption, with an ingenious crank between the wheels so that he could wheel himself with one hand. The other man leaned forward with his elbows on the table, one hand supporting his head as though exhausted. Other than that, the room held only a row of sinks down one side and a number of hooks on the far wall, some of which held filthy towels. The floor looked wet with runoff. I couldn't see much more except, of course, what lay on the table between them.

Pablo's painting.

It had been wrapped in tea towels and string. I knew then that the other man was Jean-Claude, Céline's son. The painting was partially unwrapped, to be shown to Luc, and presumably to anyone else who turned up. I looked up and saw Tom watching me, his face lit with severe shadows by the light through the floor. I nodded—*That's the painting; they're our men.* He raised his eyebrows but I could only shrug—*I don't know what happens next.* I looked down and willed myself to hear their voices. But they spoke too softly, in a kind of patois or slang that I couldn't properly understand even when I did catch a phrase or two. I had to be content to read their expressions. Jean-Claude drooped over the table, head bowed; his leg jiggled compulsively and he couldn't stop smoking. Luc was still, he barely moved, his hand gripped his glass. Both men were tense, perhaps afraid. They didn't touch the painting but instead addressed it, talking to Olga's purple face instead of each other.

There was a bang from somewhere downstairs and both men jumped— as did we. It had to be a door slamming, as footsteps rang out over the concrete with voices, harsh and masculine and definitely not speaking French. The footsteps came closer, and I mentally cursed that I hadn't brought a pistol, or even a knife, to this assignation. My wits were sharp but not literally cutting. I cursed my lack of preparation—so unprofessional. But the steps didn't come upstairs. They went into the room, pushing open the door with a bang.

There they stood, right below us, unmistakable under the washroom's naked bulb.

Fern and Hausmann.

They stood as if in uniform. Backs straight, feet at ease, coats buttoned to the top. They took off their hats as they entered, Fern placing his on the table, Hausmann flinging his carelessly, like the dandy that Bertie knew.

"Do you have it?" said Fern, his precise French loud enough to rise up to the ceiling.

"Here, comrade," Luc indicated the painting.

I watched Hausmann closely. His hair was so fair that his pomade hardly darkened it. He was slight but tall, and moved with a feline grace that suggested menace. He wasn't Bertie's usual type, but then who knew what kind of man he was with Bertie. It was clear that both Jean-Claude and Luc were in awe of him. They were stiff, almost frozen to their chairs, as Hausmann moved around them to look at the room, their clothes, until finally coming to rest by the painting.

"Let's look at it, shall we?" Hausmann said, in an odd, simpering French. He completely unwrapped the painting from its cloths, his movements mesmeric in the way they were both languid and powerful. Olga's face looked up at us. The vibrant yellows and purples, blues and oranges, made the canvas luminous in that drab room.

Hausmann caressed it, picked it up, turned it over, moved it this way and that. "Yes, it'll do, wouldn't you say?" he said.

"If you say so." Fern showed none of the charm I had witnessed at Margaret's party.

"Well done. I congratulate you both," Hausmann said to Luc and Jean-Claude.

"All for the cause, comrade." Luc was nothing if not a true believer.

"Yes, quite," Hausmann said in English. He turned to Fern. "Finish it."

Luc was startled—he clearly knew enough English to know what that meant—but when Fern pulled out his gun, both Luc and Jean-Claude started yelling. Hausmann sat on the edge of the table and calmly wrapped up the painting, as Fern directed the men to stage their own shoot-out suicide. Jean-Claude blubbed and Luc's yell became a rasp almost straightaway. Fern directed Jean-Claude to place Luc by the sink, to hit him in the face as though he'd beaten him; Jean-Claude pleaded, Luc protested and tried to appeal to their belief in the cause. Hausmann laughed at his appeals and mimicked his injured voice; he gave stage directions to Jean-Claude, cruelly highlighting the pretense of their fight.

"Go on, hit him properly, like you meant it—and once more, with feeling, man—"

"Get Luc over there, we want him to bleed into the sink."

"Don't make me, I can't do it—"

"He won't do it! You traitors! You, you—bourgeoisie!"

"Is that your best insult? Oh dear me. We're a bit loftier than the bourgeoisie. How old is your family, Ferny?"

"Norman princes and Prussian Junkers. Do I have to hit you, you sobbing fool?"

"And my mother was a princess, once upon a time. Now, put your hands—sorry, hand—up by your face, as though to shield the cruel, traitorous blows—"

This went on. I looked at Tom and his expression was unlike any of his that I knew. It was as though the skin was pulled tighter across his bones, his eyes focused, his brow creased and every movement sharp and spare. I realized that this must be the face he showed to the guns, the shells, the dawn whistles for an attack. It was his fighting face. He nodded at me. He'd need it.

We pushed ourselves up and moved quietly across the floor. I don't know how Tom saw it, but he grabbed a wrench from a table on the way down and handed it to me with a whisper. The yells were becoming more urgent and a high-pitched laugh pierced the commotion. I prayed that Jean-Claude would be able to help, as while Tom was a match for Fern, I was no physical match for Hausmann.

We had no plan but speed and surprise. Tom pushed open the door and I ran for Fern. I whacked him on the shoulder with the wrench as Tom took advantage of Fern's stumble to kick the gun out of his hands. Tom grabbed him and, after a breath, Jean-Claude helped Tom wrestle Fern into a headlock. I grabbed the gun as a shot ricocheted—Hausmann had fired at us—Jean-Claude and Tom both yelled out. I aimed the gun at Hausmann.

"No," he said simply. The room was still. His own slender pistol was pointed at me. He still sat, apparently unmoved, on the edge of the table.

"It'd be a shame to shoot you all," he said. "So messy. But needs must."

He cocked his gun.

"Teddy," I said in English, "that isn't necessary. Just the painting will suffice."

He raised his eyebrows and laughed, a girlish giggle that sounded hideous emerging from his mouth.

"Is this the one you told me about?" he asked Fern.

"Bitch," Fern spat.

"Fox sends his regards, Ferny," I didn't take my eyes off Hausmann and the sneer left on his face by his laughter. "He looks forward to seeing you again."

Fern cursed his former employer as he struggled with Tom. A vicious smile split Hausmann's face. Jean-Claude and Luc, clearly not understanding a word, were silent.

"You work for that jumped-up little Anglophile? Traitor to his German heritage. He's not worth spitting on. Well, well." He regarded me critically. "I must say, I can't see what Bertie sees in you. I wouldn't think you were his taste. Your friend, on the other hand . . . I might just take him with me. But he seems to be somewhat attached to Ferny and I always hate to break up a couple in a squeeze."

"But needs must." I shrugged. "Just leave the painting on the table and—"

"Silly girl." He stood up. "I've had enough of this."

"Quite. Action is always best." I smiled. I prayed that my aim was as good as it used to be and I shot him.

Pandemonium. The noise of the shot reverberated through the concrete and flimsy walls. Hausmann screamed, dropped his gun, dropped the painting, and clutched at his bleeding right shoulder. I kicked the gun to Jean-Claude as Luc lunged for the painting. Fern yelled and struggled with Tom, who I feared was coming out rather the worse for not being armed. Hausmann growled, more angry than hurt, and lunged towards me. I fired another shot near his ear, deliberately missing him. With that, he ran, cursing me, Fern, Luc, France, the entire human race. We heard a door slam and his voice disappeared.

I turned around and my heart sank. Tom had blood down his face and was breathing heavily. Fern spat blood, looking sullen, his arms pinned back by Tom. Jean-Claude held the gun too shakily and too close to his head to be properly useful. Luc held the painting like he'd a rescued a child.

"The betrayer is betrayed," rasped Luc. "Hausmann has abandoned you. I'm no poet, but this is justice, no?"

"Of a kind," I said. "Jean-Claude—it is Jean-Claude, isn't it?"

He nodded.

"Give the gun to Luc and get a chair and some rope. Fern has a few questions to answer."

"If you think I'll talk for that pissant, Fox—"

"Oh no," I said, sitting on the table to stop myself from shaking. "You'll talk for me." Fern laughed at that, but I just smiled sweetly. I could see Tom's muscles quake with strain and I hoped that Jean-Claude hurried back.

"Mademoiselle, when I asked you to this meeting, I never meant—"

"I know," I spoke to Luc in French, "But your group of Communists—"

"Anarcho-Communists."

"—has been compromised. Fern and Hausmann are Brownshirts from Germany"— Luc cursed at Fern—"and they've used you to further their own cause. Unsuccessfully, this time."

"But how could they pass our initiation?"

"It was ludicrously easy," Fern spat.

"They're professionals." I shrugged. "There was probably nothing you could have done."

Luc scowled at Fern and kept a steady aim on him as Jean-Claude came back with the rope and chair, and the three of us tied Fern onto it. I checked my watch—6:50 p.m., we had just a few minutes before the pick-up.

"Jean-Claude, you stole the painting from the Picassos." He hung his head. "Why?"

"For Luc—"

"To further the cause," Luc cut in.

"But how?"

"To sell, to raise money."

"For what?" But neither Luc nor Jean-Claude answered. Fern smirked through his bruised face.

"Fern didn't tell you what for?"

"They asked no questions, so I told them no lies." Fern was as smug as a man with a fat lip could be. "They assumed we were going to blow something up or some such prank."

Luc lifted his chin, proud and defiant. "The cause will triumph," he rasped. "Whatever setbacks, whatever traitors, whatever the world in its blindness—"

"Oh, shut up, you blithering fanatic." Fern resorted to English. "You're as bad as the wartime demagogues."

"Luc, I think Jean-Claude needs a drink." I put my hand on his shoulder. "And your bottle is empty." The adrenaline had caught up with Jean-Claude and he shook all over, little trembles and jerks so that he had to lean against the sink to stay upright. Luc also had no desire to stay here and be humiliated by Fern.

I took the painting gently from Luc. "This belongs to Pablo," I said. "I'll make sure it's returned."

Luc pursed his lips, but just nodded. He spoke quickly to Jean-Claude in that same incomprehensible dialect and used the crank to wheel himself out of the room. Jean-Claude followed, only just managing to light a cigarette, refusing to look at me. He caught the handles of Luc's chair by the door, but Luc stopped him.

"Mademoiselle . . ." Luc rasped.

"It's all forgotten," I said. "Give my regards to Marie—and to Céline."

We listened until the footsteps and squeak of wheels had faded away.

"But as for fanatics," I said to Fern, "I don't think you're one to cast the first stone." I sat on the table, relieved to have some way to stop my legs from shaking—the adrenaline had caught up with me too. And with Tom, it seemed. He moved gingerly to the sink to splash his face, his body turned towards Fern the whole time.

"I have no idea what you're—"

"Oh drop the mask, Fern, you're going back to Fox. Whether you tell me or tell him, you're going to talk, and I know who I'd rather talk to."

Fern's fat lip curled.

"You're a feisty little vixen—"

"What did you call me?"

He sneered as much as his swelling face would allow. "Fox's female counterpart—oh, yes, we all knew about you. Fox was discreet, but he couldn't help showing you off. I've been on the watch for your . . . interference. Though I didn't think I'd be so rewarded. You walked into my trap."

"And walked out again. Who was your accomplice?"

He just laughed. Tom was dabbing gingerly at his side. I had to hurry.

"Was it the German ambassador's nephew?"

Fern stopped laughing abruptly. Bingo. "Who told you that? Violet? That bitch, I'll tear her apart—"

"Now now, settle, petal." I kept the gun trained at his heaving chest. "It was Lazarev."

"The Russian? But . . ." He looked shocked. So, Lazarev had betrayed him too.

"But?"

Fern just spat bloody saliva at me; I steadied my aim. Lazarev's role in this business would not be forthcoming, but at the moment it wasn't what I wanted to know.

"Tell me, these Brownshirts: how did they recruit you?" I saw Tom tense in surprise. Fern sneered; my guess was right.

"Recruit? Like our industrious wartime employer, you mean? How did he 'recruit' you—by a hospital bed? Or in a camp bed with your skirt around—"

"Don't argue with a woman with a gun. Answer the question, Fern."

"Fox trained you in banter too, I see." His black eye made him look more sinister. "Eddy—Teddy, as you called him, you must know one of his perverts—I've known from school. We were both disgusted with the war—"

"Who wasn't?"

"Not enough people!" He was vicious. "Too many just accepted it! The way we ripped our enemy to shreds, we left them with no honor, no dignity! I—we—have old family in Germany, boys I've known since childhood, and then we killed them, just like the king and the kaiser, we just . . ." He shook his head.

"'Like the king and the kaiser'—what, you killed your actual cousin?"

"I couldn't, in the end." His voice had softened, he was panting from pain and the strain of talking through the ropes around his chest. "Had him by the scruff of the neck, young Johann, a full decade younger than me, should've still been in school but of course they threw every last body into the frontline's ravening maw. . . . He was wounded, lying in the mud, I was mopping up. . . . His big blue eyes looked up at me, afraid, then calm as he recognized me, then terrified as he realized what I was about to do to him . . . so I couldn't, could I? That felt like murder—more than anything I did for Fox, that would've been a cold-blooded killing. I took him prisoner."

"That doesn't explain how you came to join a group of German right-wing revolutionaries."

"Doesn't it? I thought Fox said you were clever."

I just smiled. I'd thought Fox was clever, but he'd recruited this fragile turncoat. Surely he'd have detected his fanatical strain? But then, Fern might have been different before; the war had done strange things to us all.

The tap dripped, the drop in the concrete basin echoing in the still dark of the factory, a timer, a metronome. Fern looked at me with his one good eye. If he was talking to me in the hope that Fox would be gentler with him, he didn't let on. He spoke like someone who didn't care who heard or what anyone thought of him. Like someone too in love with his high requiem to hear that his plaintive anthem fades.

"I kept in contact with Johann. I visited him in Berlin. What a mess that city is, disgusting, worse than Paris. It struck me with force: order must be restored. Honor and dignity to Europe, so that no man will have died in vain. Our lot are too insular to do it, they just want to grow roses and mumble about the weather. The French are a bunch of whiny children and the Italians are all hot air. The Germans are the only ones who know what's what. I knew that as soon as I stepped into their meeting. When I saw Eddy . . . well, that clinched it."

"But why did you steal the painting?"

"Money. Do you think a political revolution comes for free?"

"But why steal a painting to sell? Why not rob a bank, or persuade businessmen of your righteous cause, or—"

"Who says we aren't doing those things? The theft was an opportunity. Lazarev knew men who'd buy a Picasso unseen—"

"But Lazarev betrayed you."

He looked like he tried to shrug, but he was tied up too tightly.

"I came to Paris to recruit and find sponsors. There are plenty of proper men hidden among the feeble peacemakers. This Weimar government will collapse—Eddy will make sure of it—Germany will rise again and here, in Paris, is where we need to till the ground for the second coming. And with dupes like Luc to help us . . . well, it's too easy, really."

"Except that you've been caught."

"Do you think I'm the only one here?"

There was a bang and strident footsteps. A voice barked, "Button!" Tom took the gun from me as I left the room.

"Here," I called into the darkness.

A huge man with dark hair and a smashed nose, just as Henri had described, bore down on me and shook my hand in his black leather glove.

"Bacon," he said in a rough voice. "But call me Fry. Where's the worm?"

"He's in here."

Fry was almost twice my size. He could hardly fit through the door. Fern looked up at him and laughed.

"So you're still his errand boy then, Fry?" he spat. "I knew it was a joke, when you turned up in Poland."

"Evening, Fern. You're coming with me."

"How, may I ask?" But Fry delivered such a smack to Fern's face that he was knocked out. He then untied the ropes surprisingly quickly and hoisted Fern over his shoulder. For all his bile, Fern looked like a little boy, flopped over the large man's back. Fry turned to me.

"A message from Fox—tomorrow, midnight at the Rotonde."

"Again?"

"And this is your retainer."

"No, you're mistaken, I'm not being retained."

"You are. Fox said to mention your 'real' payment if you protested."

"What about my real payment? Is there more?"

But Fry just shrugged and fished a check out of his back pocket for an amount that made me boggle. His footsteps rang as he left. Tom and I were alone, in the dank washroom with its dripping tap and naked bulb, in the dark factory haunted by its gutless bodies. I took Tom's hand and led him towards the streetlights.

23

"AFTER YOU GET WHAT YOU WANT, YOU DON'T WANT IT"

It wasn't long before my washbasin was pink with diluted blood. Tom was in a state and both of us were shaky. I forced him to strip down to his underwear so I could wash every cut and tend every bruise, so I could make sure no bones were broken, so he couldn't act the hero and in doing so become ill. I washed his back along the lines of muscle, bone, and scar; I knelt in front of him to clean his face; I pressed his legs and moved his arms to check their fitness. It was so intimate, but somehow beyond romantic. I was professional in my manner, gentle in my tone, and Tom was content to take instructions. He was content to watch me soak his grazes, to ice his bruises, to let my fingers search his body for pain. We barely spoke.

But it was too chilly to remain undressed. We gathered up all my half-drunk wine bottles and sat, with our cigarettes, by the window. Tom had some ice in a tea towel for his jaw, a huge wadded bandage on a serious graze on his side, and his bare foot was elevated on a pile of coats.

"What now?"

"We return the painting to Pablo tomorrow—"

"No, I mean, right now."

"Nothing. It's done."

"That's it?"

"My mission from Fox was to find the mole and hand him over. My case from Pablo was to recover his painting. My payment from Fox—my real payment, not the check—was your incriminating letter via the careless, or devious, Bobsy."

"And your payment from Picasso?"

I frowned. "You know, we never discussed it. These walls are pretty bare. A sketch would liven them up, don't you think? Wait, I might have one in my bag . . . "

"You undersell yourself."

"Goodwill is worth more than money. Besides, he might recommend my services to other artists in need." I winked at him. I wanted to see him relax, to forget his wounds for a moment. I probably needed more wine for that.

"Do you need me to rustle up a chemist for some morphine?"

"Never again," he said. "That stuff makes me lose my head, and heart and soul along with it. I want to feel everything—even the pain."

The look he gave me then, dark and intense, his hair over his eyes, his shirt undone, his bones straining at the skin as he tried to drink me in, as though he was memorizing my every detail. I had to look away, at the lights of Paris that called to the flickering candles in my studio.

"Tom . . ." I could only address the view.

"Button."

How could I say it? How could I say no but yes but no—I want you and don't want you—can you come back in a few years when I'm ready—you're too much, I'm drowning—how could I say any of these things, when I didn't know what I wanted? Being witty with a gun was easy compared to this. Tom watched me as I lit a cigarette, avoided his gaze, fidgeted with my cuffs and my hair. I could feel him waiting.

"Our last cigarette," I said as I shook the empty packet.

"Our very last?" His voice cracked and he looked devastated. I hadn't meant that to be a symbolic sentence.

"Just for this moment," I said. "I don't think there could be a very last, with us."

He sighed and his face showed such relief. I smiled and reached out to his foot upon the coat pile. He wriggled his toes as I caressed it.

"Tom . . ." But what did I want to say? He smiled into my pause.

"No words, Button?"

"No words, Tom-Tom."

"You make me feel the same way." His feet were so big that he could curl his toes partway around my finger. "But I'm happy to wait until we find the right ones."

"In the right phrases."

"At the right moment."

"And until then?"

"We fill the space with chat, wit, rant, hoot—"

"Whisper, giggle, sigh—"

"Cackle, yodel, warble—"

"I'm sure there'll be plenty of that," I said. "Especially the cackle bits."

He grinned. He took a final drag of his cigarette and flicked the butt in an arc into the street. There was laughter in his face, the expression he had when he was about to dare me to do something dangerous.

"What, Tom?"

"Would you come to London to make sure?"

That was his dangerous dare? My heart pounded hard before I could catch my breath and regain control.

"Only if you come back through Paris."

"Deal." He reached out to shake on the deal and winced.

I made a pitying *tsk* noise, but he grabbed my hand, flipped it, and kissed my palm. He kept hold of it and I squeezed his fingers. The night smelled of tobacco and wine; the chill breeze held laughter and jazz. The candlelight sent flickers of gold up and down Tom's skin. I wanted to stay here, hand in hand, the two of us in the window, suspended in the sky above Paris.

"Button, I have to ask . . ."

"Anything." But what more could I give him?

"Why did you let Hausmann go?"

That was it? But I suppose the mission was everything. I let go of his fingers and leaned back.

"How could I stop him? It was either him or Fern, and the mission was to get Fern."

"But Hausmann is clearly the villain."

"Clearly, but those weren't my orders."

"You're taking orders again?"

I hung my head. My words betrayed me. They told the truth of my actions that I'd hidden from myself.

"You promised that you wouldn't, Button—"

"You have that letter, don't you?"

"I told you that I didn't want your help, not when it comes via Fox."

"But we're so much closer to clearing your name."

"*We're* closer? The cost is too high!"

"If you think that I won't do everything in my power to help you—"

"Once and for all, I don't need your help!"

"Yes, you do. You need me."

His eyes were dark in the soft light. I wanted to look away, to escape their stare, but they pinned me to the wall. I bit my tongue; once again, my careless words told the truth that I had wanted to deny.

"Don't tease me, Button."

Should I apologize or tease some more? As I wavered, my silence felt like sulky defiance.

"I told you that I would wait for the right words at the right time, Button, but I can't if you provoke me."

"I can't help it." My voice sounded choked. "I will help you, whether you want me to or not. If that's a tease, so be it."

"You know that's not what I meant."

"You need me," I whispered, but it wasn't what I meant. I meant *I need you*, and Tom knew it. The hair on my arms rose, but I couldn't tell if it was the breeze or my fear.

"Button . . ." His voice held tears, and I responded in kind. I couldn't utter those three little words, that revolutionary cliché, the longed-for simple sentence. It wasn't right, it wasn't the time. I couldn't commit and we'd make a mess of things unless I could. So what else was there to say but my name, his name, over and over?

"Have we run out of wine?" I said eventually with a sniff.

"Completely. And cigarettes."

"What a catastrophe! Are you hungry?"

"Always." He grinned. "I want steak and chips—"

"Mussels and fresh bread—"

"And beer, a tankard of beer—"

"Ooh, no, a crisp white wine, in some kind of flagon—"

"And pudding, an entire rice pudding—"

"With ice cream!"

"Oh, Button, yes." He put his hand over his heart.

"Can you walk?"

"For ice cream, I'll manage."

I didn't know what time it was, but I knew the Rotonde would serve us. I wanted to show off Tom to all my café people. I wanted North to fuss over his bruises and swoon at his smiles. I wanted Bertie to wink at me and dance his silly jig walk and make Tom laugh. I wanted to forget brown shirts and double agents and charges of treason, I wanted to forget Fox and his disturbing excitement, I wanted to forget the words that stuck in my throat. The Rotonde was just the place to do so. As we limped slowly up the street the lights called to us, then the music called to us, then North called to us from one of the terrace tables and she ran up to take Tom by the arm, just as I'd hoped. Bertie turned up too, just as I'd hoped, and Henri made the cook put his apron back on and make our dinner, and we only had to swap rice pudding for chocolate cake for all our dreams to come true. I watched Tom as he laughed and drank and expertly handled all the flirtations that came his way. I watched him until I didn't have to, until I knew he was happy and I could relax.

"You really care for him, don't you?" said Bertie as we danced a sweet foxtrot.

"How can you tell?"

"Oh, Kiki," he scoffed, "I'm not blind! Have you told him yet?"

"Told him what?"

"You know . . . those three little words."

"Good God, no. That would mean marriage—"

"Dreadful—"

"And leaving Paris—"

"Unthinkable—"

"And playing the little wife somewhere, with no money, under a false name—"

"And a false mustache?"

"Oh yes. It's too absurdly complicated. We're not ready for marriage yet, trust me."

"I always trust you, Kiki."

"More fool you. But . . . take care of him in London for me."

"He lives in London? Oh goody."

"Bertie . . ." I warned.

"What?" But he undercut his faux innocence with a wink. "Never fear, Kiki. If he has you on his mind, he won't easily be distracted."

Then the band changed to a fast jazz and we had no more time to chat between our laughter.

"HOME AGAIN BLUES"

Bertie had left on the dawn train with a thousand promises. Tom and I woke with the midday bells, the little sparrows tapping on the window to be let in.

"I feel fumigated," he croaked.

"I feel soaked and dried," I returned. "Can you reach out and open the window?"

His camp bed lay the length of the tiny room. His head was near me, but his feet dangled off his camp bed well before the ankle. He reached out with one foot, pushed down the handle of the window and nudged it open with his toe. I laughed as he flopped back onto the blankets.

"Too much effort, Button."

"Will it be too much effort to get coffee?"

"Never."

But neither of us moved. We let the breeze from the street slowly freshen the air in the room, the sparrows chirp and chirrup, the geraniums' perfume cancel out our toxic exhalations. The room filled with light and muffled street noises. I reached out to stroke Tom's hair and he made a humming noise. The terrible truth was that I liked to wake up with him. He pulled my hand down to kiss my fingers. We clearly liked to wake up together.

Madame Petit was back behind the counter, ready with smiles and aspirin and endless coffees, ready to tut at me and to show off her still-girlish dimples to Tom. His little bag held enough clothes that he could look decent, if a little rough and unshaven. Through our midday breakfast, kindly rustled up by Madame Petit with a wink, we went over last night's antics, laughing too loudly and too long as we pushed away the goodbye that waited for us. We continued as we caught a taxi to the station and bought his ticket. We continued until we stood at the platform, the long line of carriages in front of us, steam rolling over the steel and porters scurrying by.

My arm was linked in his. He stood still at his carriage, then turned sharply and grabbed my hands.

"Button—"

"When are you coming back to Paris?"

"As soon as I can. What are weekends for anyway?"

"They're for visiting me. Do so."

"Is that an order?" He raised an eyebrow.

"If you like." I smiled. Steam blew up around us and metal rang out its urgent clang.

"Button . . ."

"Tom-Tom."

"I know I said I that was happy to wait for the right words, but I can't wait empty-handed." His words fell out in a rush. "Tell me."

"Tell you what?"

"Anything." His face searched mine, hunted desperately for a sign, a yes, in my expression. Of course I couldn't refuse him. I went on tiptoes, pulled his face down, and whispered in his ear. He grinned, lifted me off the ground with a whoop, and gave me a huge smacking kiss on the lips.

"That will do, Button! That will most definitely do."

The train whistle sounded and the wheels began to move. He jumped aboard at the last second, waving his hat out of the window. I waved until long past the time when I could see him, until I was a lone fool on the platform. I was devastated, I was ecstatic, I was empty and full and overwhelmed. Thank God I still had to deliver the painting to Pablo, or I might have picked up any old fruit seller or taxi driver to assuage my fast, all-consuming loneliness.

◈

"Mademoiselle Kiki." Céline's smile was genuine. With it, I could picture her as a young woman, a bunch of flowers in her hand, as she walked down a summery country lane.

"Céline, I have a delivery for Pablo." I indicated the painting under my arm.

"Of course! Come in, come in"—she ushered me into the hallway—"and I have something for you, if you would be so kind as to visit the kitchen." She nodded as she opened the studio door and announced me.

"Kangaroo!" Pablo held out both arms and kissed me three times. I placed the painting, still wrapped in tea towels, into his hands.

"Your wife will love you again."

"She loves me regardless," he said as he tore off the wrappings to inspect the painting, "but now she has no excuse to make a fuss. Ah, perfecto! It's an excellent portrait, no?"

"I've never met your wife—"

"That doesn't matter. You can see that it's excellent." He didn't look at me, bent as he was on his handiwork. I had to restrain a smile. Then his attention snapped to me, his look took me in, and he laid the painting aside.

"Right, payment."

"Oh, no—"

"Don't be ridiculous. All you English-speakers are like that—you say no to the thing you want most." After that station goodbye, truer words were never spoken. "And everyone in Montparnasse wants money. How much are your services?"

"I've been paid by a third party." He looked shocked. "You can pay me by sending me more clients. If the artists of Paris need a mystery solved, I'm their lady detective."

"Ah! I'm your first client?"

"The very same. But . . . my walls are quite unbearably bare. Perhaps you could give me one of your little sketches?"

"Now that is something I can do easily. Sit." He pointed at the lounge. I wore my lavender shift today, and it settled around the lounge as I leaned back, arm above my head, one foot up on the seat to show off my stockings and my black suede boots. The sketch took almost no time at all. He rolled it up and tied a ribbon around it. As he held it out to me, he leaned in close, a kiss away from my lips.

"Are you busy, kangaroo?"

"Always. But for you, never too busy." I touched the tip of my tongue to his lips and he drew in his breath with a gasp. He was about to embrace me when there was a crash in the hall, followed by a child's cry and Russian calls and French yelled with a Russian accent. Pablo looked to the ceiling.

"Olga is home."

"I'd better go." I smiled.

"Until next time," he whispered as he ushered me out.

I heard him cry, "*Ma chérie!* Little Paulo . . ." He walked out and enveloped his wife and child with such an embrace that they couldn't see me. I slipped past and into the kitchen to see Céline. She smiled and I took her hand.

"Did you have something for me?"

"I do." She pulled out a basket. "In here are some orange spice biscuits from my sister, some burgundy from my cousin, blackberry jam I made myself, and some pâté from the village of Jean-Claude's father."

"My goodness!" I felt the intricately embroidered lace edge of the linen cloth that sat inside the basket. "And this?"

"That, I made myself, for my trousseau." She looked so proud. I started to protest, but she held up her hand. "I know I should save it for my daughter-in-law, but without your help, Jean-Claude would never have had a chance to find me a daughter-in-law. No"—she held herself straight—"I would be honored if you would accept this gift."

I took the basket in both hands and kissed Céline on both cheeks.

"The honor is all mine. Truly. How is Jean-Claude?"

"He is . . . 'all right,' as you English-speakers say." She shrugged. "Thankfully, he still has his job at Citroën. He seems to have lost his friends—which I think is excellent—except that he is lonely. That is something a mother cannot do for her son—he must find his own men. But . . . there were no nightmares last night. That is another thing to be thankful for." Céline poured me a cup of tea and placed a little, thumbnail-size biscuit in the saucer.

"Long may it continue," I said as I accepted it. I was about to sip when her name was called through the door.

She sighed heavily and I put down my cup. "No, no, it's time for me to go," I said.

"Are you still one of Pablo's models?"

"I hope so."

"Then, until next time."

◇

I had hours until Fox's call. It was a Monday, the office clerks had gone back to work and only the tourists remained. I could seek out Manuelle, but after the aborted assignation with Pablo, I didn't want to—it'd make her second best, or third or fourth best. She wasn't, and I wouldn't treat her that way.

But it was more than that. My life had revolutionized in the last week. In the last month—and had it been only a few months ago that I'd left

Sydney? Had I been footloose and fancy-free a week ago, and now I was a detective, a spy, a lover? And if so, where were my lovers, my spy-masters? For a moment, the city seemed empty, just buildings full of cardboard men and flimsy women, wooden children and their wind-up toy dogs. Then a car hooted me as I crossed the road with my basket, a flower girl called and a newspaper seller tipped his hat and offered me cigarettes. I could smell freshly baked bread and rotting vegetables; I could smell salt and fried potato and burnt sugar. A couple laughed and a horde of schoolgirls in their white gloves giggled around a corner. Paris was alive and it welcomed me. It taught me that loneliness was a core part of freedom, that my sort of loneliness—asked for, paid for, and treasured—could be soothed remarkably easily. By the sights and smells of the street. By a basket of delicious local goodies. By just knowing that Maisie and Harry were a block away, Bertie a call away, Tom-Tom just a train ride away.

The wind whipped up my skirt, but I enjoyed the breeze where it tickled my thighs. I didn't push it down again.

◈

"Kiki! Darling, where's your lovely Australian fellow?" North kissed me and looked around for Tom. We stood in the thicket of the Rotonde's outside tables, sunset and already full.

"He went back to London."

"And left you? Too cruel! When was this?"

"Earlier today," I sighed theatrically.

"Why didn't you drown your sorrows here with us?"

"I read a book instead," I said, and grinned.

"A book!" North gaped.

"Shocking, I know." I'd bought a stack of books at Shakespeare and Company, all the ones I hadn't been able to get in Sydney—D. H.

Lawrence's *Women in Love*, Virginia Woolf's *Night and Day*, F. Scott Fitz-gerald's *This Side of Paradise*. It would've been great to say that I'd read one of them. But they'd been used as a table, and instead I had ripped through a detective novel by a new writer named Agatha Christie, *The Mysterious Affair at Styles*. Her Hercule Poirot made me smile. It had been the most peaceful afternoon I'd spent since I'd arrived in Europe.

"I suppose that is why we're all here, isn't it?" North said with a frown. "To make art. But still, Kiki, you could've done it in public. How can you show off how modern you are, if we can't see you?"

I laughed and North winked. There was something in her face, a little smile that went with her wink—she wasn't as silly as she liked people to believe. I had a hunch she had never intended to make art, but had so many relatives visit her that she had to keep up the charade in order to stay in Paris. She was here, like me, to get out of the marriage market and be free.

We settled in and let all the pearls and all the riffraff swoop by our table. Fernand Léger came by with his tubular mustache, on the arm of that irrepressible Brit, Nina Hamnett. She sung bawdy songs to Mr. Monocle, Tristan Tzara, who kissed me three times on each cheek. Tzara nodded to Cocteau, who wafted by in a cloud of opium and opulent absurdity, waving vaguely at Pascin and Hermine at the tables behind us. Hermine joined us and we gossiped about the L'Ecole Grand-Chaumière, where she knew all the "so-called teachers." Californians North knew from home swirled around us; North begged me to scare them off, so I spoke French to Hermine and they evaporated. I drank but never became drunk, I ate but never became too full. I eventually went inside to buy more cigarettes, where Henri bowed to me and refused payment.

"Is it time then, Henri?"

"*Oui, mademoiselle.*"

I lit a cigarette and followed him into the office. I hoped that I was past caring what Fox thought, defiant as I picked up the receiver.

"*Oui?*" I put on my best Gallic accent.

"'She dwells with Beauty . . .'" purred Fox.

This game again; here we go.

"'Beauty that must die'? I don't think so—'no, no, go not to Lethe—'"

"Let me be a partner in your sorrow's mysteries—"

"Fox, only those whose strenuous tongue can burst Joy's grape against his palate fine can see Melancholy in her sovran shrine."

"Which is where? In a Montparnasse café?"

"In a Montparnasse studio."

"So when will you invite me?"

"When you burst Joy's grape. Do you even know joy?"

"She's my secretary."

"Ha! Why didn't you hire a Prudence?"

"Prudence is no fun. But truly, I await your invitation."

"Rubbish. You don't wait for invitations. You demand entrance."

"Not with a lady."

"Oh, so I'm a lady now? Not a messenger, rat catcher, dogsbody, whore—"

"Whore? You'd never let me."

"Ugh." I stubbed out my cigarette. I didn't mind the banter but I hated his flirtation.

"Fox, I looked around for my little follower but there was no one. I missed my flies and their haunting murmur. I almost felt lonely."

"You don't think the newspaper boys are the flies."

"Of course not. If they were, how could they sing a high requiem of honor and nation? How could their plaintive nationalist anthem fade?"

Fox hummed in appreciation, "Very good, my bright star."

"Only a Nightingale could sing such a song. Only a forlorn fox cub."

"'Forlorn! the very word is like a bell—'"

"I'm not coming to London. Dream on, little soldier boy."

He laughed then, rich and deep, and I couldn't help but think, *I will fly to thee—*

"So, why did you stop the newspaper boys following me?" I had to move on before I could finish that thought; before that thought could finish me.

"Your follower was no longer necessary."

"You knew I'd behave? That's a gamble."

"I knew you'd worked out the clues. All that was left was the conclusion of the mission."

"Although it's not quite concluded, is it?"

"Isn't it?" His silvery voice again, the one he used to entice. "How so?"

"The Brownshirts and Action Française. The exiled Russians. Hausmann."

"He'd be a catch."

"When do I catch him?"

A long pause, as he gulped some drink and lit another cigarette. I would've been impatient if I hadn't been too used to his manipulative silences. I look around the office, posters for exhibitions, dances, ballets, and operas in a palimpsest on the walls—

"Your friend's husband knows a lot of Brownshirt supporters," he finally said.

"Which friend? I have so many."

"With his record, it's not amazing that he resists their Germanic rhetoric . . ."

I waited. I suspected he meant Raymond Chevallier, Maisie's husband, but I wouldn't name my friend in front of Fox. I would protect her as long as I could.

"But he may not be able to resist a certain blond dandy's love of cabaret." I could hear him smile, but I was confused. "Or should I say, a certain blond dandy knows Monsieur Chevallier's weakness for the dark and exotic."

Raymond was on Hausmann's hit list. "And why would Hausmann need to know that?" I asked.

"Because Chevallier knows—ah, but that's for next time, Vixen."

"Next time?"

"You didn't think this was the end, did you?"

"Hardly. If only because of Tom's payment."

"Nice little letter, wasn't it? Bobsy is such a good little soldier—"

"Did Bobsy create that charge of treason?"

"Vixen, what an accusation! Don't you like what I gave Tom?"

"What you gave him is a partial payment."

"The evidence I gave him is impartial."

"Fox, where does Tom need to take that letter?"

"You'll have to work for that information."

"If that's the case, your payment isn't just partial, it's in a useless currency. You've paid me in doubloons."

"Doubloons are quite valuable to a collector."

"In shells, in beads, in a patronizing gesture to the natives."

"What else should I do, in your estimable opinion?"

"Get out of my territory."

He laughed. "That's rich, coming from a daughter of, what do you call it? The squattocracy. How did your forebears buy their farmland, with shells or with bullets?"

"That's not me—"

"Is that why you're in Europe? Are you 'getting out of the territory'? Tell me, do you still use Daddy's squattocratic money, or are my payments enough for the moment?"

"My reporter income—"

"Is hardly enough."

"But is enough."

"Stop being silly, Vixen. I did as you bid."

"Only literally."

"Then I suppose we must resort to cliché and say 'be careful what you wish for.'"

"I never wished for you." I couldn't keep the sadness from my voice.

"More's the pity," he said after a pause, his voice gentle.

"Then why do you persist, Fox? It's not the work—"

"It's always the work, Vixen. For this work, I need you."

"Give the job to another woman."

"There is no other woman." There was an edge in his voice that I wasn't familiar with. Not a warning, exactly, but something raw. I couldn't help but poke at it.

"Then train another woman."

"Vixen, you deliberately misunderstand me." The edge in his voice intensified. "There is only you and you work for me until—"

"Until?"

"Until the work is done."

"And you'll blackmail me, through Tom, to make me comply?"

I heard a lighter click, an inhale, a rush of smoke.

"I'd rather not, it's so grubby"—his smooth tones had returned—"but if you won't come willingly, what else can I do?"

"Leave me be, perhaps?"

"And would you leave me be, knowing that I can save your precious farm boy?"

What could I say to that?

"Your silence, Vixen, is very eloquent. Here are some other things you might be silent about: you find this work exciting."

Bastard.

"You find me intriguing."

Intriguing wasn't the word, but that he used that word was intriguing. I kept silent to see where he went next.

"You want to come to London to see me for yourself, perhaps to throw a drink in my face, or administer a passionate caress in the form of a slap, or perhaps just to search my drawers for evidence."

I laughed then. What arrogance.

"That's better, Vixen. Just be grateful that you have some proper work."

But that sentence properly silenced me. I couldn't deny it—gossip reporting was utterly boring compared to the thrill of Fox's mission. I hadn't felt this alive in years. Or ever, if I was being completely frank. What a bastard that Fox knew it too.

"So my next payment is . . . what, the name of a man who can help Tom?"

"If you wish."

"Don't I have to be careful what I wish for?"

"If you desire, then." His voice jingled with charm. "I like to indulge your desires."

"But I don't like to be indulged. I demand—"

"Oh, demand—you can only demand in person."

"I'm staying in Paris."

"Shame. Then we'll have to say, await my call. It will come."

"When?"

"When indeed?" And he hung up.

I stared at the receiver, the operator barking that the line was dead, the still tone of her cutoff. When indeed—would that be in a week, a month, a year? Would he wait another lifetime to swoop on me? Would I get a summons to London that I couldn't refuse? That's what I feared most of all, as I didn't trust him or trust myself in his company. He must know that, or he wouldn't tease me with it.

The office was still, the posters a modern history lesson. The café crowd, with its jazz and lipstick, its short hair and long cigarettes, its artistic revolution and modernist seduction, awaited me. There was nothing else to do but head out into it.

Henri greeted me at the door with a whisky, North waved to me with a bottle of champagne, and I danced into the night. Whatever Fox said and did, this was my Paris, and here, I was free.

ACKNOWLEDGMENTS

My gratitude is boundless and my thanks are many and various.

Firstly, to my dedicatees, Hannah Ianniello and Bridie Lunney, who convinced me that Kiki was worth a read.

Secondly, to my American readers: Katie McGuire; my excellent and precise copyeditor, Erica Ferguson; Claiborne Hancock; and everyone at Pegasus. The words 'thank you' merely gesture at my excitement.

Thirdly, to my Australian readers: my agent Sarah McKenzie, for her tireless work; Catherine Milne, Belinda Yuille and the fabulous Julia at Harper Collins Australia; Carly Williams and Patty Brown for their work on Maisie; Tania Disney for her fashion and fruit-growing knowledge; and Martin Jones for checking my German, too rusty after almost 20 years of disuse.

Research for this book has been a long and winding but entirely primrose-laden path. The books are too numerous for this page, but I want to thank Virginia Nicholson and her book *Among the Bohemians* for beginning this journey into twentieth century bohemia. The excellent Erik Lenaers drove me around the battlefields of southern Belgium and northern France, for in-the-field research so necessary for this book and the next. The Ritz Paris was also very prompt in answering my questions!

Finally, I would like to thank my precious Penny, for putting me in a Kiki mood, and my darling Dima, who makes everything possible.

DODGING AND BURNING

A MYSTERY

JOHN COPENHAVER

A lurid crime scene photo of a beautiful woman arrives on mystery writer Bunny Prescott's doorstep with no return address—and it's not the first time she's seen it.

Fifty-five years earlier, in the summer of 1945, Ceola Bliss is a lonely twelve-year-old tomboy, mourning the loss of her brother, Robbie, who was declared missing in the Pacific. She tries to piece together his life by rereading his favorite pulp detective story "A Date with Death" and spending time with his best friend, Jay Greenwood. One unforgettable August day, Jay leads Ceola and Bunny to a stretch of woods where he found a dead woman, but when they arrive, the body is gone. They soon discover a local woman named Lily Vellum is missing and begin to piece together the threads of her murder, starting with the photograph Jay took of her abandoned body.

As Ceola gets swept up playing girl detective, Bunny becomes increasingly skeptical of Jay. She discovers a series of clues that place doubt on the identity of the corpse and Jay's story of how he found it, and journeys to Washington, D.C. in search of Lily. In D.C., Bunny is forced to recognize the brutal truth about her dear friend, and sets off a series of events that will bring tragedy to Jay and decades of estrangement between her and Ceola.

In David Krugler's exhilarating wartime thrillers, intelligence officer Ellis Voigt fights to prevent the Soviets from infiltrating the Manhattan Project while running from enemies on both sides.

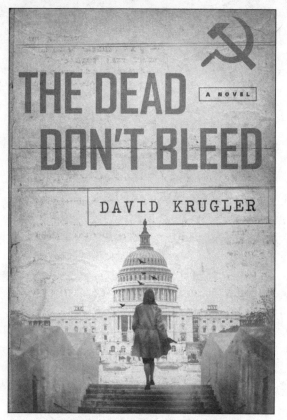

NOW AVAILABLE IN PAPERBACK

**PRAISE FOR DAVID KRUGLER'S
ELLIS VOIGT THRILLERS:**

"A good old-fashioned spy novel. The action is fast paced and the mystery is gorgeously wrought and splendidly opaque. Read *The Dead Don't Bleed* for a thrill-packed ride with a truly stunning ending." —*Dayton Daily News*

"Krugler brings expertise and authenticity to his first thriller, as well as a penetrating portrait of wartime Washington. And Voigt—a man with secrets of his own – stands out as one of the most intriguing characters in espionage fiction. Expect the unexpected in this thumping good read."
—*The Richmond Times-Dispatch*